BAKER THIEF

Claudie Arseneault

Kraken
Collective

Baker Thief
Copyright © 2018 Claudie Arseneault

ISBN 978-1-7753129-0-1

Edited by Lynn O'Connacht
Cover by Laya Rose
Interior Design by Claudie Arseneault

Published with The Kraken Collective

Kraken
Collective

claudiearseneault.com

CONTENT NOTES

Below is a list of trigger warnings for *Baker Thief*. If you need more information to navigate the story safely, please feel free to contact me for details. Numbers represent chapters.

First, general trigger warnings for **genocide**: a substantial amount of the storyline relies on villains targeting a specific caste of people and transforming them into a power source.

Breaking and entering: 1 – 11 – 14 – 19 – 27 – 29
Gunshots: 1 – 14 – 23 – 24 – 29
Food: 2 – 6 – 9 – 10 – 16 – 25 – 26 – 28 – 31 – 32
Alcohol: 6 – 8 – 10 – 26 – 27
Mob violence: 5 – 6 – 10
Human experimentation and trafficking:
2 – 4 – 7 – 11 – 14 – 15 – 19 – 21 – 22 – 29
Misgendering (accidental): 14
Fire/Burns: 14 – 15 – 17
Breathing difficulties/asthma: 1 – 14 – 15 – 16 – 20 – 22
State violence (police): 8 – 22 – 23 – 24 – 29

Val-de-mer

-1-

PENDRE LA
CRÉMAILLÈRE

ADÈLE LAY WIDE AWAKE IN HER BED, PONDERING THE differences between the unfamiliar noises of a new home and the scuffle of discreet footsteps in her living room. The occasional grating filtering through her door could only belong to the latter. Someone had sneaked into her flat.

They had chosen the wrong house.

Adèle pulled her nightstand's drawer open in a deliberate, silent movement, then wrapped her fingers around her pistol. Not two weeks inhabiting the neighbourhood and a stranger already wanted to steal from her. She might regret deciding to live in the Quartier des Bouleaux. Whoever this thief was, Adèle would make sure they shared some of that regret.

She slid out of bed, her thin night gown slinking around her. Adèle thanked God she'd put something on. Summers in Val-de-mer grew hot and humid, and she didn't always bother. Bad enough to be arresting thieves without her uniform on, she didn't need to be doing it in her underwear. Adèle breathed in deeply, both to calm her nerves and to listen to her intruder. The soft scraping of her desk's drawers drifted through the otherwise silent night. They were in her minuscule office, then. What a strange choice. The tiny room was almost a cupboard for storage and utilities. Adèle had crammed a desk under the westward window, however, granting her the luxury of sunlight when working late evenings. She used to bring a lot of police work home in her last job, and suspected the extra light would remain an essential.

Adèle progressed across her bedroom with slow and careful strides, gritting her teeth at the cold floor against her naked feet. Walls and furniture cast unfamiliar shadows around her, and Adèle thanked the lampposts outside for the meagre light filtering through her curtains. She'd needed to adjust to it, but in complete darkness, she might have hit a corner, alerting the thief to her coming. She wished she was still at her old home instead; this new flat's foreign rooms felt threatening. The presence of a stranger riffling through her belongings didn't help any.

She rounded the corner to her office, pistol raised before her.

A woman bent over her desk, clad from head to toe in black cotton clothes, including a cape and flowing skirts. A bad, stuffy choice in this weather, and the outfit surely got caught on furniture often as she moved around. Still, at least the fabric clung to her soft arms, the rolls of her belly and the thickness of her thighs, giving Adèle an excellent idea of her shape. She'd covered the upper half of her head with a black bandana, which she'd

2

folded and tied behind her head. Long purple hair flowed out of the makeshift mask, cascading down her shoulders to the middle of her back. She held a thin ink pen, sculpted from birch wood after Adèle's new quartier's Soul Tree, which her sister had bought for her upon learning she planned to move to Val-de-mer. The quartier hadn't won the Tournoi in the last thirty years, and Emmanuelle had joked that with her little sister in their ranks, they finally stood a chance. The bauble didn't warrant stealing, but Adèle hated the idea of losing it.

"I'm in a foul mood, so you'd better put that down."

The thief froze, then let the ink pen fall with a clang before turning to Adèle. Her brown skin glistened in the moonlight, but even face to face with her Adèle couldn't spot much else. She registered the details she could, memorizing the intruder's large nose and smirk, along with the brown eyes shining through holes cut in the mask, until her gaze landed on an exocore, tucked in a subtle fold of the fabric that acted as a voluminous pocket. A soft red light emanated from the gem, as if the power it should be pushing through Adèle's flat was struggling to get out. The metal casing contained most of the radiance, but, as it didn't fully cover the core, some of the glow escaped. Enough of it for Adèle to notice. Her gaze shot to the stand on the wall, where her recently-bought exocore should be ensconced. It was, of course, missing.

"Give back the exocore too," she said.

Instead of obeying without question, the thief pouted and crossed her arms. Disbelief and indignation rippled through Adèle, and she tightened her grip on her pistol. She'd had enough.

Moving into Val-de-mer had already been difficult, and she didn't need an upstart thief shattering her feeble sense of security and taking off with her flat's costly source of electricity.

"Don't make me say it twice."

"Or you'll shoot me?" The thief's voice was rich; her tone playful. If the gun scared her, she hid it well. "I don't think you would. I'm Claire, by the way."

"I'll arrest you." Adèle ignored the given name. She didn't want to know! This woman wasn't Claire; she was a thief who had broken into her house to snatch her valuables away. A criminal who didn't show the slightest hint of remorse. "I am an officer of the law."

She saw no need to mention she only started this new assignment tomorrow, and had never met her boss or colleagues. Nor that she didn't expect them to be very welcoming of her—not if her troublemaking reputation had followed her from one city to the next. If Adèle had to introduce herself tonight in order to bring Claire in, she wouldn't hesitate despite the less than ideal circumstances.

Claire clapped her hands. "Oh, good!"

Adèle scowled at the thief's pleased exclamation. Did anything get through her thick skull? Why would she ever consider this good news? Adèle's doubts must have shown, because Claire chuckled.

"It explains the revolver. Not a lot of people in the big city have legal reasons to keep a firearm within reach, and those who ignore the law… they're not the sorts I want to associate with. Or anger."

"You ignore the law! You broke into my house. You're trying to steal my things, right now!"

"You can't compare the two! I'm harmless."

Harmless? Didn't she realize harm came in other ways than through physical wounds? The nerve of this girl! Adèle stepped forward, her blood boiling. She wanted to return to sleep, to rest before her first day of work, but she doubted she'd manage to now. Especially since every word out of Claire's mouth renewed her anger. "Put my exocore back on the desk, then step away from it."

"If you insist."

"I do."

With another pout, Claire slid her hand towards the sling pouch. Adèle willed herself to track every inch of movement, to never lose sight of her. The thief grimaced as she touched the exocore, and Adèle scowled. If the thing disgusted her so much, why even steal it? Then again, perhaps she shouldn't expect the motivations of a masked and caped thief to make sense. People who sneaked into private houses costumed and laughing tended to have weird ideas about the world around them. Adèle didn't care to hear them. She wanted her exocore back, and she wanted this Claire to answer for her crime.

Yet despite her vigilance—despite the assiduity with which she watched Claire's fingers—Adèle never noticed her drop the exocore in favour of a smokestick. One moment she was staring at the hand, the next it had turned into a blur, and before her brain could even register how wrong this was, thick gray smoke erupted from the pouch. Adèle's mind scrambled to grasp how the thief had moved so fast, and her instincts took over. She shifted her aim towards Claire's left knee and pressed the trigger.

The bang startled Adèle, shaking off the last of her drowsiness. She so rarely shot, she had forgotten how hard it made her ears ring. Her bullet whizzed through thick smoke and thunked into wood. Not flesh. Adèle hurried back as Claire's cape snapped close by, loud and clear. How had she reached Adèle so fast? Would she strike her next? Where from? Adèle backpedalled against a wall, her heart hammering in her chest, inhaling the smoke in the process. It shot through her airways, burning, and she doubled over to cough. Her firearm almost slipped out of her sweaty palms as she leaned against the wall, trying to recover from her throat closing down.

Something brushed against her—a flash of purple hair and black cotton—then the soft padding of silent feet grew weaker. Adèle stumbled out of the room, cringing at the wheeziness of her breath. Hard to hear anything above herself. Had the thief fled? She peered at the smoke, slowly improving. As seconds passed, she began to relax. Then Claire's voice boomed from behind, and Adèle spun on her heels.

"Sorry for all the smoke!"

Adèle brandished her revolver again, but Claire was nowhere around. A strange absence followed, and for the first time since waking up, Adèle knew with complete certainty that she was alone in her flat. She hurried to the bathroom, snatching her bottle of vivifiants. She snapped two of the pressured-air capsules into a small chamber, and shoved the open end of it in her mouth. Adèle inhaled deeply, and fresh and stingy air flowed down, reaching into her lungs and appeasing her. With a relieved sigh, she allowed the medication to take effect then spat the worst of the mucus back into the sink. She hoped she wouldn't need the stronger but slower inhaler later; she was in no mood for the long routine of mixing medication with water and having it boil in her special tin can. Sometimes, though, the rescue vivifiants just weren't enough. When she felt better, Adèle returned to her living room. Warm summer wind slid into the house from her now-open window.

Her thief had escaped.

The woman had stridden into Adèle's home, browsing through her personal items and unhooking her exocore, stealing power and safety all at once. Worse, she had grinned at Adèle, introduced herself like this entire encounter was a pleasant chat in the nearest café, then slipped through her fingers. A walk in the park! No wonder she hadn't worried about the revolver.

Adèle slammed her palm against the wall, humiliation burning through her stomach and throat. She should have arrested Claire. Smoke drifted out of the windows, revealing walls still undecorated. Adèle hadn't turned her flat into *her* cozy home yet, and now it felt more foreign than ever.

-2-

LE CROISSANT-TOI

REASSURING FAMILIARITY WASHED OVER ADÈLE AS THE local bakery's bell rang. Every morning since moving to Val-de-mer, the lovely sound preceded the scent of fresh bread, the warmth of the bakery, and the delicious croissant she always bought. Established a block away from her apartment, Claude's *Croissant-toi* was a haven and her favourite spot in this neighbourhood. Moving had brought about many changes, but Claude's infallible smile had soon created a routine Adèle used to ground herself. It made this new area feel a little like home.

Unlike that thief, who'd smashed her growing sense of security and belonging into pieces.

Adèle heaved a sigh and rubbed her eyes. Even after this Claire had left, she hadn't managed to get a drop of sleep. She had watched the sky lighten for dawn through her thin curtains, cursing the anxious insomnia on the eve of her first day at a new job. Adèle reached for the talisman at her neck, prayed the bad timing wasn't an omen of things to come, and returned her attention to the tiny bakery.

Huge wicker baskets hung on the walls behind the counter, each filled with baguettes and breads of all types—brié, bran, nut sourdough, with white or rye flour, they spread before her in various shades of brown, their crusts almost glowing in the warm light. Claude stood in front like a proud father, round arms on his hips. Adèle's gaze immediately sought the golden croissants he prepared every day, and her mouth watered at the promise of buttery goodness. She stifled a yawn and hurried closer.

Claude cocked his head, and strands of rich brown hair fell in front of his eyes. It never seemed to stay contained in his long and loose ponytail, even early in the morning.

"Madame, have you slept at all last night?" Concern tarnished his otherwise radiant smile. Adèle wondered if he'd ever stop calling her Madame or using "vous" instead of "tu" for her. She couldn't be more than a year older, and the overt politeness and formal address both amused and irritated her. When she shook her head, he snatched a ceramic cup from his shelves. "Let me brew you my finest coffee, then. On the house."

He motioned to the visitor's counter, a small section at the rightmost end devoid of viennoiseries and fitted with seats, for customers who wished to linger, and Adèle plopped down on a stool. She rubbed her eyes again. "You're too kind. I had a rough night."

"I'm sorry," he said. "I hope the croissant is extra delicious to make up for it."

"That's a tough challenge." Adèle grinned and watched him put a percolator over the fire. Claude still powered his bakery

9

through gas, foregoing the more modern exocores. Perhaps he couldn't afford this latest technology. The upgrade didn't come cheap, even for low-energy houses, and she wouldn't have paid for hers if not for the diminished risk of fire. "Your croissants are always impeccable. It'd be a miracle for this one to surpass others."

He laughed, and Adèle allowed the sound to wash over her. His voice became deeper when he laughed, heartier, and more honest, as if every loud burst came unfiltered from within. She had never been with a man before, despite a number of romantic crushes, and listening to him now, the stiff smell of coffee drifting around the bakery, Adèle wondered if Claude might become the first. She leaned forward, her gaze following him as he hand-picked a croissant for her. Her romantic life could wait until her job had settled, for sure. Besides, it might give her time for a bond to form, and the sexual attraction that sometimes came with it. One could hope, she thought, staring at his golden skin and bright hazelnut eyes. He'd be a nice change of pace from the wild ride Béatrice had been.

Claude set the coffee and croissant in front of her. Their gazes met, and his face shifted into a more serious expression. Before he could add anything, however, the bell chimed.

A tall woman swept in, skirts flowing behind her, with short boyish hair and rich brown skin. She threw her arms up with a grin, called "Claude" in a deep and accented voice, pronouncing the "a" and "u" as two tied vowels instead of a single "o". Claude's eyes widened, but after a stunned second, his face split into a welcoming smile.

"Livia!" Then they were off, chattering in Tereaun, which Adèle struggled to follow. Despite sharing words and sounds with Bernéais, Tereaun had a completely different musicality, a sing-song rhythm foreign to her ears. She loved it, even if she didn't understand most of it. Claude had gone around the counter to embrace the newcomer, then turned to Adèle, a hand still on the taller woman's shoulder. "Adèle, this is my younger twin, Livia. Livia, Adèle is new in the neighbourhood, but one of my most regular customers already."

A little knot unwound itself in her stomach as Claude presented Livia as his sister, surprising even Adèle. Perhaps she was more interested than she'd allowed herself to believe. She slipped down her stool to greet Claude's twin, but before she could extend her hand, Livia had twisted away from him.

"Did you say 'youngest'?" Livia's accent induced a flourish in her otherwise perfect Bernéais. She poked Claude's ribs hard as he laughed, then rolled her eyes and turned to Adèle. "My brother compensates for his missing inches with the five extra minutes in his life."

"I'm not sure which is the best deal," Adèle said. "It's a pleasure to meet you."

Livia glanced at the extended hand, then ignored it to peck Adèle three times on the cheeks. "Same to you," she exclaimed, stepping back. "I hope you like your new home."

Adèle's mind sprung to the purple-haired thief in her office, all wide smile and bandana and cape. Claire had laughed and introduced herself too, remorseless at her unwelcome presence

11

in Adèle's home and her shattered sense of security.

"I did," she told Livia, "until last night anyway. I had an undesired visitor about which I really must give my report." It always amazed Adèle how little consideration for others people could have. It shouldn't—not with the horrible things she'd seen criminals and old colleagues do through the years. Yet it still did, and she berated herself each time for her naivety.

She hated to start her job this way. "Hi, I am l'officier Adèle Duclos, your new detective, and last night a thief broke into my house and slipped through my fingers." This move into the city was supposed to be a new beginning—a chance for Adèle to put her life together, closer to her favourite sibling. Not a resounding success so far. Adèle downed the espresso, smoothed her uniform, and grabbed her still-untouched croissant.

"I must head out. It wouldn't do to be late for my first day. A pleasure again, Livia—and Claude, thanks for the coffee."

It helped to know at least one person besides her sister cared for her in this city. Even if it was a distant, "I wish you no ill" kind of caring. He'd given Adèle a croissant and solid coffee, and it had soothed her tired irritation. Adèle left the rich warmth of the bakery, stepping into the heavy summer day. Stifling humidity thickened the air, holding down the stench of burning gas. Exocores might cost an arm and a leg, but they didn't stink, at least.

Adèle grimaced and threw the croissant into her vélocycle's front basket. She had a long way to bike still, and new colleagues to meet. With no idea what lay ahead, Adèle suspected the croissant's softness might come in handy to remind her she already had a friend in the city.

Claude flipped the *Ouvert/Fermé* sign on his door, then slipped the key in and closed for the day. The morning had come and gone, customers emptying the shelves of his bakery as Livia and he provided for their bread-related needs. He'd never worked the bakery with his sister before, but she fell into the role as though she'd been around for months, serving clients with a wide smile and chatting as she wrapped their loaf and handed it to them. She'd picked up a broom to clean while he counted his till and completed paperwork for the day, but as soon as he emerged from his office, she stopped and stared at him.

"This is a nice life you've got going," she said, "but you didn't write me for a bakery problem. Not after so long."

Claude pressed his lips tight at "so long". Livia resented him for not following the family out of Val-de-mer — and in truth, so did he, at times. He missed their dad's wry puns and the way their mother's singing always filled the house. But he had spent all his life in Val-de-mer, spoke Bernéais better than he ever would Tereaun, and he hadn't wanted to flee, no matter how bad the threats to magic users had become. Besides, being alone had granted him time to fully explore his genderfluidity without worrying about potential family reactions.

"Sorry, Livia," he said. "The climate grew worse at first, and then…" He gestured vaguely at the air. "You know how bad I am at giving news."

"Indeed I know. Thank God for Zita, who writes a novel every week and makes sure to check on you!" The hint of a smile pierced through her stern expression, and in that single moment she was strikingly familiar to their father when he tried to scold them.

"I get it, Livia. I promise never to go silent for so long again! Happy?"

"Yeah!" She strode up to him, her grin returning. Claude's eyes widened at her approach and the mischievous light in her eyes. Before he could dodge, she'd wrapped an arm around his neck and rubbed her knuckles in his hair, pulling even more strands out of his ponytail. "You can't blame me for wanting news of my tiny sibling!"

Her voice covered his protest and he struggled until she let go, both of them laughing. Claude tried to smooth his hair, his skull hurting but his heart full. "Maybe this kind of behaviour is why I don't write!"

"As if." She booped his nose, but her smile lessened. "Now tell me what your magical sister can do for you."

"It's the exocores." His shoulders slumped. He would rather talk about bread and family and Livia's sibling-bullying than these unnatural devices. They'd plagued enough of his nights over the last months without occupying his days, too. But Livia had crossed the Bernan-Tereaus Détroit for his sake, and he couldn't keep his suspicions secret. "Do you have them in Tereaus?"

"Not yet, but with that ugly bridge of yours it's only a

14

matter of time."

Claude grimaced. Val-de-mer nestled at the bottom of a depression, on the most southern point of Bernan. Here, the sea separating the country from Tereaus narrowed to a thin, thirteen kilometres band. Ferries had always ensured the passage of citizens from one country to the other, but during the last five years a massive bridge had been built over the water: Le Pont des Lumières. They called it a marvel of new technology, the first large-scale structure powered entirely by renewable energy. To Claude, it was a dreadful scar on the sea below, huge supporting pillars plunging into the water. And, if his fears about the exocores meant to fuel it were true, this bridge would become the most ignoble project ever constructed in Bernan.

"Let me show you." Claude led Livia through his office, to the cupboard where he stored old administrative paperwork. He rolled the filing cabinet containing them out, revealing the thin trapdoor under, then removed the key hung around his neck. Livia tilted her head to the side as he slid it in the lock, opened the way, and motioned for her to go down the ladder.

"Secret lair?"

Claude laughed. "You have no idea."

He waited for his sister to reach the bottom and step aside before jumping down, foregoing the ladder and landing behind her. After so much climbing around Val-de-mer's rooftops at nights, he'd gotten used to simple shortcuts.

Two gas lamps hung on the low ceiling of his basement, but Claude hadn't needed them to see in weeks. A huge pile of exocores was strewn on a table in the centre of the basement, each of them glowing a pinkish red, and collectively they cast enough light to move around the small room unaided. A large map of the city covered the right wall, half-buried under black and red pins marking his progress. In the Quartier des Chênes and the Quartier des Mélèzes, where wealthy citizens resided, one could hardly read the street names anymore. Claude's neighbourhood and other, poorer sections of Val-de-mer had next to no pins, not even the red ones to indicate exocores to steal. His gaze stopped at the newest addition—black, for exocore stolen.

Adèle's pin seemed to glare back at him.

Guilt dried Claude's throat, and he turned away from the map. Livia had crossed the room to the wardrobe in a corner and opened it. Her fingers trailed the black cotton of Claire's outfit, then moved to the massive skirts and beautiful dresses behind. Was she purposefully ignoring the exocores, or did she not feel the wrongness of them, as he did? Her smile widened as she continued to inspect his clothes, pulling them out one by one. "You always had more flair than I did."

Claude snorted. "Not a hard feat by any measure."

"Oh shush." Livia closed the wardrobe and her voice softened. "So that's where Claire went. Is it better? For you, I mean."

"Claire didn't go anywhere, you know this. She doesn't vanish with daylight, just as Claude doesn't go away when I put a cape on." He wished it was so simple. His gender swung between male and female, sometimes firmly on one end for weeks, sometimes shifting after a day. Claire and Claude were both full expressions of himself and they helped him handle his fluidity. "It's not perfect, but it's better than trying to suppress one gender. So, yes."

"Good." Livia frowned. "No, not just 'good'." She strode to Claude, flinging her arms around him and hugging him before he could react. The tightness of her arms communicated what her words couldn't, and a deep warmth spread through him. Livia squeezed, then stepped back. "I'm happy for you."

"Thank you. It means a lot." This, more than anything else, was why he should write more often. Livia would always be on his side. He'd shared so much of his early gender confusion with her, and not once had she belittled him while he figured it out. Now, more than ever, he wanted an ally he could trust—and no one could beat his twin in that regard. "Back to business?"

Livia stepped back and hesitated, casting a wary look at the glowing pile on his table. "These… things? These are exocores?"

The disgust in her voice surprised and worried Claude. She did feel it, then. Starting with the wardrobe must have been avoidance if even standing nearby put her off. His heartbeat sped and his palms grew sweaty. He needed to hold one to sense something off about them, but Livia had known right away.

"I've spent the last months investigating exocore rumours," he said. "I tracked down their owners and stole those I could, gathering them here. They're promoted as renewable and safe—the perfect solution to our limited gas supplies and the supposed instability of magic—but their creation process is an industrial secret. I don't trust it. I can't! Not when hovering my hand near one makes me feel... sick."

Sick didn't properly describe how he reacted to the exocores. They gave him a slight nausea, true, but the feeling went deeper, gripping him tight. Like someone had flared up an alarm, and his brain and heart and *soul* screamed in protest, repeating *wrong wrong wrong* over and over. No one else ever noticed, however, not that he could tell. After some time, Claude had concluded it might be related to his limited magic.

"Since you hogged all the magic strength when we shared a womb, I figured I'd ask you to check it out."

Livia snickered and gave him a little shove. "Jealous still?"

"You bet I am. Imagine the delicious bread I'd prepare with your power!" He was only half-joking. Sometimes he wished he didn't have to keep his small abilities a secret and could put his spells into creating unique loaves and cakes, or the butteriest croissant in the entire city. He'd need to practise a lot before he could shift the essence of his magic so significantly, however. His power naturally augmented speed and strength, and Claude had made great use of it recently, but he'd often desired something more... peaceful. "Seriously, though. You can feel it, can't you?"

Livia met his gaze, her expression turning into an impassible mask. That, more than anything, alerted Claude to the seriousness of the situation. Livia had the worst of all poker faces. Her face always gave away something, whether through wide grins, deep scowls, or shaking lips. This emotional void scared him.

"Livia?" he asked, his voice tight.

"I don't want to go nearer," she whispered, casting a glance to the exocores as though they would hear her and react. Her mask cracked into a fearful grimace as a shudder ran up her spine. "They feel so wrong. It scares me that you even have those in your basements. People use them for electricity?"

"They want to power the entire Pont des Lumières with them. Hundreds of them."

Livia stared at the pile of exocores, and Claude could follow the rise of her nausea through the twisting of her face. She breathed in slowly, inching her fingers through her short hair as her lungs filled, and exhaled. Her hands dropped to her side—an old routine of hers before distasteful tasks—then she took several determined strides to the table and snatched one of the exocores up.

A shocked gasp crossed her lips, then a loud swear. She flung the encased gem across the room, cringing as it hit the wall and clang to the ground. "Oh, no, I'm sorry! I'm so sorry!" She had addressed her words to the thrown exocore and dashed after it, scooping it up from the floor. Although her grimace returned the moment she touched it, Livia ran a finger over its surface. "It's not your fault. I know, I understand. I shouldn't have done that."

A deep unease grew at the bottom of Claude's stomach as his sister whispered apologies to the exocore—heartfelt, horrified apologies. His mouth dried, and words failed him, as if his mind snatched them away before he could form a complete sentence and ask her why. But he needed to know. He couldn't dodge out of this now, not when he'd spent months hunting down exocores, trying to unravel the secrets behind their creation, to understand what was wrong about them and if he should destroy them.

"What's going on, Livia?"

She lifted her head, tears shining in her eyes. They didn't quite hide the furious determination behind them, however, and Livia set her jaw. "These feel like people, Claude. They're... people's core, the sheer energy we draw on when we cast magic. I—touching one was like forcing them to help me create a spell. Like I could have ripped off parts of their souls for my needs."

Claude stumbled back and reached for the wall behind him for support. "Are you saying—the electricity..."

"Comes from trapped witches' lives, I think. And I... I can't tell if they're sentient or not, so throwing one like this..."

Claude's gaze snapped back to the exocores on his table. The forty-seven exocores he had stolen from various homes in Val-de-mer's quartiers, acting on instinct more than anything else. The forty-seven souls, abused and trapped, at which he'd flung a multitude of insults over the course of the last weeks. The floor seemed to vanish under him. People. Alive, after a fashion, stored in gems, in his basement and all across the city. A scream built inside, but it stuck in his throat, imprisoned there as surely as these witches were in exocores.

A light hand squeezed his forearm and startled him. When Livia spoke, her voice was steady, grounding. "You've been rescuing them, Claude. At least no one is using them while they're here. They're safe here, and we'll find a way to free everyone."

Free them. Over the last months, all he had thought about was how to *destroy* the exocores. Collect and eliminate, in short. He hadn't understood their nature, only their wrongness, and that something needed to be done. But these were people, and destroying the exocores… Claude closed his eyes, struggling with the heavy mix of guilt and relief washing into his nauseating horror. Thank the Saints he had called Livia to Val-de-mer. What would he have done, without her insight? Killed the exocores? But together, he knew they could find a solution. If he needed to break into every house of Val-de-mer to save those trapped in exocores, he gladly would.

-3-

BANDE À PART

BIKING TO VAL-DE-MER'S WEST PRECINCT SHOWED ADÈLE the brutal differences existing between some of the city's quartiers. Emmanuelle had called the Quartier des Érables the heart of Val-de-mer, and every time Adèle's path brought her to the rue Saint-Adémar, its northern edge, she rediscovered why. It breathed life. Here, three-storied buildings leaned against one another, linked by attics and balconies, housing local business, families, and artists. People greeted each other on the sidewalks, shops kept their doors open or had stalls in front of their location, and music drifted past from a nearby park.

And yet, just one street away, the scenery changed completely. Massive villas and spreading lawns formed the Quartier des Chênes, and its people averted their eyes as others biked past them. No commercial avenue brought life to the area, and the rare park remained well hidden behind ample vegetation. How many tightly packed homes had been destroyed to make room for these mansions inside Val-de-mer's old walls? Fences and hedges concealed the inhabitants from prying eyes, but the

Wansonian names on streets and individual houses served as constant reminders of who too often held wealth and power in the country of Bernan, even more than a century after conquest.

Adèle tried to ignore the street names of Preston, Ross, and Stanley surrounding her—Wansonian generals, politicians, or merchants—and parked her vélocycle in front of the precinct. She paused there, her breathing laborious. Val-de-mer's old walls enclosed the highest part of the city, and she had biked uphill most of the way, leaving her struggling for air. Reluctantly, she snatched a vivifiant and its chamber from her bag then cracked the capsule in it before inhaling the medication with relief. It was only a temporary fix, but on this first day of work, it would have to do. She wanted to appear calm and in control.

Her new workplace had no reason to envy the surrounding houses. Two massive wooden doors greeted visitors at the top of smooth, marble stairs, and on each side the structure extended, proud and solid, with columns in a style reminiscent of the first settlers to arrive. Its green roof contrasted with the red tiles of nearby manors, and the oxidized copper tiles reflected the sun, forcing Adèle to squint against the light's glare. The old architecture mixed seamlessly with the large and clear windows, the modern sign on the entrance, and clacking of heavy typewriters reached Adèle as she stepped inside.

She stopped in the grand hallway, impressed and estranged by the airy space and its illumination. The entirety of her old station could have fitted here, with its cramped space and shoddy gas lamps—all a punishment for her unit's willingness to dig where they shouldn't. A year in the mouldy, decrepit offices had almost killed Adèle's lungs, causing irreparable damage. They had wanted her to leave—to vanish along with every bit of proof of corruption she had unearthed, and which they had promptly buried anew—and she'd had little choice but to oblige. It would be better here, she thought as she studied the hall. She wouldn't have years of bad blood between her and other colleagues slowing her investigations. She hoped the latter wouldn't happen again.

Adèle strode to the secretary and asked for help finding her way through the large building. Even with clear directions, she took a few wrong turns before she reached the premises of her new team's office space: l'Unité Koyani. Someone had added a flowery "Enter at your own risk" sign under the name, and Adèle stared at it. What kind of unit had she landed herself into? All her old bosses had said was that she could either transfer or leave police work altogether. Any request for more information was met with laughter and promptly denied. She had accepted, hoping for a new beginning with less mould in her office and more chances to see her sister. Further research had revealed the Unité Koyani had a reputation for digging where it shouldn't, and tended to draw the ire of colleagues, all behaviours she was intimately familiar with.

The detectives worked in a large and open area, their desks placed in two rows of three, each with a plaque for name and pronouns. Papers and files covered all but one of them—hers, she guessed. Two separate offices lined up on the left wall, while signs on the right labelled the rooms there as the conference hall and the interrogation room. Immense windows bathed the wooden floors and dark furniture in a warm light that seemed to beckon Adèle inside.

The spacious office would have been a welcoming sight, had it not been devoid of people.

No colleague waited for her, no boss, not even a janitor. The premises were eerily silent, and wariness replaced Adèle's eagerness as she took her first stride into her new office. Had everyone gone elsewhere?

No. She spotted a cup of coffee forgotten on a desk, lacking the dark rims that would have appeared if it had been given time to cool and evaporate. When she approached and touched it, the cup was warm. Papers rested beside it, half-completed. Her new team had been around not so long ago. Adèle was wondering where they'd gone when the murmur of voices reached her. Several people talking, muffled by walls and distance, the sound coming from the right-hand doors—either conference hall or interrogation room, then.

Adèle padded through the office, unreasonably afraid of making any noises. She didn't want to break the dampened atmosphere, as if this strange silence had something sacred. Her previous workspace had been a cacophony—colleagues arguing, phones ringing, doors creaking and slamming, all underscored by the constant buzz of the ventilation system. Some nights she'd even heard screeches and clanking as the building struggled to keep standing and living. This place was all tranquility and new technology, and the stark contrast unsettled her. She was glad to hear the whispers grow louder as she reached the conference hall.

Her fingers rested on the doorknob for a moment, the metal cool against her skin. Her gut twisted with nervousness. The voices inside were engaged in a lively debate—nothing more natural than that, and nothing to worry about. She stomped down her first-day jitters, then stepped into the room.

Silence fell. Five police officers spun towards her in perfect synchronicity, fixing intense gazes on Adèle. They were all sitting around a table except one: a small woman with ferocious, deep-set eyes and olive skin, and the only one in uniform. Capitaine Koyani's black and white outfit marked her rank, and Adèle froze under the glare of her new boss.

"Officier Duclos," Koyani greeted her. "I'm glad you finally decided to join us."

Cold anger underlay the captain's pleasantness, and the corners of her full lips twitched as she smiled. Koyani gestured at an empty seat with her red prosthetic arm, but Adèle stayed frozen, her heart hammering in her chest. She *wasn't* late. The instructions she had received had said nine in the morning, and she'd checked every mural clock on her way through the building.

"Capitaine, I apologize, but…" she said, her voice tight from fear of angering her new superior even further. "I was told meetings started at nine."

Koyani's arm flopped to her side, before she raised it to rub her temple. "Of course. They know I hate lateness." She fixed her gaze on Adèle again, but her ire had slipped out of it. "Please sit down. It's fine."

"You think Poitras sent the instructions, Capitaine?" The

question came from a man in his thirties with a high-pitched voice and a flowery shirt—likely the creator of the sign, Adèle thought.

"Who else?" Koyani replied. "Petty office sabotage is just his style. But no matter. I can deal with him later. Welcome to our beloved unit, Officier Duclos. As you can see, we're quite popular with our colleagues."

"I'll remember." Adèle sat between a muscled black woman with grey cornrows and a wiry, beak-nosed man, relieved not to get chewed out. It sounded like similar mishaps were common occurences for Koyani. "What *is* the correct time?"

"We have round-up meetings every Lundi, at eight thirty." Capitaine Koyani's hands returned to ample hips, and she radiated authority as she swept the group with her dark eyes. More than that, even. Her gaze wrapped the others in pride, severity, and trust, and she cast these so naturally it made Adèle long for a similar look. The capitaine belonged in a leadership position, where she could judge others for their strengths and weaknesses, and use them as was best. So much competence and stature packed into five feet of muscles and willpower left no questions as to who was in charge.

"Let's continue, then." Koyani ran a finger over a list on the table before her until she reached their next order of business. "Yuri, please share your progress on the eau-de-vie ring."

Yuri was the slender man on Adèle's left, his blue eyes so pale she'd mistook them for white, his skin no darker. He leaned forward and detailed what he'd done over the last week, and Adèle paid close attention. Although she'd arrived halfway through the case, she hoped she could be useful in some measure. It turned out a group had been sneaking a new addictive substance into the city, pretending at first to sell a clear and strong alcohol. No one had cared until it moved from low-class revelries in the Quartier des Ormes to some of Val-de-mer's richest balls, right here in the Quartier des Chênes. Now the police had to crack down on it, but they were having no success.

Yuri explained the leads he still needed to explore, listened to suggestions, then they moved to the next order of business. The group went over two more cases like this. First, the case leader summarized their progress over last week, then everyone talked about new leads, potential problems, or hypotheses. Capitaine Koyani guided the discussions, cutting off any unproductive topic before it stretched on. They worked as a team, every officer contributing with their expertise, and all of them deferring to Koyani's final decision. The structure also provided a great chance for Adèle to learn everyone's names. The meeting progressed, smooth and efficient, devoid of the bickering that had stalled all of Adèle's previous experiences.

Half an hour into the meeting, Adèle was smitten with this team.

"This covers our ongoing cases," Koyani declared. "I'm afraid l'officier Duclos is not the only new thing this morning, however. We have a special case." Everyone perked up at once, flipping notebooks to blank pages and readying their pen. Adèle cursed herself for not bringing anything to write with, but she hadn't even been shown her desk yet! She would have to rely on her memory this time. Koyani's gaze lingered on her and she sketched a smile. "Like most of us, this case wound up in my unit because no one else wanted it."

The black woman on Adèle's right, Inha, startled her with sudden laughter. "Not our job to be wanted, boss."

"Quite true, and it would be a mistake to think otherwise. Now, about our case... Everyone dodged this bullet for two reasons. First, several politicians and commanding officers have an interest in it, which means success or failure could play big in one's career. Second, it's thievery, and we catch one of those in a hundred, so none of the promotion-seekers believe they can find our culprit. They would rather pass than fail spectacularly." Koyani paused, as if she needed to control her disdain and irritation at their attitude. The scribbling of her team's pens filled the silence, and Adèle held her breath. She had managed to forget about Claire until now, but with thievery on the table it was hard not to think of the criminal who had shattered her sleep. "It seems someone is sneaking into our wealthiest citizens' houses, taking off with their valuables. This includes jewelry, silverware, exocores... objects easy to carry around. Two witnesses indicated they wore a long cape and a mask—like some sort of vigilante—and had purple hair. All our reports come from wealthy inhabitants and I—"

"Not all." Adèle blurted the words out against her better judgment about interrupting Koyani. Once again, all eyes homed in on her with perfect synchronicity. She swallowed hard, her head buzzing so loud she was half-convinced they could hear it. But it had to be Claire. How many wretches with purple hair pranced

29

about in a cape at night, stealing? "Her name is Claire. She was in my flat last night, and it doesn't qualify as wealthy no matter how you put it. Her disguise is black, made of cotton, and she has long purple hair. Short, fat, with pale brown skin. Further details were difficult in the dim light. She stole my exocore."

"Is that so?" Either Koyani wasn't impressed, or she hid it well. "Anything else you can think of?"

"I pointed a gun at her and she didn't seem worried. She escaped by throwing a smokestick in the room, so she comes equipped to deal with potential problems."

"Good." Koyani smiled, and the implicit approval sent warmth coursing through Adèle. "I'm sure you're eager to lead hopeless cases with us, but—"

"Please," Adèle interrupted. "Hopeless cases are my specialty." She *needed* that case. Claire's nonchalance and her sudden escape had gotten to her. Adèle had no idea if her flat would ever feel like home now, all because this flimsy girl thought it was fun to break into people's homes and take off with their things.

"No." Koyani's voice cracked through the meeting room. "I'm glad for your enthusiasm, but you're too close to this. Élise gets this one. As our best source of information and a newcomer, you can shadow her. Ask questions and make as many suggestions as you want, but she is in charge and has the final say. You're not to do anything she hasn't permitted. Understood?"

Adèle cast a stiff glance at Élise Jefferson, the quiet girl who'd said very little through the entire meeting, except for her own progress report and the occasional sarcastic remark. Her dark curls framed a pale and round visage, with shining brown eyes. She'd seemed too small for police work to Adèle, but the detailed report of her activities over the last week proved she could handle herself. Competent or not, however, Adèle had wanted this case to be hers. She swallowed down her bitterness.

"Excellent. Unless someone has more to add, this meeting is over." Koyani scanned every officer one by one, and they shook their heads in answer. Once certain no one would speak, the capitaine picked up her sheets. "Good day of work, team. Duclos, in my office. I'd like to talk."

Anger still simmered in Koyani's tone, and she stomped out of the room, striding past Adèle without a glance in her direction and giving her no option but to fall in steps with her. Adèle followed, nervous yet marvelling at how such a small woman could move so fast. They crossed the larger office area and entered the spacious room on the other side, which Koyani had claimed for her own. As soon as the door clicked behind Adèle, the capitaine spun about.

"Let's clarify a few things." Metallic fingers pushed her bangs aside before she gestured at the guest's chair. "Sit."

Adèle would have rather stayed standing. Nervous energy coursed through her and, if she sat, she'd be wringing her hands and shuffling around. Yet Koyani's tone left no room for arguing, so she took a deep breath to calm her jitters and settled into the seat.

"First, about this morning... we are a team. Almost a

31

family. Lateness at group meetings is a mark of disrespect."

"I didn't—" A raised hand stopped her.

"I know, I know. This isn't on you—other police pull shit like this all the time--but you should know for the future. I don't tolerate it."

Adèle's face and throat burned with shame anyway. She tried to convince herself Koyani's anger wasn't directed at her but struggled with the capitaine's brusque tone. First impressions mattered, and even if others were to blame, this whole affaire had messed up hers. She swallowed her feelings down, her shoulders squared, and waited for the rest, remembering Koyani's smile in the reunion room, her satisfied "excellent" when Adèle didn't argue about Claire's case.

"Don't make that face," Koyani said. "You are wanted here. I asked for your transfer."

"You... what?"

"I asked for you. I'm sorry, was that unclear?" Adèle stared blankly as shock and confusion rippled through her. When she had been told she'd been transferred, she had assumed her presence in the Unité Koyani was imposed, perhaps even a form of punishment for Koyani. A glimmer of amusement shone in Koyani's eyes, but the other woman kept her face schooled as she asked, "Do you know what my team does?"

"Not exactly." She had already learned they were efficient and that they handled difficult cases that many would rather avoid, but Koyani seemed to seek a more precise answer. Adèle volunteered what she had gathered and hoped none of it was too far off the mark.

"Close enough," Koyani said afterwards. "Mairesse Jalbert created this unit to chase down cases everyone refuses to touch, either because of their political weight or because they're likely impossible to solve. We have her blessing and her protection, and more leeway than most. We've also touched enough corrupted colleagues that we're no longer welcome anywhere within police forces.

"Now, I hate wasted potential, and I've learned that when nobody wants an investigative employee, it can be due to crass incompetence, or because they have a way of digging out what everyone wants to bury. You have three months to prove you're the latter category, or I'll have you shipped back into a mould-ridden hole like the one you no doubt just left. Succeed, and you'll be part of the team for good."

Adèle recalled how they'd worked together earlier, seamlessly contributing to each other's cases, examining new angles and possibilities through healthy debate rather than by outshining others. The respect and efficiency she'd witnessed had struck envy in her, and now she learned they were explicitly allowed to investigate corruption? She wanted in. The desire burned through her stomach, stronger than her previous shame, and hardened into determination.

"We'll get her, Capitaine." She squared her shoulders and smiled back. "With your permission, I'd like to go file my report and join Lieutenant Jefferson."

"You have it. I won't wish you good luck, however. It is

only half the battle."

That still left half she could make well wishes for, Adèle thought, but she withheld any comments. If good fortune didn't follow, she would have to create her own.

The rest of Adèle's day was split between her theft report, running around the huge precinct to acquire all the necessary supplies, ensuring she was set up properly for future work, and officially meeting her colleagues.

The latter happened the moment Adèle returned with her supplies. As she stepped back through the door, the wide office area fell silent. Her presence killed the half-whispered conversations, and she knew they'd been chatting about the team's newcomer and her remarkable entrance. Adèle stared at the four gathered — a strange group of police officers if she'd ever seen one.

"Don't stop for me," she said, striding to her desk and dumping the supplies on it. "I'm sure it was a pleasant conversation."

A beat of silence, then a raucous laughter escaped Inha, who had sat on Adèle's right during the meeting. She was the unit's oldest member. Time had grayed her tight cornrows and wrinkled and marked her dark skin, but her arms retained impressive muscles.

"You've got character," she said. "Nice to have some fresh blood around."

Was it Adèle's imagination, or did it sound like they meant to hunt her down? Like a pack waiting to jump on her. Adèle pushed the idea aside. Her initial entrance hadn't happened in the best of ways, but Koyani clearly wanted her in this team, and she had no reason to believe the others were hostile to her presence. Besides, she had more than character: she had the skills to prove she belonged, too.

"And it feels good to join a team instead of rotting away in a dump," she said.

"Don't let the airy area fool you," Élise replied. "We still clean the precinct's trash."

"And get no thanks for the dirty work," Yuri added, before raising the cup of coffee Adèle had spotted earlier. She suspected its content had cooled over the last two hours, but Yuri sipped at it anyway. Perhaps he couldn't bear to waste a drop of it.

"Don't be so grim!" Marcel's northern accent needlessly elongated every vowel and reminded Adèle of home, near Lac Saint-Damase, where she had grown up. "You'll discourage our new friend before her first day is even over."

Of all the team members, he'd been the most talkative during the meeting. His hands flittered midair as he spoke, adding dramatic punctuation to every word. Where the others remained serious and careful in their estimations of the work they could accomplish over the next week, Marcel had grinned, professed hopes of important achievements, and encouraged all to do the same. An attitude that quite fitted the bright-coloured shirts with flower patterns he wore. His positive outlook had soothed

35

Adèle's nerves during the meeting, and it calmed her now, too.

"Don't worry. I have thicker skin than that." After she'd tried and failed to stomp the corruption at the backbone of her last police corp, she'd heard worse than the speculations of a small team about their new colleague. "Shall we start, Élise? I can't wait to dig through these theft reports and see what we can uncover."

A slight smile curved Élise's lips, while Inha laughed again. "Ah, the enthusiasm of newcomers," the older woman said. "Enjoy it while it lasts."

"Words of wisdom from our family's grandma."

Adèle couldn't tell if Élise was being sarcastic or not. Inha must have thought so, because she gave her a playful shove with a heavy-booted foot. Then she slid down her desk and clapped her hands—a signal the whole team immediately obeyed. They scattered back to their respective desks, all well within earshot, and soon Adèle's new colleagues had opened their case files and jumped into work. Only Élise remained in front of her.

"Let's decide how we approach this, and then you can go fishing for information while I close my other case."

There weren't a billion ways to handle thievery cases, and Claire's wouldn't be any different. They settled on a classic strategy to begin: first, they had to sort through and organize what they knew. Make lists of everything she'd stolen and everywhere she'd stolen it from, to see if patterns would emerge. Many thieves weren't careful and picked targets too close to their homes.

Élise showed her where they stored large cork boards, then helped her find a map of Val-de-mer. Adèle didn't waste a moment to start, reading through the victims' reports and listening to her colleagues' frequent banter. Those who had to stay at the office chatted as they worked, ate together, and continued their on-and-off conversations in the afternoon. The helpful dynamic Adèle had witnessed during the morning's reunion never really died, and the team alternated between unravelling cases and discussing their private lives. Yuri recounted his weekend shopping for binders with Marcel while Inha shared her night in the Quartier des Sorbiers' clubs with her two polyamorous partners, hoping to meet new women. Half the time, Adèle found herself forgetting her work to listen in to the stories. She loved the group's ease with one another.

At the end of the day, Adèle's desk had returned to a more normal state for a detective: it was covered in files to read and scribbled notes. She stared at the mess, then at her map, on which she'd pinned several of the locations Claire had presumably stolen from. These were her weapons—information and her wits. More than the revolver at her belt would ever be. Koyani had called the case hopeless, but only determination filled Adèle. They would find the thread connecting these thefts, and they would arrest Claire.

-4-

LES DESSOUS DE MONTRANT

THE FACTORY LOOMED BEFORE CLAIRE, ITS MASSIVE walls blocking out the stars. Grime clung to its bricks, left by decades of harsh winters and dusty summer, and rust half-covered the side entrance's door. Everything in the Quartier des Épinettes had this rundown look—most street lamps no longer even functioned—but if Claire had walked past this particular building unknowingly, she would never have pegged it as Montrant Industries' local exocore production factory. She turned to Livia with a frown.

"Are you certain this is the place?"

"It's the right address," her sister answered with a shrug. "They could have moved, but there's only one way to find out for sure." She gestured at the door and grinned, unable to quite hide her excitement.

Claire snorted. On Livia's second day in Val-de-mer, while Claude had distractedly prepared coffee and croissants for

38

customers, she'd ensconced herself at the public library, browsing through newspapers and records for everything she could dig out about Montrant Industries. Most of the articles had been published almost two years ago, when the exocores had officially launched, and apart from a couple in *Le Quotidien du Val* few newspapers bothered to give more than surface information. Mairesse Jalbert had visited one of their factories, however, and journalists had been granted a one-time opportunity to tour the premises. Neither Livia nor Claire had such an authorization, but judging by Livia's excitement, this only made the excursion better.

Claire had to admit she would rather have come alone. Standing next to her twin while wearing her mask, purple hair, and heavy black cotton skirts and cape felt weird. Besides, Livia had always been the expressive and noisy one, and Claire would wager stealth would prove difficult tonight. They had found a second piece of cotton to hide her face and Livia had changed from her flowing skirts into more straightforward pants. What a strange turn of events—never had Claire expected to break into a factory with her twin. And yet she suspected things would only get weirder from now on.

"Ready?" Livia asked.

When Claire nodded, Livia stretched out her left hand towards the metal door. Ice covered her fingers, reflecting moonlight, then jumped through the air and onto the knob. It crackled as it spread across the surface and slipped into the lock, and the door gave a long, plaintive creak. Claire gritted her teeth as it echoed in the otherwise silent night, hunching her shoulders as though taking up less space could quieten the door. Livia's hand balled into a fist, and the ice expanded into the lock until it gave in with a final crack. Smiling, she stepped to the door and opened it with a slight shove.

"Here we go! First obstacle crossed."

"I hope no one heard that," Claire pointed out, before heading into the building. "Let's not wait to find out."

Livia followed with a shrug. "I doubt busting it open with your strength would have been any more discreet."

True enough. Whether they'd forced the door with ice or muscles wouldn't have changed the noise it would have created. They only needed to become more subtle now. Claire gestured for her sister to stay silent as she scanned their surroundings. The back-entrance led into a wide area with several conveyor belts and large machinery. The relative obscurity concealed most details, and she cursed the destroyed street lamps outside. Grime in the windows kept any starlight out of the factory, and they would need their own source to navigate the factory. Nothing to do about that, however. Claire reached into her outfit's front pouch and slipped out a torchlight. She pointed it to the ground before spinning the crank on its side, generating enough power to bring it to life for the next five to ten minutes. Sweat covered her palms by the time she finished, and she wiped them both on her skirt before sweeping the beam around.

The factory looked bigger than she'd expected, as this area spread over two stories and most of the floor. She spotted an overseer's office above, across from them, but the huge machines blocked most of their view to the right, towards the entrance. Nothing was moving at the moment, not even clouds of dust, but Claire could easily imagine the place teeming with workers operating the equipment, their conversations buried under the continuous humming and clanking of exocore production.

"The newspaper's picture had the mairesse in front of a large, closed off room labelled charging station," Livia said. "We could start there, or we can sift through the papers and hope for a clue."

"Do you think... how would they do that? Charging with witches?" Claire hadn't exactly thought of what she expected to discover here. Would they keep witches prisoner? Did they need to be alive? Her stomach tightened as she tried to imagine the repulsive process—she didn't *want* to consider anything remotely close to this. She had forced herself into emotional numbness since finding out about the cores, stalling the horrendous possibilities her mind sought to conjure with the familiarity of her bakery work, but she could no longer maintain that state while standing in Montrant's factory. Nausea gripped her, and her mask and cape felt hot and stuffy.

"Can't wait to find out so I can wreck it into tiny pieces," Livia answered, deep anger almost turning her voice into a growl. "I want to ice this whole place over."

"I'd rather we find who did this and ice *them*. Let's check the office first."

Claire started off again, careful not to illuminate too far ahead. She stopped every few steps to listen to the surrounding

41

sounds, convinced a security guard would come by sooner or later. The eerie silence troubled her, fraying her nerves further. Shouldn't the factory be under constant surveillance, considering what they were producing? Why wasn't every door watched? They couldn't be *that* confident no one would find out. Who would take that risk? The longer she and Livia explored, walking around conveyor belts and past large cisterns without interruptions, the more stressed Claire became. Her heart was hammering so loudly she half-expected *that* to raise the alarm. When they reached the stairs leading to the overseer's office, Claire sighed in relief. She couldn't wait for this to be over.

Livia forced the door open with ice once more, and they stepped into the tiny room. It held a single desk facing the wide window, offering them a diving view of the main area below, a chair on wheels, and a filing cabinet. Dust covered every surface, and the only paper on the desk was a blueprint of the factory.

"Take the desk. I'll check the cabinet," Claire said, striding across the narrow space. Something about this place didn't feel right, but she couldn't put her finger on it. Hopefully they wouldn't have to stay for long. The first drawer resisted her when she pulled, and she let her magic strengthen her arms before trying again. The lock snapped, revealing folder after folder of paperwork to Claire. She grabbed a few and flipped through the papers. Delivery schedules, lists of equipment, suppliers… All utterly fascinating stuff. She scanned it, not too optimistic, until she noticed the dates marked on them. None of these were more recent than the last six months. Had they not had a single delivery since?

Claire set the papers down, frowning, and moved to the next drawer. This one had employee files! Her heart sped at the thought, and she flipped through the folders eagerly, opening each in turn, checking for the position within the industry, and closing back anyone who wasn't part of the management team. She didn't care about the lowest rung—they likely had no idea what they were producing here. But the bosses? Those were the names they sought. Except... none of them seemed to have files here, not even the overseer. Who occupied this office, then?

"We have any names on who's in charge here?" she asked Livia. "Anything personal in the desk?"

Her sister straightened, then shook her head, dismayed. "I'm half-convinced no one's ever sat here. Everything's so orderly."

"What did the newspaper articles say? Who guided the mairesse and journalists?"

Livia's frown deepened as she tried to remember. "It talked about a representative. I'll check when we get home."

Claire shoved the drawer closed, and the sound of it slamming shut spread through the empty factory, an echo of her frustration. She cringed at the loudness of it, then ran a hand over the lower half of her face, slipping her fingers beneath her mask to brush some of the sweat away. "I hate this place, and I'm not spending hours squinting at pointless papers in the dead of night. Let's see this charging station."

Livia checked the factory's blueprint for its location, and they left the overseer's office behind. Part of Claire feared they had missed important clues, but she convinced herself they could return if needed, later tonight. She followed her sister as they headed to the right portion of the production area.

A belt lead straight into the wall in front of them, only to reemerge five metres to the right. Between them was a display area, with several indicators and, in rusted letters above, the words "Zone de chargement". Despite the bright light on them, Claire couldn't read what any of the gauges meant. She gave up with an annoyed grunt, instead shifting her attention to the door just beyond the belt's exit, with the telltale "personnel autorisé seulement" on it.

"We're about to authorize ourselves," Claire said. "I'll take this one."

"Suit yourself."

She shouldn't, really. Livia's magic ran so deep she could draw on it almost endlessly, but Claire's power was more limited and replenished more slowly. She hadn't quite recovered from the bursts of speed she'd used to dodge Adèle's shot two nights ago. At least she wouldn't need as much energy tonight. With a flicker of thought, Claire infused her muscles with extra strength, grabbed the door's handle, and pushed. The lock snapped, and this time the echoes bounced off surrounding walls instead of losing themselves in the night's air. Claire hissed at the loudness of it, and both sisters held very still. Seconds passed. No cries of alarm, no footsteps rushing. *Nothing*, so much nothing that Claire almost threw the door at arm's length, just to see if *that* would provoke a reaction.

Livia released a breath and ran a nervous hand through

her hair. "I want to scream," she whispered.

"Same," Claire said, and she smiled, glad Livia had followed after all, and that she didn't have to endure the oppressive silence alone. "Let's get this over with."

She strode into the charging room with a grand sweep of the torch, like a detective revealing the last piece of their puzzle, and found... nothing? A handful of empty crates lined the wall, and in the centre stood a single machine, with cables leading in and out of it. The conveyor belt entered on one side and exited on the other, but it didn't look any different from all the industrial apparatus outside. A few newly charged exocores lay on the exit belt here, too, and Claire reminded herself she needed to steal them. Livia stepped over to it with a frown and placed her hands on each side of the central piece. Claire fought to keep the thousand questions on her lips silent as her sister moved her palms to different portions of the machine. What was she doing? Could she sense anything? Shouldn't this room be *more*? Though more what, she would be hard-pressed to say. Livia removed her hands and cast her gaze about.

"I don't understand. I can't feel anyone within it, or in the tubes. Not even something diffuse to help me tell how the energy flows."

"Maybe it's empty because it's turned off." Claire didn't want to turn it on, either. What if it required setting the entire production chain in movement? And wouldn't it just create *more* exocores? She refused to sacrifice whoever would get shoved into a gem while they figured it out. Livia drummed her fingers on the conveyor belt while Claire strode to the crates and sat down. She cranked the torchlight again and examined her surroundings once more, hoping for a clue of how to proceed, more than a little discouraged. "We might have to search the entire factory."

"No… I don't think so."

Livia scooped up one of the charged exocores from the belt. Determination had replaced confusion in her face, and a satisfied smile curved her lips as she held the core. Claire leaned forward. She'd recognize that expression on her twin any day — Livia wore it every time she won an argument between them. She flipped the exocore up, catching it again with a grin. "This is a fake, Claire. There's no one in it."

"But it glows, and it's after the charger… Why would — oh. You think it's all make-believe?" It would explain why the entire factory was empty. Why hire guards when you had nothing to hide? Maybe a single man made rounds every now and then, but any more than that would be money wasted, and Montrant already injected loads of cash into this facility every day. "They're paying workers and power and rent to run this place, all for a façade? No wonder these things cost a leg and an arm."

"It's handy when you need to give a mayoral tour of your premises, or when journalists want to snap a few pictures of this brand-new product. Too much mystery and everyone tries to unearth your secrets. But this? It's enough to convince anyone without magic of its realness and keep intruders snooping around satisfied." She set the exocore down on the belt again. "I wish we hadn't broken the doors, though. Now they'll know we came this far."

"We wouldn't have made it this far otherwise," Claire pointed out. She slid down her crate. "It's okay. It also explains why the papers in the office were all outdated, and why they don't have any real management. Think it's worth staying?"

Livia scanned the room one last time, as if worried she had missed something. "No… We could tour some of it, to be sure, but let's leave soon after. Then we discuss Plan B around one of your marvellous coffees. I suspect we'll need a lot of those in the coming days."

Claire laughed, less nervous about the sound level now. Even if someone caught them, she and Livia could escape, and they would get nothing more out of this place. It irked her to have run into a dead end immediately, but their investigation had only just started. Considering the lengths Montrant Industries was obviously willing to take to cover up the true nature of exocores, Claire doubted they would fall easily. With Livia by her side, however, she knew they could unravel their lies one by one.

-5-

POINT DE CONTACT

CLAUDE'S SIMPLE SHIRT HAD FELT WRONG TO WEAR ALL day, and the feeling had only worsened now that the sun had set. Nights had been Claire's long before he had started stealing exocores, and over the last few days his gender had slipped firmly to woman. He had picked up his shirt with embroidery and laced a purple ribbon into his hair—little reminders of femininity that helped him deal with the *wrongness* brought by male presentation—until he could bust out the skirts again.

Tonight wasn't one for stealth and thievery, however. He and Livia couldn't get to the bottom of this by sneaking into Montrant Industries' factory, that much was clear now, so they'd chosen their next tactic. They had discussed their options in the early hours before dawn, while Claude rolled and folded the dough for his next batch of croissants. Livia had watched the process with fascination, more than once losing track of her exocore-related plans to ask questions about his technique. The morning's work had taken twice as long as it should have, but explaining the importance of the butter's temperature for its incorporation or how the many folded layers became flaky pastry down the line had kept him grounded. They used the mundane as a shield against the horrible and managed to discuss human souls imprisoned in gems for power by a secretive corporation without being overwhelmed by the scope of it all.

Livia had suggested contacting Val-de-mer's mairesse early on. Denise Jalbert wasn't only one of the most prominent politicians of these days, she was an old family friend. Claude remembered sitting in their living room, learning string tricks from her, his clumsy child fingers struggling to imitate her deft movements. She had worked closely with Claude's father for years, before the threats to their family had pushed them to leave. Maybe she *would* listen to Claude and Livia, but what did they have to show her? Their only proof was Livia's senses—a witch's word—and even if Denise Jalbert believed them, as a mairesse her hands would be tied. She certainly hadn't managed to curb the waves of violence against magic users in her city. No, if they wanted her help, they needed to have concrete proof. And since the factory couldn't provide that, then perhaps they would have better luck with the start of the process. In order to force witches' souls into exocores, Montrant Industries needed those witches. People were bound to have disappeared, and they hoped the witch community had noticed.

Claude spotted their destination: a wine shop with a small hanging sign claiming *Le Vin-Coeur* in dark red cursive. They had walked across the city and followed the rue Saint-Phidéas as it wound its way up the hill on which most of the Quartier des

Sorbiers was perched. Claude loved this area of Val-de-mer. All types of crafts lined the streets, from the most gorgeous paintings to the simplest wood carvings, including hand-dyed scarves and wool, and intricate bead art from the Yahnema community farther downriver. The Bernéais living here hailed from all over the world, and the neighbourhood thrived on their unending creativity. The Quartier des Sorbiers had always been a refuge for outsiders, and as such it had remained one of the main gathering spots for witches. *Le Vin-Coeur* sold wine and alcohol both local and imported, but it also served as a gateway to the hidden witch network.

When they stepped into the tiny establishment, a single customer was paying for his bottle, chatting with the old lady behind the counter. Massive and frizzy grey hair framed her wrinkled and spotted face, and the dim light deepened her already dark skin. She laughed at her customer's joke, an honest and throaty sound that immediately set Claude at ease. He had steered clear of the community over the last few years, getting his rare news from Zita's visits, and diving back in now stressed him. It shouldn't, there was no reason they wouldn't be welcomed, but it had been long enough that he felt like a stranger in it.

Livia obviously held no such worries: as soon as the customer left, she strode to the counter. "Excuse me, Madame?"

"Oui?" The owner leaned forward, peering straight at Livia.

"I'm looking for a special vintage. Château 1608. Perhaps you've heard of it?"

"Somehow, I knew this would be your kind of bottle the moment you passed my doorway," she said. "Follow me. We keep them in the back." Her gaze slid over Claude, and she smiled. "I assume you want the same?"

"Please."

She heaved herself down her stool in stiff movements before muttering about bodies not being like fine wine when it came to age. Her pace was still brisk, though, and she led Livia and Claude down a row, into a backstore, and to a flight of stairs heading into a basement. "Can you find your way?"

"It's been a while, but we should manage. Right, Claude?"

He was surprised she had even remembered the code to access this tunnel, considering how quickly he'd forgotten it. Livia's memory had always been better than his, however. Whenever they tried to recall joint birthdays or other events, she provided so many details he was half-convinced she'd invented them. His mind instead retained random numbers with ridiculous ease. "I'll blame you if we get lost."

The old lady laughed. "As long as it's not me. Glad to see the Loureiro kids are back in town. Send your parents my regards when you next see them, will you?"

"I will!" Livia chirped.

Her warm tone jarred Claude—how had the owner known? Had he introduced himself when he'd last come here, years ago? He remembered her and the existence of a code, but no extensive conversations. Perhaps she'd known back then, too. His parents had always been popular figures: his dad as a politician, and his mother as a powerful witch, very active in the community. Claude had forgotten what that meant for his private life, and how many people knew he existed.

A single round lamp at the top illuminated their way down and their bodies cast long shadows as they descended into progressive darkness. Claude kept a hand on the railing, his grip tightening with every resounding creaking under his steps. He was heavier than Livia, and the wooden planks were so rotten half of him was convinced they would give in under his weight. Once again, he found himself wishing for Claire's clothes. The mask and cape helped manage his stress, like a permission to accomplish dangerous and sometimes illegal acts—like dressing up for an important interview, except more complicated, with an added layer of being himself that well-tailored outfits could never grant him. They were only here to gather information, however, and the outfit had to stay hidden. Perhaps if this was to last, he ought to explore feminine presentations that didn't involve purple hair or the type of colourful, flowing skirts he had always favoured, even before he had stolen his first exocore.

They reached a low doorway with no handles. Livia set her hand against it, and a soft blue glow traversed the wood, following its veins outward from her palm. Before long, the door shimmered from top to bottom and with a last flash, it vanished. Bright light flooded the corridor from beyond, forcing Claude to squint against it. Livia had to duck under the frame to continue on, and she winked back at Claude when she noticed he passed without leaning forward. He stuck his tongue at her and raised five fingers—the number of minutes he was born ahead of her. Her laugh was lost in the murmur of conversation from the room.

The cave stretched in a half-circle, and its stone walls had been polished to a sheen. They reflected the greenish glow of mushrooms spread across the ceiling, shedding a soft light over the tables beneath. The space could fit about twenty, but a stone-brick corridor extended from the darkened area on the other end, even deeper into the hill. The rich inhabitants from the Quartier des Chênes often mocked the Quartier des Sorbiers as an anthill teeming with useless poets, but Claude doubted they understood how accurate their metaphor was.

Zita waved at them from one of the tables, tiny arms stretched as far up as she could. His friend was built like a barrel: short and stocky and muscular, with a crown of short-cropped and curly hair, a flat nose, and a large mouth she typically had a hard time keeping shut. Everyone knew Zita couldn't keep secrets. She was the community's biggest gossip, and an invaluable source of information. Plus, her Seeker powers allowed her to track down almost any witch in town. If anyone could help them find missing people, it would be her.

"Now that's a surprise!" she exclaimed as Claude and Livia sat at her table. "Who would have thought Claude would visit *me*, instead of the other way around?"

He threw a grin at her, as if it could hide part of the guilt. She teased him, but they could all see the truth in her words. Zita was his closest friend, yet if not for her weekly stops at the bakery, they would have lost sight of each other. He had always struggled to keep in touch with people who mattered.

"Life is full of twists and turns," he said.

Zita cocked her head to the side, eyeing him. She must have seen right through his smile—more perceptive of her than she usually was. "Are you feeling all right?"

"I'm… mostly, yes. Why?"

"That grin is tell-tale Claire, friend. I've told you, your smile changes depending on how masculine you feel. Not so much now, huh?"

Claude laughed, and shook his head. He didn't see his own smile often enough to tell, but Zita certainly would have. "Not so much, but I'm fine, I promise. How have you been?"

"Super dandy! It's calmer in the summer. People spend more time outside, enjoying the weather, and less inside, buried under six feet of snow and writing letters to their families. I haven't delivered much over the last few days." She slid down her chair. "What brought you here?"

"Questions," Livia said. "We're looking for something and thought you could help."

Zita's eyes widened in curiosity. She jumped up with barely contained enthusiasm. "Let me get you a drink, then! And if we finish before your glasses are empty, we can just hang out. It's been so long! They have some unique wine samples here—you ought to taste them, Livia. Claude, still no alcohol?"

"Please."

Zita grinned and skipped away with a pleased "you got it". Claude watched her head for the counter, drumming his fingers on the table. They had forgotten to discuss one important detail before coming here. "How much do we tell her?"

"As little as we can." Livia met his gaze. "I love Zita, but she can't keep a secret from other witches. If we say anything about the exocores, everyone will know."

"Maybe that's a good thing. They deserve to be warned."

"Yes, but against what? We still don't understand how they do this, or what to watch for." Livia shook her head. "I worry *they* will learn and be on their guard. Let's inquire about disappearances and missing witches. The community will know something dangerous is happening, but we might avoid a panic."

Claude grunted in agreement. He had no real idea of how to go about this. His initial plan hadn't gone past stealing the exocores and figuring out the source of his malaise. Now that he knew what had set him so ill at ease with these exocores, he had trouble forming concrete plans. The sheer awfulness of it all obliterated his thoughts. That's why he needed Livia. Her calm and foresight would get them through.

Zita returned with three glasses. Rich red wine filled hers and Livia's, but she handed Claude a glass of clear yellow liquid.

"Sparkly apple must! Alcohol free and delicious, from an orchard not an hour away from here." She swirled her wine around, breathing it in. "All right, question time?"

"Has the community grown smaller recently?" Claude asked, figuring it'd be a prudent formulation.

"Witches are disappearing," Livia added. So much for subtlety. "You talk to everyone, no? Noticed anything?"

Zita frowned. "They're just leaving, Livia. The climate here is downright hostile. All you hear is how we're scum, a waste of space and resources, dangerous criminals driven to chaos by their powers. It hasn't gotten better since you moved away." She shifted her gaze to Claude, obviously expecting him to confirm it. When he said nothing, she pouted. "It's the same exodus as fifteen years ago, except slower."

"Then where are they leaving for? Our community in Tereaus hasn't grown. Do they have another haven?"

"Maybe? I don't know everyone's whereabouts."

"Yes, you do." Livia smirked. "You're a Seeker, and the biggest gossip in Val-de-mer! Knowing these things is what you do."

Zita laughed and brought her fist over her heart. "You do me too much honour."

"Please. Think about it?" Claude asked. "They might not have seemed like violent disappearances, but something is wrong. We're sure of that."

"You two are hiding something from me." It wasn't a question, and neither of them bothered denying it. Zita nibbled at her lower lip, her silence stretching as she considered his request. Her expression darkened as seconds flew by. "People are leaving Val-de-mer, more than usual. I've passed along several messages about sick loved ones, job opportunities in the countryside you can't refuse, old friends suddenly coming in town during a roadtrip… It started months ago. Perhaps even years?"

"And they never give news again?" Claude pressed her.

"Let me think! It's been a long time, and I suck at keeping track."

They fell silent. Livia and Claude sipped from their drinks while Zita very dramatically rubbed her temples while emitting thinky noises. Despite the seriousness of the situation, Claude couldn't help but smile. He loved Zita's expressiveness, and how she didn't care for the ridicule. She was always herself, fully and completely.

"You're right," Zita admitted after a moment. "Over the last two years, we lost contact with almost all of those who left the city. They don't even send letters back." She lifted her head and stared at both twins in turn. "What happened to them?"

Worry laced her words. A heavy silence hung between the three of them. Livia stared at her wine, as if the rich liquid had become the most absorbing element in this entire room and letting Claude answer the awful question however he could.

"We can't say for now." He would rather be honest. His lies sucked, anyway. Omission was the only way he could get away with secrets. "We're not even sure. All we know is that it's bad, and we need your help. All of it."

Zita leaned forward, hands wrapped around her glass, and held Claude's gaze. "You don't have to ask. I wish you'd tell me! But fine, keep it secret. Just promise I'll be the first to learn of it once you unravel this."

"Promise," Livia and Claude answered at once.

"Then I know who you need to talk to." Her tone had returned to its natural cheer. "Do you remember Clémence? The community organizer your mom often met with? Ol still does a lot for the community, and with so many people gone, ol has become an important point of contact. I gossip, but ol has everybody's trust, and the real news. If something's up, Clémence ought to know, and ol can probably help."

Not only that, but Clémence had asked Zita to deliver quite a few of the messages to now-vanished witches. Ol could help them track these even farther up until they found Montrant Industries. Zita promised to set up a meeting for them in two days' time, and not-so-subtly reminded them they could always find her here, in this pub, if they decided to share more information. Once that was settled, they moved away from the disappearances to reminiscing about their teenage years together. At first it felt wrong—they shouldn't play catch up while people went missing—but Claude forced himself to relax. Livia hadn't been in Val-de-mer for years, and they could jump back into their mystery tomorrow. Besides, the night was still young, and there would be ample time to rescue more exocores after his chat with Zita.

-6-

LE NID FAMILIAL

ADÈLE RAN NERVOUS FINGERS THROUGH HER SHORT HAIR once more, hoping she didn't look in desperate need of a new cut. Her sister would never let her hear the end of it, and Adèle didn't have the time or energy to freshen up. Besides, beautiful hair wouldn't mask the bags under her eyes. Heavy make-up might, but the one woman in Adèle's life skilled enough for such a feat was the very one she wished to hide her exhaustion from. Emmanuelle had warned Adèle not to move into the Quartier des Bouleaux' neighbourhood, insisting that she instead take residence in her manor. Plenty of room for one's little sister, she promised, but as much as Adèle loved Em, she needed *her* space—a place that belonged to no one else.

Claire's break-in had robbed her of that cocoon. Adèle had spent the last night waking up at the slightest sound, tensed, convinced another intruder had slipped inside her home. She devoted entire days to tracking down that thief, only to imagine her returning during her sleep. Adèle might have been calmer if their investigation had progressed, but they had no real leads. It had stalled quickly, and while her new coworkers didn't give her a hard time over it, she knew they were assessing her skills in silence. She needed to succeed.

Between proving her worth at work and rebuilding her trust in her cramped flat, the one place Adèle felt safe and unjudged was Claude's little bakery. She had started arriving earlier to chat with him—fifteen minutes of meaningless, fun exchanges—and wished he was open in the late afternoon, when she passed his shop on the way back from the precinct. Flanking her day of work with these conversations would do wonders for her mood. Hopefully Em wouldn't press the issue of Adèle's tiredness and tonight would provide a well-deserved break from the upheavals of the last week. Adèle replaced her rebel bang one last time, smoothed her blouse, and headed out.

Summer had grown old, but evenings remained warm, shedding off the stifling humidity of Juillet and allowing Adèle to walk through the city without feeling like the air itself was trying to strangle her. She loved this period of the year. In a few weeks the leaves would turn all manner of yellow and red in a last burst of colour before winter. Adèle headed off, ignoring her vélocycle in favour of a stroll. She had ample time ahead of her, and Em had always preferred for people to show up a quarter hour late, rather than before. She relaxed more in that short extra walk than she had in the entire week, her quick stops at the *Croissant-toi* excluded—a good omen for the night, she hoped.

Em lived at the edge of the Quartier des Mélèzes, where the fortification wrapped around wealthy manors—once a protection against invaders, now a screen from the other citizens dwelling a rock throw away. Two-storied houses with clean white walls and lush vines lined one side, while grimy low-roofed buildings of the Quartier des Saules hunched on the other. Unlike the Quartier des Chênes, the manors here had no large yard to accompany them, and the street names remained in Bernéais. This neighbourhood had been the home of Bernéais lawyers, doctors, and other liberal practitioners for decades—those few who had achieved wealth despite the obstacles before them.

When set against the neighbouring residence, Em's home was modest. It still dwarfed Adèle's tiny apartment and left her with an uneasy sense of inadequacy. She would never be able to afford such a big house. Not that she really wanted to, but she wished she had the money to have the option. She could dream — most promotions in police corps required greasing palms, turning a blind eye on doctored reports, and keeping your mouth shut when asked. A manor like Em's would cost Adèle more than a large amount of cash.

At least Em never had to make that sacrifice. Thirteen years ago, she had designed coal chambers twice as efficient as those widespread across the country. Her invention had come two years after the Meltdown Massacre, when Val-de-mer's magic-powered reactor had exploded, razing the Quartier des Épinettes, killing thousands, and annihilating the city's main power source. Adèle remembered grabbing a newspaper every morning, trying to follow the chaos propagating through Val-de-mer, worried sick about Emmanuelle. Then the letter had arrived, late in the

61

afternoon: Emmanuelle's husband, Julien, had been stabbed to death while defending fleeing witches. Adèle had seen Emmanuelle three times since: once for Julien's funeral, another when Em's new invention had earned her a national award, three years later, and for a family reunion almost eight years ago. On all occasions, she had seemed exhausted—stretched and thin. As Adèle strode up the slow ramp and to the ornate door, she prayed time had given Em the space to recover.

She used the bronze slammer to announce her arrival, half-expecting a butler to answer, but after a minute she heard the clack-clack of high heels, and Emmanuelle threw the door open. The last five years had metamorphosed her. The long curls once tumbling down to her shins had been snipped and now bounced at shoulder length, while round glasses perched on her nose. Emaciated cheeks had turned round and full while her arms had thickened. Her breasts remained small—almost flat—but she had gained a large belly, giving her a pear shape. The fat enveloped her, cocooned her. Adèle recalled the spindly woman, stretched by stress, grief, and exhaustion, and she thanked the Saints for the change. Em laughed, and Adèle realized she'd been staring in silence, too shocked for words.

"I wish you could see your face!" Em said. "But wow, Adèle, it looks like I changed for the both of us. You're the exact same."

"Minus some naive illusions, yes." The admission slipped out before Adèle could hold it in, and she wished she had kept the subject far from the conversation. Adèle had hit her first solid lead on political corruption a month before Em's award ceremony and thought she could unravel it all. And she had, only to see her entire operation and case shut down as they prepared to prosecute. "You're fabulous, Em. Your letters don't do justice to how much you're glowing."

"I'm happy, yes. More than I have been in a long time. And now my little sister lives nearby! Letters aren't the same."

"Definitely not." Adèle grinned and stepped inside, wrapping Em into a hug. "Letters don't allow that."

Em squeezed back. She smelled of mint—fresh and sweet all at once. Adèle probably stank of sweat and coal and stress. But that had always been the case with them: Adèle in pants and dirt, Emmanuelle in lush dresses and perfume. Even today, despite Adèle's efforts to pretty up, Em outclassed her. She wore a gorgeous yellow robe with delicate white laces, with a simple and elegant cut. Gold ribbons twirled among her curls, tying part of them back to keep the hair out of her face. Adèle admired her talent. With the right outfit and make-up, Em always managed to shine.

Emmanuelle clasped Adèle's hand and pulled her out of the entrance hall and into a small vestibule. Tall windows allowed the slanted light of the setting sun, casting a warm glow on two pristine, wide armchairs. They flanked a low table of forged iron, and large potted plants completed the scenery. Two orange cats had piled atop one another in one of the two armchairs, and Adèle smiled; Sol and Gaia still didn't miss an opportunity to laze in the light. Emmanuelle didn't need much more in decoration: the mouldings around every frame and crossing the room halfway were all intricately carved and provided the place with the extra touch that made it beautiful. Emmanuelle always managed to balance her taste for complex and sometimes overbearing motifs with a room's or outfit's needs of simplicity.

"I should have you decorate my flat," Adèle said, knowing full well she preferred it as it was: barren, save for a few items.

"As if you'd let me hang a single painting on your walls."

They laughed. Emmanuelle displaced her two cats to settle into their chair, inviting Adèle to do the same. Sol left the room, but Gaia jumped back on Em's knees the moment she could. While her sister petted the fluffy orange cat, their chatter moved to the latest details of Em's scientific life. There had been an important energy conference in Val-de-mer over the last week, with a large focus on renewable, witch-independent technologies. Apparently, speculation about the exocores' fabrication methods ran wild through the community.

"We're like teenagers with an incomplete bit of gossip," Em said. "Everyone wants to discover the rest, but we don't even know who's the genius behind the tech! The brevêt is under Jean Tremblay—not a name anyone in our community bears, and as fake as they come if you ask me. Besides, no teams have published anything like it. These things just appeared on the market, proper papers all filed in, and now Montrant Industries are cashing in, their secret held tight."

"Jealous?"

Em laughed at Adèle's teasing. "Curious, more like, and a

little nostalgic. My name is no longer enough to keep our team's funding intact. They don't care how many breakthroughs we make: my tech would first require witches to collaborate, and no one wants anything to do with magic anymore, even if it's emulating it. But without it, I have no idea how we could catch sunlight!"

Catch sunlight. Adèle smiled; what a beautiful thought, yet it seemed ridiculously impossible. What even was sunlight? It shone down on them and kept their planet warm, an invisible force they could neither deny nor explain. Like magic, really.

"A gearhead like you? You'll find a way."

"I know." Em grinned. "I have all it takes: a cool head, a good method, and the right spark of imagination."

"Don't forget the Duclos' legendary stubbornness!"

Em laughed again, and Adèle joined in. Her sister's easy happiness was contagious, washing away the week's hardships and the tight knots they'd left in Adèle's neck and shoulders. She'd missed family reunions, with the warmth and inner peace they often brought. The six Duclos siblings rarely fought, and while Em's motherly nagging sometimes annoyed Adèle she wouldn't trade her sister for anything in the world. They were lucky everyone got along so well. What a shame they hadn't bothered to gather in years.

"I've missed you, Em. We ought to write the rest of the family and hold a bigger party. Something grand. You have the room to house everyone, don't you?"

"Them and a whole other family, if need be! Have you seen

the size of this house?" She threw her arms up. "I hire students from the Académie to clean with me. This helps pay their bills, and I get to talk about science I'm not immersed in all the time!"

"Oh, so that's why you insisted I should live here. It has nothing to do with the house being empty. You just want hands for the dirty work!"

Em laughed and gave Adèle a little shove. "I would never. I miss family, is all. You're right about seeing each other more. Even six cats can't make up for all of you."

They moved into the dining room, and it was all Adèle could do not to gasp. The massive table could have held fifteen, and heavy wooden chairs flanked it, with soft red cushions. A large chandelier occupied one end, shedding bright light on their silverware. And amidst all that luxury, in a big iron pot, the most traditional of their mother's meals.

"Tourtière!" Adèle exclaimed. "I can't believe it. I haven't eaten any in... I don't even know how long!"

"I figured," Em said, grinning, "so I wrote Mom and asked her the recipe. What you have here, my dear Adèle, is my first attempt at a Duclos tourtière, as per traditions handed down through our ancestors by the Lac."

"It looks delicious. I can't wait to taste it!"

"Then don't."

Adèle hurried to the table, and within minutes she had two spoonfuls in her plate. Three types of shredded meat had stewed with small potatoes and spices for hours, all wrapped in a delectable crust. She breathed in the greasy, homey scent before reaching for the sweetened canned beets and tomatoes and pouring a ton on a corner of her plate. Emmanuelle laughed at the heavy addition—she never put anything on her tourtière, going as far as calling them contaminants. With the delicious meal came a red wine so deep it seemed to absorb the candlelight. Adèle had no doubts about its quality.

Adèle dove into her plate. After the quick and cheap meals she'd eaten all week, this dinner was an explosion of flavours and memories. She relished each bite of the sweet beets mixed with the salty goodness of the tourtière, and for a moment her conversation with Em gave way to food and wine.

When they restarted it, they talked of their youth growing up around the Lac Saint-Damase—of their moms' small house on its bank and the first spring dip in its cold water, of David's wooden cabin in the great oak tree, of picking up blueberries in the fall, along with the *one* time Adèle had devoured so much she'd been sick. One memory led to another, until they'd retold every classic family story in the repertoire, laughed at the endless antics of six children in the same house, and drank almost two bottles of wine. Adèle had no idea what time it was or if she could take two steps without falling, and she didn't care. A happy buzz covered her thoughts, erasing the stress of the last few days.

Em brought it all back in a single question.

"But enough of the past. How has the city been treating you?"

Heaviness crashed back on Adèle's shoulders. She grimaced, inebriated enough not to try to hide her pain. "Badly."

She sighed, filled her glass with the last of the bottle, and leaned forward, elbows on the table. "Some purple-haired thief broke into my flat the night before I started working and stole my exocore. Couldn't stop her, even though I had my firearm pointed at her, and now some high-placed chump wants her in jail. She's landed my first special case—but only as a colleague's shadow."

"Isn't that a good thing? You've seen her. Won't it make finding her easier?"

"She had a mask. Unless someone's parading in lilac hair around Val-de-mer, it won't help me much. Thievery cases are the hardest because of how little clues they leave behind, and if I fail this one, they'll shove me back into a mouldy underground office with a shitty job." Thinking of it clenched her stomach. Proving her worth to Koyani's team stressed her; she had never desired a position so hard in her life. "I can't lose this new job. It's everything I dreamed police work would be! This unit knows the meaning of teamwork. They trust and respect each other, and they wanted me to join." She flattened her hand on the table, staring at it with an intensity born of the high volume of wine consumed. "I can't let them down."

"You'll do great. It's not even your case, Adèle. Breathe deeply, calm down, and contribute however you can. Besides, if thieves are so hard to jail, they'll understand if it takes time, no?"

"They might." Adèle avoided looking Em's way. Her sister was already trying to cushion her potential future fall—to break the pressure Adèle was putting on this particular case. "I don't want them to have to."

"Adèle…"

"Have you ever been to *Croissant-toi*?" That was the least subtle change of subject in existence, but Adèle didn't care. She knew the lecture that would come—about putting too much pressure on herself, or too much weight on a single event. Em thought it was unhealthy behaviour, but she'd already made her name and fortune. That single event had happened for her, and she no longer needed recognition from her peers. "It's a nice bakery near my flat."

"We weren't talking about—"

"With an even nicer baker," Adèle continued, pushing the topic firmly into a territory that would catch her sister's attention.

"Oh?" Em perked up, a knowing smile spreading on her lips. "How nice?"

Adèle would regret this maneuver. Em loved romantic gossip too much to let Adèle hear the end of it anytime soon. But, well, Adèle had clung to fresh croissants, hot coffee, and friendly talk all week. Claude's tranquil warmth was an oasis of calm in her rough days—a feeling Adèle already cherished. She would be a fool to deny she'd love to know him better, maybe even start something with him. Thinking of all the ways it could go wrong dropped stones at the bottom of her stomach, and she tapped the table with her fingers to pass some of the discomfort.

"His name is Claude. He's peaceful and kind. Always has my coffee ready in the morning and listens to me ramble. I know I'm a customer, but he treats me like an old friend—like my coming to the bakery is a personal pleasure to him, too."

Em clapped her hand, and Adèle suspected she'd fought her desire to squee. "Maybe it is personal. You're cute and bright and entertaining! He ought to see that."

In addition to cute, bright, and entertaining, Adèle turned a deep shade of red at the idea that Claude's kindness could hide more. Had he noticed her? Claude treated everyone with the same care. Part of his job, and part of who he was. Surely Em was getting ahead of herself and imagining things. Adèle cast her gaze about, looking for another convenient topic change, and spotted a calico cat slinking through the room. Its fur was extremely short and wavy, and Adèle didn't remember ever seeing it around.

"Who's the new cat?"

"That's Aurora. She's very friendly and petting her feels like suede, but she's nowhere near as interesting as your baker. You should ask him out."

"Aurora, you said?" Adèle replied while her mind all but panicked at the idea of asking Claude out. They barely knew each other! She grabbed her glass of wine and downed it, hoping to camouflage part of her intense flush. Emmanuelle was not so easily duped.

"You heard me, Adèle Duclos, and I won't let Aurora be your distraction." Em grinned from across the table, cocking her head to the side. "Why not, really? Go on a date. It'll be fun, you'll get to know him elsewhere than at work, and it could evolve into more! Who knows, you might even add sexy to his list of qualities after a while."

"One can hope."

Em laughed at her answer and Adèle cursed herself. She hadn't meant to imply she was *that* interested. She was, but did Em need to be encouraged? Hell no. Besides, Claude might never draw any flutter of desire from her. He had a beautiful smile and laugh, and was easy on the eye, but her mind balked at the idea of kisses or more this early on. They hadn't known each other all that long, though, and she was demisexual. Strangers did not raise goosebumps across her arms, or send her heart hammering with want. When it happened to her, it was with people she felt deeply connected with, and was wrapped in a need for a new kind of intimacy. Even without that attraction, however, her romantic interest in Claude was undeniable.

One look at Em's insistent stare warned Adèle her sister demanded more than a vague agreement and wouldn't let go until she had a concrete promise. Adèle clacked her tongue.

"All right. I'll set something up with him and investigate. Happy now?"

Em clapped her hands. "Sure am! It'll be good for you. You can let off some steam from your work."

Adèle wondered if she would be exchanging one type of stress for another but pushed the thought away. She didn't want to rush Claude and would pick something casual, from which either of them could escape with ease. It'd be great: fun and simple. Exactly what she needed these days.

With a slight smile, Adèle raised her glass of wine. "To my future date, then."

Em clinked her glass to Adèle's. "May Claude the Baker

prove worthy of your attention."

They drank to that, the last of Adèle's wine joining the rest of the alcohol in the pit of her stomach and the heady spin of her mind. Walking home tonight promised to be its own adventure.

-7-

UNE FRACTURE DANS LA GLACE

CLAUDE SPED THROUGH VAL-DE-MER'S STREETS, HIS MUSCLES screaming as he pushed his vélocycle to new extremes, boosting himself with magic whenever he climbed steep hills. He cursed the old lady who had hung around his shop way past closing time, and his generally wonky sleep schedule. Between his illegal thievery at night and the bakery from dawn to mid-afternoon, Claude didn't have a lot of time to rest. He often counted himself lucky to have five full hours of sleep. Today, he'd meant to cut it even shorter in order to make the rendezvous with Clémence and Livia, and instead he had snoozed right past the time.

He'd be late no matter how much he sprinted, but he hoped to catch the tail end of their conversation. At least Livia would have spent another day investigating Montrant and talking to witches while he ran the shop. She'd be well equipped to question Clémence about the disappearances. Yet Val-de-mer was Claude's home, and he'd touched dozens of exocores. This was his

73

fight, too, and they would always be better together.

He rounded the last corner, releasing his magic as he turned onto the rue Saint-Agathe, in the Quartier des Mélèzes. The smooth lane sloped down then circled around a park filled with lilac trees and the quartier's great larch, its Soul Tree, towering above them. The soft scent of lilacs already drifted up to Claude, calming him. Far behind, slightly on his right, the Pont des Lumières loomed over the city's roofs. No lights illuminated the massive frame, belying its name and leaving nothing but a black shape against a dark sky.

Claude preferred it this way. A wide tower rose above the bridge on this side of the Bernan-Tereaus Détroit, with intricate glasswork at its center, and would one day spread its light on the water below. They'd promised lamps along the entire frame—a brilliant monument to the most recent advances in power technology: exocores. The whole Pont des Lumières was meant to be powered by hundreds of cores, and the thought of it shining in the night sickened Claude. They had two weeks left before the grand opening. He and Livia needed to get to the bottom of Montrant's machinations before hundreds of souls burned for so-called progress.

A glint caught Claude's eyes, scintillating among the lilac trees below. He squinted, trying to figure out what reflected the moonlight in such a way, then dropped the vélocycle and stalked forward. His heart beat faster, a chill creeping up his spine.

Ice, his instincts said, but his heart stubbornly refused. Why would there be ice in a park in the heat of summer? Livia could conjure ice, but she wouldn't. Not with the dangerous climate surrounding witches and magic, not in the middle of Val-de-mer where the reactor exploded and killings started, not around a Soul Tree. Not unless she believed it absolutely necessary.

Not unless she thought her life depended on it.

Claude stopped at the end of the slope, his heart sinking. Ice patterns expanded from the park's centre, climbing along the lilacs' trunks to create crystalline structures around their leaves and flowers. The sight might have been enchanting if Claude hadn't known who had provoked it and feared the reasons behind. He advanced under the trees, his throat so tight he thought he'd choke. Livia's flash-freeze had covered the larch and created a deep fissure in its bark. If the tree died… They said quartiers lost their souls with their tree, and their prosperity declined through the years. The Quartier des Épinettes certainly had never recovered from their Soul Pine dying, though the reactor's destructive explosion had much to do with that. How would people respond to another witch killing a Soul Tree? Claude forced the thoughts away; nothing he could do about it, and he needed to figure out what had happened to Livia.

Her ice radius didn't form a complete circle. It had stretched out from a central point—Livia—and around, but the shape slanted forward, as if reaching for a target. Claude's gaze trailed the frozen cobblestone path until the ice came to an abrupt end. A perfect arc stopped it, into a clean edge unlike the usual fingers of frost normally extending out of Livia's magic. Something or someone had stood there, blocking Livia's attack.

Claude stared at the demarcation, his body shaking and his legs turning to wool. Livia's inner strength rivalled that of Val-de-mer's best witches. Incredible raw power underlay her ice blasts, and it'd take someone with similar abilities to stop her. Who could have done that? Where was Livia now?

He stumbled back until he bumped into a frozen bench and crumpled into it. This couldn't be happening! What if he'd been on time? Could he have protected Livia or would he be gone with her? What was better: suffer through what came next together and escape it, or have a chance to rescue her from the outside? Guilt climbed up Claude's throat. He'd called Livia to Val-de-mer, brought her into this mess, and now he'd failed her. Would Livia become Montrant's next exocore? How long did he have? He couldn't let it happen.

Claude rubbed his face and gave himself several small slaps on the cheeks, hauling his spiralling thoughts back into more rational patterns. Livia wasn't there to calm him, and he would have to stifle his feelings. No one but them, Zita, and Clémence knew they'd be here tonight. To think they had come to learn more about witches disappearing, and now Livia was gone! Had Clémence done this, or had ol also been captured? Claude shivered, the bench's cold seeping through his pants and keeping even the summer heat at bay.

Zita would know where to find Livia. She was a Seeker and could track down any witch in Val-de-mer. This wasn't over. He had options still, and the nine saints willing, he would get to the bottom of this. Dozens of souls imprisoned in exocores already relied on him for a solution. He needed to create one before his sister joined them.

By the time Claude reached the *Vin-Coeur*, a low panic had settled firmly in his mind. He almost tore the door right off its hinges to go faster, only to force himself to cool down and pick the lock. It felt wrong to do so without his mask—although, really, if he'd had time he would not have spent a single hour presenting as Claude tonight. The sooner he reached Zita, however, the sooner he could pursue Livia's assailants. He needed to get a grip on what was happening before he even considered changing. He hurried down the stairs, withholding his magic through a difficult effort of willpower, and his heart squeezed as he passed the low doorway and remembered his twin's gentle teasing. He would find her. He had to.

Zita occupied the same table as last time, as promised. She spotted him immediately and rose with a grin. "Wow, Claude. I didn't think I'd get news so fast. Is the meeting already over?"

"They took her."

"What?" Zita then swore, and Claude cringed. Hopefully the nine saints wouldn't hold it against her.

"Livia. I got there late, and she had vanished. The park's iced over and she was gone, Zita. Exactly like the witches we're looking for!"

"That's…" Dismay replaced Zita's initial confusion and

77

she clasped the side of the table. "I-I don't understand. Was Clémence there? Is ol all right?"

"How should I know?" Why should he care, too? He didn't have time, not now. "Please try to find her, Zita. Seek her out."

"Of course! We'll be on their trail in no time, you'll see." Zita snapped her fingers with a grin, and her confidence soothed Claude's panic. She closed her eyes—half to focus better, half for show, he knew—and for long minutes not a word passed between them. Zita's smile slowly diminished, and a line barred her forehead. "I... I can't find her. That's not possible. Livia's so powerful, I would never miss her particular aura!"

"No..." Claude's throat tightened, killing his voice. He had spun hundreds of questions in his mind as he rushed here, imagining every way this conversation could go. Yet now that he stood before Zita, nothing would come out. Fear and frustration clogged his mind, blocking all calm thoughts and swirling panicked lies. He would never find Livia, his brain whispered. It was all his fault—his fault for calling her, his fault for being late, his fault for stealing exocores or getting involved. Claude wrestled his strong urge to kick the nearby chair and instead pulled it back to sit down.

"Here's what I saw," he said, surprised by his own sudden calm. He described the scene as he found it, his voice hollow as he related the ice covering trees and pavement alike. "Only one section was spared, cut off by a perfect arc. As if something had dissolved Livia's ice midair."

Zita gasped. She'd just decided to sit down and jumped

right back to her feet. "It wasn't dissolved," she said. "It was negated. That's Clémence's power. Ols magic is like... a void of magic, if that makes sense? It takes incredible strength to pierce through it. That means ol was there with Livia and still is: that's why I can't detect her! Maybe someone attacked them as they met, or —"

"I don't think so." Claude's throat had gone dry. Livia hadn't been aiming her ice away from the negating circle, but towards it. Like an assault. "She was defending herself against whoever blocked her magic."

"N-no. Clémence wouldn't..." Zita's voice faltered, and she shook her head emphatically. "It doesn't make any sense. Ol would *never* betray us. Clémence is a protector for this community, and without ol hundreds more would have died after the reactor meltdown. The negating power made our gathering spots impossible to find, allowing the community to go underground and become near invisible."

"So when we hid together in these bunkers..." Claude remembered large rooms with soft blue lights and a constant flow of witch families. Children cried, adults whispered, and fear permeated the air. Claude hadn't understood their panic: so many of them wielded incredible powers, couldn't they defend themselves? But not everyone would survive a fight, and every time a witch struck back, things became worse. So they had hid whenever they'd caught wind of a raid. "We had Clémence's magic masking us?"

"We still do." Zita looked away, rubbing her forearm,

strangely subdued. Claude's friend could usually barely contain her energy, but the years following the meltdown had been particularly difficult for her. Militias had hired or coerced Seekers into hunting other witches. Most of her family had been approached this way. Some, like her parents, had refused and died; those left behind found it harder to say no. Zita had never shared the details. She had sought refuge in Claude's home and buried most of her grief away. Even now, years later, she preferred to skirt around the subject. "Clémence managed to infuse part of ols magic in crystalline stones. We keep one in every major underground witch gathering spot, just in case. The hunt might be over, but it's better safe than sorry."

On that, at least, Claude agreed. Just because people no longer mobilized in public spaces to discuss how best to find and kill witches didn't mean they weren't actively looking for ways to do so—the exocores proved that well enough. Claude ran his fingers through his hair, further pulling strands out of his loose ponytail. Zita's words only confirmed his impression Clémence was involved in this mess—after all, it seemed ol had devised a technique to hold ols magic in stones already, and what were exocores if not a more advanced version of this? But it didn't make sense for someone so integrated in their community to suddenly betray it. Why would Clémence contribute to this massive and secret extermination of witches if ol had put so much energy into protecting them in the past?

"I need to talk to ol." Claude pushed himself back to his feet and met Zita's gaze. "Can you find Clémence again?"

Zita crossed her arm. "Will you explain what's going on if I do?"

"Zita…" He didn't have time to argue, or for lengthy tales. "Just tell me where to go. I need to hurry. Livia's life could depend on it, and I have no idea how much time I have. *Please.*"

She huffed. "You're always keeping secrets from me. Don't think I'll let you off the hook if you don't come back, but fine. I can find Clémence. Negating magic does leave a trace—a sort of void you can detect, if you're careful enough. Ol lives in the Quartiers des Mélèzes and was still there when I searched for Livia earlier. I checked."

Back to their starting point, then. It made sense: Clémence wouldn't want to carry Livia halfway across the city. "Good. And ol is stationary?"

"Yes." Zita leaned forward. "Let me come. I'll tell you if ol moves."

"I can't. I'll sprint across Val-de-mer, and I can't waste energy on strength to carry you."

Zita pouted, then reluctantly gave Claude a more precise location. At least the bakery was on his way back to the Quartiers des Mélèzes: if he was going to run recklessly across the city burning through his powers, he would rather have his mask on. Besides, he'd rarely felt like a man over the last two weeks, and that had intensified since Livia's arrival. It would be a relief to have presentation match gender again.

Zita had him promise twice that he wouldn't attack Clémence unless absolutely necessary, and her anguish at the thought surprised him. He had expected Zita to encourage him to give Clémence what ol deserved, if it turned out ol had captured Livia, but instead she insisted not to. Claude suspected his friend's care for ol went beyond the public figure, though he had no idea why, and no time to find out. He thanked Zita again, then hurried out of the underground pub.

-8-

COLLISION

CLAIRE SLIPPED HER BLACK TIGHTS ON, AND THE SHAKING in her hands diminished as the fabric encased her foot then leg. Her panic subsided as she pulled on the other half, then the short skirt going over it. Her heart still pounded, but the frenzied beat shifted into a more controlled cadence—an urgent demand to act rather than a confused run forward. She snatched the cloak out of the wardrobe, flung it around her shoulders, and grabbed her mask. This was her battle gear, and this short stop at the bakery helped refocus her energy and harden her resolve. No one got to hurt her sister. She turned her hair purple—a simple trick that had taken hours of practice to master, but which she *loved*—then tied her mask on and slipped into the night.

On most outings, Claire climbed onto a nearby roof to survey the city first. Val-de-mer had an odd shape. The thick of it sprawled in a crescent around the ancient fortifications enclosing its heart and the richer quartiers, as if the dirty houses of the rabble were laying siege to its pristine manors. Yet on the left rose a second heart, beating far differently from the old families and newcomers residing inside the walls: the Quartier des Sorbiers, full of artists and revolutionaries, where alcohol was the least of illicit substances one could acquire. Claire had hung around it long before she had stolen exocores, freer to experiment with her genderfluidity there than anywhere else in Val-de-mer. Between the Quartier des Sorbiers' hill and the fortifications' cliff, the terrain dipped, reaching down to sea level. Several quartiers sprawled in that area, including her own, the Quartier des Bouleaux. From her little bakery's roof, she'd watched the Pont's slow construction at the end of the Tronc, Val-de-mer's main avenue—first with fascination, then with increasing dread as her fears about exocores deepened.

Claire skipped her usual climb tonight, sprinting out without even a vélocycle. She restrained her use of magic, trying not to burn through her small reserves. She had already expended too much getting to the initial rendezvous. She could clamber up rooftops without the extra boost, anyway. Still, each lost minute frayed her nerves. What was happening to Livia now? Was she scared? Defiant? Angry at Claire for being late? Her sister had room in her for all these emotions, and much more. She had to be frustrated to be without powers. The ice had always been a part of her, just within reach. Did she feel incomplete without it? And if having it blocked felt awful, Claire could only imagine what having it sucked out of you to make exocores would be like.

The streets passed in a blur, small houses becoming two-storied properties and more tightly packed as she approached the wall. They flanked her, tall and menacing, as if threatening to fall upon her and block her path. Claire tried to push back against the impression, to convince herself it was only her brain playing tricks on her, that the city wasn't out to stop her. Every corner she turned sent a rush of fear as she imagined someone—something, *anything*—hurtling into her, ruining her chance. She thanked the Saints when she reached the fortifications and avoided the gates: at this time of year, many enjoyed late night strolls, and this close to the Quartier des Mélèzes, she'd rather be seen by as few as possible. She slipped into an alleyway instead, close enough to the gates that the terrain hadn't become a cliff yet.

Claire climbed over the wall, muscles straining under the effort, her grip sometimes slippery on the friable stone. Exercise often created empty space in her mind, a refuge from the day's anxiety. Perhaps that was why she always thought of her nights as less stressful than the bakery, despite the breaking into houses and thieving. She tried to reach this haven once more, to focus on the cold stone under her gloves, the gusts of wind hitting her full force as she left the buildings' protection, the strain in her muscles... Maybe if her mind was otherwise occupied, it would discard her gnawing fears about Livia for a time. Slow down. Give her space to breathe and steady herself. But she couldn't escape the haunting iced park, glittering in the moonlight, or the mound of exocores glowing red on her table at home—the awful fate of those witches now threatening her twin. It was too much, the dread reaching too deep to be so easily dismissed. With a sigh, Claire leaped back on the other side of the wall and dropped to the ground.

She had never liked the manors around here, even before

CLAUDIE ARSENEAULT

most of them became exocore-powered. It felt wrong for rich people to have claimed Val-de-mer's heart, and she wished more of the intra muros city resembled the Quartiers des Érables, with its tiny boutiques, active street life, and mix of wealth levels. At least this quartier hadn't been built by throwing down several houses to make room for conquerors the way the Quartier des Chênes had. The lawns didn't sprawl as extensively, and the ornate manors stayed compact, mindful of the space they occupied. Here, the well-off had *always* lived and dominated others—a thin consolation, really. These houses were among the best protected of Val-de-mer. It had stressed her when stealing exocores, but tonight it made her downright queasy. Livia couldn't afford her to be caught.

She reached the general area indicated by Zita with a grim smile and leaned forward, spying into the street ahead. A few stragglers were enjoying a late-night stroll, the lamps overhead casting plenty of light on the cobblestone path. Elegant fences flanked the street, protecting lush gardens and fancy manors. Clémence's place had brick walls, white columns, and large balconies on two floors. Good for breaking in, those. Zita had warned Claire she might have the precise location wrong, but considering the size of the building, she doubted it. All Claire needed now was to slip into the house unseen.

She withdrew into the alley and reached for the nearest window ledge when quick footsteps echoed close behind. Way too close, she thought, and running.

Firm hands grabbed Claire, yanked her back, and spun her

to the ground. She hit the street hard, and the shock reverberated through her teeth and skull. Tears stung her eyes as her breath was knocked out, and she struggled to keep her wits about her. A knee jabbed into her back, holding her down, and the stench of alcohol washed over Claire as her assailant leaned forward.

"I have you now."

Instant recognition flashed through Claire, and the wave of panic turned her voice into a squeal.

"Adèle?"

Several swear words danced around Claire's mind, and she buried them with a pang of guilt even though none crossed her lips. She couldn't deal with Adèle here and now, right in front of Clémence's location. What if the commotion of an escape alerted ol? Claire gritted her teeth. What was Adèle even doing in this neighbourhood?

"You're mine now," the policewoman grunted.

Heat rose through Claire at the possessive tone. Three words and suddenly she was very aware of Adèle's body over her, of powerful muscles holding her down and pressing her into the stone, and she hated herself for the immediate wave of desire. Smoking hot or not, this police officer would arrest Claire if she let her. Now was not the time for pinned-down fantasies about her cute morning customer! Adèle stood between Livia and her.

"You're drunk," she said, trying to buy herself time, to find a way to escape. "Is that how you like to work? Hammered to deal with the lies and corruption you help cover?"

Adèle scoffed, and her weight shifted as she leaned back

up. "I'm coming out of a pleasant evening with one of this city's most upstanding citizens. Someone entirely unlike you."

The sneer underlying Adèle's tone hurt more than Claire was willing to admit. Adèle sounded so different from when they chatted every morning. That Adèle worried about the wild cats meowing all night, debating the best option to feed them extensively. Yet now that she was talking to a thief, spite replaced the woman's compassion. Claire scowled, pushing away memories of the week's banter. If Adèle could see the thief but not the person, then Claire would force herself to see the officer, and not the woman wearing the uniform. She hated it, but Livia needed her to.

Claire drew upon her powers, imbuing her muscles with sudden strength and speed. She twisted her hips, reaching for Adèle's arm and tugging her forward. Without magic, she'd have no grip and no angle to put weight behind the move, but with it she surprised Adèle. Two seconds later they'd flipped around, with Claire on top, staring at Adèle's confused shock.

"I don't have time for you." Livia didn't have time for her, she added mentally. She had to go—what if Clémence fled? Took Livia with her? Every second counted.

Adèle glared at her. "Too many jewels to steal? Too busy depriving people of their wealth and power source?"

A bitter laugh escaped Claire. It hurt that Adèle would think this was about money, even though she had stolen more than exocores specifically to mislead others. The judgment was a punch to her guts, and more than her nerves could endure tonight.

"You have no idea what's going on!"

Her voice pitched high with anguish. People were kidnapping witches and shoving them into exocores, draining their lives to power the city. Her sister had been taken just a few hours ago. She was here, so close, within reach. But here was Adèle, snarling at her for a handful of necklaces, as if they mattered in this overall mess. Claire's anger built, and her grip tightened as it did, until Adèle could no longer hide her pain. Her face contorted, and Claire realized she'd been squeezing her harder against the ground, magic still coursing through her muscles. She released her hold.

"I'm sorry, I—"

She stopped herself. She didn't have to apologize, even if she hadn't meant to hurt Adèle. Claire pushed away her purple hair, leaning up and gritting her teeth, forcing pride into her shoulders and face. She was doing this for Livia; her motives were good. As her focus widened from Adèle, she discovered they were no longer alone. The stragglers from earlier had gathered on each side of the alleyway, too cautious to come closer but too curious to miss the show. Claire cursed and jumped to her feet, releasing Adèle entirely. Clémence was bound to notice the noise under ols window. Ol might even be in the crowd right now.

Adèle struggled up as fast as her drunken balance allowed, keeping one hand on the wall. Despite the slump in her shoulders, her heavy breathing, and the dirt smearing her white blouse, she managed to look both imposing and incredibly sexy. Or perhaps because of it. Sometimes it was best not to question these things.

"Claire." Adèle laced her name with anger, bitterness, and

disbelief. "If I'm so ignorant, enlighten me."

Could she? What would happen if she told Adèle about Livia's disappearance? The exocores? Would she stop chasing Claire and help instead? She wanted to believe it, but she couldn't know for sure. The way Adèle had hardened earlier, smashing Claire to the ground, full of spite and anger. Claire would trust the Adèle she saw every morning—quick-witted, compassionate, helpful—but that woman was nowhere tonight, all because she was talking to a thief, not a baker. What if Adèle thought the same of witches as she did of criminals? Many believed these two went hand in hand, and police officers had often returned home to join witch-hunting militias. Claire barely knew Adèle, and Livia's life was hanging in the balance. She couldn't risk this, nor could she waste time around with witnesses and a police officer. She needed to get out now if it wasn't too late already.

"I can't," she said. "Not now."

"Then you're coming with me."

Adèle lunged for Claire, but the drunken swipe had nothing against her augmented speed. Claire dodged out of the way with ease. She forced a smirk back to her lips, willing the bold, mocking Claire to resurface.

"Sorry to disappoint, Madame l'Officier, but I have other plans. May we meet again!"

With a burst of magic, Claire leaped to a balcony above. Adèle's enraged cry followed her, and she glimpsed the officer patting at her side as if she had a revolver. Claire climbed to the rooftop in a hurry, her heart speeding as she recalled the close shot

Adèle had taken the first time around. Anyone willing to shoot her down like that could not be trusted.

She sprinted off, leaving the area she'd been so eager to investigate, dashing across the relative safety of Val-de-mer's roofs for a few minutes. She didn't want to get too far away, knowing she'd need to return and search for Livia. Deep down, Claire suspected Clémence was gone, but she had to check and be sure. What if ol was still there, or even Livia? What if she found clues about their location? She skidded to a stop on a roof near the fortification and sat down, her legs and heart heavy. She could only pray to the nine saints that Adèle hadn't ruined her best chance of saving Livia. She didn't know if she could ever forgive her.

Adèle watched the dark shape vanish over the rooftop, impotent rage coursing through her muscles. She cursed, one loud and heartfelt *calisse*, before leaning on the wall behind her. Alcohol spun her head and her shoulder throbbed from being thrown to the ground, but her pride hurt more than either of these.

She had been so close.

Fifteen minutes of silent stalking through the streets had given her a golden chance to catch Claire, and she'd wasted it. It confused Adèle that she'd even managed to remain undetected for so long despite her shaky balance, but her target had never once looked back. And while tailing her across Val-de-mer, Adèle had imagined herself bringing Claire in, showing Koyani's team how she could seize an opportunity and solve cases and savouring the unexpected, blessed victory of securing her position within the team and arresting the thief who'd broken into her home in less than a week. The perfect way to conclude an already successful evening.

"Madame? Madame l'Officier, can I ask you a few questions?"

The question snapped Adèle back to her surroundings. Now that the rush of adrenaline had passed, it became hard to focus under the pleasant throbbing of one-too-many glasses of wine. She turned towards the crowd gathered at the alleyway entrance and her gaze settled on a tall and slim, dark-skinned person with short curly hair, holding a fancy graphite pencil and a notepad. A journalist. Adèle grunted. Bad news, that.

"My name is Nsia Kouna, they/them pronouns, and I work for *Le Quotidien du Val*. I just witnessed what happened here," they said, "and I can't help but wonder: who is this caped person? Are they behind the series of stolen exocores in this neighbourhood?"

Adèle stared at them, silent as her mind slowly registered the questions. She was in no state to engage journalists in a verbal spar. "I'm afraid I can't answer your enquiries." She hoped her voice didn't slur horribly. "I have to go."

"You seemed quite familiar with her."

Adèle gritted her teeth. Reporters rarely gave up easily. "I said, no comments."

"But you do have answers, do you not?" Kouna strode forward, detaching themself from the crowd still eagerly listening in. Curiosity lit their eyes, and in a moment of drunken stupor, Adèle marvelled at how expressive they were. "She called you Adèle—would that be l'officier Adèle Duclos, recently added to the special unit led by Capitaine Koyani? Was your team not just assigned a new case that concerned the numerous break-ins and stolen goods throughout the city?"

Calisse. This time, she kept the swear inside. How did this journalist know so much? This wasn't widespread information; they must have done research. Brief panic jolted through Adèle. She met Nsia Kouna's confident gaze and swallowed hard. *Calm down*, she berated herself. "I'm off duty," she repeated, her tone harsh. "No comments."

She turned heels and started in the other direction, hoping Nsia Kouna wouldn't pursue her. Koyani hadn't discussed what her politics related to journalists were, and Adèle knew from experience that the best would be to say as little as possible. Not that the case had progressed much over the last few days. Until she'd caught sight of Claire leaping between roofs, Adèle had had no idea how they could find her. Tonight's opportunity should have sealed the deal. Claire would be in custody now if not for her unnatural strength. No one magicless could have reversed her grip like this. Adèle tampered her frustration with this new knowledge: Claire had magic. She'd dodged Adèle's bullet on their first encounter with it, and used it just now to escape again.

The murmur of conversations died behind her as she got farther away, and Adèle focused on this information. Perhaps the possibility should have crossed her mind earlier, but very few witches remained in Val-de-mer. Many had fled when the reactor had exploded, killing hundreds and destroying the Quartier des Épinettes. More than a decade had passed since, but the scars from this event ran deeper in Val-de-mer than anywhere else in the country. Revealing your powers here always carried a risk. People often assumed most witches had gone into exile and congratulated themselves on getting rid of them.

What could have brought Claire here? Or had she always been around, keeping her powers under wraps until necessary? Adèle frowned. How many witches still lived in Val-de-mer, hidden? She'd never stopped to think about it, and now it bothered her. These things shouldn't have to remain a secret. Citizens should be safe no matter what, but Adèle wasn't foolish enough to think the police force could or even would protect witches if they needed it. They certainly hadn't in the past—many officers had helped organize and led the militias hunting down witches. Adèle only hoped none of her new team had done so, or would in the future.

She reached her home and slipped inside with a sigh. Her head throbbed, her inebriated elation destroyed by the encounter, leaving nothing but a fog. How much of Claire's escape was due to Adèle's alcohol level? Would she have reacted faster? Been less angry and controlled her words more? But she couldn't have predicted this encounter, or how it would unfold.

Adèle's mind kept returning to Claire's exclamation—*you have no idea what's going on*—and the raw emotion in it. In that moment, her smirk and easy banter had vanished, and the fear behind had been a punch in Adèle's guts. She believed Claire. She

94

shouldn't, had no reason to, but she did. This case had an extra layer to it, one she couldn't see yet. That was fine. Digging deeper was part of her job, though she might need help to do it right. That reporter... Adèle wracked her mind for their name. Nsia Kouna. They knew more than expected and might have clues. Afraid she would forget again, Adèle moved into her office and scribbled the name down, using the very birch ink pen Claire had tried to steal. Adèle stared at it, her determination building. She'd get past the surface, to the heart of this case and the key to catching Claire.

-9-

À LA UNE

CLAUDE DIDN'T REMEMBER GOING THROUGH THE MOTIONS OF opening the bakery, yet for the second morning in a row since Livia had disappeared, he was standing behind the counter, greeting customers with a smile. The latter came naturally to him— even on his roughest days, Claude always found the strength to smile—but it was empty. A reflex without meaning or depth, its usual mirth stolen by Livia's absence. He had returned to the Quartier des Mélèzes the following night, hoping to find a clue, risking detection from journalists, policemen, and residents on high alert. He'd broken into four large manors—just in case—and drained his entire reserve of super speed to search them from top to bottom. But Clémence was gone, and the mansions contained no hint about whether or not Livia had even been there. Claude had almost decided to close shop for the day, but he felt listless and lost. Better to keep himself busy while he tried to figure out the next step. He was rearranging his display for the third time when Adèle entered the bakery for her usual coffee and croissant.

Claude's smile stiffened.

She hadn't come on the first day, perhaps nursing her hangover too much for his rich pastries, and he was grateful for it. It was hard not to blame losing track of Clémence on her ill-timed interception. He'd reviewed the night's events in his mind, over and over, and each time he grew a little angrier at Adèle. Yet when her gaze fell upon him and the crease of worry on her forehead smoothed, giving way to a genuine smile, Claude naturally relaxed. He scolded himself—this was the police officer trying to arrest him, and a smile shouldn't melt his willpower like this!—but thoughts of an arrest only brought back memories of her strong, lean body pressing against him. His cheeks burning, Claude busied himself with his percolator, eager to hide his sudden flush of desire.

Adèle didn't come straight to get her order, instead moving to the side counter, where a few stools allowed customers to pause. He didn't have much of a bistro area—two tables and six chairs near that counter—and he couldn't afford more space for it, but many enjoyed resting at the counter itself, to read the newspaper or chat with him. Adèle had always preferred the latter, but this morning she reached for the newspaper and started flipping through the pages, examining each of them with great care. He wondered what she was looking for.

"Do you have yesterday's?" she asked as she neared the end.

"I do. I keep them because customers love the extra-long game section in weekend issues." He retrieved one of the copies of *Le Quotidien du Val* from under the counter. "Is something up? You

97

don't usually read any of them."

Adèle's gaze flicked up. "I should have. We often run into journalists during our work, and it's good to know who writes what."

Except she was actually browsing the articles, searching for something, sparing titles only a glance before she moved on. Claude would have sworn it was related to the exocores, but he didn't dare ask. Fear built in the bottom of his stomach, climbing up his throat. Had a reporter spotted him that night? What did they know? Should he look over his shoulder for a tail the next time he crossed the city? Claude moved away from Adèle, towards the back of the counter, and squeezed his eyes shut. Almost two days had passed since Livia's disappearance, and he still didn't have a clue what to do.

Adèle closed the *Quotidien* with a rustle of paper, and Claude straightened in a hurry at the sound. He snatched the ready percolator, serving Adèle's coffee as if he hadn't been lost to his slow-building panic moments ago.

"So, how does this morning find you?" she asked, leaning forward.

Numb, anxious, and minus one twin. He silenced the thought before it could cross his lips. He'd considered confiding in Adèle about Livia's disappearance while omitting details, but any investigation would involve digging into his life—if they even looked into a vanished witch. The moment they discovered his basement or the nature of his powers, however, Adèle would connect him to Claire. Part of him still wanted to tell her everything—for help, and to shove the consequences of her interruption in her face.

"Claude?"

Worry tinted Adèle's question, and her voice drew him back to reality. He'd been so focused on not either snapping or spilling everything, he'd forgotten to answer at all.

"Good, good," he said. "I'm fine."

"You don't seem fine. You've been staring into space."

He had always been a terrible liar. Livia teased him ceaselessly for it. Or she had, anyway. "I haven't slept well. Bakery life can be unforgiving."

He tried to laugh, but even to his ears, his chuckle sounded empty and strained. Claude tapped on the counter briefly, the awkwardness weighing on him, then he hurriedly grabbed a croissant out of the pile and put it on a plate. Adèle sipped her coffee, staring at him over the rim. She set the cup down as he handed her the pastry, and shattered the remnants of his professionalism with a few words.

"Do you want to go out with me?"

"I'm sorry, what?"

He stared at her—her long nose, pretty freckles, and beautiful smile—his heart in a frenzy. That was the last thing he'd expected this morning, and he wasn't ready for the mix of want and stress it brought. She wanted to go out? With him, and his *very aromantic* ass?

"To talk about it—about what keeps you from sleeping." She closed her eyes, obviously trying to control the flow of awkward words. Claude stared at her in amazed disbelief. Two nights ago, she had interrupted his best chance at rescuing Livia, and now she was asking for a date. "I'm sorry. Was that too forward? I'm not used to this. It's my sister. She keeps telling me if I want someone, I need to stop pining and go for it and—"

"You want… me." Each word came out slowly, weighed by Claude's doubts. Adèle was hot—undeniably, breathtakingly so—but this would be a mess. How many layers of complications could a night out with her bring? Besides, she wanted a date, not an escapade, and his gut twisted at the idea of romancing Adèle.

"Maybe?" she replied.

A shy smile flitted across her face and sent his heart racing. Claude clenched the counter, struggling to control his feelings. His mouth had gone dry as he considered his situation. He had more at stake than someone misunderstanding his aromanticism. Claude had no desire to get involved with people without being open about his genderfluidity, but if he let Adèle in… Livia was missing, and juggling a nascent relationship, no matter its shape, with the risk of an arrest didn't sound pleasing.

Still. She wanted him, and that was hard to ignore.

"I don't do romantic dates. I don't do romantic anything, actually. I'm aromantic, and not interested." He had tried for a time, with Zita. It had not ended well, and piecing back their friendship had demanded a lot of work after that.

"Ah." She didn't bother to hide her disappointment. "Just a drink between friends, then. I'd love to get to know you better. Every morning I come here and leave calmer and more ready to tackle the day. You've helped me with a rough week, and I'd like to give it back."

"You don't have to." She had, technically, worsened his week. But what if he could learn more about her and what she believed in? Could he push Adèle to reveal what she'd been looking for in the newspaper or, even better, information on her investigation? "Between friends, though... I think I'd love that."

He couldn't believe himself. A night out with Adèle would only make his life more complicated, and agreeing was unfair to both of them. Guilt punched through Claude instantly, yet Adèle smiled at him again, and it evaporated his desire to take his word back.

"You decide when and where," she said, renewed chirp in her voice.

This is a terrible idea. Claude reminded himself she'd caused him to lose Livia, and that in comparison this was a small betrayal—that the lies and deceiving that would come from this had a good purpose, one Adèle would hopefully agree to, if she knew. He could bring her to the *Tinashe* and at least discover what she thought of witches. If he found anything else useful about Montrant Industries, exocores, or Livia, it would be worth it. In the long run, Livia's life would always take precedence over Claude's growing desire or Adèle's hurt feelings.

Nsia Kouna's article came in the following day's edition of

the *Quotidien du Val*, à la une, filling the front page with bold letters.

EXOCORE THIEF DODGES ARREST

The title was located over a black-and-white sketch of Claire leaping from one roof to another. Even without the tell-tale purple in her hair, the precise rendition left no doubts about her identity. This artist had reproduced the exact shape of her body, including belly fat and large thighs, and Adèle was certain they had seen Claire. She sought the credit, and discovered without surprise that Kouna themself had drawn it. Adèle set the paper down with a sigh and looked up to her capitaine, who had brought it to her desk.

"How bad is it?" Adèle asked.

"They know a lot," Koyani answered, "and they use it to build up what they don't."

The evening after her dinner with Emmanuelle, Adèle had fought through her hangover and cycled to the police station. She had immediately sent word to both Koyani and Élise about her encounter with Claire and Nsia Kouna's presence, in part hoping they would be allowed to interrogate the reporter. Koyani had ruled to wait: they had no idea how much Kouna knew yet, or where that information stemmed from, and it would be premature and might only raise more questions.

"Honestly, it's below a journal like the *Quotidien du Val* to publish this," Élisa called from her desk, before pushing her chair back and joining them. "Considering what's in there, I'm surprised their editor accepted it at all, let alone front paged it. But that's what the word 'exocore' gets you these days: publicity."

Adèle had glanced at it earlier at the *Croissant-toi*, and now she was dying to read the article more thoroughly. She hadn't understood why Nsia Kouna was tying Claire's crimes solely to exocores that night, but despite all the jewelry stolen, that's all the article had focused on. And now they had dubbed her "the exocore thief". "I suspect Mx. Kouna has been investigating this for as long as we have, if not longer. They knew who I was as soon as they heard my first name."

"There could be something to their allegations," Koyani said. "Élise, we'll have several interview requests coming in now. I trust you can handle them?"

"Of course. Shall I tell them this is nothing but wild speculation?"

"Let the world know Nsia Kouna is publishing unconfirmed information and that our investigation will remain private and based on evidence. I don't want the whole city following our work." Her frown deepened and she spread prosthetic fingers above Claire's sketch. "Once the worst of the storm has blown over, drag Mx. Kouna here and learn how they reached their conclusions. Cases that land in this unit... they're always a bit unique. Perhaps they can help us see how, and why this one caught our bosses' interest."

"Understood," Élise said. "I'll prepare my standard responses."

Koyani left them to their work. Adèle's gaze returned to

the newspaper and she read the first few paragraphs. Despite Élise's assertion, Nsia Kouna had done more than string a few sensational clues into a shoddy article. Their writing was solid and concise, backed by facts Adèle knew to be true. It did deviate after a while, elaborating on the mysteries of Montrant Industries and the exocore process, casting both as looming, secret forces. The beginning, however, stayed spot on: several of Val-de-mer's wealthiest citizens had complained about their disappeared exocores, realizing only upon reporting to the police they'd also lost other valuables. The rest of the city remained mostly untouched. Kouna concluded this thief targeted the rich—if one discounted Adèle, but Kouna couldn't know that—and that she was after exocores, which left Adèle pondering.

Was she?

Adèle rummaged through the piles of paper for the complete list of what Claire had stolen. Her heart pounded as she scanned it. Exocore. The word showed up everywhere. Without fail, no matter which house Claire broke into and what else she pilfered, she left with the exocore. Once, she'd even taken the resident's reserves, stealing six exocores. Adèle's mouth went dry and a slow certainty crawled into her.

The exocore thief. Nsia Kouna's snazzy nickname was spot on, their groundless guess backed by evidence.

Adèle snatched the newspaper and spun in her chair, to face everyone else's desks. Most of the team was out of the office to plug away at their respective cases, but Yuri and Élise had remained. Yuri glanced up from his pile of documents with an inquisitive eyebrow while Élise ignored her, writing intently on a pad. Conversations always flew across the workspace, and no one bothered to stand up to strike one. Neither did Adèle.

"What if they're right?" Adèle asked. "What if Claire is after the exocores?"

Élise set her pen down and looked up from her notes. Her gaze flitted between Adèle and the newspaper. "You're not serious."

"We can't ignore the possibility that Kouna is right. Claire always steals an exocore, I checked. She sure snatched mine."

"This is not about you." Élise's soft voice had a hard edge. "Everyone makes a huge deal of exocores, but they're just new-fangled batteries. They hold electricity, and they're worth a shit ton of money. That's all there is to it, and that's why she's stealing them. Don't let their shininess distract you."

"I am not." This wasn't about the cores' novelty. Nothing could change the fact Claire kept stealing them. "We thought she targeted people with wealth, but I'm not rich, and it's the only thing she took. We should investigate this, and Montrant along with it."

Her forceful suggestion drew a groan from Élise. "It's a dead end, Adèle, and the only reason you cannot see it is because it's *your* exocore that breaks the pattern. Listen, I know it makes for a nice story, but we're police investigators, not journalists. We can't choose our leads based on what makes a good front page. Let others get riled up about exocores and spin sinister secrets around their fabrication. I see nothing surprising about a company keeping the lid on its main product's creation. Montrant Industries isn't big enough that it can afford to offer its competition all this information."

Adèle willed herself not to scowl. Her instincts screamed that they should look into it anyway, and her ego struggled with the solid refusal, but Claire's case belonged to Élise. She called the shots, and if Adèle wanted to be a part of their team, she'd have to refrain from arguing with colleagues. Once her frustration settled down, she nodded. "All right."

Back at her last job, the "all right" would have been a lie—a front to placate superiors while she went off on her own. Here... She needed to give this team a chance. Élise's piercing gaze studied her, perhaps sensing this. Her lips curved into a thin smile Adèle had grown familiar with over the last week—the one she used for small victories.

"Thank you for not arguing further," she said. "I don't think it's worth our time, but we can do minimal investigation. Good police work doesn't follow narrative laws, but it also doesn't ignore possible trails. We'll put ears out to several fences and pawn shops across the city. With the current price of exocores, we might catch wind of Claire. She stole them—why wouldn't she be selling them? For now, however, you go back to witness accounts."

She did not seem convinced, but Adèle didn't care. She could prove Élise wrong later, and if exocores were a dead end, then she'd at least have her peace of mind. But she didn't think so. This was *it*, and the only reason she didn't insist further was to avoid getting shoved back into a mouldy office. Time and good police work would support her theory either way. Whether it took days or weeks, they would catch Claire, and she would have done so *with* her colleagues rather than without.

-10-

ENTRE QUATRE MURS DE CRISTAL

DESPITE SPENDING SO MANY NIGHTS ACROSS VAL-DE-MER'S rooftops, Claude had never explored its pubs and restaurants outside of the Quartier des Sorbiers—the only place he'd gone out to, which had something of a bad reputation—and the immediate area around his bakery, here in the Quartier des Bouleaux. What did Adèle even eat, except coffee and croissants? Funny how little they actually knew of each other. They'd talked every morning for a few weeks, but he'd only ever seen two sides of her: the fuzzy-brained, pre-coffee and stressed Adèle, and the aggressive, stubborn officer Adèle. And she had only met the friendly baker who listened to her. He hid too much—his shifts in gender, his powers, his nightly activities—and it bothered him. He hadn't meant to compartmentalize and knew it couldn't last. He just didn't have a better solution for now.

Nor did he have time to look for one. He had reduced the *Croissant-toi*'s opening hours during the last two days to focus on searching for Livia. He'd tried returning to the Parc des Lilas, but that, much like his scuffle with Adèle, was all over the newspaper. The ice had cracked through the Soul Tree's bark and no one was certain the larch would survive the damage. Several customers had mentioned the whole affair in hushed tones to Claude, as if voicing the possibility of another lost Soul Tree could make it happen. They were scared the Quartier des Mélèzes would dwindle and go into disrepair along with its tree. He had nodded in faked compassion—that larch would have perished because Livia defended herself, and he couldn't bring himself to regret it.

In addition to the park, Claude had returned to Clémence's alleged residence and to Montrant Industries' cover-up factory. Neither of them had held any clues for him, so he'd switched to performing Livia's daytime activity and gathered her notes. She had extended her search past Montrant itself and to everything related she could find, and one name had caught his attention: Emmanuelle Duclos, energy engineer and inventor of the coal burners still common in Val-de-mer. When the first exocores had appeared on the market, many had speculated she might be involved. She had refuted it, but a quick look at her current research topic—the potential use of a solid matrix of magic as a solar energy captor—struck doubt in Claude's mind. Exocores might not need the sun, but they were certainly a concrete support for magical energy. Close enough to warrant investigation. As if that wasn't enough, Emmanuelle Duclos lived in the very same neighbourhood Clémence did. The one in which Adèle Duclos had intercepted him. One too many coincidences not to raise the hairs on his arms.

Claude hated the idea that Adèle was associated with this horror in any other way than her stubborn pursuit of Claire, but he needed to know for certain, and this friend-date was a perfect opportunity. Despite his lack of experience with the city's restaurants, he knew exactly where he could start poking at the subject and gauging her reactions.

The *Tinashe* had been crafted from top to bottom by its owner, Basir, a witch with the power to shape, shatter, or solidify crystal into anything his imagination could conjure. He'd chosen a restaurant. Claude had always marvelled at that—how someone with such amazing powers could settle for a simple business not even directly related to them. He understood, though. Kneading dough helped calm his mind, and every tingle of his doorbell rang in his heart, too. He loved to bake and serve and would do so regardless of his powers. It would be nice to create a bakery as special as this place, though. The front crystal wall rose before him, unpolished to obscure most of the inside. Claude could distinguish vague shapes through them: customers sitting around transparent tables or standing at the counter. Round sections of the crystal wall remained clear—the restaurant's theoretical windows.

"What is this place?"

Adèle's question startled him. She'd walked up to his left, her usual uniform replaced by a cream-coloured blouse with slightly puffed sleeves and a delicate pattern of laces up front. Still in pants, Claude noted without surprise.

"My favourite spot in Val-de-mer. The bigots avoid it

because it's magic-built and witch-owned." He laid out the words with calculated casualness, but every fibre in him waited for her reaction, tense. If she refused to go on, that was it. He could break their friendship fast and clean, and he wouldn't need to worry about faking kindness if either Emmanuelle or Adèle was involved. Adèle was so absorbed in her contemplation of the glass wall she didn't give sign of even hearing him, however. Perhaps that was good. "Shall we?"

"Yes!" She grinned and strode to the entrance. "I can't wait to see what their seats feel like. This sounds great, Claude!"

Hard to resist her enthusiasm. Or to superimpose this almost childishly excited Adèle with the woman who'd slammed him into a wall. His heart fluttered at her approval, however—no one could look at the *Tinashe* and believe magic hadn't been involved. He followed Adèle inside, and despite his regular visits, the eerie beauty of the restaurant still stole his breath away. Sunlight bathed the pub during the day, but at night Basir lit handmade gas lamps across the ceiling. The blue tint of their glass encasing and its triangular pattern cast strange shapes through the room. At times the light hit the red crystal chairs, turning purple, and the resulting painting gave a velvety ambiance to the pub.

They picked a table nestled in a crescent of crystal and Adèle trailed her fingers on the surface, lips parted in gleeful amazement. Claude stared at her, his optimism rising. He should quell it—contain himself—but he couldn't. He had prayed to the nine saints she would enjoy the magical nature of this place and could get through the evening without slandering his kind, and it looked like he might have his wish.

"I've never seen anything like this," she said.

"I don't think anything like it exists." Not so publicly, at any rate. The underground pub had its charms and was safe from those without magic, but it remained a hideout. Claude wished more of them could flaunt their powers like Basir did, but he knew the risks involved. Basir's establishment lived in the Quartier des Érables, where people had always shown more tolerance and loved more eccentric venues, and it still saw trouble.

"How did it even survive? So many businesses like this got sacked after the Meltdown, especially in Val-de-mer. Why would they spare the *Tinashe*?"

A third, deep voice answered before Claude could. "They didn't."

The floor near the foot of their table shifted, first turning murky then rising from the ground. It took a humanoid shape, gaining colours and limbs until an olive-skinned man stood before them. He would've looked entirely human if not for the glassy texture of his skin, his transparent eyes, and the crystal spikes he had instead of hair and beard. Those had grown since Claude's last visit, and he smiled at the imposing structure.

"My apologies," Basir said, "I did not intend to listen in, but it is difficult to ignore discussions of the *Tinashe*, especially when one of those involved is an old friend. It's been a long time since I saw you."

Basir cast Claude a meaningful look. Perhaps a reproach, perhaps a way to underscore how he'd avoid using Claude's name.

Thoughtful. When they'd last talked, Claude had been considering changing it. Had he sent word of his final decision? He couldn't remember. With an exaggerated sigh, he replied, "Yes, I know. Livia already scolded me. 'You don't give enough news, Claude!' It's a theme."

Naming Livia twisted his guts, but he kept smiling, maintaining the mask. He would find her, and she would be fine. *Fine*.

"You two know each other?" Adèle asked. "And what…" She made a vague gesture towards Basir. "I'm sorry. That might not be an appropriate question."

"We're old friends," Claude said. "Basir taught me a lot about starting and owning a business."

"They did attack the *Tinashe* and me," Basir said, his voice grave. "They shattered entire walls. Shot at me, too. I should have died. It's… difficult to explain what followed. Sometimes, on the brink of death, your powers take on a new shape. I could become this—save myself and save my home—and I did."

"Oh, I'm sorry." Adèle leaned forward, and although her tone was sincere, her curiosity quickly overcame the damp on her mood. "Are you in the walls, or attached to the general area, like a ghost would be?"

"In the walls."

Claude had heard Basir explain before, but he'd never considered the larger implications of his condition. When you boiled it down, his magic and soul had transferred into an appropriate recipient for it, granting him continuous access to his power and complete sentience. Not unlike exocores, except Basir had chosen this form, and his magic wasn't forcefully sapped out of him. Livia had questioned if the people trapped in exocores remained conscious, and as he listened to Basir detail the limits of his body to a very inquisitive Adèle, Claude concluded they must be. Basir certainly felt and heard what happened around his restaurant. Claude's stomach tightened. What must it be like, to stay stuck in his basement, knowing someone was trying to help but deprived of news? He ought to update them, talk to them. Livia had always greeted them when she went downstairs, but he had never *really* understood. Watching Basir speak of his transformation, a full human being made of crystal, drove it all home. Every single exocore in his basement contained a person. Livia had instinctively seen them for what they were, and he wouldn't fail to do so again. First, however, he needed to know if there were any here he should come back for. He waited for a lull in the others' conversation to shift the topic.

"Can I ask you a business question? You haven't changed to new power sources either?"

"You mean exocores?" Basir pursed his lips. "I have not, and I never intend to."

Disgust had flitted through his expression, as if the very thought sickened him. Had Basir felt it, too? If they'd unsettled Claude, then several witches must have been uneasy around exocores. He ought to ask Zita if any rumours had spread in the community. In fact, he *really* should go back to talk with Zita and explain what he could. He had completely forgotten her, too.

"Why not?" Claude asked. "Not cost efficient?"

Basir stared at him, measuring his words. Claude recognized that expression: he didn't know what was safe to voice. "You could say I'm old-fashioned like that. Besides, if local news is to be believed, a bright and young thief would come along and snatch them away from me."

Adèle stiffened, her gaze hardening at the praises uttered by Basir. Claude struggled not to smile. It helped to hear his trusted friend subtly agree with his latest enterprise. More would if they knew the reasons behind it. Perhaps even Adèle, provided she managed to step back… and that her sister wasn't a part of this. The very idea nauseated him, and he'd had to set down her profile when he had first run into the speculation about Emmanuelle and exocores. But this was something else he could probe during the evening: how much did Adèle know, and was her sister involved at all? He hoped not.

"But enough of me," Basir declared, drawing Claude out of his thoughts. "I'm sure you came to be together, not to listen to me. The menu's changed a lot, Claude, but I still have my tagine."

He'd blushed at the slight inflexion on "together" and all it implied, but opted not to correct Basir. "Let's go with that, and drinks."

Adèle ordered an apricot beer to accompany the meal, and Basir walked away. His feet fused and unfused with the ground at every step, their colour sometimes shifting with the floor. Adèle's gaze trailed him until he reached the back wall and strode straight through it. They could see his form on the other side, blurred by

115

the glass between but still moving. Claude paid more attention to Adèle's reactions than Basir's steps, afraid to perceive hints of disgust in it, but he found only bewildered joy. An invisible knot untwisted in his stomach.

Adèle returned her focus to him. "I'm glad I let you pick our spot. I haven't been in Val-de-mer long enough to know interesting places."

"I've lived here my whole life but always visit the same handful of venues, honestly. Basir's deserves more love. Besides, it helps spark conversation." Especially regarding certain sensitive subjects, but even in general it gave people a first topic to discuss, from which they could flow into others. Claude smirked at Adèle and added, "Perhaps I was worried you'd have nothing worthwhile
to say."

She laughed, her smile widening as she pushed his leg with her feet, under the table. "You wouldn't. You're too nice for that."

"I have a mean streak, but I mostly use it on... Livia."

Why did he not think his words through before he started his sentences? Claude's voice had broken before the end, fear and grief overtaking his control and forcing an awkward pause. Adèle frowned at his reaction, peering carefully at him.

"Your poor sister hardly seemed deserving of your mean streak. How is she, by the way?"

"I'm not sure." He knew better than to lie outright. Adèle would see through it instantly and only question further. "She left earlier than expected to deal with personal problems and I worry about her." Almost not a lie, and the closest Claude could get to the truth. "But sometimes you need to trust your siblings can take care of themselves, right?"

"Watching from the sidelines is always the hardest." Adèle leaned back into her chair and sighed. "Don't stay far away too long if you can help it. I regret not being with Em more often after her husband died."

"Em? Is that your sister living here?"

Guilt surged as Claude pushed the topic away from Livia and closer to Adèle's sister. It didn't feel right, this fishing for information, but what choice did he have? He hoped he'd have a chance to explain one day. Whatever mess he created searching for Livia, he could deal with it once she was safe.

"She is," Adèle said. "Emmanuelle Duclos, the star of the family!" She laughed, casting an arm out as if introducing a celebrity. "She's the mind behind the coal burner powering your bakery, and a pioneer in energy tech."

Claude's heart hammered in his chest. How was he supposed to stay casual? This was what he'd come to hear. "So she worked on the exocores, too?"

"Nah. She doesn't even know how they managed it. Says the entire scientific community is kept in the dark."

"No pun intended?" Claude asked, burying his relief under a snort of amusement.

She could be lying, but he didn't believe that—didn't want to. Light-headed from hope, he clung to the small bit of humour to keep himself grounded into the conversation. Adèle frowned, and it became obvious she hadn't meant to use such an appropriate expression. Claude's laughter redoubled until she caught on.

"Oh! No, actually." She grinned, and Claude's insides melted away. "I guess I'm witty even when I don't try."

Basir arrived with their respective plates and drinks, and for a while they both forgot about conversation and ate heartily. Claude's recent diet had consisted mostly of leftover pastries and quick tomato sandwiches, and the solid food in his stomach felt wonderful. Adèle wasn't halfway through her plate by the time he'd finished his. Between her constant smile and his delicious meal, a pleasant buzz covered his mind. Part of him wanted to talk about everything except exocores. He forced himself to continue the conversation where they'd left it anyway, hoping to learn more about Adèle's sister.

"So if she's not behind the cores, what does she think of them?"

Adèle's eyebrows shot up. She finished her bite slowly, mulling her words over. "You know that feeling when someone teases you with a secret, but won't say what it is? That's her relationship with exocores. She'd love to discover how they work and what's renewable about them."

So would Claude. Witches were not a source of infinite energy, unless they planned on force-breeding people. The very thought sent a shudder up his spine. Would they, if they needed to? At this point, he didn't put it past them. And they had Livia... He tried not to let his frustration, fear, and disgust affect him. All these questions got him was more guilt. If Emmanuelle Duclos was directly involved, Adèle had no idea. Neither could lead him to Livia, either, and right now he cared about nothing else.

"Wouldn't we all?" Claude asked.

"Maybe Claire does."

Claude tensed. Adèle had dodged that topic earlier, but perhaps her now-empty mug diminished her reluctance to breach the subject. Did he want to hear what she had to say? It might hurt more than it'd help. Yet the opportunity to get an honest opinion was not one he could pass up.

"Your thief? So you think the article is right about her?" Reading it had left Claude breathless and exposed. He hadn't expected to wake up with his likeness on the front page, and that day he doubly thanked his binder and the looseness of his clothes. He both loved how the rendering captured his fatness in action, climbing and escaping, and he feared others would recognize his body shape. The article itself had felt like Nsia Kouna had been trailing him the whole time, taking notes, exposing his strategy and casting suspicions on Montrant. Claude hoped people would read and believe it, and it had been an immense relief not to be presented in a negative light. He'd wondered if he ought to track *them* down and make an ally out of them.

"Parts of it, perhaps. We always verify, but some patterns are too strong to be a coincidence. You learn to investigate. Élise thinks it's a waste of time, but…" Adèle shrugged, and determination widened her smile. "We'll see, won't we?"

Claude hoped they wouldn't. They couldn't have gathered

that much information on him. He'd been careful to pick his targets almost randomly, changing quartiers and streets on a regular basis. But Nsia Kouna had pulled back his jewelry-stealing cover, and rich people would be warier and protect their cores. At least he knew his next steps: Emmanuelle herself, then Nsia Kouna. Judging by their article, Nsia Kouna had had no more luck than Claire and Livia digging out precise names to track down, or they didn't have enough evidence to publish. Emmanuelle, however, could very well be at the heart of this mystery. He prayed to the nine saints Adèle's sister had nothing to do with it, and that either her or Nsia Kouna would help him crack Montrant Industries' secrets.

He had a harder time staying focused through the rest of their non-date, his mind drifting back to the exocores and the newspaper while Adèle chatted about her old job. Only when she mentioned the bakery she used to frequent did he successfully set his worries aside. Claude leaned forward as she described the selection of baguettes they had sold, and which types she missed. He took mental notes, promising himself he could experiment along those lines. He'd never specialized in baguettes because of his competitor down the road, *La Bague Étoilée*, which offered a wide array of them. They didn't have counter space and coffee, however, and customers dropped by to leave almost as quickly. Claude had favoured a rest area and pastries, allowing him to fill a different purpose in the neighbourhood. Adèle eventually admitted she *did* grab baguettes at the other place every now and then. He laughed before absolving her of her guilt, and the smile she answered with melted his insides. He was glad he had accepted this night out, and not only for everything new he'd learned. Talking about dough and business allowed him to relax, and he had needed to recharge.

He might not get another chance.

-11-

LA NATURE DES EXOCORES

CLAIRE LANDED ON THE BALCONY WITH A SOFT SQUISH from soaked boots and the splash of water. The day's downpour had slowed without quite stopping, making her rooftop trek across Val-de-mer more dangerous than usual. At least she'd arrived. Emmanuelle Duclos lived a single street away from the manors Claire had investigated, searching for Clémence—close enough for her initial suspicions to resurface. Adèle's smile had melted them, but Claire knew better than to let that be her final guide. She'd been attracted to assholes in the past. Her desire was a terrible judge of goodness.

She hurried inside, glad to escape the water pounding on her head. The patter of rain on windows followed her as she entered a guest room. Her cape dripped on the beige rug. Claire wrung it—she preferred to leave a pool here rather than a trail all over the house, where anyone could spot it. Her damp clothes clung to her thick thighs and belly, and she wondered if anything

122

was more disagreeable than drenched fabric hugging her skin like that. She tugged at it with a sigh, then put that thought out of her mind. Comfort would have to wait.

Claire stalled at the guest room's door for a moment, listening for sounds and moving into the corridor only once she knew it would be safe. Clouds obscured the dim moonlight, so she progressed extra slowly, one hand trailing on the wall. Where to, though? With exocores, she began her search with basements and cupboards under large staircases, where people often installed the metal casing supporting them. Tonight, however, she needed to find the master bedroom. Claire hoped a methodical sweep of the manor would suffice, and, since she'd landed in a bedroom on the second floor, she started there. It might have others.

Claire did her best to stay silent, but the squish of her boots and slosh of her clothes echoed in the corridor. It didn't matter how much she crouched or walked on the balls of her feet or held the cape, rain had made her noisy. She often paused, listening for sounds—any hints that an alert had been raised. None. Emmanuelle's manor seemed unstaffed and unguarded. Empty, even. Good.

Claire opened doors as she went, her lips pursing at the amount of wealth casually displayed. Nothing distasteful exactly, but between the huge house, numerous paintings, and nice rugs, she couldn't help wonder how much money Emmanuelle Duclos had made from her coal burner. Unless part of it came from exocore payments, too. Claire suppressed the thought—she had no proof yet, and she hoped never to find it. Her hands clammy from stress and rain, she moved past the door... only to be assaulted by a fast and dark shape. Claire quelled down a surprised scream as a tortoise cat dashed for her cape and snatched at it, claws out. She shooed it away, her heart hammering a million times a second as the cat changed direction and ran off, proud of its hit-and-run. Claire stayed put, certain she would die from the sudden panic, torn between laughing and crying. She should have expected pets: Adèle had mentioned her sister's love of cats before. When the shaking in her hands returned to normal, Claire set off again.

She eventually reached an area where the rooms no longer seemed unused. Instead of being tidy under a film of dust, they contained small clutters on tables and the furniture was slightly ajar. Someone lived in these. And... was that light around the corner? Claire squinted, her heart pounding. She'd found her target.

As she crept closer to the door, Claire reviewed her plan — if it could be called that. She wished she'd prepared for this conversation better. Either Emmanuelle Duclos was involved in the exocore mess, or she could become a great ally. An insider in witch-related power technology might point her in the right direction, get Claire moving forward again. Because right now? Time was ticking for Livia, and Claire's only other lead was a journalist who was liable to ask for interviews and scoops in exchange for help.

She curled her fingers around the cool doorknob, stopping for one last deep breath, to steady herself. *Drip.* Every drop of water on the lacquered wood unnerved her, sinking deep into her

124

bones, cold and accusing. *Drip. Drip.* They reverberated in Claire, marking the seconds slipping by as she paused, the seconds lost for Livia. *Drip drip drip.* Your sister is dying, they said, you're running out of time, stop wasting it.

Claire shoved the door open, nervous energy slamming it against the wall on the other side. She jumped at the sound, surprised by her own strength, then snapped her attention back to Emmanuelle. Adèle's sister sat rigid in her bed, clad in nothing but a loose nightgown. A sharp gasp escaped the woman at the intrusion and she clenched the thick tome on her lap. The resemblance with Adèle was unmistakable: long nose, dark hair, and strikingly beautiful.

Like the rest of the manor's decoration, Emmanuelle had picked her bed and sheets with tasteful opulence. Intricate motifs covered the heavy duvet and were echoed in the top of her four-poster bed. The thick pillows made Claire wish for a nap, and she fought the cumulated exhaustion of the last days. Emmanuelle stared at Claire, plump cheeks flushed in the dim glow of her nightlight, her frown eerily similar to Adèle's. The silence stretched, words flitting away from Claire, refusing to form a coherent sentence. She really should have prepared for this.

"Yes?" Emmanuelle's flat tone surprised Claire. No fear in there. "Are you waiting for me to call the police? I know one, at least, who'd love to get her hands on you."

And not, sadly, in the way Claire would have enjoyed. She cleared her throat. "N-no! I have questions." Eloquent. She closed the door behind her, buying herself time to sort her thoughts. "I'm sorry for intruding. Well, not really, but I would be under different circumstances."

"You should be. You're interrupting an incredibly important read on the thermodynamics of magic and how they defy our current understanding of physics. I might forgive you, but only provided you bring significant contributions to a new framework and revolutionize our obsolete models."

Emmanuelle slung one word after the other without the slightest hint of mirth. Straight-faced, mildly offended, utterly confusing to Claire. Was she joking? She had to be!

"A tall order," Claire said with an awkward chuckle. "You can't expect me to help with…" She gestured at the air.

"I don't, no." A smile softened her expression. "I wasn't serious. Except for the part about the important read. You did interrupt that."

"Whew!" Claire grinned. "What a relief. I did come to talk science, though."

"Really?" Emmanuelle set her bookmark down, closed the tome, and pushed it aside. "You could have knocked and asked, then."

"With my likeness on the city's biggest newspaper? Doubtful." Claire readjusted her mask. She preferred to enter uninvited than to have police after her before she could even ask questions. At least Emmanuelle Duclos never had a chance to call for help. Still, it was best to get straight to the point. "Tell me about exocores."

Emmanuelle's eyebrows shot up. "So it *is* true. The

Exocore Thief. That's what you want."

Claire had yet to decide if she loved or hated the title. They didn't understand; she wouldn't care about the cores if not for the souls imprisoned within. But, if her fame could bring attention to the evil at hand, all the better. She might use that against those behind Montrant Industries and the witches' disappearance once she knew precisely who to blame.

"People thought you were involved in their creation," Claire said. "Is that how you pay for this marvellous mansion?"

"No. My wealth stems from my first invention."

"That's quite a few years ago," Claire stepped forward, hoping to impose enough to draw more helpful answers.

"Yet no one imagined better," Emmanuelle said, spreading her arms, "and every house needs power."

True enough, and one of the reasons exocores terrified Claire. Sooner or later, witches' souls would provide for every building in Val-de-mer. They had to stop it before it came to that.

"What are you working on now?" she asked.

"Is this an interrogation?" So far, Emmanuelle had remained calm, her tone casual. An edge slipped into her voice now and she leaned forward, and although the woman continued with a quip, Claire immediately knew she'd had enough. "Have you been taking lessons from Adèle?"

"I wish." Oh no. She had not meant to say that. The mask made her daring, and now she thanked the relative obscurity hiding her intense flush. She was the worst liar, and too impulsive to boot. Emmanuelle quirked her eyebrows and Claire hurried to another topic. "Please. I'm trying to understand all this energy science. I need your help to track down who could fabricate the exocores and where."

"We know who. Montrant Industries created them."

"Montrant is a front. They exist, but you can't find their owners and employees. There's never any name attached! No director, no scientists, nothing! Even their factory is a fake." Words spilled out, days of frantic research and investigation blurted out all at once. Her hands flitted through her hair with them, and she stepped forward. "I don't have proper access to their files, no idea where they would be, and no time to stalk the few officially involved hoping to find a culprit. I-I need better, and I need it now."

"You're... something special." Emmanuelle tilted her head to the side, brow furrowed into a puzzled expression. "So you seek to discover who fabricates exocores because... you want to steal more? Provoke them? Why did you think I would be your chance to find a faster path to them?"

A lump blocked Claire's answer as it dawned on her how much information she'd given away. It should've been the other way around! But while she had never studied interrogation techniques under Adèle, Emmanuelle clearly had. She'd flipped the conversation over, knocking Claire off balance and opening the door for a big slip. No more. Claire spread her legs then crossed her arms with a huff, trying to steady the panic swirling at the bottom of her stomach. She stared down at Emmanuelle, ready to reassert control of the situation.

"Never mind that! Just tell me about your research. Don't all scientists love to do that?"

"If that was a universal law, we'd have heard of the ones behind exocores, wouldn't we?" Emmanuelle replied, still utterly calm, as if the shifts in Claire's emotions were of no import to her. "You're trying to dodge my questions."

"I am. I don't see any reason to answer."

"Neither do I." Emmanuelle smirked and leaned back. "What a troublesome stalemate."

Her smirk smothered Claire's sympathy, giving full berth to a burgeoning anger. She stalked forward, scowling. Lives were at stake here, whether Emmanuelle Duclos realized it or not, and Claire didn't intend to waste her night in verbal sparring, especially not with someone better at it than her. She grabbed the bed with a single hand, shoved magic into her arm, and lifted the end off the ground with ease.

"You misunderstand the power dynamics here," she said, and Emmanuelle's eyes widened in justified fear. "I did not come to hurt you, or break anything, but I need answers and I *will* get them. Please. This is not a game to me."

Emmanuelle half-slid, half-backed away to the other end of the bed, her smile gone. "I'm not convinced I can trust you with this information, and you're not helping."

"I'm not asking for your trust." Claire glared at her, putting all her fears and exhaustion and hope into the look, desperate to give it enough intensity for Emmanuelle to fold. She didn't know if she had it in her to actually strike Adèle's sister, or even flip the bed on her, and she did not want to find out. Emmanuelle held her gaze, unflinching, but her expression softened as seconds trickled by.

"We try to create a flexible matrix interwoven with magic that could capture the sun and use it as a power source. Our understanding is incomplete, but magic flocks to certain live physical vessels and must have one to be used, whether by witches or as energy. This is why spell casters have a limited pool of strength. They can't harness ambient magic, only what has gathered within them."

Emmanuelle's brow furrowed as she continued and sank deeper in thoughts. Claire marvelled at how the woman's technical explanation matched her lived experience: when she burned through too much magic, she became tired, unable to call more forth. Yet time dispelled that fatigue whether she rested or not—it was just faster if she slept.

"We don't want to use magic directly as power anymore," Emmanuelle went on. "It proved too time-consuming and costly to ask witches to refill the batteries constantly, and… Well, after the Meltdown, it'd never pass the politics test. Even our project gets rejected as too dependent on witches when we apply for subventions, which is several layers of bullshit and—" She stopped, glanced at Claire single-handedly holding the bed, and licked her lips. "I'm sure I don't need to explain why this is ridiculous bigotry to you. The point is, creating a matrix of magic that captures another type of energy—the sun, for us—means we only require a small amount of it, during initial production. And studies have already demonstrated how great magic is at transmitting or transforming energy from one type to another without much lost, so we think we'd have an efficient final product. But the matrix itself is proving to be a difficult beast to tackle, and I have no idea how any of this is supposed to help you, but there you go, that's my research."

Claire stared at her, trying to parse through all the science jargon. They wanted witches to create a magical container to capture the sun and turn it into electricity. But magic was hard to imbue into physical objects. Claire only knew of two instances: Basir, who had transferred not only his magic but himself, and Clémence's protective artefacts used to conceal the witches' hideouts. Claire wondered what ol had used, and if it resembled the exocores.

"Are you having problems finding the right receptacle for the magic?" she asked. "Objects aren't supposed to hold it."

"Yes. And it is near impossible to do methodical research and testing for this. The materials used for the old witch-powered batteries only store raw magic, not other types of energy, and all our attempts with them failed. To be systematic, we'd need to study witches themselves, which would require either large scale statistics or invasive procedures."

Invasive procedures. She doubted that had stopped the exocores' creators. With a shudder, she prevented her too-vivid imagination from detailing what that entailed, before she projected everything on Livia and panicked. "Right. These aren't options available to you."

Emmanuelle tilted her head to the side and straightened up, her interest clearly piqued. "Not to *me*, no."

Claire sighed. Had she said too much again? It didn't matter. She had her explanation, and while she didn't understand the minutiae of Montrant Industries' technique, she could see the general scheme of it: transfer people into gems without their consent, hold them in this physical shape, find a way to draw only the magical power out, transforming it into electricity. Did this mean they left bodies behind? Her stomach clenched from nausea, and her palms turned sweaty. She pushed aside thoughts of the more gruesome, technical details. She could imagine those later, alone and at home.

She dropped the bed, certain Emmanuelle wouldn't have anything else useful for her, and cringed as Adèle's sister almost fell off it from the shock before quickly burying that guilt. She needed to find a way to crack the opaque shell Montrant Industries had built around the exocores. There *had* to be a network of activities still existing, starting with the capture of witches and ending with the production of new cores. But how to uncover it? Perhaps she should look at the places selling exocores. They had to be shipped in from somewhere, after all! Claire headed towards the bedroom's private balcony, preparing herself for the rain, but stopped at the door as a thought struck. "Wait. Do you have any exocores?"

Emmanuelle laughed, and the mirthful sound erased the tension hanging between them. "You're asking me to tell you if I have any of those things you love to steal? Why would I answer?"

CHAPITRE ONZE

Claire smirked and turned around with a shrug. "A girl can try. It'd have spared me the trouble of looking."

"I could call for help while you do," she pointed out.

"A girl can try," Claire repeated, her grin widening. Even if Emmanuelle did find police officers or willing neighbours, Claire would outrun them with ease. She'd take the risk if it meant one more saved exocore.

Emmanuelle stared at her in silence for a moment, evaluating Claire and the chances of catching her. It lasted long enough for Claire to shift awkwardly and worry help was already on the way after all, and Emmanuelle was just buying time. When would she have called them, however? No. Everything was fine.

"I don't have exocores here," Emmanuelle said. "It's silly, but I can't switch to another power source yet. I'm still too attached to my little burner. This entire house runs on the prototype. Go check it out, if you don't believe me."

Claire did believe her. She couldn't explain why she trusted Emmanuelle's word—something about her pinched frown, so similar to Adèle's, or the candidness of being caught reading heavy science in her night robe. Perhaps Claire was deluding herself, but she decided to accept her instincts and trust herself, too.

"One last thing… You'll tell your sister I came, won't you?"

Emmanuelle Duclos nodded. Claire swallowed hard. She probably shouldn't talk about Adèle, but when would she have the opportunity to get a message to her? Adèle wouldn't give her a chance to say two words before trying to arrest her. Besides, she

133

didn't want Emmanuelle's story to only contain "she threatened me for information."

"Tell her I'm sorry I broke into her house. But… tell her I'd steal that exocore again any day, and she's right, that was always the point. She has good instincts."

Claire shoved the balcony door open and sprinted into the heavy rain. It soaked her instantly, seeping through cape, mask, and dress as she leaped off the railing and to the closest rooftop. She didn't know if her words would only infuriate Adèle more, but she'd had to say something, to at least acknowledge she grasped what she'd done. And maybe, with a better context and understanding of what was happening, Adèle could one day forgive her.

Claire strode into her basement and threw her mask off. It fell to the ground with a wet slap, immediately followed by the heavy thump of her cape. Every piece of cloth on her body was drenched and she couldn't wait to remove them all. She struggled to pull off her gloves, then fumbled at the buttons of her dress, fingers made clumsy by the cold rain that had seeped through, and undressed in a hurry. Claire flung her wardrobe open, grabbed a towel from the top shelf, and dried herself with great relief. Such awful weather. Just the kind of heavy downpour Livia loved. Claire closed her eyes and lowered the towel, fighting the void growing in her heart. Livia would see more of these terrible rainy days, she promised herself. She would never give up on her sister.

Claire dressed back up, slipping into comfy pants and a loose shirt she usually wore only during the day, but not bothering with the binder or the removal of her hair colour yet. Presenting and being read as a man grated her more and more these days, and she wished she could've spent the entire week in Claire's disguise or another nice dress. At least when it was the other way around — when her gender leaned towards male for several full days or weeks — she could stay as Claude all day. Her evenings were flexible. No such luck with the bakery, however. She should have made clear that her gender shifted from day one to avoid this problem and wished she had been more confident in her identity. So many others presented outside the binary without issues, so why not her? But doing it now, while Claire was being pursued, was a terrible idea.

Once her drenched clothes were hanging to dry, Claire returned to the exocores. She'd avoided them since Livia's disappearance, unable to deal with the sickening unease provoked by so many of them in a single place. It'd been subtle when she'd only had a handful, but ever since they'd covered her entire table the whole basement gave her chills — an excellent reminder of everything at stake, and how many counted on her. She worried about Livia, of course, but Claire couldn't forget those who'd already paid for this inhuman industry.

She wanted to do more than remember. Ever since talking with Basir again, she'd tried to imagine what the victims' lives were like, stuck in a gem which drained their souls to power houses. Claire hoped that had at least stopped since she'd brought them here, but did the pain linger? Could they recall it, or their pasts? How sentient were they truly? She suspected the answer to that was "very", which meant they'd heard or seen nothing but Claire rummaging and changing since Livia had vanished. Guilt overrode Claire's unease, and she reached for the closest exocore, running her fingers over its surface.

"It's going to be okay, everyone." She meant it. She'd find a way, no matter what. "I've been busy."

She sat at the table for hours, narrating the last days to imprisoned witches who might not even hear her. She had to, just in case. Claire poured out her fears and hopes and suspicions, and voicing it helped clarify her thoughts. The exocores never answered, but, by the time she was finished, Claire's determination had hardened. She understood exocores, the potential tech behind them, and the pieces of her puzzle better now. She could do this. She thanked them for listening, moved to her desk, and reached for her large file on Montrant Industries. Dozens of notes, newspaper articles, and archive files, compiled for her perusal. Adèle would be impressed.

"This is my enemy," she said, to herself, to the exocores, and to Livia, wherever she was. "Somewhere in there or on the street is my damning evidence, and I'll find it. I'll find a link I can follow to the top. I promise."

-12-

ET POURQUOI PAS MONTRANT?

"CLAIRE DID *WHAT?*"

Adèle's voice rang through the Parc des Bouleaux, where the quartier's emblematic birch Soul Tree grew. The park spread behind an old theatre, and the greenery helped alleviate the dark mood instilled by the heavy clouds still hanging over Val-de-mer. Humidity and cold made it harder to breathe, but she hadn't wanted to stay inside. She had managed to keep her calm during Emmanuelle's story, her teeth clenching as her sister explained how the damnable thief had snuck into her manor and busted into her room while she was in a nightrobe, but that was too much. Adèle couldn't believe the gall of this girl. How dare she? Breaking into Adèle's flat and ruining her feeble sense of security was one thing, but doing the same to her sister? And worse, she'd—

"Lifted the bed," Em repeated with exemplar calm. "It did get a little scary then."

A little. *A little.* "I'll find that no-good invader and—"

"Adèle, calm down." Emmanuelle laughed and grabbed her arm as Adèle's strides lengthened, as if she could've run after Claire here and now. Her sister squeezed her arm, forcing a steady pace as they walked along the park's pathways. "I'm fine. Of the two of us, I'm certain Claire had the worse night."

Hard not to believe it, with her level tone and bright smile. Em was as chirpy as if she'd had a massive scientific breakthrough. She had knocked at Adèle's door early in the morning, in a flowing pink robe and beautiful hat, and insisted on "sharing some great news and checking out that cute baker." Their first stop had thus been the *Croissant-toi*, and this time Emmanuelle did not miss the pun in its name. She'd spent the entire walk from Adèle's flat to the bakery expounding on how adorable and uplifting it was for the name to say "believe in yourself", provided you slightly mispronounced it as *crois-en toi*.

Claude himself still worried Adèle. Their night out hadn't helped, and this morning a faint smoke scent lingered in the bakery. Burnt loaves of rye bread from a distraction, he said, and Adèle hoped the fire hadn't been too bad. Perhaps his mistake explained why he'd shown so little enthusiasm at meeting Em. New customers typically excited him, and, considering how interested in learning more about her he'd been, Adèle had expected huge smiles and a warm welcome. They did receive a free croissant, yet he acted like a man who knew he had to go through these steps but couldn't conjure the energy for them. Whatever he didn't want to talk about, it was worsening. Adèle promised herself to check back on him and she had found it hard to focus on

Em's chatter as they entered the park and set down a gravel path…
until her sister had mentioned Claire breaking into her mansion.

"I don't care how horrible her night was. She doesn't get
to assault my sister like this. Are you sure she didn't steal
anything? Have you searched the whole house? You don't even
have an exocore!"

"I'm sure. She only asked questions."

"And lifted your bed."

"Well, I wasn't answering." Anger must have flashed
through Adèle's expression because Em quickly added, "I think
she's scared, Adèle. You talk about an arrogant and mocking girl,
and when she entered it's true she had that air, like the world
belonged to her, but it crumbled so fast. Under it she's frazzled and
desperate, and perhaps a little directionless."

"Am I supposed to pity her?" Despite her rock-hard tone,
Adèle thought of Claire shoving her off during their second
encounter, of the panic in her *you have no idea what's going on*, and
she wondered. What was she missing? Pity or not, she would have
to understand Claire in order to catch her.

Em huffed at her question. "If that's what it takes to
remember the very real human under that mask, then yes, perhaps
you should."

"I—" She stopped her protest. She had always been
unwilling to give Claire a chance to have good reasons. It made her
job easier. "Right. If stealing those exocores isn't a get-rich-quick
scheme, then I won't find her looking for black market sales. You
think she's keeping them?"

139

"Definitely." Em paused as their path vanished under a large puddle, left over from yesterday's rain. She hiked her skirts with a pout and attempted to avoid the deepest parts as she continued. "She was trying to figure out how they worked. And when I couldn't tell her, she wanted to know as much as possible about my research."

"About solar energy and magic?" That was new. What did either have to do with the exocores?

"Yes." Em's smile widened. "It's been a while since someone took such an… intense interest in my research. She asked how magic could create a solid form of electricity, I think? So I detailed how we didn't seek to use magic as the source of power itself, but as a sort of trap for it, embedded in a fabric that would only require its magic during the initial steps of production. But you know that. I need to stop rambling." She chuckled and sipped her coffee. "I didn't think I'd ever have to explain my research to a wet and masked witch!"

Adèle marvelled at her sister's ability to form fond memories about Claire's intrusion the very morning after. Em had always rolled with the punches more easily, however—all except Julien's death. Adèle required time and space to deal with others crossing her boundaries, and she'd yet to get over Claire breaking into her home. No matter the reasons, it'd always be a breach that had thrown Adèle off at a moment when she'd needed stability.

"What do you think she's doing with the exocores? Why would she want them?"

"I don't know. That's your job, isn't it? Perhaps she wants

to use them, or is testing stuff on them. I do hope it's not the latter. Without the proper equipment, concentrated energy can be dangerous. The Meltdown could never have killed so many without such a huge amount of magic localized in a single spot."

"So she could still be dangerous."

Em glared at Adèle, obviously disapproving of the conclusion. "She had a message for you. First, she confirmed she was after exocores, and that's where you should look too. Second, she said she was sorry she broke into your house, even if she would do it again should you have another exocore."

"Great. I almost feel better about it." Sarcasm aside, and despite her better judgment, she *did* feel relief. All it'd taken was a half-assed apology for her stomach to unwind and her anxiety to lighten, and that made her angry. "Not safer, though. Is she watching me? She knew we were sisters, if she told you that."

This time, Em's smile vanished. She stopped and tensed. "I had never considered that. It's sinister, but... I don't think she came because I was your sister. She just used the opportunity."

"You'd better be right, for her sake." Adèle already struggled to forgive Claire for breaking into her flat. If she'd sought her sister not only for the information, but to intimidate Adèle... it wouldn't go well once Claire was caught. Adèle tore into her croissant and shoved a bite into her mouth, using the chewing time to control her anger. "You heard her questions. What do you think she'll be doing now?"

"Investigating Montrant Industries again." Not an ounce of doubt lingered in Em's voice. "Perhaps more aggressively than before. Their secrecy frustrated her, and talking about them is when she lost her façade, really."

"Makes sense. If she's after exocores or their secret, she'll look into unravelling their network and stealing their exocores. She might search either for warehouses where they store the cores or the scientists behind the technique."

"She tried already, but I think she will again."

In which case, Adèle would have to get to these things first. She could do it; she had the law behind her. "Thank you, Em. I didn't expect to learn so much when you knocked this morning."

"Thank Claire." Em laughed when she frowned. "She's the one who braved heavy rain to talk science with me and reveal so much, knowing full well I was your sister."

Adèle stopped dead. Why would Claire let so much information slip? She'd covered her tracks about exocores before, disguising a precise theft by stealing random valuables. Did she think the charade was no longer worth her time? Perhaps Nsia Kouna's article had blown it open too widely for her to care anymore. Yet she'd given away more than her designs regarding exocores. Em had enough information to predict her next step. Did Claire doubt Adèle could catch her? She was in for a bad surprise if that was the case.

"I don't like it." She stared at the trees around, as if one would lean forward and whisper the answers into her ears. Claire could be misleading her, too, offering red herrings for Adèle to chase. Any of this information she'd dropped to Em might turn out false. She might be a fantastic actress. Yet they had nothing better and she had to pursue it. Or as Élise had put it: a good investigator never ignored a lead. Adèle shoved the rest of her croissant in her mouth, pondering how to approach this.

Emmanuelle's hand on her shoulders brought her back to the conversation. Her sister stared at her with a determined expression, confidence and seriousness shining in her rich brown eye. "Whatever is going on, Adèle, I know you'll get to the bottom of it. You'll do the right thing."

A soft warmth spread through Adèle. This was exactly why she had missed her siblings so much. They all had a way to recenter and support each other when they needed it.

"Thank you." Adèle wrapped her arms around Em and squeezed. "I'm glad she didn't hurt you. I'd never forgive myself if bad things happened to you because of me."

Em laughed—not at all the reaction Adèle expected, and one that left her a little offended, too. "Sweetheart, I know if anyone dared, there would be hell to pay."

Well, she wasn't wrong either. Adèle squeezed her sister again before stepping back and resuming their stroll through the park. They'd both have to return to work soon, to dig into their respective mysteries, but until then Adèle intended to take every ounce of comfort and strength she could from her sister's presence.

Nsia Kouna sat straight as a pole on their chair in the barren interrogation room, their fingers deftly playing with their pencil as they studied Adèle and Élise. The lanky journalist had accepted to come without protest, and between their wry smile and the quirk in their clearly defined eyebrows, Adèle had the distinct impression Kouna found the entire situation amusing. They must have talked with police before, and would not easily be intimidated. If anything, Kouna obviously expected the upper hand in this interview. They turned their attention to Adèle, smile widening.

"I'm glad you're on duty now, Madame l'Officier. Will I finally receive the answers to my questions?"

Élise snorted. "Doubtful. We're asking the questions today, Mx. Kouna, and you're providing answers."

"Or so you hope, at any rate." Kouna leaned back into their chair, and a spike of anger rose within Adèle. "You've read the article. What more do you want to know?"

"How you acquired so much information, for a start." Élise pulled a chair and sat down in front of Kouna. They had agreed earlier that she would conduct most of the interrogation while Adèle listened, ready to pick up on nuances in Kouna's words. She remained standing, hands clasped behind her back. The journalist was so tall that Adèle doubted her height would intimidate, but she was afraid she'd fidget if she sat. Focusing on others' words was always a struggle, especially when her hands didn't keep busy, and she needed to stay alert.

"Am I to understand you confirm what is in my article?"

"This does not answer my question."

Kouna shrugged with calculated calm. Strange, how

144

expressive their thin and long face was while still betraying nothing of their thoughts. Their entire body language shifted with a smile, yet Adèle had no idea whether they felt tense or relaxed, amused or annoyed. "Perhaps we could trade. I answer one of your questions, and you answer one of mine. We both get what we want."

"Absolutely not." Élise flicked her head, sending dark curls flying back. "You're in a police station, Mx. Kouna, and I have no times for games. We have a thief to catch."

"An *exocore* thief," Kouna said.

"And we believe you have information that could help us," Élise continued, as if they hadn't said anything.

Kouna leaned forward, putting down the pen and linking their fingers. They looked down on Élise, who instinctively straightened her shoulders to compensate. Adèle couldn't help but think the journalist knew exactly what they were doing. They had been through this before. "Let's not waste our respective time," they said. "I have but one question for you: will you be investigating Montrant Industries, or are you only interested in arresting this thief?"

Adèle's breath caught. Now she wished Kouna hadn't arrived at the police station before Adèle could tell Élise about Claire's intrusion in Emmanuelle's manor and the conclusions they had drawn from this. Élise would have no idea Claire was actively trying to unravel their network. Élise studied Kouna in silence for a long moment, her lips pursed. "Placing Claire under arrest for her numerous illegal acts is our first and main goal. We will do whatever it takes to achieve it."

"Then I'm not sure I can help you." They pushed themselves up in one graceful movement. "What I know of Claire is in the article. I can't tell you who is behind the mask or where to find her. All I am certain of is that she discovered a trail—something sinister—and she's following it. Guess you'll have to do your job to find her, though."

"I *am* doing my job," Élise retorted. "Please sit down. We are not done."

"We are." The pleasantness vanished from their tone. "This special unit is exactly the same as the rest of police—tied up by politics and money, supporting those above rather than dismantling their corruption. But since you are investigating Claire and I have no further information to give, I am not hindering your investigation. You have nothing to hold me. Mesdames, call me back once you decide to sniff around Montrant Industries' business. Until then, I'm afraid I cannot help you."

They swooped their pen off the table, bowed in salutations to both of them, then strode out of the interrogation room. Élise did nothing to stop them, her jaw clenched, her breathing coming in and out slowly. The door clicked behind Kouna, and she finally sighed. "Well, that was unhelpful. I'll get a proper warrant for interrogation and drag their ass right back to this chair."

"I think we *should* investigate Montrant." Adèle dropped the words like she would a bomb, steeling herself for impact. Élise had not been very receptive to the idea the first time, so why would she be now? She spun around to stare at Adèle, gesturing for an

146

explanation. Adèle obliged. "Claire busted in my sister's bedroom last night to ask questions about the exocores' fabrication and the science involved. My sis works with something similar at the moment. She told me Claire was quite insistent on piercing the secret behind Montrant. I think if we do it before her, we'll be able to anticipate her next step and catch her."

"Perhaps... Certainly, nothing we have tried so far has led us closer to her." Élise's hand started drawing circles on the table beside her, a habit Adèle had come to identify as nervous thoughts. "If we do so, however, we must be subtle. Montrant Industries is a secretive organization and its network reaches deep. Investigating them will require a delicate touch, or we risk upsetting the beast."

"I thought 'upsetting the beast' was why we existed," Adèle said. Kouna had clearly hoped so, or they would not even have agreed to talk with them. "What if they are up to something wrong?"

"Then we can dismantle them *after* we catch Claire," she replied. "Don't get ahead of yourself. Our target is Claire, not Montrant Industries. If we can use them as bait, however, we might be able to achieve a quick result. I'll speak with Koyani about it. We could use Mx. Kouna's eagerness to leak it out." Élise's smile widened as she voiced her thoughts and the idea took a clearer form. "Thank your sister. I believe she provided the honey with which to trap our fly."

"I will."

Yet instead of the excitement she ought to feel, a quiet dread filled Adèle. Based on Nsia Kouna's words, Claire was working solo to dismantle a mysterious and dangerous entity. Worse, Emmanuelle had clearly described the girl as frazzled and afraid—which she had also been, the night Adèle had drunkenly tried to arrest her. *You have no idea what's going on,* she'd said, raw and angry. Adèle still didn't, and now she feared she might never learn. Adèle knew the kind of hunch building in her mind: whether or not they brought Claire into custody before investigating Montrant Industries, she would dig into their business and see what she could find.

-13-

L'AIDE-XUBÉRANTE

LOUD KNOCKS ON HIS FRONT BAY WINDOWS STARTLED Claude awake. He scrambled out of bed, his heart racing as his visitor hammered again, harder and harder. Did they want to break the glass? Claude let out a low moan and rubbed his eyes.

"I'm coming!" he called. "Just a moment."

He grabbed his binder and pulled it on carefully, before slipping a loose shirt over his head and retying his long hair. Part of him wished not to, but with all the hammering, he didn't have time to think on gender and presentation too carefully. The problem with sleeping in the late afternoon was that some people had no respect for his wonky schedule. They barged in at ungodly hours of the day and rammed his door until he answered. This visitor was assaulting the bakery's window, too, which meant he could expect an angry customer ignoring the *Fermé* sign.

Or perhaps it was Adèle. He hoped not. Keeping a straight face during her short passage with Emmanuelle had drained him, and he didn't think he could succeed again. This charade needed to end soon. Every new meeting with Adèle tired him. All those omissions, those lies… it felt too much like pretending he was someone else, that Claire shouldn't exist instead of allowing her to shine as the very essential part of him she was. Not knowing *when* he could clear that up and simply be was as exhausting as the lies themselves. Eyes still beady, his heart increasingly turning into a shrivelled, tired mess, Claude emerged into his shop to check who was at the door.

There was no mistaking the stocky frame and frizzy hair of the woman gesturing at him from the wide display windows. "Zita?"

Zita pointed to the door and vanished from sight. No doubt if he didn't open, she'd beat at it again, and those tiny arms of hers could pack a punch. Claude opened, and a look at Zita's scowl warned him something was wrong. He probably knew why, but trying to drag his half-asleep brain to provide an answer was too much at the moment.

"What's going on?" he asked.

"You tell me!" She strode inside, slammed the door, then whirled on him. "You promised you would come back to explain. But no, *poof*, no news for a week!" Zita threw her arms up and poked his chest. "You can't push me around swearing Livia has been kidnapped and it might be Clémence and refuse to elaborate—just saying 'not now'—and never return, leaving me to stew in my fears and confusion. That's a shitty way to treat a friend."

Claude reeled from the onslaught, trying desperately to wake himself fully. He wasn't ready for Zita, and she deserved him to be. She was right about this: he shouldn't have forgotten her. "I didn't mean—"

"I'm not done," she snapped, and her intensity shocked his mind into full awareness. Zita's unrelenting cheerfulness had vanished, and the seething anger under it frightened him. "I didn't just sit on my ass for a week. I was scared out of my wits, so I tried to find Livia again. And when that didn't work, I started Seeking the other witches that had gone missing—all those I'd passed Clémence's messages to and who had disappeared? I applied all my knowledge to their signature energy, going off what I remembered of them and what I've learned of my powers through the years. I figured if I could track down one or two of them..." She laughed bitterly and shook her head. "I sensed dozens of them. They're different, I'm not sure why they don't feel the same, but it's them. And most of their locations were split between two places—two gatherings of people. I picked the smallest, to check it out, see for myself what was going on since you wouldn't tell me... and here I am."

Claude's stomach tightened. He forced himself not to glance down and tried to keep panic off his face. *Here*, under his feet, in a pile of exocores. What could he say now? "You mean..."

"They're in your bakery, Claude." Her tone was colder than Livia's ice magic. "I don't like being played for a fool, and I won't be kept in the dark. You're lucky you're my friend, or I would have gone to the police, even at the risk of revealing my powers. You better have a good explanation, though, and no more dodging me!"

151

A tight ball of fear clogged his throat, and Claude struggled to get any coherent thoughts in his mind. He stared at the floor, twisting his body to the side, away from Zita, as if he could escape her glare while she stood right before him, hands on her hips. Ever since Livia had been kidnapped, he had endured the weight of the exocores' secret alone. His own fault, perhaps, but dodging police pursuit and lying to Adèle and keeping his business running while trying to find a single clue to uproot Montrant had left him completely drained. And every day that passed, Livia's time slipped away. How long before they turned her into an exocore? Had they done so already? He couldn't think clearly anymore, and he needed help. He should have asked ages ago.

Claude lifted his gaze and met Zita's. "All right. Brace yourself, though."

He motioned for his friend to follow him and led her down his secret ladder without a word. Zita remained silent, another unusual reaction for her. He wished she'd break the tension with a snappy joke and bring their relationship back to better-known grounds. Considering what he was about to show her, however, that might never be a possibility again. Claude entered his basement, then stepped aside to give her a full view of the exocore pile on his table.

Zita crossed her arms. "You're just adding more questions, not explaining anything."

"The disappeared witches you followed here? They're in the pile. They *are* the pile." Claude strode to the table, his stomach

152

squeezing. It still hurt to even think about it, despite spending over an hour talking to them last night. "They're likely conscious to some degree, too. If you don't believe me, Seek them out. You'll see."

Zita's expression had gone blank, and she closed her eyes to use her powers. More receptive witches would have detected the shift in magic, like an imperceptible change in the air, but Claude's strength had never been there. He wielded his shallow reserve of power in either low burns or sudden bursts that always affected him, not his environment. As such, his sensitivity to his surroundings remained less-than-stellar. He waited for Zita to finish. Horror darkened her eyes when she met his gaze again, and he instantly felt less alone.

"You've been stealing them, haven't you?"

Claude couldn't help but snort. "Don't you read the newspaper? The Exocore Thief. I even have a nickname!"

"Avoided them as soon as I heard the larch Soul Tree had been attacked by a witch. I didn't want to deal with the fear-mongering."

"Zita..." Claude rubbed his forehead, struggling to word the irony of this. Zita had stepped back fast enough to avoid the one detail that mattered. "It wasn't any attack. It was ice. Livia's ice."

Zita's eyes widened and she released a soft curse. Mentally, Claude added *Don't let the Saints hear you*, but he didn't reprimand Zita. Most people cursed these days, anyway, and the situation certainly warranted it. Instead, he strode to his desk, where all his files on Montrant Industries piled up, and he rummaged through them until he found the *Quotidien*. Recognition flashed in Zita's eyes the moment she saw Claire's portrait.

"No wonder you no longer invite me to wild escapades in the Quartier des Sorbiers. Here I thought you'd grown old and preferred to rest at home!"

"No… I've been using Claire as a cover to steal exocores. Kinda regret it now. Been feeling more like a woman for a few days, but I don't dare present accordingly at the bakery in case someone puts one and one together. Even without the mask and purple hair, Adèle might recognize me."

"Adèle?"

"The police on this case. She's a customer. You'd like her, I think."

"No? Why would I? She's trying to arrest you!"

"But she's *gorgeous*."

"Claude!" Zita snorted, folded the newspaper in two, and slapped him with it. "This is not the time. But do point her out to me as soon as you have the chance," she added with a wink.

Claude stifled a laugh—Zita was right, this was really not the time, but joking with her lifted a huge weight off his shoulders. They exchanged a smile before he turned towards the pile of exocores. "When I started stealing them, I had no idea what was happening, only that I disliked the way they made me feel."

"Yeah, it's… icky. Sorry, buddies. How did you even run into one in the first place? These things cost the skin off your ass."

"Looked into them for the bakery. I use a lot of energy for

the ovens and I wanted to save. When I touched one, though…
something was wrong. That's why I called Livia over. She was
always more perceptive, and she knew instantly. So we started
investigating together and…" He trailed off, unable to finish—not
while staring at the exocores, their red glow filling him with dread.
What were the chances even that Livia wasn't a gem now?

Zita moved behind him and set a hand on his shoulder,
reaching up. "I'd sense her if she were an exocore. I think she's still
with Clémence, and ols suppressing magic is blocking me."

She might be dead, or too far away for Zita to sense, but
Claude didn't point out either of those things. He refused to believe
Livia was lost to him forever. "Right. We think an exocore
connected to a power grid forcefully removes magic from the witch
it hosts. Soul-sucking, really. I have no idea what I'll do with all of
these. We'll need to figure it out once Livia is safe and we've
stopped exocore production."

"You could have told me," Zita said. "I'm helpful."

Helpful, and talkative. Had they known Zita could sense
the witches even in exocores, however, they would have tried.
"This is a secret, Zita. We thought our chances were better if it
didn't spread because we had no idea who would do such a thing.
Not you, of course, but…"

"I'm not good with secrets." She finished for him, without
a hint of resentment. Zita knew herself, at least. "I can keep
something this big to myself, Claude. I've been sick with worry!"

"I'm sorry. After Livia vanished I really lost… perspective,
I think? Tunnel vision. I couldn't think past the next step, or

anything around." Even before she'd been captured, knowledge of the exocores had hit him like a brick. His twin had steadied him, and without her he'd quickly sunk into a frenetic confusion.

Zita squeezed his shoulder, then leaned on him. "Just... don't do it again."

"I won't. I'm glad you're here, Zita. Clémence works with them, so that's at least one witch greedy enough to sell their community. Who knows how many others there are?"

"Clémence isn't greedy. They have something on ol."

Claude pressed his lips tight and crushed any thoughts of arguing with Zita. At this point, it didn't matter whether or not ol had been coerced into helping, only that ol had kidnapped Livia. "You said you sensed a lot of others in a second location, didn't you? Even more than are here?"

"Y-yeah. Tons of them. Are those all exocores too? How many could there be?" Her voice cracked towards the end, and she stepped back, away from the table. "These things... they're all over the rich neighbourhoods, aren't they? Oh dear..." Obviously, the enormity of this was beginning to sink in. Tears shone in Zita's dark eyes, and she stumbled back until she could crumple into a seat and drop her head in her hands. "Why are people so horrible? First they hunt us down, and now they devise an entire industry out of our souls and deaths? How are we supposed to fight that and–and do anything?"

Claude wished he had an answer, even a small one. Despair like Zita's had been hammering at him for days, and in truth he saw no way out of this. Montrant Industries wasn't a single person: it was a system, built in the shadows to slowly exterminate them, and it wouldn't exist without the approval of people in power. Once again, he wondered if the mairesse knew, or even suspected. Hard to imagine Denise Jalbert, unyielding and loyal to his parents, accepting this. He didn't want to, either; she meant too much to him, had taught him to value his aromanticism. Claude would rather think of her as someone else to ally with, if they could gather proof.

Thinking too far ahead would overwhelm them, however, so Claude focused on the next steps. He sat beside Zita, put a hand on her stocky shoulder, turned her his way. "It's not over. This second location might be a storage for Montrant Industries. Take a few hours to wrap your head around everything and help yourself to the pastries upstairs. I need to sleep, but when I wake up again, we'll investigate together. We'll save everyone."

Empty promises, perhaps, but Claude couldn't help it— not with the hollow despair settling in Zita's eyes. She straightened and met his gaze, searching for the lies in his word. He prayed that, just this once, he'd prove a good liar. Zita smiled, nodded.

"Okay. Yes. You're right." She clenched her firt, and determination returned to her expression. "We can't give up. Go to bed, and I'll be ready when you're rested!"

Claude squeezed her shoulder before standing up. "We'll crack their mystery open," he said, before climbing back upstairs.

Exhaustion settled in his muscles as he heaved himself up the ladder. Zita's sudden appearance had terrified him, but sharing his burden had lightened it considerably. Maybe they did have a chance. He had options still, could go to Nsia Kouna if this didn't work. Claude returned to his bed and sat on the edge for a moment. He had a friend with him now, someone he trusted with his life. He knew he'd sleep better this afternoon than he had in days, and hopefully, by the end of the night, he'd have saved several more exocores and gained a solid lead on Montrant Industries.

One could dream.

-14-

LE FEU AUX POUDRES

ADÈLE STARED AT THE WAREHOUSE, ONE HAND ON HER revolver, the other deep in her pocket, fingers tight around the anonymous tip that had led her here. She had returned home frustrated by the interview with Kouna and Élise's persistent focus. Claire and Montrant Industries couldn't be separated, and she wished she could investigate the exocore producers while they prepared their trap, not after. Clearly, someone else was of the same mind. The note read "1162 Rue des Quenouilles, Quartier des Grands Sapins, Tonight" and she suspected a certain journalist had left it for her. At least it had been slipped under the door. Adèle had still checked every room and window when she arrived, half-convinced she would find traces of Claire's passage. The last thing she needed was proof someone had broken in again considering how slowly her sense of home was piecing itself back together.

She'd stared at the note for a long time, then set it aside to fix herself a quick summer dinner: grilled corn, a cucumber sandwich, and a delicious chickpea, parsley, and tomato salad she'd prepared the previous day. Adèle preferred to keep heavier meals for rainy fall days, and her stomach felt particularly tight as she contemplated her options. If she waited until tomorrow, she might miss one of their best opportunities to investigate Montrant. And if she showed Élise... what if she again insisted not to look into it until Claire was caught? Adèle didn't want to dawdle if Montrant hid sinister activities, but feared Koyani would consider going a lack of team spirit. She ate through her meal slowly, her decision changing with each bite.

Ultimately, Adèle changed into comfortable civilian clothes, grabbed her revolver, and headed to the Quartier des Grands Sapins. She stopped at a messenger station on the way and paid a young man to cycle to their headquarters and drop off the anonymous note, with her "investigating" scribbled beneath the address. Just in case. She could explain later, and good team members relied on each other's individual initiative too, no? Her gut insisted she check this out, and she had long ago learned to trust herself.

Adèle parked her vélocycle some distance from the warehouse and approached on foot, to scout the surroundings first. Coming here without a partner was already a risk—no sense in rushing in. She couldn't help but note that this would make a perfect stakeout spot if they needed to trap Claire. Several buildings around offered shadowy hiding locations from which to spy on the warehouse, and one had an abandoned floor for a full team to lie in wait. The warehouse itself didn't have many entrances: a large double door in front, a back door, and four flat and high windows which would require effort to use. It'd be easy to watch the old wooden structure, and hard to escape unseen. Ideal.

Her survey finished and fairly certain no one was watching her, Adèle returned to her vélocycle, grabbed her lamp, and entered the building from the back. The door creaked as Adèle stepped in, and chills ran up her spine. Had the air turned colder? Long shadows surrounded her as she advanced one deliberate stride at a time, weapon at the ready, lamp held high. Large crates flanked her on the left and right, nailed shut, and the scent of old dry wood filled her nostrils. No dust covered the surfaces or drifted in the air; this place had seen recent use. Hard to tell when they had moved the exocores in, but not long ago. Adèle tried to peek inside but none of the crates glowed red within. Perhaps inactive exocores lasted longer when protected from light.

After a summary inspection of the area, she sidled to a door along right wall. Adèle stored her pistol long enough to grab the cold handle, and stopped short as she turned it. Was that... weeping? She froze, fear tightening her throat, and listened. A strangled sob, a sniffle. In the eerie nighttime silence, someone was crying.

Adèle doused her lamp to a minimum, and pushed against the door, sighing in relief when it didn't creak. Whoever was in there might not have heard her yet, and until she knew what was happening, she wanted to go unnoticed. The crying was coming from another exit, barred with a heavy metal rod. Adèle advanced into this second, near-empty storage area. The only crates piled under a narrow window, glowing grey in its light, or on the opposite side of the weeping sound. Neither provided cover for her to move across the room safely. She slunk in the shadows along the wall, lengthening her stride, until she noticed a third source of light from inside her target room, slipping out through the door's cracks.

Adèle extinguished her lamp and set it down—if she didn't need it, she would rather have her hand free. When she approached, her revolver led the way. She slid the metal rod away, wincing at the scraping sound. No response emerged from inside, only the continuous whimpering and the light flickering. Adèle's heart pounded. What was going on? She set her palm flat on the door, inhaled deeply to steel her nerves, then shoved it open and stepped in, brandishing her firearm.

Frightened screams greeted her, and Adèle stopped short, her urge to use the weapon drained in an instant. Only habit kept it up as horror seeped into her bones.

A dozen people curled up on the floor, their limbs a sickening thinness. Some had scrambled to their feet to stare at Adèle through greasy hair while others held themselves tighter. An old lady angrily hummed a lullaby to herself, as if willing the rest of the world away. Her eyes never left the ground. The red glow came from a teenager with long red hair shining like embers. She retreated on all fours, and her light glinted off metal bands at her wrists. Adèle had seen those before: police corps used them to restrain witches and negate their powers.

"No, no! I wasn't doing anything. I didn't—please, it's not my fault. It hurts. I don't want to, but you took her and her ice and it hurts so much."

Flames flared for an instant along her thin arms, only to be snuffed out. Her metal bands hissed with a red glow and she gasped. Adèle lowered her firearm in a hurry, eager not to increase the young girl's panic.

"It's okay. I won't hurt you. I won't hurt any of you." She cast her gaze around the room, her stomach twisting, shock slowing her thoughts to a crawl. Whatever was going on here could not be good. Questions bounced in her head, a disorganized whirlwind, slipping away before she could work through an answer. Who were they? Who had locked them in here? Had they eaten? Did they need medical assistance? Adèle silenced the questions for now. She could piece everything together once they'd left this ridiculously small room—once everyone was safe. "Let's get everyone out."

She put her revolver back in its holster and walked to the flaming girl, crouching next to her. Age varied widely in the group, but she couldn't be more than sixteen. She withdrew at Adèle's approach and stared without a sound. Adèle extended a hand, and she wrestled horror out of her tone, to speak calmly and firmly.

"I am l'officier Adèle Duclos, and I'm here to help. This nightmare is over." She would do whatever she could to make it so, at any rate. The horrible experience would cling to them, surely, but at least nightmares would be confined to this girl's nights from now on. Her voice soft, she continued, "I don't know what happened to you. We can find out together. But first, you need a safe place, food, new clothes—time to breathe and settle. Come with me?"

The girl cast a glance back to the others, and they in turn looked at a dark-skinned woman with short-cropped hair — one of those who had stood up at Adèle's entrance. She met Adèle's gaze and studied for a brief moment. "We'll follow."

The whole group reacted. They stood up, helping each other up but shying away from Adèle, always staying behind their leader. The teenager grabbed Adèle's hand and pulled herself up. She swayed on her feet for a moment, and the ember glow of her hair diminished as she settled. Adèle smiled at her encouragingly then helped her towards the door. They'd need to find someone and call for help as soon as possible. Would any of them be in a state to bike and fetch reinforcements? She'd rather not leave the group alone and unarmed.

"What's your name?" The heavy silence weighed on her, and she hoped her voice would help. Only the shuffling of weak bodies and the groans of pains from behind broke the stillness otherwise. She wished she could make everyone instantly better — as if even time would ever erase this experience completely.

"C-Celosia." She stumbled over the name, then swallowed hard. Adèle squeezed her hand as encouragement, and Celosia leaned more heavily on her. "Please help. My wrists — they hurt so much. I can't control it… this is too much."

"Your wrists?" Adèle stopped, picked up her gas lamp on the other side, opened its valve bigger, and cast the light on Celosia's wrists. Deep burns marred nir pale skin under the metal bands, and Adèle recalled the way they had hissed when flames had flickered along the teenager's arms. Witch cuffs would suppress powers in two manners: many had dampening magic embedded into them and, when that didn't suffice, they turned white hot and seared their owner. Their goal was to inflict such overwhelming pain that witches judged dangerous wouldn't manage to maintain dangerous spells. Adèle still remembered when the cuffs only contained the dampening effect and no pain; after the Meltdown, however, people had been quick to clamour for more "efficient" methods of containing magic users, ethics be damned. Despite the constant pain Celosia must endure, her powers seemed to have a mind of their own.

Adèle grimaced. "I don't have anything to remove them. We'll get it done as soon as possible, I promise." Celosia swallowed and avoided her eyes, bright hair sticking to her forehead. Slowly, Adèle brushed the strands aside and met her gaze. "I'm sorry I can't offer better," she added.

"I'm so afraid," Celosia whispered.

Adèle wrapped her hand around Celosia's shoulders then turned towards the rest of the group. They had started filing out, everyone staying behind their leader, wary eyes on Adèle. A part of her didn't understand their collective suspiciousness—she was saving them, wasn't she?—but then she noticed everyone had metal bands like Celosia's clamped on their wrists. Her breath caught. No way that was a coincidence. "Wait, everyone here is—"

A loud bang interrupted her. Pain blossomed in her side, sucking out her breath. For a moment the world vanished behind a white light, its sounds drowned out by an intense buzzing in her skull. Her mind slugged through the sudden agony, finally reaching the obvious conclusion: someone had shot her.

Adèle stumbled back and fell. As she hit the ground, her senses snapped back into place. Screams from the others, crying. Pleading. Adèle reached for her wound and cringed at the blood welling out of her side. Her head spun, her focus slipped. *Good shot.* She tried to sit up, but furious pain slammed into her belly and kept her down. Adèle cursed and punched the floor next to her, steeling herself for another attempt.

"Everybody back inside, or you're next!"

The voice echoed weirdly, distorted by Adèle's mind, firm yet cavernous. Feet shuffled. Celosia screamed. A wave of heat washed over her, and flames licked the ceiling, above Adèle. *I can't control it,* Celosia had said. She was burning her wrists and the whole warehouse around them. Adèle pressed a hand on her wound, gritted her teeth, and pushed herself up again.

Most of the witches had slipped back into their original prison, and as their attacker advanced, the rest of them followed — all except Celosia. Tears blurred Adèle's sight, and at first all she could see was the shape of someone muscular, with short blond hair and a dapper vest. Details added themselves as they came into focus—a square jaw, slender hands, clean pants and shoes.

"Don't come closer!" Celosia's shrill voice covered the fire's growing roar. Jets of flame flew above Adèle, straight to her attacker, but they died long before they reached them. Cancelled out. Gone.

"Continue and you'll be next, Celosia." The cavernous

voice had vanished, replaced by soft words. Was she imagining the pain in them, projecting her own burning agony? Adèle shivered despite the heat. "Some things are worse than death."

Celosia answered with a burst of flames and a raw, heart-breaking scream. Adèle flinched away, her skin sizzling under the intense fire swirling in the air around. Nothing touched their attacker, and as they stepped over Adèle, the fire stopped too, cooling the air. Celosia crumpled to the ground, her powers drained and the pain finallytoo much. Dry wood cracked above their heads and the warehouse kept burning, even without help. With a sigh, their assailant picked up the iron bar and slid it back into the door, trapping everyone else.

They would die in this fire if Adèle didn't stop it.

If only she could.

Her arms gave in and Adèle slumped back to the ground. Propping herself up had become too difficult. Her strength was escaping through the bullet hole, following her blood, and her thoughts were threatening to do the same. She needed to get a grip on herself. Stop this asshole, at least. Maybe even manage to remove the iron bar again. Adèle focused her attention on a single beam across the ceiling, pushing out all other sensations—heat, smell, pain, despair. With shaky hands, she reached for her revolver.

A shadow fell over her, and she froze. This time, the air remained hot. Adèle found herself looking down a barrel gun. An intricate design lined the left side. Useless, that. It wouldn't shoot any better for it. Not any worse, either, and at this distance it couldn't miss Adèle's head. She lifted her own weapon, only to have it kicked out of her hands. The sharp pain in Adèle's fingers made her forget the one radiating from her side for an instant.

"You have a reputation for digging into others' affairs," they said.

Indeed. It had gotten her transferred into the shittiest jobs, but she had never thought it would get her killed, too. Perhaps she should have.

"Too bad I need a death," they added.

Adèle's stomach twisted. She thought of Emmanuelle and the rest of her family, of how difficult a second burial would be for them, and how she once more wouldn't be there for her sister. She didn't want to go. Moving to Val-de-mer was supposed to change her life, not end it.

A thick shape barreled into Adèle's attacker, all black skirts and purple hair. Another blast exploded, but this time the bullet lodged itself in the wood, inches from her head. Relief flooded through Adèle, dampening the pain. *Claire.* Now her life and those of the witches trapped inside depended on the very thief she'd been trying to catch. Adèle squeezed her eyes closed and prayed to God she would hold on against the pain long enough to know which it would be: dead or alive.

-15-

À LA RESCOUSSE

ZITA LED THE WAY THROUGH THE CITY, STOPPING EVERY few blocks to concentrate on her Seeking. Claire slunk into the shadows nearby, trailing her and only coming out when no one else was around. After her likeness on the front page, she didn't want to risk being seen, especially with someone else. That would only put her friend directly in a police interrogation room.

"This is super weird," Zita had said at one point. "I didn't know what to expect, but you following me in the night was not it."

Claire had shrugged it off. Once you'd come to terms with the idea of humans as exocores, everything turned more mundane. She had been breaking into houses, stealing, lying, and even threatening people over the last few weeks. Zita hadn't known for long, however, and although she seemed calmer now, she must still be unused to the exocores. Or to thinking of Claire as both her friend and a thief. As they headed into the Quartier des Grands Sapins and the docks area, Zita paused more and more often, readjusting her direction, until she stopped in the middle of several old warehouses. She gestured for Claire to come closer.

"It's this one," she said, pointing at a large building. "Something is wrong, though. Most of the witches I detect are muted, like in your bakery. That means they must be exocores, too. But a few... they must be alive—or, well, still human, I mean. Their presence is too strong. They feel real."

Claire's heart squeezed. "Any of them Livia?"

Zita shook her head, avoiding her gaze. Of course not. No such luck for Claire. She forced a long, deep breath into her lungs, pushing her frustration and dread away. At least she would save others tonight, before Montrant Industries transformed them into exocores. One step at a time. "Right. Let's get going."

Zita agreed, took a single step, then froze. Her eyes widened. "It's gone." She closed her eyes, focusing on her Seeking, before glaring at the warehouse. "My powers are blocked. Claire, I think Clémence is in there."

Claire's head buzzed for a moment. Clémence. Ol had escaped once, but she wouldn't let ol slip away again. Even if the witches inside couldn't lead her to Livia, ol certainly could. What was ol doing there, though? Judging from Zita's reaction, Clémence had entered the warehouse, not been there all along, otherwise Zita would never have detected anything. And if ol could move about freely... that didn't bode well for ols innocence.

"Let's try to get the drop on ol and ask a few questions. Where do we enter?"

"I'd say by those large doors?" Zita pointed at the main entrance. "I think ol is in an area behind them, but it's hard to be precise."

"Got it. We'll find ol."

Claire filed "searching through a warehouse packed with crates" with all the fun activities she'd never expected would fill her nights and approached the warehouse. When she noticed the high and small windows, she strode up to the wall under one of them. A quick shove of magic into her legs, then she leaped up, catching herself on the windowsill and taking a peek inside.

Unexpectedly, the main room contained very few boxes. A dozen of them lined the walls on her left, with perhaps more under her, but otherwise nothing filled the warehouse. Had they moved the exocores out already? Or did they not need this much room? Either way, this meant less to save, and maybe even that fewer existed. Doubtful, though. The open space also gave her a clear view of the warehouse interior. It would have been pitch black, if not for the dim light on the other side. Claire squinted, trying to spot anyone, when two shapes emerged from a room at the back.

Her heart flipped instantly. Was that Adèle? How had the officer found this place? Either she had been investigating Montrant Industries long before Claire had babbled to her sister, or she'd tracked down the warehouse in a single day. Skillful… and a little scary, too. At this rate, Adèle would snap handcuffs on Claire before she'd saved Livia and uncovered proof of Montrant Industries' horrible activities. But perhaps… perhaps Adèle would help. She was here, wasn't she? And she seemed to be helping a teenager out, with other people following behind. Emmanuelle had turned out more open than Claire had expected, and it'd gone so well with Zita! Hope sped up Claire's heart, coalescing into determination to at least try to get Adèle on her side. It would be so much easier if she didn't have to hide anymore.

Light flashed at the periphery of Claire's vision and a powerful bang echoed from the warehouse. Her breath caught as Adèle stumbled back and fell. *No no no*. That had been a gun. A *gun*, and Adèle was wounded. Claire dropped back to the ground, but before she could rush to the door, Zita grabbed her arm.

"Don't run towards the gunshot!" She hissed. "Do you have a death wish?"

"It's Adèle. Ol shot her."

"Isn't she—"

Claire yanked herself out of Zita's grasp. "Yes. It's complicated. I'll explain later." Their earlier quips didn't cover the extent of her appreciation for Adèle. How did one explain she'd befriended the police investigator trying to catch her, and also wouldn't mind grabbing her by the hips, pushing her against the wall, and kissing her hard? All of a sudden, Claire was hot and slightly dizzy, goosebumps running across her skin, and glad for the mask hiding her flush. "I spotted the other witches too, and they need our help."

As if to confirm her words, bright flames erupted from inside, shattering the window Claire had been peeking through a few seconds ago. Several screams followed the wave of heat out of the warehouse. She and Zita swore simultaneously, then Claire rushed for the door. When it wouldn't budge, she called upon her magical strength and kicked the door in. So much for subtlety.

172

Claire added speed to her powers in case a bullet came her way and dashed inside.

The flames extended from the teenager that had been with Adèle, a whirlpool of bright fire reaching towards the ceiling. She stood at its centre, her red hair glowing, metal bands on her wrists shining. And she screamed so loud Claire's ears rang, only to collapse a second later. The raging inferno barely diminished, eating away at the dry wood around. In the shifting and blinding light, Claire struggled to find Clémence or Adèle.

Her stomach sprang all the way into her throat when she did. Clémence's muscular figure loomed over Adèle, a firearm pointed at her, and a pool of blood already glistened under the police woman. *So much blood*. Claire blocked the image from her mind, sprinting ahead with a renewed surge of magic. Ol was preparing to shoot again, and if she arrived too late…

Claire crossed the warehouse in less than a second, releasing all of her magical speed at once. Just as she shifted her weight to tackle Clémence, her magic vanished, breaking her balance and timing. Her momentum carried her forward and she slammed into Clémence with the grace of a seal on land—which didn't stop ol from pressing the trigger. Her stomach lurched at the terrible sound. They both fell and rolled on the ground, and Claire scrambled to her knees as soon as she could, checking on Adèle: eyes squeezed shut, face contorted in pain, but clearly breathing and no new blood splatters. Good.

Her relief was short-lived. Clémence grabbed her from behind, wrapping an arm around her neck and squeezing. Claire

173

tried to shove magic into her muscles, but Clémence's suppressive magic overpowered hers, nullifying her efforts. She cursed, trashed, clawed at ols forearm. Clémence smashed a fist into her belly to force her to stop, and stars danced before Claire's eyes. She had to get out, but her lungs were empty, her throat crushed.

Worst. Rescue. Ever.

Something flew in from the side, hitting Clémence's temple. Then another, like a red flash through the fire's shifting light. Exocores, Claire realized as the chokehold lessened. Zita was throwing exocores at Clémence.

"Those are *people!*" she exclaimed. "You can't just fling them around!"

"Sorry!"

Zita rushed at them and smacked a gas lamp hard on Clémence, knocking ol over. The fire around them *wooshed,* briefly growing more intense where oil splashed into it. Claire rolled away, hacking and coughing, then struggled to her feet. Clémence didn't stay down for long. Ol crouched, hands lifted, ready to fight if need be. Soot and dust marred ols white shirt, but Claire doubted ol would hesitate to get more dirt or blood on it. When Clémence's eyes fell upon Zita, however, they widened and ol paled. She snorted at ols surprise.

"How long did you think you could lie to my face?" Bitterness and anger laced her words. "How can you–"

A large beam overhead cracked, then snapped. It crashed down between Claire and Clémence, flames clinging to it as it fell, sending a wave of intense heat their way. Claire and Zita stumbled back, shielding themselves with their arms. Clémence hadn't moved, still staring at Zita with a torn expression.

"Zita, I—" Ol stammered and stopped.

Then ol turned heel and ran.

"Oh no, you don't," Zita exclaimed, before dashing after ol. Her short legs couldn't keep up with Clémence's long strides, but Zita could track ol, at least, following the void that ols cancelling power left in her Seeking. Perhaps Clémence would finally lead them to Livia. Claire resisted the urge to chase them too; she had to trust Zita with this. She hurried to Adèle's side instead and was relieved to find her clinging to consciousness. The warehouse's creaking and groaning grew more intense with every passing second—they needed to get out of there.

Claire brought Adèle's hands on top of her wound, then lifted her, drawing a small frown from her. She kept applying pressure, hoping to staunch the blood flow, and pushed magical strength into her limbs before heading for the main door. Cumbersome as another adult was, Claire had no trouble carrying Adèle. She bent her knees as much as possible to avoid the thick of the smoke, but her already burning lungs protested immediately. She was glad for the fresh air outside when she escaped.

Adèle moaned as Claire put her down. Her eyes fluttered open and she dug her fingers into her forearm. "The others... Free them."

"As you wish, Madame l'Officier." She straightened and saluted with a slight smirk. Claire would've gone back in anyway—she remembered the screams and knew what they meant—but her quip dragged a thin smile out of Adèle. "But don't you die on me. I'm getting used to running into you wherever I go."

Adèle raised a glassy gaze on her. "I—I can't. No dying until I've caught you."

Her voice slurred, each word weaker than the one before. Claire hated having to leave her—what if she did die? Yet if she didn't move, everyone stuck inside would burn. Them and all the exocores stored within. She couldn't save Adèle and abandon everyone else. How could she ever get every soul out to safety, though? The warehouse was already threatening to collapse.

Claire gritted her teeth and plunged back in. She zoomed for the door on the other side and reached for the metal bar, stopping less than an inch from it. That thing was radiating pure heat. She searched the room for a tool to help, to no avail. Claire unclasped her cape, whispered farewell to it, and wrapped the fabric around the iron bar. It caught fire immediately, but with her super strength she needed only seconds to remove the rod. Claire flung it away, smoke still filtering into her lungs. Then she kicked the door in.

Heat rushed in with her. She found a dozen women huddling in a corner, as far from the thickest part of the fire as they could. A black woman stood as Claire entered, spreading her arms protectively. Claire hacked from the smoke in her lung for a moment, then straightened.

"Hi. I'm Claire. Can you wonderful people make a bee line for that exit? Adèle is bleeding right on the other side. Anyone who has the strength to grab a crate would be welcome to do so."

"What of Celosia?" The leader had a deep and marvellous voice—the kind Claire could've listened to for hours. "Is ne all right?"

"Fire teen?" Claire asked, reframing her initial assertion of Celosia's gender before she misgendered nir further. "Ne fainted. Might be a little burned out?" She winced at her phrasing. Some puns were better kept for later. "I didn't check on nem. Came straight here."

And she needed to go. What had seemed like a minuscule number of crates to salvage now stressed her, and she'd spotted a second door. There could be even more on the other side. She had no time to waste. "Good luck. I'll join as soon as I can. And seriously. Grab a crate if you can."

Claire sprinted right out again, dashing left to avoid a shower of sparks and smouldering wooden chips. Her gaze sought the crates of exocores. So few, she had thought upon arriving, but now... how could she save them all before the warehouse collapsed? So few, and yet too many. She gritted her teeth and pushed some of her dangerously low pool of power into her muscles as she reached a first pile. She had to save them before they burned to the ground.

Seven crates.

Claire had saved seven crates of exocores before another

wooden beam had crashed down. Every time she'd entered the warehouse, heat had assailed her skin. Her clothes clung to her, drenched in sweat, sizzling in the blazing inferno. She'd removed her mask and resettled it over her mouth, tying the holes at the back, but smoke still filtered through. Soon Claire had been hacking and coughing every few steps. She'd managed two trips inside and had already been wondering how she'd survive a third when the warehouse had given a long plaintiff groan and dropped the beam.

The building, too, might not endure long enough for Claire to save more exocores. But she had to try. Too many still waited inside, heat building around them, powerless to stop the melting death coming for them.

Claire wiped her forehead and basked another moment in the pleasure of fresh night air. The witches stared at her with wide eyes. Three had taken a crate on their way out, but they all seemed at the end of their strength. They had been discussing leaving earlier, when Claire had first reemerged, and she was glad they'd remained. One of them held cloth to Adèle's bullet wound. The police officer looked past her, to Claire, her gaze somehow focused despite all the lost blood.

"Cl-Claire."

For a brief moment, Claire thought she'd say "Claude", and her heart had squeezed painfully. "You're doing good. Keep on staying alive."

Adèle grimaced. "Don't go. The danger…"

Was she… worried? *Finally.* She wouldn't care if she still

perceived Claire as a dangerous criminal and an enemy. "I have to risk it. I can't let them burn. Hang on."

She could explain later. At the moment, lives depended on her—so many of them. Claire plunged back into the roaring fire. Every inch forward became a fight against the unbearable heat. She expected her clothes or hair to catch fire any time, or the roof to collapse, or flames to suddenly eat her. So many things could kill her in this smoky, burning hell.

Claire drew upon her almost depleted magical pool, speeding across the simmering floor to another group of crates. She tore the lids open with bare hands, gritting her teeth against the pain. She'd count her blisters once everyone was safe. Inside, the exocores' gems reflected the fire's light as if it was their own—as if they shone an angry red, calling for help. Claire piled three crates on top of one another and lifted them, wishing she could balance more. She had risked four on the first run and almost stumbled into the flames, however, and the constant use of her powers was taking its toll. She dared not risk it. The warehouse groaned as she hurried back outside.

She almost dropped the crates when she found the witches in a quiet panic over Adèle. The black woman Claire had pegged as their leader had both hands on the bullet wounds and ordered the others to back off. Claire dumped her load with the rest of the exocores and crouched near Adèle, taking their place. Sweeping cheekbones and bright eyes made the leader's glare formidable, but Claire ignored it nonetheless.

"What's happening?"

"She's slipping and I can't heal her." She huffed and clenched the bloodied rag tighter. "The bullet is still inside, and I'd say she has internal bleeding, but without a proper hospital or my powers, I can do very little to save her."

Sudden despair had constricted her chest at the description of Adèle's state, but hope battled it. It wasn't over, not yet. "You're a healer? And a doctor?"

"Docteure Zuri Adaho, of the Hôpital Général de Val-de-mer, yes." A tired smile curved her lips, and she lifted her wrists. "I cure ailments through both mundane and magical means, but these witch cuffs are keeping my powers at bay. They'll slam me with pain and knock me out if I try."

"That's all?"

Zuri scowled at her dismissiveness. Claire ignored it, hooked her fingers under the metal band—one hand on each side—then pulled. The bands resisted. Claire shoved more her magic in her muscles, not caring if she couldn't drag herself out of bed for days after. Adèle was dying. Searing pain lit in her hands as she tried to pull again, sizzling her skin and everything under. Claire's sight whitened, her thoughts blanked. It *hurt*. Sudden intense agony, washing everything else away. Less than a second later, the band snapped, leaving her panting and dazed. Every finger throbbed. She swallowed down nausea and tears and extended her hands.

"The other wrist…" Her voice cracked, but she met Zuri's gaze without hesitation. "She can't die."

Even knowing how painful it'd be, Claire couldn't prepare

for the second band. The metal seemed to sink into her hands when she activated her powers, burning skin and muscles into a crisp. One moment she'd grabbed the witch cuffs, and the next she was staring at a billowing cloud of dark smoke, blocking the night's sky. The blinding pain had knocked her out. She rolled over and retched, and her palms burned as she set them on the ground. Claire risked a glance at them. Thick crusty lines of dark red crossed them and the tip of her fingers, and her hands shook uncontrollably. Her head spun at the sight, the edge of her vision blackened, and sounds grew distant and dissonant. At first, she didn't hear Zuri talking to her.

"Please," the doctor said, finishing a sentence forever lost to Claire. "She'll be fine. It's your turn now."

"What?" Claire blinked to clear her mind and looked around. A golden cocoon enveloped Adèle's belly, thicker above the bullet wound. The sight sent an immense wave of relief coursing through Claire. "You healed her."

"I did. Give me your hands now."

Oh! Of course. Claire offered her palms, her throat tightening again at their constant shaking. She could barely hold herself together because of the pain and exhaustion. She had no idea how she'd get through the night, but she needed to stay strong. Her gaze returned to the warehouse, its flames reaching high into the sky. If the good doctor could protect her hands, she might have the endurance for another run. The warehouse still contained a handful of crates.

Just as the thought crossed her mind, the ceiling gave a

181

long, plaintive moan and snapped. The warehouse crumbled inward, its roof collapsing. Claire jumped to her feet with a loud "no!" but the world spun, pulling her balance away with it, and she fell back down. Zuri caught her and firmly forced her to stay on her knees.

"It's over." Zuri clasped her palms flat against one another then spread them apart slowly. A web of light emerged between her fingers. She picked at the strands, weaving them one into the other with quick movements, creating a tapestry out of nothing. As she worked, she approached Claire's heavy burns and laid it over her hands. The immediate cooling sensation cleared Claire's mind. The doctor smiled. "Help will be on the way soon. Someone's bound to have seen the fire."

Not good. Very few people worked in the Quartier des Grands Sapins at night besides guards, but the doctor was right; someone would come. Claire had to be gone before they arrived — she and the exocores. Those she had saved, at any rate. If only she'd been even faster and stronger. If only she'd continued, instead of stopping for Adèle. Would that have been enough? How long had she been knocked out? How many had burned because of her choice?

"I can't stay. I… listen, I'll need help. These exocores can't go to the authorities." They'd hand them right back to Montrant Industries. Leading a dozen women to her bakery could prove dangerous, however. Claire racked her brain for a solution. Her gaze eventually found Adèle, unconscious on the ground, and an idea emerged. The police officer would want to kill Claire over it later, but it was their best option. She turned to Zuri. "I'll give you an address. Adèle's sister lives there, alone in a huge mansion. She'll take care of your group and hide the crates. Tell her I sent you. Just… explain what happened tonight."

"Are you not coming?" Zuri finished her healing weave and leaned back, quick brown eyes studying Claire. "Your wounds could infect. You need a doctor."

"I'll drop in." Claire struggled to her feet and managed to stay standing this time. She stared at the still-burning ruins and wiped her forehead. In her mind and heart, she could hear the screams of the dying soul trapped inside. Emptiness filled her. So many lost, and she hadn't even saved Livia. Perhaps… She hoped Zita was safe, running after Clémence like that. She ought to try and find them, but she'd had no idea where to start, and no energy to do so. "I need to be alone."

"Be careful, then. Don't uselessly touch anything."

"I won't."

She had no strength left, and very little willpower. The weariness settling into her bone wouldn't vanish anytime soon, if ever. It felt as though the dead souls had found her and solidified as guilt inside. Claire gave everyone instructions about how to reach Emmanuelle Duclos' manor and turned away, eager to be alone.

"Wait!" The voice came from the red-haired teen who'd initiated the fire. Nir companions held nir up so ne could stand, and ne was still pale. "Claire, wasn't it? Thank you. You saved us."

Claire forced a smile on her lips. She *had* saved them, along with the hundreds stored in crates already out. She needed to remember that—to think of what she'd accomplished in a night, rather than what she'd failed. Or try to, anyway. No amount of self-congratulations could get through the numb emptiness in her heart.

"No problem," she said. "Just don't let it go to waste."

Claire left the warehouse behind, sprinting away from it. Under the cooling weave, her skin felt like it was stitching itself up, adding a scratching itch to the continuous pain. She should slow down and take it easy, but burning through her reserves of magic left her with no time to think, no energy to review the events, consider the dead, and lose control over herself. She wanted to exhaust herself so much she would fall asleep without a thought once home—just collapse into darkness. Yet as she grew farther away from the warehouse, the weight of the night's events overwhelmed her. She turned into the first isolated alley she found and leaned against the wall. Once certain she was alone, Claire slid down to the ground, knees to her body, and finally cried.

-16-

ON RESPIRE

THICK SWEAT COVERED ADÈLE'S BODY WHEN SHE WOKE UP.
It had soaked the bed under her, and her nightgown was clinging
to her. Her head hurt, as if a vice had tightened around it, her lungs
were on fire, and her every breath turned into a prolonged, difficult
wheeze. She grimaced and pushed herself up, eager to clean up
and change. Sudden pain shot through her belly when she moved,
drawing a yelp from her. Adèle fell back, shocked and confused,
and her sluggish mind started piecing her situation back together.

She had gone into a warehouse following an anonymous
demand for a meeting about Montrant Industries, expecting to find
Nsia Kouna waiting. Instead of the journalist, she had discovered
a group of witches, imprisoned and famished. Someone had shot
her and threatened to finish the job—something about needing a
death? Her memories blurred. There had been fire, her blood
spilling, and then… Claire. Adèle closed her eyes. Claire had saved
her life. Overwhelming pain had washed most of the night away,
but she recalled the flash of purple slamming into her assailant. She
remembered being carried out. Promising not to die. And Claire

had gone back in. For exocores.

It left a bitter taste on her mouth. She had dumped everyone outside and plunged back for the cores—what else would have brought her there in the first place? At least she'd freed the girls, but they could have used moral support, someone to calm Celosia—general help, in short! But where one-tracked minds were concerned, Claire would win competitions. Hard to believe her level of obsession. There had to be a reason, but Claire had vanished again, and Adèle was… where was she, even?

She frowned and propped herself up long enough to examine the room. What had happened after she had lost consciousness? They hadn't brought her to her flat or to a hospital. Could this be Claire's place? Paintings decorated the walls, and the furniture seemed recent and of high quality. Perhaps Claire had been selling exocores after all, even if they hadn't traced the source. Or she'd always been rich. But something about the overall disposition and tastefulness felt both familiar and reassuring, and although Adèle had never been here she found the room relaxing.

The door clicked as Adèle examined her surroundings, and she held her breath. Latent exhaustion and pain muddled her mind. She wasn't ready to talk with Claire. She knew she'd miss important clues and get emotional—mistakes she couldn't afford if she wanted to reach the bottom of this.

Emmanuelle stepped into the room, carrying a small tray with a glass of juice and porridge. Aurora slipped in behind her.

"Em?" Adèle half-gasped the name. "What are you–" She stopped her question. No wonder the surroundings felt familiar.

"Am I at your manor?"

Em chuckled, sweeping closer to the bed. "Awake and questioning already, I see. It's good to have you back." For all the teasing, worry shone in her eyes. She set the tray on the side table, dragged a chair nearby, and picked up Adèle's hand. "It doesn't matter how often the medic assures you your sister will be fine, it doesn't ring true until she smiles again. Or starts interrogating you."

Adèle laughed, and the movement sent jabs her pain in her sides making her gasp before throwing her into an awful coughing fit. Blackness spread across her vision as she struggled for oxygen. Em pressed something hard into her hand—her medication chamber.

"Steady," Em said, and the familiar snap of a vivifiant followed. "Now breathe it in."

Adèle obeyed, bringing the chamber to her lips and inhaling as deeply as she could. Distantly, she marvelled at how wonderful it was to hear her sister's voice again—to be here, alive, even through the pain in her lungs and throat and side. She squeezed Em's hand as the drug loosened her airways, allowing her to breathe a little easier. Em watched in silence, eyes still bright with tears, and Adèle needed all her patience not to remove the chamber immediately to speak. She counted up to sixty, slowly, forcing herself to remain calm before she tore it away.

"For a moment, I thought you'd have to bury someone again and…" She stopped, a huge lump blocking her throat. She was a mess—fear and pain and relief crashed into her all at once, as if they, too, had waited for her to finish with the vivifiant, and tears spilled down her face. At least everyone should be allowed to be a mess in front of their siblings. She wiped her tears away. "I'm glad you're the first person I see upon waking."

Although the smile remained firmly set on Em's lips, her eyes became glassy too. Neither sister said anything for a while. Adèle would appreciate the silence more with a cleaner bed and gown, but she didn't mention it. She'd almost died, and that put perspective on her discomfort. She spat out some of the horrible goo still clinging inside her throat, stifling another full-blown coughing fit. Aurora—Em's newest cat—jumped on the duvet and curled up at Adèle's feet, sadly out of reach. Adèle wondered if her short fur did feel like suede, but she'd have to discover it later. Minutes slid by, peaceful. Part of her wished they could last forever, but as the cobwebs in her mind cleared, she found the pressure of work waiting.

"Em... how did I wind up here? Where's Claire?"

"Beats me." She shrugged and yawned. "A group of people knocked at my door in the middle of the night, carrying crates of exocores and you. Apparently Claire didn't want me to sleep last night, either. She gave them my address and promised safety."

"She sent everyone here." Adèle's mouth turned dry. Did she think this was a game? Last night had proven that the people behind this would kill without hesitation, and Claire had pushed the threat right to her sister? Adèle gritted her teeth together. "It's dangerous, Em. You can't get involved—"

Chapitre Seize

"Yes, Adèle, I gathered this entailed a high risk when I laid eyes upon your dying body." The sharpness in Em's voice surprised Adèle. Her sister scoffed, then started fussing over her, helping Adèle sit up and placing the pillows behind her back to make her comfortable. Her abdomen was a constant series of sharp and stinging tugs and she struggled with the pain as her sister went on. "I am hereby choosing to get involved. This is big, and these people need a safe place to stay. Claire's instincts are good: I have no intention of turning them away. Besides, I want to know what's in those exocores, why they were keeping witches prisoner, and why Claire risked crushing fiery death on several occasions to salvage what she could."

"That was always what she was after. She said it herself." The new position made her head spin, but Adèle refused to lie back down. Not yet, anyway. She'd need more sleep later, but she wanted to get her bearings first. "If she has a good reason, she hasn't deigned to share it."

"Then we shall piece it back together ourselves. But first you need to eat." Em grabbed the porridge and offered it. Adèle threw a doubtful stare at it, suspecting it wouldn't stay in her stomach, but there was no mistaking the look in her sister's eyes. Em would brook no refusal. Adèle set to work, her hand shaking horribly as she brought the spoon to her lips. She hated her own weakness. This wasn't worth the effort. As if reading her thoughts, Em added, "Docteure Adaho said your stomach would remain upset for a while, but it's essential that you eat anyway. Don't try shirking on it."

189

"Yes, mom. I promise."

Adèle smirked at her sister, then forced the food down her throat. Em shifted the conversation to the group of witches she now housed while Adèle ate. They had broken the witch cuffs and put her numerous guest rooms to good use. Most had been delighted to receive a warm bath, clean clothes, and a comfy bed.

"None of them had been beaten after their capture, and apart from Celosia, they managed to keep their magic in check and avoid the witch cuffs' punishment," Em said. "Food was minimal, however, and they didn't know what their purpose was. We don't think it's safe for them to go back to their families and friends, so they'll stay here until we figure out better. I'll be buying more food and clothes this afternoon."

"Good. I agree. Whoever found them once could do it again." Montrant had more resources than a local company should have, if they could pay for so many witch cuffs and kidnap people without anyone noticing. Did the exocores bring in that much money, or did they have outside sources that predated their quick economic rise? The questions floated in her head, but no trace of answers showed up. Adèle set her spoon down with a sigh. Her sluggish mind couldn't analyze properly at the moment. "I need more sleep. I'll never figure it out in my current state. I can't even add one and one."

"You do that. I might, too." Her sister stifled a yawn, and Adèle suddenly noticed the bags under her eyes and the slump in her shoulders. Em gathered the leftover porridge and empty glass on her tray and headed for the door. She stopped before leaving.

"We'll get to the bottom of this. Someone has to."

And that was Adèle's job, wasn't it? To solve the cases everyone avoided, because someone had to. With Claire's case turning into Montrant Industries'—the rising star of Val-de-mer's and even the country's energy technology sector—this would become truer than ever before. Even Élise hadn't wanted to push this, but what choice would they have now? Someone had tried to kill Adèle and people had been kidnapped. She would need to send word to Koyani about what had happened and at least let them know she was safe. But as Adèle struggled to figure out what else to say—what mattered, truly, in the confusing string of events— her migraine returned in full force. She closed her eyes to focus, and sleep claimed her immediately.

-17-

ET TOMBENT LES MASQUES

HUGE, BRIGHT RED BLISTERS COVERED CLAIRE'S PALMS, and she wondered if she'd ever manage to hold something again. A tad overdramatic, perhaps, but damn did it hurt. Even with Zuri's quick healing, her hands throbbed and every movement shot searing pain up her arms. No baking today, for sure. Or tomorrow. At first, she'd thought not to return to Zuri, but since the doctor's protective cocoon had vanished, she had barely been able to function. She'd stayed in bed for the whole day, emerging from her cave only as the sun set once more. As worrying as entering Em's manor a second time was, she needed the doctor's help, and it'd allow her to make sure everyone had made it there safely.

The mask chafed at her face and she wished she could trade her cape and skirts for the comfort of cotton pants and a loose shirt. A day of rest hadn't put Claire back on her feet. She didn't think anything ever would, not after last night. Questions persecuted her, as tiring as the constant pain of her burns. How many had died in that fire? Had they suffered when their physical support was destroyed? Or was it like falling asleep, getting slowly less and less tethered to the world? None of them should have had to find out. She wondered if she could have saved more. How much time had she wasted on Adèle? Should she have carried out another pile of crates instead? She'd sacrificed so many souls for a single friend—one who might hate her once she knew the whole truth. How could Claire justify that?

She wanted out. She wished she could spend a day kneading dough, putting bread in the oven, and relaxing as the delicious scent spread through her bakery, playing a tranquil game with Zita and Livia. Being herself, at home, with friends and family. Or perhaps offering coffee and a croissant to Adèle, as she used to before Livia's kidnapping. Anything *ordinary*. She'd slammed her hand into heavy machinery when she'd stolen that first exocore, and now it threatened to eat her entire arm.

She wished she could escape it and have her simple life back, and, as she longed for that pause, she wondered if her gender was shifting again, or if her growing urges to bind and present as a man stemmed from how strongly she associated that with the bakery. Sometimes circumstances pushed the fluidity, sometimes it happened on its own; either way, she'd rarely felt less like a woman than she did now. Admittedly, she felt more like a wretch than anything else, but that was another problem entirely. No matter how intense her desire to give up, she knew she couldn't.

Sharp knocks, coming from her back door this time,

stopped Claire before she could leave. She'd always had a second entrance into the building to go in and out of her home without having to pass through the bakery, even though she lived right behind it. Only a few friends knew of this access, and her heart sped with hope. It had to be Zita! Claire hurried to the door, reaching for the handle. She stopped before she could pull wide open, remembering just in time she had her mask on and skirts and purple hair, and if this *wasn't* Zita, opening it would destroy her cover. She peeked through the peephole, and the distorted face of her friend left her grinning. As her palm met the cold metal of the handle, though, Claire gritted her teeth and flung the door open.

Zita hopped inside, and the spring in her steps warmed Claire's heart. It spelled good news at last. "Please tell me what put you in such a mood. I need it." Despair laced Claire's tone and knocked the smile off Zita's face.

Zita studied her, her frown deepening with every passing second. "You first. You don't sound okay, and one should always start with the bad."

On most days Claire would have agreed; now it irritated her. She didn't have the strength to argue, though. "Downstairs, then. I've yet to tell the witches in exocores." Guilt over those she'd lost had slowed her. Guilt and exhaustion and pain. Zita's mere presence and the promise of good news helped to drag her out of that ditch, however. She couldn't stop now—couldn't let her grief sap her energy before the fight was over. How many more would die if she gave up? Keeping everyone safe and unravelling Montrant's network was all... It was too big a burden. At least she had Zita with her. She didn't have to deal with it alone.

She made her way into the basement with her friend and settled onto the couch, gathering her thoughts before retelling the evening. Claire started earlier than necessary for Zita in case people in the exocores were listening. Words followed one another in rapid succession—Clémence and Adèle, the fire, the crates, removing the magic-suppressing witch bands, giving them Emmanuelle's address. She skipped nothing except her breakdown, but, by the time she'd reached the end of her night, tears were running down her cheeks again. She really needed a croissant break. Maybe she could show Zita how to bake. She had some leftover dough in the cooler, after all.

"Now I have to return for more healing, and bring the crates back here, so everyone can be together and safe." Everyone except Livia. Livia and the hundred exocores that had burned down the previous night. In short, not everyone at all. Claire sighed and wiped her tears. "I hope that's very good news you have, Zita, because I could use it."

Zita reached into her pockets and offered Claire a handkerchief. "How much do you love her?"

"What?" That was not a logical question to continue this conversation.

"Adèle. You rushed in there without second thoughts and you burned your entire palms to save her. I was promised more explanations, and I want the juicy bits!" Zita grinned, then gestured at the exocores. "Come on. Confess it before witnesses!"

"I'm not going to put myself in another romantic

relationship. I'd hate it." Zita would understand more than anyone else. They'd tried dating for almost an entire year before admitting it didn't work. The experience had instilled a constant sense of unease in Claire—as if everyone expected something new of her, a different kind of feeling, and it refused to show up. She had struggled to get "je t'aime" past her lips, and even then she had known on the deepest level that she did not mean the same thing as others did. She had felt like a liar and hated herself for it. "She's important to me, though. I wish it was simpler, that I could work something out with her! Instead I've found myself lying through half of our relationship and I'm afraid I've ruined my chances. But I can think more about that and what to do with it, if anything, once Livia is safe and Montrant Industries' atrocities have been exposed."

Zita stifled a laugh. "Sounds reasonable. And the time might come sooner than you think! Ready for the good news?"

"More than you know."

"I found their factory. Not the publicity stunt one—the real thing." She paused, turning a haunted gaze to the exocores on the table. "It's smaller than I'd expected, and perhaps not the only one, but it's definitive proof of their... process. And research, if I'm not mistaken."

Claire froze. A factory. Imagining it made her nauseous, but her heart rate picked up. At last, a breakthrough.

"I need to see it. How did you get there? Clémence?"

"Yes. I tracked ol all night, and at dawn ol went there. It's under the Centre de Recherche, where Clémence works. Ol has had

196

a team studying energy-related projects—not sure what, the science is always too much for me and ol stopped trying to explain. But it's not… really there, either. You access it from an elevator, but I could sense the portal magic as I passed through."

Claire gritted her teeth. It felt weird for Zita to speak of Clémence as an old friend, no matter how true. Plus, she didn't like this lab business—it meant Clémence worked in the same building as Emmanuelle Duclos, on similar topics. What were the odds they didn't know each other?

"I wish I could give their secret factory the same treatment we did the warehouse."

"You don't. They have people in there. Unconscious, encapsulated in a weird tank, with tons of tubes going in and out. Don't ask me what all that shit does, though. All I know is that it blocks my Seeking, and once I noticed, I reached around." Zita closed her eyes and allowed a tense silence to stretch on. Claire struggled not to push her forward with the story. "It extends deeply and contains a lot of people. I think… Claire, they might have Livia somewhere in there. I'd concluded Clémence kept me from detecting her, but these tanks also fill that purpose. It makes more sense than someone staying near her at all times!"

"It… it does." They had located her. They *must* have. Somewhere in these labs would be Livia, and Claire would find her. She'd been right about Clémence—following ol had led Zita to Livia! "Let's go! We need to save her." Claire jumped to her feet, but dizziness slammed into her at the sudden movement. She slumped back into the sofa with a groan.

Zita couldn't help but chuckle. She put a hand on her forearm and smiled. "How about we heal your palms and secure the other exocores first?"

"But—"

"It's been a week, Claire. And even if one more day does make a difference, you're not in any condition to go. How will you climb, sneak, or lift anything with those blisters? You're on the verge of collapsing and in no state for heroics."

Claire opened her mouth to protest, but Zita glared at her. She shut it again, knowing how right her friend was. Exhaustion had crawled into her being and settled in her bones. Just an hour ago, she had yearned for a break. If she rushed headlong into these labs, she would get herself killed and no one would be saved.

"All right." One thing at a time. Healing, exocores, rest, and then the factory. "Let's pay Emmanuelle Duclos a visit."

They stared at each other for several minutes, heavy silence crushing the words before they could cross their lips.

Adèle couldn't believe Claire had just strode in. Right through the door, as if she owned this house and wouldn't be intruding. Then she remembered they'd first met in Adèle's new flat, and that Claire's conceptions of property and privacy were fundamentally skewed. Claire walked into forbidden places every day of her life. Why would one more bother her? Yet no carefree smile lit the face under her cotton mask today, and a new slump weighed her shoulders. A strange pang twisted Adèle's stomach—sadness, tinged with confusion. Perhaps Claire's unapologetic behaviour had been an act, projected to keep others from seeing the person behind it. Now the thief seemed a shadow of herself, bathed in the golden glow of the healing magic cocooning her hands but radiating no life herself. Adèle tried to think of something meaningful to say—after the events of last night, she should have dozens of ideas—but her tired mind came up short.

"Docteure Adaho told me how you got your burns," she eventually started. It had bothered her. Not only had Claire saved her life in the warehouse, but she'd repeated the exploit immediately after. Twice in the same night, despite Adèle's relentless attempts to arrest her. "Why would you…?"

Claire flinched away, almost as if Adèle had punched her. "*Why?* Is that an actual question?"

The profound hurt in her voice surprised Adèle. It shouldn't have, really. She had just suggested Claire was the kind to let her die even if she could help it. Adèle pinched the bridge of her nose and leaned back into the pile of pillows Em had set up for her. She'd slept most of the day and her fever had passed, but sitting in bed was starting to make her restless and rude. "I'm sorry. What I mean to say is 'thank you'. I owe you my life."

"You promised not to die. I like to think not all policemen are liars." She flashed a grin at Adèle, and the dynamic Claire who'd first broke into Adèle's home returned. Her eyes shone, her shoulders straightened, and the entire room seemed to light up. Adèle's breath itched, and her mind tried to complete Claire's face

199

with the top half she'd glimpsed the previous night, blurred though it had been. Warmth curled at the bottom of her stomach, tingling, and Adèle found herself staring again.

Somehow, despite the limited time they'd spent together, Claire's demeanour had become deeply familiar. A smile, and Adèle noticed the detailed changes in her posture, the release of tension, the way she flicked her hair back as she chuckled. As if she'd seen these movements dozens of times, not a handful. She tried to pinpoint where the familiarity emanated from, without success.

"I did my best," Adèle said. "We all do, no?"

At times, the best way to get someone talking was to open a door and let them step in, especially with a sheen of compassion. Claire bit her lower lip, her gaze lost in the distance. *Come on,* Adèle thought, *tell me what your best is.*

"It's not always enough," Claire said.

Adèle frowned. So much guilt had laced those words. What had Claire failed at, despite saving Adèle? What could her best have left behind? "They escaped, didn't they? Whoever assaulted me." Hours in bed had given Adèle time to piece her memory back together. Claire hadn't been alone in the warehouse. Someone else had helped, someone who'd thrown objects at their attacker while they were strangling Claire. Wait. Not just anything. Exocores. And suddenly, Claire's voice echoed in Adèle's mind, spinning her head.

You can't just fling those. They're people.

"People," she whispered, before snapping her gaze to

Claire. "That's what you said, isn't it? They're people."

Claire froze, her body tensing as soon as the affirmation crossed Adèle's lips. She stared at her, her mouth thinning into a line, and even with her upper face covered, Adèle sensed the emotions battling in her—should she deny it? Admit it? But her hesitation only convinced Adèle she was right, that *this* was why Claire had gone back into the warehouse to get the exocores. She waited, hoping Claire would choose to share what she knew.

The thief's shoulders slumped. "Witches, to be more precise."

Adèle closed her eyes, nausea itching its way up her throat. How could anyone transform a human being into a power source? Even disregarding how cruel the idea was, the very process seemed beyond their current technology. Em was struggling to create a physical matrix from magic, so how had Montrant managed that feat? But she remembered Basir, how he'd instinctively transferred himself into his crystal shop to save his life. Perhaps they'd found a way to force and bastardize that. Were the people in the warehouse being prepped for this? How many more were imprisoned across the city? How many had already been shoved into tiny red gems?

"That's horrible."

"You don't know the half of it." Claire stepped closer, then changed her mind about advancing and stayed put. Adèle wished she would sit near the bed. "We think they're sentient. That they're... aware of their surroundings, at least. And I... I left so many crates in that warehouse. It just collapsed on them."

201

"Oh. *Oh no.*" When Em had spoken about the crates now in her manor, she'd said she'd never seen so many exocores at once. How many more had burned in the warehouse's inferno? Adèle stared at Claire, perceiving new depths to the weight burdening her shoulders. No wonder guilt laced her every word. "Then why *did* you save me? Why choose me, of all people, over them?"

A wistful smile passed over Claire's face. "Who knows?" She shrugged, but her casualness felt forced. She knew, and it bothered Adèle. One of Claire's masks might have fallen but several remained, blocking Adèle out. If only Claire would let her in more—let her help with this! "Montrant Industries is behind this. Their official facility is a fake. We think we've found the real one, however, and I'm investigating tonight. You should rest."

Adèle scowled. She didn't intend to stay back while Claire dug deeper into this mess. "No way. Give me a day and I'll be right there."

"Madame l'Officier, I mean to break into a highly protected compound, steal, and possibly destroy private property. You cannot come."

"Then you'll have no legal proof. Let me get a warrant."

Claire laughed, but no mirth filled her voice. "If this goes to court, I'll pay and they will walk free. I'm not out for a trial. I'm out to dismantle them. Run them into the ground."

Which good police work should do, but Adèle had experienced first-hand how untrustworthy the justice system could be. "We can back you up. Koyani's unit is not your regular police team."

"I don't trust them," Claire said. "This… all of this reeks of corrupted money and power, and I've yet to find a uniformed person that could be called an ally to our community."

Adèle slunk deeper into her pillows, unwilling to argue with Claire about methods. She had good points, and the kind of trust required by an alliance with Koyani's team was not something she could demand from Claire. "Will you tell me what you discover, at least, or should I expect you to vanish once more?"

Claire hesitated. Perhaps she'd never planned to include Adèle in her quest and had only come to check on her. Why put your faith in the officer who'd threatened to arrest you twice already? Adèle doubted Claire would want to get involved with someone who'd tried to shoot her knees on their first encounter.

"I… I think I will," Claire said at length. "There's a lot I'd like to tell you."

Her voice had softened, full of secrets and withheld words. Adèle bit back a scream of frustration. She knew thousands of thoughts lay below the surface, layers upon layers that Claire kept to herself, and Adèle wished she could learn them all. Her intense desire to delve deeper in Claire's mind took her by surprise. When had caring replaced her anger this thoroughly? Claire had broken into Adèle's home to save a person, who'd been transformed into a gem, and Adèle found the crime instantly forgiven.

"I'll be ready to hear it whenever you want to share," she said.

Claire's smile returned, and once again her entire stance changed, going from tense and closed to casual and welcoming.

"Thank you. With luck, it will be sooner rather than later. Keep your wits sharp, Madame l'Officier!"

She didn't give Adèle time to answer, slapping a grin on her face, turning heels and striding out. Exiting with the same confident carelessness she'd shown entering. Only this time, Adèle saw through Claire's posturing. No assured walk or grand cape gesture would ever cover the deeply caring and exhausted woman underneath again.

-18-

SUR LA PISTE

CLAIRE REGRETTED SPEAKING WITH ADÈLE WHILE exhausted. She couldn't control herself enough, and her feelings had slipped out unwanted, a crack through her wall. Adèle had already asked twice why Claire cared so much about her well-being. How long before she wondered who hid behind the mask or how Claire had first tangled with Montrant Industries? Adèle'd been exhausted and feverish and still managed to understand the truth about exocores. How long before she pieced it all together?

Should Claire tell her everything now? A part of her was dying to peel away the last of her secrets, but she didn't have the emotional fortitude to face Adèle and deal with her potential reaction. Both of them were hurt and tired and stressed—a fight waiting to happen. They'd just reached a delicate truce, and she didn't want to tear it apart.

It would be easier to avoid Adèle if she wasn't so dreamy, of course, but Claire thankfully had a lot of important fears to help ignore how her heart hammered. Something in Adèle's long, pointed nose, in the way she bit her lip when she smiled, in the curve of her breasts and the muscular body under that uniform... all of it left Claire a little breathless, her lower body throbbing, her imagination requiring to take over. All in good time, she told herself. For now, she had an evil industry to destroy, and witches to save—including her sister. And for all that, she needed to find her friend.

Zita was in the gardens outside, sitting around a delicate white table, having an intense discussion with Emmanuelle and Zuri... about exocores? Claire stopped nearby and listened, caught in their debate about magic transference, body survivability, and the creation of exocores. Doctor and scientist were working together to pinpoint the actual techniques, with Zita occasionally chipping in with the impressions her powers granted. Before long, Claire lost track of the debate, her tired mind receiving the words without analyzing them. When she realized she'd been staring blankly, she cleared her throat to interrupt.

"I need to bring the crates home, Zita." It'd be more efficient alone than with her friend, but she worried about overexerting herself. Her magic pool had only just started to regenerate. She didn't want to empty it pointlessly.

"Leave them," Em said. "I promise to take good care of them. Zita told me... I know what they are—who, really."

Claire reeled at the idea of leaving exocores behind. She'd been their sole protector for what seemed like ages now, and it didn't sit well with her to abandon any of them here, especially after everything she'd risked to save them. But she trusted Emmanuelle, and it would be a relief not to carry them across the city while trying to dodge notice. Claire looked at Zita, who nodded.

"Okay. Don't... don't let me down."

"I solemnly swear on my husband's head," Emmanuelle said, raising a hand. "Everyone is safe with me."

"Thank you." Claire's knees weakened and the intensity of her relief surprised her. She hadn't expected help, she realized, and was still calculating her actions as if she needed to do everything by herself. But she had Zita now, and Emmanuelle and Zuri and even Adèle. Their support stalled her growing despair. She was not alone. Together, they could do this. They could find Livia and take on Montrant Industries.

Zita jumped to her feet and grabbed Claire's forearm. "There's something else. Can we talk?"

Claire tilted her head. Only a limited number of topics would push the very open Zita to ask for privacy, most of which were Claire's secrets. "Sure. Let's walk."

They could have returned inside, but the sun was shining in an almost cloudless sky. Claire wished the two others a good day and started off. Emmanuelle's backyard wasn't as extensive as those in the Quartier des Chênes, but a large maple grew near a corner, offering shade for the bench underneath. A white bird feeder hung from the branch, and a pair of chickadees clung to it, eating their fill. Claire moved closer, and they stayed silent for a while, their eyes drifting from birds to the intricate flower arrangements around. Claire sweated under her mask; the hot sun reminded her of how unsuited to summer days this outfit was. She always stalked the nights, when the rapidly approaching fall cooled the air. She settled on the bench and took in the cold metal under her fingers.

Whatever Zita wanted to discuss ate at her until she couldn't hold it in. She stopped squirming and blurted it out. "Livia was with them, in the warehouse."

Claire spun to face Zita. "She... was?" Two words, yet her voice cracked and the cool bench vanished from her perception. *Livia. Alive.*

"Powerful ice witch with a strong accent who disregarded the witch cuffs to stall Celosia's flames in her first panic attack? Sounds like her. Besides, she gave them her name." Zita put a hand on her shoulder, but Claire could barely feel it. "Talk to Celosia. Ne'll know more. It has to be her, though."

Who else? Claire's head was ringing, and her heart filled with hope. Over the last weeks, the belief that Livia had become an exocore had grown into an overwhelming certitude. She had denied it relentlessly, afraid she'd stop searching and give up. Finding a dozen witches but not her sister at the warehouse had cemented her fears. "Zita, this is..."

She didn't—couldn't—finish her sentence. It'd require pushing words past the lump in her throat. Zita pulled Claire into a hug, squeezing until neither could breathe. Solid arms around her calmed the dizzying whirl of hope. Zita's news tasted sweeter than fresh brioche dripping with glaze. Not even the first batch of croissants on a bright morning compared to the warmth spreading through her now.

"Thank you. Zita, you have no idea how much you've helped."

Zita laughed and set a proud hand on her hip. "I told you I could be handy. Should've taken me along for the ride from the start."

Claire grinned at her friend's laughter, the honest sound washing her fatigue away. News of Livia had been the coup de grâce to her grimness, and Zita's good spirits instilled in her the energy she needed to fight again. She bowed and wished she still had a cape to complete the movement with and properly honour Zita. "I have learned my lesson. No more staying apart or bearing burdens alone. My friends are few, but they're the best."

After Zita gave her directions, Claire turned away, light-headed and excited at the prospect of hearing more about Livia, of getting so near to her at last. Renewed energy filled her to the brim, and although she knew she should conserve her magic, she couldn't help infuse her muscles, sprinting to the house and leaping straight to the second-floor balcony. Zita whistled behind her, and Claire dropped the enhancements as she entered the manor. Kind of silly to ignore regular doors now that she was welcomed in here, but it amused her and she *needed* that whimsy in her life. With a smile, Claire sought Celosia's room.

Unlike with Adèle's, she knocked before entering. It didn't feel right for Celosia. Barging unwanted into the other's life had been a core element of her dynamic with Adèle from the start, and Claire had walked into her room without second thoughts. Not here, though. Not with an agender teen prone to panic attacks, who'd chosen to hide in nir room despite the bright day. Celosia clearly needed space, and Claire preferred to invade as little as possible.

A long silence followed the knocks, but an uncertain voice did call eventually. "Yes?"

"Can I come in? This is Claire. I'm the one who—"

"I know. They told me everything." Silence again. Claire leaned towards the door, trying to listen to the muffled sounds. Footsteps? A second later, the handle turned. The freckled teen Claire had seen crumpled on the floor stared down at her, large bags under nir eyes. "Is it urgent? I'd rather be alone."

Nir tiny voice drained Claire's excitement away. Overbearing joy also didn't feel right here, and she forced herself to calm down. "Kind of. I won't linger, however, I promise."

Ne nodded and stepped away from the door, opening up the room to Claire. Heavy curtains kept the sunlight from coming in, and the very air constricted Claire's chest. She cast a worried look around, then at Celosia.

"How are your wrists holding up?" she asked.

"Is that why you knocked? Here." Ne lifted nir arms, exposing nir wrists. Dark red lines marked them, the same as Claire's palms, but Zuri had obviously tended to them. No blisters spread across nir skin, and the pockets of rosy colour looked like long-healed burns rather than recent wounds. "Happy?"

Nir aggressiveness surprised Claire. Perhaps it shouldn't, after everything Celosia had been through. She shook her head. "It's... not why I came. I was worried."

"If you wanted to see the damage the unstable fire maniac did to nirself, you should just say so. I *know* they're saying it, outside. They've been muttering about me since I first panicked."

"Well, I haven't talked to them." Considering how concerned Zuri had been about Celosia, Claire doubted the doctor would utter those words, but she didn't know the others. They might. The last thing she wanted was to question Celosia's impression of how strangers perceived nem, though. How often had ne heard similar accusations before? Been blamed for a crisis instead of helped through it? "I wanted to ask about Livia."

"Livia?" Celosia's eyes widened, and nir entire body language softened, nir shoulders slumping. Grief spread over nir face and ne stared at the floor. "Why? She's gone."

Claire closed the door behind herself. She pulled her mask off—that, too, felt wrong here. "I need to know. She's my sister. My twin. I've been searching for her."

"Your..." Celosia stared hard, then snorted. "You don't look alike at all! She's tall and stunning, with deep brown skin and eyes to die for. You're..." Ne gave Claire a once-over. "Well, you're kinda cute too, but not in the same way. Purple hair's great, though. I love it."

After the initial surprise passed, Claire laughed. She would take that as a compliment. It's not like she'd ever aimed to compare to Livia. "Yeah, Livia's dreamy all right. We're not identical twins."

"I didn't mean..."

"Don't worry about it." Claire moved into the room, settling on the bed, and Celosia joined her. Ne sat with nir arms

211

apart and nir palms turned up, minimizing contact with nir burns. Claire glanced at her own hands. The golden glow had vanished and the skin was a lighter brown where new. "My friend told me Livia was with you, in the warehouse—that she helped you."

Celosia's expression darkened once more, but nir cheeks remained flushed red. Ne was kind of cute nirself, with nir intense freckles and strong pointed nose. "I… have panic attacks. Once my brain takes off, it's near impossible to stop it. It used to spin on itself, and I'd feel horrible and certain my life would crumble into ashes and everyone hated me, but it never triggered my magic. Not until they kidnapped me." Ne ran fingers over the burn marks and stared at the bed. "I guess I knew I was being threatened. And their witch cuffs hurt *so much*. They're meant to overwhelm concentration, but what does panic care about that? Out the flames came, but Livia…"

"Nobody does ice like her."

"Her wrists won't look as good as mine. She iced the cuffs to lessen the effect, but it can't have been enough, and no one's there to heal her." Celosia threw nir head back and turned to Claire. "They took her three days ago. We never knew where or why they left with one of us. They said they needed someone powerful like her, and that they might return for me later. I hope she's okay…"

Claire put a hand on Celosia's. "I think I know where to look for her. I'll find her, and she will be okay. Perhaps not *now*, but one day she will. Leave it to me."

"Please!" A fierce expression settled over nir youthful features and ne grabbed Claire's hand, squeezing it. Claire flinched at the sudden pain from her burns and gritted her teeth, trying not to show it. "You gotta. Th-they mean to turn her into an exocore too, don't they? We can't let it happen."

"I don't intend to. Too many people are trapped in those gems already. I won't let my sister become one more." For the first time in days, Claire believed herself. She stood up and smiled at Celosia. "I'm glad she was there for you."

"S-so were you, no? Without you, I'd have burned everyone. I try to tell myself it's not my fault—that they took away my means of coping—but the end result doesn't change. I turned that warehouse to cinders."

Claire swallowed hard, unsure what to answer. In a way, Celosia's guilt was as justified as her own over not saving the remaining exocores. She should have prioritized the crates, not Adèle, but she knew she could more easily forgive herself for the hundred souls than for her friend. It wasn't *right*, but it was human, and she would have to accept that. "You're right, though. This isn't on us. We're just... people with flaws, and we did our best. But they made this happen. All of it."

In fact, they were still making it happen. Somewhere under a research lab, they had a whole factory dedicated to extracting people's magic and creating exocores. Claire didn't doubt more warehouses existed across Val-de-mer, and perhaps even in other cities—an entire industry built on enslaving witches and using them as an energy source, hidden in plain sight.

"I'll put an end to it. Don't allow guilt to devour you. The best you can do is continue to work on control and coping. People here will support you." Doubts marred Celosia's expression, but Claire let it go. Whether the teenager asked others for help was entirely up to nem, and she didn't want to push it. "One last thing… Livia being my sister needs to stay a secret. Zita knows, if you want to talk about it, but it cannot reach Adèle. Can you do that for me?"

"Of course. I-I hope you find her quickly."

"Thank you, and me too."

Claire wished nem good luck, then headed for the balcony, gaining in speed with every stride. She tied her mask on as she passed the doorway, and Celosia had time for a "what are you—" before Claire leaped down.

She cushioned the landing with a burst of strength magic and sprinted away, grinning at herself. Needlessly extravagant, perhaps, but she clung to her whimsical show of strengths as outlets for her good mood, and necessary indulgences to help her cope with the horrors of the last days. Besides, it allowed her to dodge anyone inside the manor and return straight home. Hope lightened her muscles, but her exhaustion would catch up soon enough if she didn't rest. The last thing she wanted was to slip while she infiltrated Montrant Industries' secret factory.

Three firm knocks with a metal ring heralded Capitaine Koyani's arrival and jostled Adèle from her partial rest. She'd been dozing off ever since Claire had left, losing her fight to stay awake and continue unravelling the previous night's events. Something still escaped her—she knew it—but she kept slipping back into half-sleep, cozy under her duvet and the reassuring warmth of Gaia and Sol. The two cats had almost never left her bed since arriving, and Adèle was glad to wake up to their grumpy, flat-nosed faces. Not that either of them could help her figure out what she was missing.

"I'm awake," she called, silencing how it had not been the case before the knock.

Koyani strode into the room, and it took a moment for Adèle to remember she'd asked Em to send word. Her capitaine's clean-cut uniform had vanished. She wore bright red shorts matching her prosthetic arm, a loose t-shirt with large white and grey stripes, along with simple sports shoes, flat and comfortable. The laidback outfit was a striking contrast with her usual sharpness, and Adèle's surprise must have shown, because Koyani burst out laughing.

"Some days I have a life out of the office," she said. "We received your sister's message, but you were sleeping when I came earlier. I did not want to wait for tomorrow. How are you?"

"Exhausted." Hard to rest properly when your lungs felt like smoke still coated their insides and no amount of asthma medication cleaned it out entirely. Adèle touched the bandage over her wound. It had begun hurting again during the last hour, and she hoped Docteure Adaho would swing by soon. "I hurt, and I keep coughing, which doesn't help my stomach at all. Otherwise well enough."

"Perfect." Koyani headed for the bedside chair Emmanuelle had occupied in the morning and sat in it, back straight. Her posture didn't match the outfit, and the inherent tension in her stiff shoulders worried Adèle. Would she get scolded for going to the warehouse alone? "We're glad you're safe, despite taking an incredibly risky and hotheaded decision." Scolding, then, but without the anger Adèle had expected. "This is exactly why you never leave without a partner."

"I know." Nothing could have prepared her for what she did find, though, even with the obvious risks involved. "I thought the anonymous note came from Mx. Kouna. They did not seem dangerous, and I feared wasting the opportunity."

"You can get other opportunities. You can't get another life." Koyani's clipped tone would not allow for more protest. "I have no desire to lose our new team member so fast."

New... team member? Koyani rarely acted like Adèle belonged, and she had been clear that Claire's case was a test—one which Adèle might not want to pass anymore. Yet her capitaine had just casually included her, as if the decision about her had already been taken. Warmth and excitement spread through Adèle. Maybe, for all the scolding, Capitaine Koyani approved of her impulse. Maybe it wasn't anger that drove her but worry. Adèle could accept that.

"I'll be careful," Adèle promised. She knew she wouldn't, and she suspected Koyani did, too.

"Good. We'll drag Nsia Kouna's ass back to the interrogation room to ask about your anonymous tip. You can make your full report once healed, but is there anything I should know immediately?"

"Mx. Kouna didn't shoot me. Someone else was there. A tall person, very muscular, with short blond hair and a dapper vest. Claire… saved me." She'd hesitated. She didn't have to explain everything, not now. Talking and keeping her head clear was already difficult. "The exocores are souls, capitaine. Witches that were transformed. I found kidnapped people in there, with witch cuffs."

Koyani accepted the new information with perfect stoicism. Her eyebrows quirked, but she did not gasp or blanch at the idea that someone had shoved people into gems. Perhaps she didn't believe it.

"This doesn't make sense. Why send you a note with a location where you would discover something if they only aimed to trap you? Why not a random warehouse?"

Adèle frowned. Her head pounded, but memories flittered at the edge of her mind. "Perhaps they're not related or… they said something about needing a death. I don't understand either."

"I don't like it." She pushed herself to her feet, her frown deeper than ever. "I will leave you to your rest. I'm surprised you're in such good shape, but more sleep cannot hurt."

"One of the witches freed can heal," Adèle said, and the corner of her lips twisted in a half-smile. "A sliver of luck in my night. You'll have me back in no time, capitaine."

She didn't want to stay away. What if they decided to continue prioritizing Claire? It felt wrong to rest after she had busted so much of this case open. She wanted to finish the job—to find proof beyond doubt of Montrant Industries' crimes and expose them.

"Excellent. Your dedication is noted, but don't come back only to fall over. There'll be plenty of work no matter when you return."

Adèle laughed—a sharp bark that turned into wracking cough, sending pain down her stomach. She grimaced and promised herself to have her inhaler boiling soon. "I believe you."

Koyani's smile matched hers. She wished Adèle a pleasant evening and strode out, more relaxed than ever before. Perhaps the civilian clothes were adding to that impression, but Koyani had never felt so approachable before. Or perhaps, and here Adèle could only hope, she was truly becoming part of the team.

-19-

LES LABORATOIRES

REACHING THE ELEVATOR HAD BEEN EASY ENOUGH. EITHER these scientists didn't worry about people stealing their research, or most of their security protected the floors they actually worked on. Claire had to evade a single guard at the entrance—a massive man engrossed in a tiny book—and had then slipped unseen into the Centre de Recherche's corridors. Two main elevators flanked by stairs led upward, but Zita had been clear on which one Claire was looking for. It was marked as broken.

Heart pounding, steps as light as she could, Claire kept searching for the disguised portal. Only the emergency lights remained in most corridors and she clung to the shadows, hoping she wouldn't come across anyone. The longer she stalked this building, the more stressed she became. Why hadn't she asked Zita for specific directions? Claire groaned. As much as she wanted to blame it on exhaustion, she knew thinking ahead wasn't part of her strengths. At least she had brought her smokesticks this time, just in case. She gritted her teeth and continued looking until— *finally!*—a single elevator stood at the end of a darkened corridor.

219

A sign with "HORS SERVICE. ATTENTION" warned people away, and a huge lock kept it sealed. Claire crept to the web of rusted metal bars blocking her path and peeked down. Not much to see from this angle, except more darkness. She grabbed the lock and prayed to the nine saints that the guard up front wouldn't pay too much attention to the strange noises she was about to make. At least she'd had to get deep into the building to find this elevator, so unless it echoed all the way to the entrance, she should be good. With a long breath and a burst of strength, she snapped it in two and flung it away.

Claire slipped her fingers into the grate holes and pulled it open by force, cringing at the loudness of it all. Even with the distance… Better to hurry, before someone checked on the elevator. She strained against the web, and as soon as the space sufficed for her small belly and her, she squeezed through to the other side. The elevator must be all the way down, hidden in the darkness, but she didn't want to risk calling it—not when she had a better, more thrilling option. With a smirk, Claire jumped down. Her hair caught in the wind as she sped towards the bottom, drawing a grin out of her. The brief and intense thrill of the fall could almost make her forget where she was heading—then she felt a shift in the air, like shimmering freshness, come and gone in an instant. Portal magic. She grabbed the iron cable, gritting her teeth against the burning friction piercing through her gloves as she slowed her descent. Her poor hands would deserve weeks of care after these last days. Still, better that than making a racket twice. Claire climbed down through the hatch atop the elevator and smiled as she found the grate there opened. Her relief vanished as she entered the secret labs proper.

A strange smell permeated the air, as if the stiff odour of acid tried to mask a more disturbing scent. Dulled white ceiling lamps cast an uncertain glow on the area, illuminating two rows of working space half-covered in glass containers. What weird shapes. Claire wondered why a regular bowl wasn't enough for them, but discarded the thought. She could speculate on evil scientists' habits another day. She moved on, heading for the double doors across the workspace.

As Claire approached, the stink of acid grew stronger. It irritated her throat and squeezed her heart. She paused at the doors, her itching left palm set against it, and steeled herself. Tiny windows allowed her to glimpse cylindrical shapes on the other side. She did not want to get closer, not in a billion years, but she had to.

The doors swooshed as she opened them, and Claire noted the clothes at their bottom, trailing the ground and blocking the small space under. To keep odours out, or worse? Should she have a mask covering her nose and mouth too, in addition to most of her face? Zita hadn't fallen sick, though. Not yet, at any rate. Claire clung to that fact as a reassuring shield and advanced, into a noticeably colder room.

She strode down one of the main aisles, flanked by rows of tanks—massive contraptions of metals, more than eight feet tall, with a ventilation system on the side and a dozen tubes connected to the top. Blue electrical lights lined the floor and cast a cold light upward, just strong enough for long shadows to turn into darkness as they reached the ceiling. Each tank had a glass container, human-sized. Her pace slowed as she realized what would be within, and she squeezed her eyes shut.

Stillness followed. Nothing but Claire, standing in the middle of dozens of tanks holding humans, acrid vapours stimulating her too-wild imagination. It didn't matter how hard she focused on the blackness behind her eyelids, her mind filled with horrible imagery—frail human bodies resting in every container, hollow, suffering. Claire exhaled, slow and steady, preparing her already erratic heart for the real sight.

Voices caught her attention before she opened her eyes. They came from farther down the aisle, moving closer.

"This is a fiasco," the first speaker stated, her voice soft, calm, and cold. "We lost hundreds of exocores in a single fire, you were sighted, and the witches escaped. I hope you have an explanation for this."

Claire dashed for the tanks on her left, creeping into the shadows away from the aisle. Relief flooded her, spinning her head—she didn't have to look at the bodies just yet. She could focus on this conversation, and perhaps steady her shaking hands.

"I have no idea how your police found the warehouse."

Claire froze as she recognized the second voice. *Clémence.* Now that she'd heard it again, she would never forget ols voice.

"Anonymous tip." Disdain filled the first speaker's words. "Mx. Kouna might think themself wise, but I know they've been digging in our yard. I should have taken care of them sooner. What were *you* doing there, however?"

"I needed a new test subject. The process' efficiency caps and using powerful witches only means we lose more of their energy. I didn't want to waste assets while I was trying to circumvent our current issues." The way Clémence spoke of other witches as nothing but resources to plunder chilled Claire to the core. How could ol forget the people ol had once protected? "I don't have much hope. This is becoming too dangerous. You should quit while you're ahead."

"I won't, and you can't."

A long silence followed the unmistakable threat. The voices had reached her level, and Claire inched forward to get a glimpse at the pair. What a strange combo. Clémence, tall and muscular, was speaking with a tiny woman, dark curls framing a delicate face. Yet the woman clearly held the upper hand in this conversation, and Clémence shifted away from her to busy olself with the tank before ol. Ol readjusted a tube, then reluctantly returned to the discussion at hand.

"Our current transformation process is too slow to replace the exocores lost in time for the Pont des Lumières' grand opening," ol said.

"Find a solution, or you'll be the one explaining to the gouverneure why her pet project has failed."

Claire stifled a gasp. La gouverneure. Of course Montrant Industries had political support shielding them from investigations and public questioning, but you could hardly have a higher office than this, unless you asked the Queen herself.

CLAUDIE ARSENEAULT

Despite ols height, Clémence seemed to shrink back before the woman's gaze. "I have one—the ice witch—but we won't be able to turn her into an exocore."

A deafening buzz exploded between Claire's ears at "the ice witch", drowning out what followed. *Livia*. Had they experimented on her? Others? What did they mean to do with her? Where was she now? The questions bounced around her mind, disorganized and fleeting, until Claire realized their answers might be in the very conversation she'd stopped paying attention to. She cursed herself mentally and forced her focus back.

"Make sure they're all ready for the big day," the woman was saying. "If we're not the main source of power for every large-scale project in the country after this, we've failed. *You* have failed. Understood?"

"Yes. You don't need more threats."

Panic drummed through Claire's head. They were shifting the subject. She'd never forgive herself if her instant of distraction had caused her to miss invaluable information about her twin. Not that she'd know. The conversation also grew harder to hear as they moved away from her, and Claire straightened up. She needed to stay close.

"Sometimes I wonder," the curly-haired woman answered. "Adèle Duclos found her way to her sister's mansion, yesterday. Your escaped witches might be with her. I'll get an address to you as soon as I can."

Claire gritted her teeth. How did this woman know so much? Claire had chosen Emmanuelle Duclos' house to avoid

224

detection, not to send Montrant Industries to her door. Unless Emmanuelle had always been involved... No. Claire brushed the idea away as soon as it popped into her mind. She refused to believe it. Adèle's sister had been the first to help Claire understand Montrant's horrible scheme. Claire trusted her sense of people, and by extension, she trusted Emmanuelle. Doubts and second guessing would lead her nowhere. She stalked after the pair, eager to know more.

"I will see to it. What about that thief? You were supposed to—"

Claire's foot hooked in a thick tube running along the floor. She hissed from the unexpected stab of pain and caught herself on the nearest tank. A hollow metallic echo travelled through the lab chamber, killing the conversation.

"Élise. Someone's here," Clémence said.

An annoyed huff followed from Élise, then the click of a gun's hammer. Claire's stomach dropped like a weight. She strode backward, one carefully silent step at a time, and tried to keep track of the pair's shuffling feet. They spread out, Clémence walking down the aisle while Élise slid between the tanks. The room's shadows no longer seemed large enough. Claire froze, panic cementing her feet to the ground until Élise reached her column of tanks. Her instincts kicked in, and she hurried to the next series, ducking before they spotted her.

How long could she play this game of cat and mouse? If she slipped past them, she could dash for the elevator, but they'd notice her going through the double door and follow. Clémence might be armed and ol could cancel her magic. Claire didn't like her odds against two guns. She reached into her stomach pockets. Super strength and speed had saved her often, but she had other tricks in her bag. She hadn't been forced to smoke anyone since breaking into Adèle's flat, but it'd combine wonderfully with the uneven lighting to provide cover.

Claire cracked two of her smokesticks, flung one across the room and a second towards Élise, then sprinted off. Gunshots greeted her when she passed Élise's row. One bullet whizzed through her hair to tink into the tank behind, and Claire marvelled at the woman's accuracy despite the smoke and super speed. At least the glass behind hadn't shattered.

She stopped before reaching the lit aisle and leaped upward, grabbing the metal top of a cylinder and heaving herself onto it. Claire fought her nausea as she set her feet between thick tubes. Body warmth emanated from the tank under, a subtle reminder of its content. Was this Livia? Was she even here? Claire wished she hadn't stumbled. She wanted to know where the tubes led and to comb the entire place for her sister. Instead, she had to flee. And her only way out wouldn't be safe in the slightest—not with Clémence in the main passage, gun at the ready, waiting for her to show up.

Her muscles tensed as she prepared to jump, magic building up in them. If she could leap across the aisle, Clémence might not have a good shot at her. One jump, then she'd dash into the smoke created there and use it as cover while she padded her way to the exit. All she needed was to make this leap.

226

Claire sprang from her perch as a strange feeling slid into her, like a thick and distant sickness—like a vital part of her suddenly missing. *My powers*, she realized, but it was too late. Her magical strength vanished before she'd fully launched herself, and she jumped only to flail midair and slam hard into the ground, right in front of Clémence.

She was going to die.

Claire tried to push herself up anyway. If she was meant to die with a bullet to the head, she wouldn't die waiting for it. A hard boot kicked her belly, and pain snapped through her, sapping away the strength in her arms. She fell back, curling in on herself, her mind cursing her body's weakness. A second kick stole her breath and left her stunned. Claire stared at the heavy boots and more delicate shoes next to her, wondering how long she had before they put an end to this.

"Kill her," Élise said. "She heard too much."

"Only because you talk too much," Claire retorted, and while she couldn't believe the words had crossed her mouth, she was instantly proud of them. Why not sass them? They didn't need to know the terror crushing her insides right now. "Shouldn't be my problem."

"I'm afraid it is."

Clémence tapped the ground with ols heavy boots, but reluctantly pointed ols weapon at Claire. "I could use her for experimentation," ol said. "Her magic is weak, but she's our ice witch's twin. It's as good a test subject as I'll get."

Élise's eyes narrowed. "You know who she is?"

227

Claire froze, her throat tightening. The tests terrified her as much as immediate death did, but something here was terribly wrong. How did Clémence know she was Livia's twin? Did it mean ol had discovered the bakery and the rest of her life? If so, why hadn't ol destroyed it already? But even disregarding the horrifying prospect of Clémence knowing exactly who Claire was, ols pretense of needing a twin to experiment didn't work. Clémence would realize they weren't identical twins, that their family link didn't matter for science. By now, ol must have understood their magic was nothing alike, either.

Clémence stared briefly at Claire, ols eyes calm and calculating, before turning to Élise. "Not really. I know she's the first one's twin, but that's the extent of it."

Élise huffed and shook her head. "Whatever," she said. "I'm not taking that risk. Kill her."

She turned her heels and started down the aisle at a brisk pace, her order evidently final. Clémence's pistol hadn't moved, and the sickening feeling of Claire's missing powers remained lodged in her stomach.

"Very well, but if the Pont des Lumières' network short-circuits and explodes on the opening night because you refused to let me test this new technique as thoroughly as possible, I won't be the one explaining to the gouverneure why her pet project failed."

Élise stopped in her tracks. "Can't you use *any* of the dozens of witches in tanks here?"

"No. They're being transformed already. The natural characteristics of their magic and bodies have been altered and that makes them poor test subjects. This is why I went to the warehouse, but now…"

Claire didn't dare to move or breathe. It sounded perfectly logical, but after perceiving the lies about twins… It didn't make sense for Clémence to save her—not after ol'd tried strangling her in the warehouse. Perhaps ol really thought twinship changed a thing, or ol'd needed any living witch for ols horrible tests. Every second in which Élise considered her options extended into infinity, until finally:

"If you must, then, but remember what is at stake. Should you fail this, I will ensure his death stretches on painfully."

"Understood," Clémence answered in a clipped and seething tone.

Ol crouched down as Élise pushed the double doors. Relief shot through Claire—she might live long enough to escape. She would try, for sure. Her gaze snapped back to the blondx giant towering over her and she gathered her magic and punched out, desperate to overcome the nullifying aura. For a moment she thought she was moving faster, but Clémence caught her fist with ease. The slimy feeling of absence hadn't left, either. Claire had time to meet Clémence's steady gaze before ol grabbed her head and slammed it to the ground. White pain burst through her forehead, and, on the second strike, Claire lost consciousness.

-20-

L'ESPOISSON SPATULE

THE STRANGE HAZE IN THE INTERROGATION ROOM convinced Adèle she was still running a fever. Or, if she was honest, it confirmed the sluggishness she'd been experiencing since dragging herself out of bed and it explained the occasional shivers. Docteure Adaho had advised against going to work today, but disregarding medical counsel was a speciality of sorts for Adèle, and she'd returned home to put a uniform on then headed out. She'd passed by the *Croissant-toi*, only to discover she'd have neither croissant nor coffee to help her through the day. The bakery was closed—and that, more than anything else so far, had made her doubt her decision to leave her bed. What wouldn't she have given for Claude's familiar smile and laugh this morning? She'd hoped the darkness beyond the large windows didn't spell bad news for him. Worry still needling at her, Adèle had sought a vélotaxi to bring her to the Quartier des Chênes. She didn't dare bike herself.

When Adèle had stepped in, only Yuri was at his desk, bent over a thick document, one finger trailing columns of numbers as he worked. He paused to compare something to a second sheet every now and then, but quickly stopped as she approached.

"We prefer it when newbies don't get shot," he said, lips pinched into an expression Adèle had come to identify as a kind smirk. "Glad to see you're back on your feet."

"If we can call it that," she replied. The ground seemed wobbly, so she set a hand on her desk. "Where is… everyone?" Especially Élise or Koyani, but it felt strange for the office to be so empty. Over the last week, most of the team had been tying up cases and filling out paperwork, and their presence had sparked endless conversation and livened up the space.

"Collecting your favourite journalist, along with any documentation they might have related to Montrant Industries. Not that Mx. Kouna knows about the latter." Yuri's clear blue eyes examined her, then he nodded towards her chair. "Sit down. You don't look well, and you have some time before they return."

"Yes." She grabbed the chair and slid down, sighing in relief as the world stopped spinning. Yuri studied her a moment longer before standing. His steps echoed weirdly across the airy space, fleeting and deep all at once. Her fever, probably. He brought her a glass of water with condensation glistening along its sides. Adèle reached for it, her throat parched. "Thank you."

"Don't mention it," he said, before returning to his work. Yuri never chatted extensively, but it hadn't escaped Adèle how he was often the first with subtle and kind attentions. He listened, and, behind the clipped conversations and long silences, he clearly cared.

Adèle settled back and closed her eyes, trying to rest before Élise returned with Nsia Kouna. She was hot and sweaty, but a gulp of cold water sent intense shivers down her spine. The cool glass grounded her when her head swam too hard, and she kept her focus on it, reviewing her greatly changed case. She suspected they wouldn't waste time setting up traps for Claire anymore. If they ignored Montrant Industries after last night, then they were as corrupt as her previous colleagues, and she'd want no part in it.

For a while, only the occasional scratches of Yuri's pen filled the room. Then the first footsteps echoed down the halls. Adèle's head snapped up, she downed the glass of water, and she straightened as the door swung open. Capitaine Koyani led the way, back in her regular uniform, and Nsia Kouna followed, trailed by Élise. Surprise flicked through Koyani's face, but she masked it quickly.

"Officier Duclos, we're pleased to have you back. Will you be joining the interrogation?"

Adèle nodded, and the thrill of returning to the case at hand and discovering not only who had shot her, but on whose orders, washed part of her feverish daze away. As she moved to fall into pace behind Élise, however, she caught the strangest expression on her colleague's face. Élise wasn't glad to have her back; she seemed furious. She flung her black curls back, glared at Adèle, then continued without a word, her hand tight around Kouna's wrist. The quick interaction left Adèle confused, her heart pounding.

Koyani pushed the interrogation's door open and

motioned for them to go on. "I'll let you two handle it. There is still a lot of paperwork to fill and a few of Mx. Kouna's fellows to placate. Keep me updated. And, Lieutenant Jefferson, don't forget our discussion."

Nsia Kouna strode to their seat with a casual pace belied by the tension in their shoulders. They leaned against the chair after they sat, one arm cast over its back, as if waiting peacefully for the first questions, yet their eyes darted between Élise and Adèle, soaking in as much information as possible. Adèle tugged on her uniform, smoothing it to the best of her ability, and prayed she wasn't too pale. She stayed by the door, resting against the wall, wondering what discussion Koyani had referred to. Was that why Élise was so angry? Élise left them to retrieve a file, and in the brief moment she was gone, Nsia Kouna tapped on the table with their index finger, leaned forward, and whispered, "I won't talk to people I can't trust."

They straightened back with a smirk as Élise returned, their nonchalance perfectly practised. Élise sat in the chair before them, and her clipped tone as she spoke didn't need to be faked.

"Welcome back, Mx. Kouna. I hope you're looking forward to a longer stay."

"Of course! It's always a pleasure to be battered with questions to which I have no answers." Kouna smiled, and the perfect lines of their eyebrows raised in a mocking expression. "It will be a privilege to dance around your thinly veiled accusations, Miss Jefferson."

Élise returned their smile, but the ice in it would have

doused even Adèle's fever. Then the interrogation started, a constant back and forth between Élise and Kouna, like a winter tug-of-war contest in which every question from Élise was a sharp pull, but none managed to drag Kouna forward.

"How often have you met with Claire?"

"I never talked with her."

"Do you own firearms?"

"What would I do with a gun?"

"That's not an answer."

"No, I don't own any."

"How long have you been digging around Montrant Industries?"

"Is that a concern now? I'm free to write what I want."

"Should we worry about the legality of your methods?"

"There's nothing illegal about my methods, that's absurd."

"Your partner doesn't worry about stealing."

"She's not my partner. I said this. Try again."

The exchange continued on, and Adèle had an increasingly hard time maintaining her focus. What was the point of this? Nsia Kouna had dug their heels in too deep, and no ice hid under the snow to make them slip. They had only shown hints of impatience and had obviously been through this routine before. So had Élise, however, and she didn't seem of a mind to stop.

"So you've never talked with Claire?"

"Never."

"How did you know she was stealing exocores?"

"I used my brain."

"She didn't tell you."

"No. We never communicated. No talking, no written messages. Nothing."

"How did you notice, then?"

"By paying attention to exocores."

"So you were already investigating Montrant Industries."

"How else could I have written that article?"

"What do you truly know about Montrant Industries?"

At this, Nsia Kouna's expression shifted away from boredom or slight amusement for the first time since the questioning had started. They leaned forward, and although their smirk hadn't weakened, a new light shone in their eyes. Adèle perked up too. Kouna had promised not to talk unless they trusted their interlocutor, and she doubted they did Élise.

"They are not the small and local company they project." The journalist put dramatic weight behind every word, as if they were revealing a great secret — as if that hadn't been written in their article anyway.

"We read the paper," Adèle interjected. "Can't you be more precise?"

Kouna ran a hand over their bald head, then threw a smile at her and leaned back. "I could."

"Mx. Kouna, you may want to prove yourself more cooperative," Élise said.

"Am I a suspect?" They cast their long and thin arms out with wide eyes. "What am I accused of?"

"Nothing for now. We're investigating. Just answer the

questions, Mx. Kouna. You don't want to hinder us."

"Is this a threat, Miss Jefferson? Should I find a lawyer?"

Adèle couldn't see Élise's expression, but she read her amused smile in the way her shoulders squared and she leaned back. "Not unless you've done something reprehensible. We're all allies here—or we should be."

Kouna's eyebrows shot up, and they allowed doubts to shine clearly through. Journalists were often difficult, but Adèle couldn't shake the feeling this went beyond the usual reluctance. Nsia Kouna and Élise stared at each other, and in the silent communication that passed, Adèle had the distinct impression they both wanted the other to know they thought of them as an enemy. She gritted her teeth. Both Nsia Kouna and Claire had figured out Montrant Industries hid horrible activities long before she and Élise had, and she wished to understand how, not alienate them.

Yet as Élise started again, she continued keeping back all their information and avoiding the questions Adèle really wanted to ask. Did Kouna know the exocores were made of witches? Had they traced Montrant's network? Did they have any idea who could have sent the note? They weren't making any progress, and she didn't have the patience to draw information out of Kouna through convoluted badgering. At this rate they would still be trading pointless questions with them by nightfall.

Sharp knocks on the door startled Adèle, and Koyani entered before the verbal tug-of-war could fall entirely silent. With the door opened, they could hear someone's insistent request to see

Adèle, and Yuri's amused "I suspect you want to talk with her, too." Koyani gestured for both of her officers to join her outside, then turned to Nsia Kouna.

"We apologize for this interruption," she said. "I'm sure it won't be long."

They laughed. "Take your time. I know the routine and will make myself comfortable."

Koyani frowned and her gaze swept the table. Élise's file had remained closed and unused, but when the capitaine looked her way, she raised her eyebrows, shrugged, and stood to follow out. Adèle wondered if she'd imagined the silent reproach there. Koyani wouldn't critique Élise in front of an outsider, but it had felt like she'd expected progress or exchanges. It would, at least, explain why she treated Kouna as a guest, not as a suspect.

A small, barrel-shaped black woman was waiting in front of their desk area, arms on her hips, shifting back and forth on the balls of her feet in impatience. Adèle had seen her before, she was *certain* of it, but her slow brain wouldn't place it. Relief spread over the woman's face as she stepped forward.

"Oh, Officier Duclos," she said, and her intensity surprised Adèle. "I'm so glad you're here."

Adèle's eyes widened as she identified the voice—Zita, Claire's friend who had been in the warehouse that night, and with the witches at Em's house later. Why had she come here? Did she seem… afraid? Icy fear curled at the bottom of Adèle's stomach as she remembered Claire's promise to investigate Montrant's actual industry. Had something happened? If it had, and Zita gave away

Claire's location... they were still supposed to arrest her. Adèle shot a quick smile at Zita then interrupted before she could say too much.

"Capitaine, this is one of my... informants. From the warehouse." She hoped Koyani would take that to mean one of the imprisoned witches. "They discussed a new lead on Montrant Industries."

"An informant, yes." Zita stared at Adèle, obviously a little confused. To Adèle's relief, she decided to play along, straightened, and added with a grin. "Codename is Spying Paddlefish. Can we talk alone? This is highly confidential information."

Adèle exercised extreme self-control as not to laugh. *Spying Paddlefish?* Nevermind that informants rarely walked directly into a police station to spill their beans. That would put them at risk. Zita just didn't seem to realize that. Or she had more pressing concerns...

"Absolutely not," Koyani said. "This investigation into Montrant Industries is now under my control, and I want to hear it. We're a team. Nothing you'd tell Adèle wouldn't reach us either way."

Well, that was untrue, and Adèle couldn't stave off her sharp guilt at betraying Koyani's trust. Beyond that, however, her capitaine's words brought new but not unwelcome surprises. She followed Koyani as she led them to the conference room, trying to understand when the investigation had shifted from Claire to Montrant, and changed from Élise's hands to Koyani's. Was that

238

their earlier discussion? It might explain why Élise had glared at her this morning. Adèle's decision to respond to the anonymous warehouse tip had flipped this entire case on its head, and Élise had never been eager to look into Montrant. She entered the conference room last, slamming the door behind them.

"All right. Tell us all about this new lead."

The obvious sneer in her voice startled Adèle. Élise had always been helpful and understanding. What was up with her? Adèle glanced at her as Koyani and Zita spread around the table. No one took a seat—they could all sense this wouldn't drag on like Kouna's interrogation had. Adèle nevertheless gripped the back of a chair, trying to ignore the knots in her stomach and the thumping in her head. Zita continued to move from one foot to the next, wringing her hands. When the silence stretched on, Koyani broke it.

"Please don't turn into Stalling Paddlefish and share your information."

A nervous laughter escaped Zita. "All right. Okay. It's just… My friend went to investigate new clues about Montrant Industries last night, and she never returned. And I *know* what happened to Adèle and I'm just-I'm terrified."

Her voice broke towards the end. Adèle clenched her chair until her whole hands hurt. She'd expected this—what else, really? Yet to hear it out loud had struck a bigger blow than she'd anticipated, leaving her reeling. Her throat tightened, her breathing turning shallow as it sped up. The conclusion was obvious: Claire was dead. Why wouldn't they shoot her down? She should never have gone in there alone. Adèle should have stopped her at least long enough to be there.

"So this is more than a lead," Koyani deduced, and Adèle was thankful to her for taking charge while she fought her increasingly panicked breathing and growing tunnel vision. "Someone could be in danger."

"Yes!" Zita's head shot up, hope gleaming in her eyes. "I know where she went—it's under the research labs—but I can't go there on my own without winding up dead myself. So I came here, because I know she..." She trailed off long enough to meet Adèle's gaze. "She trusted you. You have to go."

Adèle's breath caught, and the room seemed to close down on her as everyone turned to stare. She hoped they would attribute any paleness and shakiness to fever, even though adrenaline was starting to wash that away. Zita was asking *her*, after all the energy she had spent trying to put Claire under arrest. Now she needed saving, and Adèle was more than ready to go. She released the chair and squared her shoulders.

"Right. No time to waste."

"In your state?" Koyani asked.

"I can handle it." Probably. Adèle struggled to keep her breathing steady and wished she hadn't forgotten her vivifiants at Em's. She really hadn't been in any state to leave this morning. And now, if she collapsed before she reached Claire, she would be of no help. Koyani examined her, perhaps weighing the truth of these words against the possibility Adèle would run ahead anyway, then grunted her approval.

"So what's your plan?" Élise asked. "Rush in on the off chance your second informant isn't already dead?"

"No." Koyani tapped the table repeatedly with her index fingers. She had leaned back, her gaze unfocusing as she considered their options. "Élise, get us reinforcements. I'll head to the lab with Adèle and Sprinkle Paddlefish here to scout out the area. I'll ask Yuri to stay in the office in case the rest of the team returns."

"Capitaine—"

"Those are orders, Élise." Her tone brooked no disagreement. Élise clenched her jaw, muttered a "yes, capitaine," then strode out of the room. She didn't slam the door this time, but Adèle had the distinct impression she would have loved to. Koyani stared after her, unimpressed, and sighed. "I'll get motorcycles ready. Adèle, take a moment to gather yourself. Adrenaline can only carry you so far and you've been shot not even two days ago."

Koyani exited, and Adèle couldn't help but feel she'd meant to leave them alone and offer them time to speak more with one another. Perhaps she suspected who this second informant was, although she gave no clue what she thought of it. Perhaps it didn't matter as long as Claire's life could be on the line. After that, however...

"You realize I might have to arrest her," Adèle said.

Zita startled. "What? You can't do that. She *trusts* you."

The words stabbed at Adèle. She didn't want to betray that, especially knowing how little she'd done to earn it, but it wasn't so simple. "So does my boss. How can I explain to Koyani that this informant we're rescuing is none other than the thief I'm supposed to track down?"

"She doesn't need to know!" Zita threw her arms up with way more flair than necessary. "Destroy your hierarchy! Rebel and keep a secret, for once!"

Adèle snorted, amused despite her best efforts to remain serious. Something about the tiny woman's flair for the dramatic managed to ease her worries and make her smile. Judging from Zita's pout, it was entirely unintentional. Adèle shook her head. "I'll do my best, I swear. Let's start by making sure she's safe."

And alive, of which they had no guarantee. Adèle preferred not to acknowledge how large a hole the thought of Claire's death cut into her. She had glimpsed a different person the other day, one who had always existed but whom Adèle had willfully ignored. She wished she could make up for it and help instead of hinder her, but she might never have the chance.

-21-

UN PEU DE CLÉMENCE

BLINDING LIGHTS GREETED CLAIRE WHEN SHE CAME TO. HER mind had turned into a thick fog through which only throbbing pain emerged. She could feel it radiate from the base of her skull, where Clémence had smashed it to the floor twice. Fabric stuck in the wound, and she realized belatedly she was still wearing her mask. Unexpected, that, though if Clémence already knew who she was, ol may not have bothered. As her consciousness slowly spread from her agonizing head to the rest of her battered body, Claire found a lot more to worry about.

Cold metal dug into her wrists and ankles. She'd been tied to an inclined table, and when she squirmed, a tube brushed her arm. Panic jolted through her—were they draining her magic? Experimenting on her already? She flexed her muscles and a needle pinched through her skin. Claire struggled against the bonds, her breath shortening, bullets of sweat rolling down her neck. Her magic wouldn't obey, locked away, denying her the super strength she sorely needed. If only she could see beyond that light!

"Hey!"

Her voice bounced on a nearby wall, all around her. Glass, she recognized, and it surrounded her. Claire knew what it meant, even as her mind fought to refuse it. The hot air turned stuffier and more difficult to breathe in.

They had put her in a tank and hooked her into the factory.

"Clémence!"

Despair and anger had ripped the scream from her, and Claire startled when the blinding light vanished. She blinked, her eyes adjusting to the sudden darkness. Scratches marred the glass casing around her, but she could make out the shapes on the other side. Clémence stood before her, ols lips pinched in a thoughtful expression. As if ol was studying a specimen.

"Relax," ol said. "It's for show."

"Relax? For show?" Claire choked on the words. She should retort with something wittier, but the shock stole her meagre sass. It left only anger behind. "There's a needle up my arm, and I'm in this... this human capsule! You can shove 'relax' deep up your ass."

Woah. Bad words. Even plugged into their factory, horror and outrage and fear coiling inside, it had felt wrong. The saints were listening! Claire grimaced. Livia had always been more adept at vulgarities.

"It's not running," Clémence explained. "You have friends who will come, yes?"

Claire stared at Clémence. Did ol think she would answer that? "I'm bait, is what you're saying."

"Yes, except it's not a trap, and there would have been no

need if you had listened silently without getting caught. You're not a very good thief, are you?"

"I'm—"

"A baker, yes." Clémence interrupted with a dismissive wave. "The one with the cutesy pun name. 'Believe in yourself'. I wish it were that easy."

Claire froze, staring hard through the scratched glass at Clémence. Ols expression gave nothing away. How long had ol known about the *Croissant-toi*? Was ol mocking her or was the casual dropping of her identity a threat? Why would Clémence even waste time with that when ol had her trapped in a tank? Once again, Claire tried to work out the inconsistency, but it felt like the tank was closing in on her, stifling her breathing and chilling her bones. Her head pounded, refusing to think through everything in composed, logical steps. She needed time and calm to figure out what game Clémence was playing—because ol certainly was, one way or another—but how could she stall?

"No one pretended it was simple," she countered. "That's why it's the bakery's name, so that the reminders are all around me. Every day as I work, I see the message and remember that I am who I say, when I say it. Even when it feels like my business will run into the ground, or like my mind can't decide what it wants, or like I should be loving people, with a capital L. Even when I'm tied to an experimentation table giving life lessons to the very person trying to turn my sister into an exocore!"

She pulled against the straps, on impulse, knowing full well that without her magic it would get her nowhere. Clémence

245

remained stiff and silent, like a parent waiting for a child to calm down.

"We won't be transforming Livia," ol said. "She'll power the Pont des Lumières. The tower contains a secret chamber, behind the glasswork hall. Three witches will be wired into the electric circuit to lend their magic strength to the hundreds of lights across the Pont. I've capped how much energy I can transfer into gems and the process is too long, so we need to use these three directly."

Claire leaned her head back against the table, nauseated. She had *not* wanted to know the details. "Don't discuss them like they're nothing but measurable energy. They're people, and you're dragging their souls into gems and light bulbs. It's disgusting."

"It is, isn't it?" Clémence's tone hovered between bemusement and regret. As if ol was contemplating this from a distance, debating the ethics of what someone else had done, applying logic to a situation which should grip ols gut and twist it. "Emmanuelle's solution would have been more elegant, but we've wasted years without achieving promising results. So they… wanted me to find another way. I shouldn't have."

"No kidding." Claire's fear had receded. If Clémence had wanted her dead, the deed would be long done, and ol wouldn't have told her about the Pont des Lumières or Livia's location, or any of their plans. Which meant ol needed Claire alive, and she could afford to speak her mind and rough ol up. Ol sure deserved it. "You better not be expecting some late mercy or compassion from me. I've been collecting imprisoned souls and digging at your

246

organization too long to have a shred of it left."

"You've been digging like I want you to." Clémence leaned closer to the tank until ol could meet Claire's gaze through the scratched glass. "I'm trapped here, but you… When you made the front page, I knew the city's eyes would follow your story. I knew I would need to trigger something dramatic to confirm Nsia Kouna's claims about Montrant Industries—how could they not investigate if a police officer died in one of their warehouses and a dozen witches were found beside her? You almost ruined it by showing up."

"I'm almost sorry I saved all these people, wow." Claire squirmed against her bindings again, if only to pass her frustration. She hated this tank.

"At least you came with Zita. Did you think I never noticed her following me? She's not exactly the queen of discretion. I led her here, gave her ample time to snoop around then leave to spread the word."

"So, what's the point of reviewing your entire plan?" Between the sharp pain at the base of her skull and the discomfort of a needle in her arm, Claire was out of patience, especially for a long explanation of Clémence's actions. She didn't care why and how. "Let's not waste time reenacting the worst villain tropes. Just get to the point. The needle, tank, and table are cheesy enough already, and we both know you want something."

For the first time, Clémence lost control of olself. Ol slammed a palm against the tank's glass and stalked away. "I'm not–This isn't a game! I can't–" Clémence stopped as ol reached a console of sorts, placed a hand on it, and inhaled deeply. "Zita will know where you are, and people will find this lab. Then you can interrupt the Pont's grand opening. And maybe while you're wrecking havoc…"

Ol's voice trailed off, anguish snipping the rest of the words. Clémence clung to the console, ols broad shoulders hunching forward, and, despite Claire's determination to have neither mercy nor compassion, a twinge of both twisted her heart. Ol was Zita's friend, or had been, and Montrant Industries had done something to ol. Reluctantly, more because Zita would want to understand than for herself, Claire asked.

"Okay, so what do they have on you?"

"A little brother."

"Oh."

Claire's mind went straight to Livia and cold horror swept through her. Would she have worked against other witches if her twin's life was on the line? She'd like to believe she'd know better—that she could force herself to prioritize hundreds of lives over a single person, but she'd pulled Adèle out of the fire instead of crates without a second thought. On impulse, perhaps, but was it that different?

Clémence ran a hand over ols face with a sniffing sound, then tilted ols head back to inhale deeply. Was ol fighting tears? Claire gritted her teeth, trying to squash her growing sympathy. *Hundreds of exocores*, she reminded herself, to no avail.

"Sorry," she muttered.

"He's dead the moment they realize I'm helping you. He

turns five next month… if he's lucky. We only have each other."

"Can't Zita find him?"

"Perhaps." Clémence turned around and rubbed the back of ols neck. Ol wouldn't even glance at Claire. "Zita alone would've gotten caught and killed, however. I couldn't send her to her death like this. With help, though…" And now ol looked up, straight at Claire, and she couldn't help but wonder how much of this was planned—how much of the guilt and fear had been acted out. Not all of it, surely, not when the prize was ols little brother's life.

"Zita will want to try. She likes you for some reason."

A brief smile shot across Clémence's expression. "She would."

"So will I." Not for free, however. And Claire suspected she could get more out of Clémence, and ruin Montrant Industries more thoroughly. "But only if you gather every scrap of proof you have of this happening—of the exocores and the people involved— no matter how anonymous or pointless they might seem, and you send them to Adèle."

"I can't. Élise would know who they're from. She heads Montrant's operations in Val-de-mer."

Claire barely held back a "so what?" The name had rung a bell when she had listened in, but, when she hadn't recognized the curly-haired woman, she had discarded her impression. Now, though… During how many morning conversations had Adèle talked about her wonderful colleagues and their teamwork? How they shared everything with one another? And about the police she shadowed for her first case—her investigation on Claire. "That was

Élise Jefferson?"

It cast half of the eavesdropped conversation in a new light. A dozen swearwords flew through Claire's mind, but she kept them all in, apologizing to the saints even as she thought them. She trusted Adèle, but what if she showed her partner this information?

"The journalist, then. Nsia Kouna? They're onto you."

"Hm. They might live long enough to be useful."

Claire's stomach twisted at the implications. How could anyone speak with such disinterest of others being murdered? Then again, Clémence had transformed hundreds of witches into exocores. What was one more person to ol?

"Deal. You get Kouna what they need to dig the rest of your network out, and we'll save your little brother."

Clémence stared at Claire for a long time, then agreed with a slight nod. "Gouverneure Lacroix will be at the bridge's opening. She made sure no one would question the industry and ordered the investigation against you. Get her if you can."

"What about the mairesse? Did she know?" Claire couldn't picture her parent's old friend involved in this. She remembered family dinners with Denise Jalbert, or afternoons at the park when she babysat Livia and Claire. She'd ask Livia to cool her water when summer became too hot, as if the ice powers were no big deal. She'd let a younger Claire assault her with questions about aromanticism later on, helping her work her identity out. Claire needed to know for sure, however.

"Not that I'm aware, but they don't tell me everything."

Clémence stepped back from the tank again. "I have to go. You have all you need to finish what you started. Pray your rescue doesn't take too long to come."

Ol tapped the glass once then moved to the console. Before Claire understood what ol meant to do, bright light filled the tank again, blinding her to the outside. She pushed down a pained cry of surprise and called after Clémence, only for her voice to bounce back on the tank's wall. She snapped her eyes closed, anger roiling at the bottom of her stomach. The ties holding her to the table dug into her arms and ankles, her head still pounded, and her palms were slowly starting to throb from the burns. She tried to tell herself Zita was on her way, that at least now she knew exactly when and where to find Livia, that they would save her and everyone at once, but already pain was chipping away at her optimism. One thing was sure: she would indeed be praying for a quick rescue.

-22-

UN FEUILLETÉ DE COMPLICATIONS

ADÈLE HIT THE BRAKES AND ALMOST JUMPED OFF HER motorcycle, letting it crash as she advanced on the entrance. Beads of sweat ran down her neck, collecting in the collar of her uniform, and the machine's constant rumbling had stirred the pain in her stomach again. Zita zoomed past her, stopping only when she reached the stairs leading up to the Centre de Recherche. She treated her motorbike with the same lack of delicacy Adèle had, and this time Koyani's voice snapped them into order.

"Everyone falls in line behind me," she called. "And don't let me catch you mistreating our property again. Motorcycles aren't cheap."

Cheaper than Claire's life, though. Adèle wanted to argue that every minute counted—Claire had proven that by barrelling into Clémence at the last possible moment, in the warehouse. Adèle reined in the temptation and waited for Koyani to stride past them, using the chance to cough out some of the mucus clogging her

252

airways. Again she wished she had vivifiants to ease her breathing. The lack of fresh air didn't help her stay calm, and rushing could also prompt fatal mistakes. She couldn't let panic grab a hold of her. Though the crushing sense of urgency threatened to obliterate rational and methodical approaches, she'd promised Zita her best.

Koyani shoved the front doors opened, and the guard at the entrance desk leaped to his feet. The protest died on his lips at the sight of the uniforms, and he fumbled his way to a calmer question. "Can I help?"

"We're going into the basement," Zita declared, and then she proceeded to ignore him and turned to the left.

"The elevator's broken!"

"If it's broken, then I'm the tallest lesbian in Val-de-mer!" Her voice echoed down the corridor, and they hurried after her. Zita needed a few turns before she reached the infamous elevator — an old apparatus blocked by a metal mesh and clearly marked as out of order. She pulled the lever beside it and the noisy clank of a mechanism dragging the cabin upward answered her. Zita turned to them, hands on her hips, a triumphant grin illuminating her face. It creaked to a stop behind the fence, and she spread her arms in victory. "Today is not the day I rise above five-foot-tall, I'm afraid."

"Was there no subtler entrance?" Koyani asked.

"You wanted one? I thought your types always barged in through the front door, yelling."

Adèle choked, suppressing her urge to laugh. "We try to cover all exits. So that would be 'barge in from everywhere, yelling'."

Koyani's gaze went from one to the other, and Adèle couldn't tell if she was holding back a smile or a sigh. With the calm of someone used to schooling their emotion and expression, Koyani strode into the elevator. "Let's move. Stay sharp; this is no game. If anyone's waiting for us, they know we're coming. Paddlefish, I cannot guarantee your safety. You should —"

"I am *not* staying upstairs," Zita interrupted. "I'm tired of everyone wanting to leave me behind! Let me help. Please."

Koyani huffed, then motioned for everyone to join her without another word of protest. Zita grinned as she shuffled inside, but Adèle clenched her revolver, tense.

They stood still in the rattling elevator, and the cabin shook as it crawled into the bowels of the Centre. With every passing second, a new knot appeared in Adèle's stomach. What would they find down there? Claire had spoken of a factory, and Adèle tried not to imagine the precise form this could take. She might lose her focus.

"For the record, there was no other way down." Zita's voice almost didn't cover the elevator's racket. "This isn't truly under the Centre de Recherche. We just passed through portal magic."

Koyani hissed and clenched her teeth. "Any... requirements to this portal? Do you know the distance it travels and how many can go through?"

Requirements? Adèle glanced at her capitaine, surprised by the precise questions. She must understand the basics of this magic, or she wouldn't have known what to ask. Zita's eyes also widened—she must not have expected it either.

"Not that I can tell."

"And the landing is safe? We won't find an entire squad waiting to shoot us at the bottom?"

Zita froze, horror painted across her face, and she stammered her answer. "Didn't find anyone when I first came."

"Stay back." Koyani gestured for her to stand away from the door.

They fell silent once more until the elevator slowed down. Koyani cleared her throat. "For the record, I expect the whole story once your informant is safe. *All of it.*"

Zita shot Adèle an alarmed look, but she ignored it. She'd known this would happen. Her short time working near Koyani had taught her the capitaine was both perceptive and decisive. Adèle feared her reaction to Claire, or to her disappearance if she vanished. No matter what she did today, she'd betray someone's trust. And while Adèle didn't understand how or why she'd earned Claire's, it seemed as precious and fragile as Basir's crystal walls, and shattering it would amount to a heinous crime.

The grate slid open in a cacophony of rusted metal. Adèle and Koyani raised their firearms, ready for resistance.

Deadly silence followed the ear-piercing shrieks of the door's opening. Nothing moved. Nothing breathed, even. The stringent aseptic smell reminded Adèle of Emmanuelle, but what little warmth the thought brought was killed by the lifeless light cast by ceiling lamps. Her sister didn't belong in a place like this. Adèle scanned the rows of science benches for a sign of ambush, but, if guards were waiting there, they were hiding well.

"All right!" Zita exclaimed, making both officers with her flinch. "Let's get searching!"

She strode forward, all careless enthusiasm. Adèle's heart climbed into her throat, and her ears rang from the gunshot sure to follow. In the stunned and expectant moment Adèle wasted, Koyani grabbed Zita's shoulder and pulled her back.

"What are you doing?" she hissed. "Listen here, Spanking Paddlefish—"

"Spying," Zita muttered, just loud enough to interrupt.

"Whatever." Koyani snorted, but her scowl hid the flicker of a smile. "Until I declare this area safe, you're to stay behind me at all times. I don't want a shot civilian on this mission because you're a reckless enthusiast. Keep yourself together or you'll be dead before we save your friend. Is that clear?"

Instead of answering, Zita turned to Adèle. It earned them both a glare from Koyani.

"She's in charge, not me," Adèle said. "And she's right. Let us do our jobs."

With Zita's reluctant agreement acquired, Adèle and Koyani stepped out of the elevator to properly explore these hidden laboratories. A beginner's nervousness crawled through Adèle. She'd never teamed up with her capitaine before, and despite years of experience, she felt as though she'd landed back on square one: the rookie needing to impress her boss. Adèle had run into so many complications since starting with Koyani's unit, this would be a chance to prove she could perform without problems, too. At least until they found Claire. Then the troubles would begin anew.

They swept through the first room without a hitch, clearing one row of workbenches after another. Despite her excessive self-consciousness, Adèle coordinated her movements with Koyani with practised ease. Whenever one advanced, the other covered her back, and they continued to alternate until every corner had been explored, and every side office cleared. Zita had stayed behind, rocking on her heels, until Koyani motioned her forward. Only two doors remained, each branching into a different direction.

"Take one," Koyani ordered Adèle. "Be careful. Do not engage without me if you can. I'll cover the rest with Squiggly Paddlefish."

"It's Sp—"

"Forget it, I'll never call you that." Koyani didn't hide her smirk this time, and Zita's eyebrows arched, as if she had just been challenged to a contest of wills. "Stay close. If you can't contribute, I need you to stay out of my way."

"I can be of use! I'm a Seeker." Zita straightened, and for a moment she seemed taller than her actual height. "I track down people."

"Can you sense her?" Adèle regretted the question as soon as Zita's smile fell off. She'd have said so already, if she could. Now the three of them were left to consider possible explanations for Claire's vanished signature, death foremost amongst them.

"I still think she's okay," Zita said in a subdued voice, "but

I don't know for how long. We should hurry."

Adèle nodded, turned, and stalked to the other set of doors. Behind her, Zita started to explain Seeking, only to be hushed by Koyani. Then they passed the doors in silence, and Adèle stayed alone with her increasing sense of dread and unfaltering determination. She couldn't fail. Claire had saved her life along with so many exocores. She had cracked Montrant Industries' secret on her own, and now she needed help to get through it alive. Adèle refused to let her down.

Investigating the secret labs quickly became a horror trek. Adèle strode down an aisle of tanks with growing nausea, her gaze resting on each frail body contained within in turn. She forced herself to stare at them, to examine the withered muscles and hollowed cheeks, to take good note of the sick and paler tones of their skin. They looked dead. Perhaps some already were, their life force drained through the tubes sticking out of their bodies. Somewhere, in another room, that magic became exocores. Adèle's mind reeled at the idea, and in the otherwise silent room her wheezy breath sounded like a death rattle to her. The edge of her vision darkened as her consciousness tried to slip away, shock and lack of proper oxygen pulling at it.

She crouched, shaking her head clear. Between the asthma and the fever, she was struggling to keep steady, and this entire expedition without help was turning into a mistake. No time for regrets now, however: Montrant Industries' goons could walk in at any moment. Once both Claire and the area were secure, they could figure out how to save those encased in glass and still within their reach.

Adèle pushed on, leaving the tanks' zone with relief. She paced down the corridor and past strange rooms with unknown purpose—no doubt Em would have a guess. One had two set of doors with only a small space between, while cold air slipped from another. She ignored them in favour of the third, from which white light spilled into the corridor. Revolver at the ready, Adèle pushed the door open and stepped in. Her heart dropped as she took in the room.

A large desk leaned against the wall on the right, filled with notes and textbooks, an exocore-powered lamp hanging above it. Further down the room, closer to the left wall, stood what could only be described as a test station. The white light came from a single prototype tank, and through its scratched glass Adèle immediately spotted Claire's characteristic purple hair, flattened over her head. Lifeless and heavy. Her gaze followed the tubes jutting from Claire's arms to the top of the tank, then out of it. She trailed them to a small console in front of the apparatus with levers and switches.

Adèle sprinted to it and stared at the machine.

One of these switches could save Claire. So many tubes stuck out from her wrists, and terrible images of witches and exocores spun around Adèle's mind. The distant disgust she'd always associated with transforming humans into physical energy coalesced into a solid horror, which lodged itself in her stomach and blocked her throat. Claire had grown pale, clammy, and a grimace twisted her mouth. Anger and fear built inside Adèle as she watched Claire hang limp, held to the tank through mechanical braces. Exhaustion lengthened her traits. Even her mask seemed half undone and tired—or perhaps that was Adèle's fever returning. It didn't matter. She wanted her brazen and cheeky thief back.

Adèle hesitated between levers, bent over the console, her hand flitting from one to the other. Which one stopped this machine? Would Claire be all right? She had to save her, but what if she hit the wrong button? Could it kill her instead? Sweat trickled down her forehead, a slow crawl across her skin marking every second wasted.

Adèle stepped back, gritting her teeth. Her gaze fell upon a power cable, running out of the control panel. Blood beating against her temples, half-convinced she'd make a huge mistake, she crouched and ripped it out in one strong yank—no time for doubts or regrets. The lights inside the tank turned off, the metal clasps released Claire's wrists and ankles, and the glass hissed as it unsealed. Claire slid from the tank, waking up with a surprised gasp, and Adèle straightened. Their gazes met, and she waved the torn cable with a slight smile.

Claire touched her mask, and relief rippled through her body once she was reassured it had held. When she took a tentative step forward, however, her strength faltered and she grabbed an open clasp to keep steady. Adèle rushed to her, one firm hand stopping further movement, before wrapping her other arm around Claire's waist to support her.

"Slow down," Adèle said. She reached for the needle still stuck in Claire's arm, pinched it, and slowly pulled it out. Claire tensed against her, making Adèle acutely aware of their proximity. She was warm and soft, and Adèle didn't withdraw after unplugging Claire. "There."

"You... you came for me." Claire was shaking, in voice and body. Adèle longed to squeeze her or run a hand through her hair and promise everything would be fine. Her cheeks flushed and she tilted Claire's chin up, towards her. She was alive, and *safe*, and beautiful. A dizziness washed over Adèle, her vision blurring at the edge as she forgot to take a few too-precious breaths. She wanted to hold Claire tight, to wrap herself around her, breathe in the warm sweet scent and touch her lips, so close to her — too close for comfort. If she just bent forward a little...

Adèle withdrew with an awkward cough, forcing her mind back to practical matters. Koyani was searching the labs nearby, and sooner or later, she'd be upon them. Adèle tried to ignore the disappointment that'd flashed through Claire's expression, or how she panted, clearly out of breath too.

"I might have to arrest you," Adèle said, hoping to break the charm. She knew the way her heart was hammering now, the flutters of "say the perfect thing and please *please* let her be as nervous as I am," the growing desire to build something magnificent and everlasting.

"Is that how you call it now?" Claire asked. "Or is the

charge 'seducing an officier de la loi'?"

Claire's mischievous grin lay a honeyed trap, and Adèle wanted nothing more than throw herself in it. *Exercise some control,* she scolded herself. They could figure this out later. "Claire, this is not the time. Others have come. If—"

Two fingers on her lips stopped her. "I know there are layers of complicated here. Heavy prohibitions and problems looming ahead—some you can't even see. I get it." The depth and seriousness of her tone stunned Adèle, but Claire's smile quickly reclaimed its rightful place. "But… if that is your desire, Madame l'Officier, you should kiss me before they crush us." She moved closer, impossible to ignore and impossible to resist. "Kiss me."

Claire waited, giving Adèle full control. *She trusts you.* Zita's words echoed in her mind. Her head spun, and the world zeroed in on the chubby woman in her arms, this thief she'd pursued relentlessly yet had somehow grown to trust and love, too. The last few days had been a blur, but Adèle's unexpected fondness was crystal clear, even through the fever. Claire held on to her, still weak from the tank, her eyes shining behind her mask.

Layers of complicated. Some in clothes, others inscribed in the law. When had that stopped either of them?

Adèle closed the gap, her lips meeting Claire's thin mouth, her hands pulling the soft body closer. Claire leaned into her, clutching Adèle for strength, fingers digging into her arms with unnerving desperation. How long had Claire desired her? Since Adèle had first pointed a revolver at her, standing in her doorway with nothing but a nightgown and her anger? Instant attraction baffled her, but thinking of Claire right now sped her heart rate. She pushed Claire against the tank, drawing a muffled cry out of her, and Adèle savoured the sound as much as she did the taste of Claire's lips. She grew more insistent, until a sharp cough behind her smothered her desire.

"Let me guess: this informant's code name is Ultimate Kisser." Koyani spoke in a controlled tone, leaving nothing of her thoughts filter through. "Or perhaps Exocore Thief would be better suited?"

Adèle froze. Pain constricted her chest. The sudden switch from dizzying elation to dismayed fear sent her reeling, too stunned to react. Claire pulled back an inch, her smile full of mischief, and she giggled. *Giggled*. Adèle's heart swelled at the sound, and she found herself grinning.

"Looks like one layer of complicated has arrived," Claire whispered.

"That's Capitaine Koyani." Adèle straightened and placed herself between Claire and her superior. The capitaine was leaning against the doorframe, her arms crossed, clearly unimpressed. Adèle knew she should explain—say something, try to defend herself—but how? This kiss was exactly what it seemed, and pretending otherwise would insult Koyani's intelligence.

"You know your orders, Officier Duclos. Respect them." Koyani snatched a pair of handcuffs from her belt and slung them across the room, to Adèle. "She is still a thief."

"No!" Adèle cried out. "Capitaine, this is where they make exocores out of people." Whatever qualms Adèle had about defending herself and her kiss had vanished. "All the tanks and tubes here, that's how they make them. She's been stealing conscious people, trapped and used against their will."

"One could argue that makes it kidnapping," Koyani said, and for a moment Adèle thought she'd detected amusement in her tone. Had the hint of a smile danced on her capitaine's lips, or was she imagining what she desperately wanted to see? Whichever the case, Koyani had no intention of letting Claire go. "We'll sort this out at the station. Between Mx. Kouna and her, I'm sure we can figure out our next step and what... deals can be struck."

Claire's hand on her forearm stopped Adèle from protesting further. "Argue all you want. What matters to me is that they're safe from Montrant Industries' greed. Some laws have to be broken." She picked up the handcuffs and offered them to Adèle, meeting her gaze. "Looks like you finally got me. Will you do the honours?"

Adèle didn't want to take those handcuffs, and she didn't understand why Claire encouraged her to. How could she remain so calm at going from plugged into a tank to being arrested? Did she trust her enough to think she'd be protected at the station? Adèle hoped that trust wouldn't be misplaced. She wouldn't leave Claire if she could help it, but it most likely wouldn't be her choice. Wouldn't it be wiser to escape now? Faced with Claire's steadfast nods, however, Adèle slowly cuffed Claire's hands.

"Why?" she whispered.

Claire shrugged, and smiled again. "We should leave, no? I don't have it in me to fight."

"All right." Adèle kept a hand on Claire, leading her out of the room and subtly supporting her. Something about Claire's cool bothered Adèle. It was forced, hiding a plan or some thoughts she couldn't guess at.

"You'll have to take off the mask, too," Koyani pointed out. "That particular game is over, I'm afraid."

Claire tensed against Adèle, yet she flicked her hair back with a wide smile, forcing the casual cheerfulness she so often projected. "May I keep it until we reach the station? I would be grateful if I could avoid immediate public identification. The mask exists for a reason. Who knows what Montrant will do once it knows me?"

"Favour granted."

It had taken a whole second for Koyani to decide, but in that brief moment, Adèle's mind had flooded with questions about who hid under that mask. Part of her was dying to see, as if a full face would explain Claire's familiarity—her shrugs, her quick laugh... even her smell. This girl scratched at her memories, both a mystery and a comforting presence, and her investigator inclination pushed her to try to fit the pieces of the puzzle together. Yet she feared finding the answer by herself: she would rather have Claire tell her. Zita claimed that she trusted Adèle, but she obviously needed time to determine how far that trust extended. Adèle could wait—forcing the issue would be breaking that faith—and relief washed away her hint of disappointment at Koyani's decision.

"Thanks," Claire chirped, and a wide grin spread across

her face. Adèle suspected her attitude was another mask, maintained for Koyani's sake. "So I'll be sharing a cell with my number one fan?" she asked. "It'll be nice to meet the one who put my name on the map."

"I don't know that I want the two of you in the same room," Koyani replied. "Unless you both plan to cooperate and tell us what you've learned. Mx. Kouna has not been amenable in that regard."

A slight frown marred Claire's carefully pleasant expression. "How long have you been battering the poor journalist?"

"A few hours," Adèle answered. "It's well into the afternoon now."

"So they… haven't been at their office today."

Claire bit her lower lip, her countenance deflated. Why was that a problem? Kouna had been clear about their lack of interaction with Claire, and Adèle had believed it. "No… Why?"

Claire's gaze flickered to Koyani. She didn't answer the question, and Adèle didn't push it. No point in drawing attention to it and causing Koyani to peg Claire as uncooperative from the start. The capitaine didn't notice the brief lull in the conversation. They'd crossed back into the area with rows of tanks now, and she was staring at them. Koyani had rarely seemed so small to Adèle; despite the captain's actual size, she often filled a room with her presence. Now she hunched over herself, her flesh hand clutching the prosthetic arm, her mouth twisted in a grim line.

"We left Kouna when Zi—your friend barged in to call a

rescue," Adèle continued. "I rushed here with her and Koyani while Élise gathered reinforcements. We expected guards to be crawling through these labs."

Claire stopped dead in her tracks, leaning against Adèle's subtle support as if her legs would give in. What colour their kiss had blown into her cheeks vanished again and her fingers dug into Adèle's arm.

"É-Élise is on her way with troops?"

"I wish I had asked for doctors," Koyani answered, her gaze still fixed on the tanks. "They will be needed if we want to care for everyone here." She reached out for one of the containers, as if to brush her hand over it, but retracted her arm before she touched it. "Let's move. They should arrive soon. I asked Paddlefish to wait for them, but I don't like leaving her alone."

"N-no." Claire stumbled back, releasing Adèle's forearm from her vice grip.

"What's wrong?" Dread crawled into Adèle's heart at Claire's reaction. Something had been off about Élise all day, and now this? Koyani snapped her attention fully back to the conversation as Claire's back hit a tank.

"It's Élise. She's—when I arrived yesterday... She was—" Claire flailed and placed a hand on the glass behind her. "This. This is her work. Montrant needed an executive arm and—"

Booted feet and shouts from the next room interrupted Claire, and Adèle's throat dried as she recognized Zita's voice, screaming at "wild brutes" to "let her go" and repeating her fake code name. The conviction she put into Spying Paddlefish amused

Adèle for a flickering second—just long enough for the consequences of reinforcements led by a hostile Élise to sink in.

"Capitaine, if she's with Montrant Industries…"

Raw anger shone in Koyani's dark eyes as she slowly turned towards the two large doors leading out. Her voice remained steady, a solid rock for Adèle to rest upon. "Then someone on my team had even bigger secrets than you. Congratulations. I'll deal with her."

The hesitant, almost diminished Koyani briefly witnessed earlier vanished. Adèle's capitaine strode towards the double door with determination, as if nothing could stop her. Wasn't she afraid of what they could do? Montrant Industries could never have built their network without legislative help. Who else worked with them, and how far up did it go? Adèle struggled to calm her thoughts and stay in control.

"Claire?" she asked. They might have other options— other exits to escape through while Koyani bought them time. It would mean leaving her alone, however, and Adèle hated the idea of abandoning her capitaine like that.

Claire lifted her chin and flung her hair back, her smile widening as her countenance returned. "I like this Koyani's style. Better to face death head-on than cornered in a hole. Let's go kick their butts so we can kiss again!"

Warmth bubbled from Adèle's chest, climbing into her throat and erupting into an elated, slightly hysteric laughter. Her fever was still running high, sending shivers down her spine. Two days ago, one of Montrant Industries' goons had put a bullet through her, and now she would walk straight at several soldiers ready to obey their orders. It was wild, in a sense—wild and dangerous—but with Claire by her side, she couldn't find it in her to worry.

"With great pleasure," she replied, and followed Koyani through the room.

-23-

JE CROIS EN TOI

POLICE OFFICERS FORMED A CRESCENT AT THE ELEVATOR end of the labs, several of them splitting from the group to go down the rows of benches and better surround them. Two of them stayed near the door, fingers clamped around Zita's arms. Koyani scowled at them, but her attention focused on Élise, posing at the front and centre of her scattered troops. "The area is secure. Everyone can stand down."

Her commanding tone left no doubt about the nature of her words, but no one obeyed the order. Several glanced at Élise instead, and Adèle's blood boiled. She shifted closer to Claire, her arm lifting protectively over her. It wouldn't do much against that many soldiers, but she couldn't help it. She regretted even coming. What a shitty rescue this turned out to be.

"I'm afraid you have been relieved of your command, capitaine," Élise said.

Koyani barked a laugh. "Have I?" She started forward, one confident stride after another, her gaze fixed on Élise. Soldiers redirected their firearms towards her, and their stance tensed with every step Koyani took between the rows of science benches. "You are making a big mistake, Lieutenant Jefferson. Do you think you can lead my unit with a snap of your fingers? You have broken my trust, and I am relieving you from your position. Everyone else still answers to me."

Fury simmered under her cool tone, and when Koyani stopped less than a metre away from Élise, the other woman moved back. Adèle knew she'd have done the same, and every officer around the room shifted away, as if they desperately wished to be elsewhere. Koyani's brutal honesty and willingness to put investigations over hierarchy had led the mairesse to grant her a special investigative unit, and it seemed the gathered police officers knew not to stand in her way. When she thrust her wrists forward in a mock "arrest me" gesture, several of them flinched. "What is the charge? Is there even one?"

"Not for you." Élise didn't bother to hide her displeasure. She must have asked for leverage against Koyani beyond destitution from her position. Did her influence stop there, or would it come later, when she'd had more time to contact help?

Koyani snorted in derision. Her voice dropped to a whisper, yet Adèle had no doubts everyone in the room could hear her. "What about you? Looking forward to answering for all the people you sucked into gems?"

Élise laughed, but her control and mirth felt forced. She was afraid of what Koyani could do—of how far down the capitaine could drag her by speaking up, even if Élise won. Adèle squared her shoulders, pride filling her at the certainty Élise

271

wouldn't escape unscathed... unless she had them shot right now. Would the guards obey such an order? Judging by Koyani's confident walk to Élise, the capitaine didn't believe it.

A quick pull on Adèle's sleeve distracted her from the exchange between her two colleagues, and she turned to meet Claire's deep brown eyes.

"Will you be all right?" she asked.

Adèle choked down her surprise. Wasn't the risk higher for Claire? "Me? What about you?"

"I'm not the one running a fever and struggling to breathe," she pointed out. "I will be fine. Do you trust me?"

She dropped the question casually, with a heartwarming grin and excitement in her eyes, yet tension laced every single word in it. Do you trust me? Adèle wanted to answer "I kissed you, of course I do" but not everyone had such clear-cut standards, and the question had legitimate roots. It had taken everything for Adèle to stop seeing Claire as a thief and believe she had rightful motives. No wonder Claire desired reassurance. Adèle smiled at her and squeezed her forearm. "I have the most complete faith in you."

"Good. I... I need you to listen and to... try to understand."

Guards started to pivot towards them. Adèle's heart hammered against her chest as Claire stepped back and met her eyes. A second passed in silence, the longest in Adèle's life. She could sense Claire gathering her courage, turning careful words over her normally loose tongue. Whatever she meant to say, Adèle's stomach twisted in anticipation.

"I also..." She stopped, looked long and hard at Adèle.

"Moi aussi, je crois en toi."

I believe in you. Adèle frowned—didn't she already know that? Then her mind heard the slightly off way Claire had pronounced it, linking her words with an audible "s", transforming a simple profession of faith into a beloved bakery name: *Le Croissant-toi*.

I… Croissant-toi.

Adèle didn't need the "am" in the sentence to understand its meaning loud and clear. Suddenly Claire's rich and warm scent clicked as that of fresh bread, along with the striking familiarity of her demeanour—her shrugs and quieter smiles and occasional laughs. Even her worry over Adèle when in dire straits herself—all of it, really. Everything Claire was and did reminded her of Claude, with a hint of daring and playfulness he might keep under wraps at work.

In the brief moment Adèle needed to absorb the connection, Claire snapped her handcuffs open. She grabbed a stunned Adèle by the shoulders, called "à la prochaine!" and spun around, flinging the surprised woman full force towards Koyani and Élise. Adèle yelped as she flew into the others, her head ringing from the impact, the gunshots that followed, and, more than anything else, Claire's most important words.

Adèle, Koyani, and Élise landed in a heap on the ground, and Élise shoved Adèle aside and sprang to her feet, firearm at the ready. Koyani snatched her lieutenant's ankle and yanked her back down, just in time for Claire to sprint past them, a streak of purple hair flying above the three women. Zita shouted wild encouragement above the din of a first salvo of gunshots, cheering her friend on. Adèle started to push herself up, but Koyani's metallic hand forced her down. Bullets whizzed through the air above them, and Adèle belatedly realized she might have gotten shot again if not for her capitaine. Was that why she'd yanked Élise down, or did Koyani aim to protect Claire?

Adèle tried to catch a glimpse of Claire, but between the officers converging on the escaping thief and the workbenches, Adèle couldn't spot her. She flinched with every gunshot, half-convinced a cry of pain would follow, yet the chaos endured. Élise had found her feet and shouted orders, and Adèle's heart sang with the palpable frustration in her tone. Even as rough hands grabbed her and Koyani, pulling them to their feet, she couldn't help grinning. Claire had walked free from Montrant Industries. She had never given up her pursuit before, and Adèle knew she wouldn't do so now, either.

No matter what happened to them, Adèle had the utmost faith Claire would see this through.

Super speed turned out insufficient against a hail of bullets. Pain flared through Claire as she sprinted across the room, bent over so the lab benches would catch most of the shots. Two grazed her anyway—one along her right arm, and another past her thigh. Every step sapped her strength, but she kept pushing her exhausted body, drawing upon her magic to finish her escape.

Fatigue and pain blurred the edge of her vision as she ran past the stunned bundle of limbs she'd turned Adèle, Koyani, and Élise into. She'd have to thank the capitaine for clearing her path. Her own mind buzzed with a strange elation—the adrenaline from opening up to Adèle and dodging literal bullets all at once, her heart hammering against her chest, threatening to burst. Every tink of a bullet landing into the floor at her feet or the benches around warned her of potential brutal death. Claire kept moving, praying the saints would protect her. By the time she reached the elevator, it was already a miracle she'd only been grazed twice. She sprang up, breaking fists first through the panel giving access to the cabin's roof. Her knuckles would hurt for years, but she had no choice. Either she gritted her teeth and climbed despite the pain, or she'd be shot down mercilessly. As Claire grabbed the elevator's cable, she heard a friendly voice cheer her on.

"You show 'em!" Zita called, and though she lifted Claire's spirits, it came with a pang of guilt.

None of the others would escape, and who knew what Élise would do? Would she force Zita to hunt Claire down, the way Seekers had been used after the Meltdown? Or would Zita, Adèle, and Koyani all be filed under "knows too much" and executed as soon as possible? Claire fought against her rising nausea and started pulling herself up. Every swing of the cable—every inch climbed—sent waves of white-hot agony through her arm, and her right sleeve was soaked with blood, but she pushed on, forcing magic into her muscles. Claire remembered how quick the fall had been and wept inside at how endless the way up seemed. By the time she reached ground level and ripped the grate open, she was drenched in sweat and wracked with pain. Shouts echoed from below, and she leaped to safety just as bullets flew past her.

Two officers and the lounge guard scrambled to attention. The instant she noticed their firearms had remained in their holsters, Claire burst into action, speeding right between them and leaving their surprised cries far behind.

Sunlight hit her in full face, and she hissed at the sweltering day as if it was the tank's hot white lamp. A month ago, she would have been in her bakery, greeting late customers hoping for leftover bread, slowly cleaning the place after a busy day. Instead, she was fleeing law enforcement in broad daylight, bleeding and exhausted, while her best friend and her maybe-something-special stayed trapped behind.

Claire dove into an alleyway, passing under rows of bright white-and-yellow flags, and released her magic. She staggered for a moment, surprised at how heavy her limbs felt again, weighed down by exertion. She considered hiding there, in a corner, and praying no one would find her while she recovered, but the risk was too high. She forced herself into a brisk pace, heading north and more or less towards the Quartier des Bouleaux, but despite the pursuit which would soon follow, her mind drifted away, to Adèle and their brief, intense encounter after Claire'd woken up in the tank.

She hadn't expected Zita's rescue to involve Adèle. She'd expected it to involve a kiss even less.

It had felt so good to lean into Adèle—to just let go and

allow protective arms to hold her up, even if only for a few seconds. Then Adèle had lifted her chin, and they had been so close, and exhaustion had washed away what inhibitions she had left.

She had wanted a kiss—just a kiss, this whole horrible and complicated world be damned—and Adèle had blessed her with it.

The world, of course, did not like being damned.

She should have known better than to curse, even in her head. Koyani had interrupted, reinforcements had arrived, and Claire had been forced to make the most terrifying snap decision of her life: to drop the last mask, or to escape with her secret.

It would have been easy to say nothing. She could have broken her handcuffs and dashed away without a word about the bakery, trusting Adèle to find her again, or running across the city to the Quartier des Mélèzes and Em's manor. It would have been the sensible thing to do—one that gave them both time to prepare, absorb, and discuss. Claire had never been patient, though, and dozens of guns pointed your way added a sense of urgency. What if she never had another opportunity? What if Adèle died, or learned elsewhere?

No. Claire had wanted Adèle to know, and she had wanted to tell her. She had held back before in case Adèle sought to arrest her and hinder her chance to find Livia, but after that kiss? That fear had vanished. Even now, as she darted between houses, pain in her arm and thigh flaring from gunshot wounds, a strange elation filled her. Je crois en toi wasn't a scared admittance: it was a profession of faith. Adèle respected her—she believed in her. What stronger foundations could Claire ask for?

If they could both make it out alive, it would be okay. They could kiss again, with significantly fewer layers of complicated. And maybe, just maybe, they could work out a relationship that fit Claire.

Shrill police whistles shrieked, too close for comfort, snapping Claire back to the present. She needed to ditch pursuit, and fast. She kept ahead through bursts of magic, ducking into alleyways or clambering upon rooftops when the vélocycles got too near. More than once, she thought she'd left them far behind and relaxed, only to be proven wrong by the renewed scream of whistles. The sound would haunt her dreams for weeks to come, sending her mind in a frenzy. Long minutes turned into an hour, and her exhaustion grew as the number of pursuers diminished.

By the time Claire was truly clear of police, the Centre de Recherche was far away and she had entered the Quartier des Sorbiers—nowhere close to home. At least the law wouldn't know where to look for her, but the run had completely, utterly drained her. She had burned all her magic, leaving nothing behind but an empty buzz between her ears and the desire to sleep an entire week. Claire headed deeper into her alleyway and sank against a wall. The Quartier des Sorbiers was rife with snaking narrow streets that climbed up its hill, houses lining against each other and creating unexpected pathways through the city. This particular alley had clotheslines crisscrossing above, and the clothes and buildings blessed Claire with shade and privacy. She removed her mask, used it to wipe her sweaty face, then covered her hair with it. Nothing she would do could conceal her properly—not with her bloodied sleeve, snapped handcuffs, and black cotton outfit—but if Claire had to trek all the way back to the bakery, she would do her best not to draw notice.

She dragged her feet down the twisting streets of the Quartier des Sorbiers, striking north first to avoid coming anywhere near the Pont des Lumières. She'd grown light-headed from blood loss, and the longer she lumbered through the city, a hot sun beating down on her, the harder it became to continue. Part of her wanted to collapse in the shade and let the world roll on without her.

She needed her bakery, her safe place. Nothing else would soothe her ragged nerves. The overwhelming last days had emptied any reserves Claire had left. She had dodged death twice since dashing into the warehouse, saved Adèle and countless others, pierced the until-now ghost network, and spent an entire night strapped in one of those horrible tanks. Her hands still tingled from the warehouse burns, and the lack of proper rest, climb up an elevator's cable, and new gun wounds left her utterly battered. She clung to what she had accomplished—to her kiss with Adèle and the certainty of her support, to Clémence's dangerous change of heart and the papers making their way to Nsia Kouna, to her desperate escape and the fact she was still out there, alive and free. More than anything, however, she clung to her new, essential knowledge:

In a day's time, the Pont des Lumières' grand opening would gather the country's finest people, including Gouverneure Lacroix, the mind behind this project. What had started as a few stolen exocores and a lot of questions had turned into a nightmare, but it would be over soon. Claire couldn't wait to crash their party, save her sister, and expose this industry once and for all.

And then, perhaps, she could return to the blessed routine of chatty customers and delicious croissants.

Two groups of policemen had gone into the elevator and travelled back to the Centre de Recherche since Claire had punched a hole through the ceiling and escaped. Élise was watching the procession with controlled cool, but her pinched lips and occasional sigh betrayed her displeasure. As the third team started its noisy way up, she turned towards Adèle and Koyani.

"Impressive powers." Her appraising tone sent a shiver down Adèle's spine. She sounded like a lieutenant Adèle'd once seen testing firearms, and whose appreciation of their power had completely disregarded the lives they could take. Élise spoke of Claire as a tool, not a human being. The lieutenant snatched her handcuffs and smiled at Adèle. "Too bad you can't do the same, is it? What did she tell you?"

Warmth spread through Adèle. Claire had removed the last mask, trusting Adèle with the fullness of her complexity. She was still reeling from the shock, but the more this reality settled in Adèle's mind, the more she appreciated Claire's faith in her. She wasn't certain she had deserved it, and she certainly wouldn't betray it now. She smirked. "'Enjoy the spin.' Like the smartass she is."

Élise tsked, unconvinced by the lie, and strode to Adèle. "I'll get that info out of you." She grabbed Adèle's wrists and snapped the cuffs on them. "You'll find prison way worse than the dump in which you used to archive."

Adèle wished her mind would devise a sharp reply, but the cold metal against her skin stole her words. She shifted towards Zita, who'd acquired her own pair of handcuffs. The small witch forced a grin to her lips. "You'll have better company, though! We'll have great fun."

Adèle chuckled, then the elevator returned. They pushed Zita, Adèle, and Koyani into it, and Élise followed, her hand hovering near her firearm. No one said a word as they shoved the rusted gates closed and the elevator clink-clanked up. Koyani stared straight ahead, stiff and tense. She might not have any charges to her name, but she was in as much trouble as her and Zita. Not to mention how much Élise's betrayal must hurt. Koyani had made one thing crystal upon Adèle's arrival: her unit was family. They were a team, relied on each other, trusted each other. Except, clearly, Élise.

And her, too. She'd hidden a lot, uncertain of her grounds, of whether she counted as one of theirs. How did one pass such a test? Shame burned Adèle's cheeks as she lowered her head, and her gaze fell on fresh drops of blood. Claire's, and more than Adèle cared to see. Her stomach twisted; she hoped the injury wasn't too deep. Her intense worry washed away her brief guilt. She hadn't let Koyani down: she'd juggled with the trust and secrets of more than one person, and done her best.

The elevator winced to a stop, and Élise led them out, through the lobby, and into the harsh sunlight. A crowd was waiting outside, the heat bearing down on them, speculation running wild. Adèle squared her shoulders and slid closer to Zita. These handcuffs proved they'd dug where they had to, and she met every stranger's gaze without flinching.

Until she encountered Emmanuelle's worried, hazelnut eyes. Adèle started—she'd forgotten her sister worked just a few floors above. She must have seen the police and come rushing down with other colleagues.

"Adèle! What's happening?" Em tried to push forward, but officers blocked her path. She glared at them, attempting to impose despite her welcoming traits. "That's my sister you're arresting, you doof!"

Zita snickered, and Adèle found the strength to smile. She sobered up when she noticed Élise's attention on them, though. Better not to have it linger there. "It's fine, Em. These are just a sign I'm doing my job right. Don't get into trouble over it."

At first it looked like Emmanuelle would protest, but their gaze met once more and Adèle's sister caught on. She had refugees hiding in her manor, and, if Élise decided she wanted it searched top to bottom, she could likely get the required authorizations. Em shook her head. "We used to think you were the calm one, following rules and staying safe."

"I like that illusion. Don't tell mom how wrong she was." Adèle winked, her way of saying goodbye. With everything that was happening, she had no idea how long it'd be before she could talk with Em again. She forced herself to turn away, and a heavy weight settled in her stomach the moment she lost eye contact.

Before them stood the jail carriage, its doors reinforced with metal, its tiny windows covered by bars. The horses at the front snorted, perhaps nervous in the thick crowd. Every stern-faced guard around was watching the civilians, tense. Had Claire's magic-powered escape made them wary of witches assaulting them? Resentment still ran high, and, while everyone acted like most witches had left Val-de-mer, they all had to realize many had simply hidden.

As they arrived at the carriage, Koyani helped Zita up the high step and inside, lifting the other small woman's elbow to subtly push her up and make the climb seem natural despite Zita's handcuffs. Before the capitaine could follow, Élise grabbed her forearm.

"You're not under arrest. You don't have to join them." It sounded like a plea. Élise gestured to the bench near the horses, where the driver waited. "Sit in the front with me. I'm sure we can arrange something."

Koyani tilted her head to the side, and for a brief moment she seemed to consider it. A flush rushed into Adèle's face, bitterness coiling at the bottom of her stomach, but she pushed her doubts away. Koyani wouldn't, not after what she'd seen below the labs. The blank horror on her expression as she'd reached for a tank still remained with Adèle.

Koyani jumped on the step, allowing her to look down on

Élise despite her short stature. "Let's not pretend I'm safe." Her voice carried across the crowd, loud and clear. "I belong with my team—with those unravelling your inhuman industry. If you think you can transform people into exocores without anyone noticing, you've got another thing coming."

Several gasps rose from the crowd, Adèle's among them. Élise's face hardened into a stone mask. "You're right. You do belong in there."

Koyani laughed, then slipped into the carriage. Adèle couldn't believe her capitaine had stated it so loud and clear. Wasn't that playing into their hands? If no one found the labs again, they would have no proof to back their claims! Perhaps they'd reached a point where it no longer mattered, and any hindrance was a good one. The more people knew, the harder it would become to smother this story. And between Koyani's declaration and Mx. Kouna's article, many would have heard now, and some might believe it, or want it investigated. And hadn't the mairesse herself appointed Koyani to head this unique team? The Spinster might listen. Adèle clung to that certitude as she followed Koyani into the carriage and settled next to her capitaine. Others would take up the lead, their own unit and Claire first among them. She had to believe in it. After all, neither Montrant Industries nor Élise had any reasons to let Koyani, Zita, and her reach headquarters alive.

-24-

LE TOUR DE CALÈCHE

ADÈLE'S DREAD HAD ONLY GROWN SINCE THE CARRIAGE'D set off, and every time she glanced through the windows' bars at the sun-baked streets, she doubted that she'd one day be free to roam them again. The handcuffs weighed on her wrists, and Adèle found herself with plenty of time to review her mistakes—every time she'd brought up Montrant to Élise, only to be rebuffed, and every hint Kouna had given that they didn't trust her. She'd missed the clues right in front of her, too caught up in her desire to arrest Claire. How upside-down the truth turned out to be. Adèle leaned forward with a groan, putting her head in her hands.

"It'll be fine," Koyani said with exemplar calm.

How could it? Adèle stayed still, ignoring her boss's reassurance. So far, the carriage continued to travel through large avenues, even taking the Tronc, but Adèle expected it to veer into lesser streets any time now. And once they were out of sight…

"They'll kill us before we reach headquarters," Adèle countered. "You know that."

"What?" Zita jolted up, eyes wide. "They wouldn't. They

can't! How would they explain that?"

"Accidents," Koyani said. "They could scapegoat one of the guards and pretend he lost it because we sympathize with witches. They've all seen Claire escape, and the Lark Soul Tree hasn't recovered from its witch icing a week ago. It'll be easy to stoke fear again if they need it."

Adèle hunched her shoulders further. How could Koyani declare it'd be fine then calmly explain how it wasn't? "At least she's out there. She'll never let this slide. They can't bury the truth while Claire is free."

"I must say, if I had expected her to break these, I would have thrown witch cuffs your way. I'm glad I hadn't reviewed your case properly."

Adèle bit her lower lip. Earlier it hadn't crossed her mind that Claire could snap off the handcuffs. Perhaps she'd discarded the idea because she'd barely been standing, or her fever had limited Adèle's ability to think it through, but she suspected Claire had known she could escape any time. She'd only panicked when she'd learned about reinforcements.

"I... I admit I forgot. She surprised me, too."

"You forgot and you put them on?" Zita glared at her from across the carriage, trying to convey the full extent of her disappointment. Before Adèle could point out Claire had given permission, she went on. "She must have felt *awful*."

The corners of Koyani's mouth turned up, and she leaned back. "Yeah. Who has the gall to kiss someone and arrest them an instant later?"

"Capitaine!" Adèle's cheeks burned—in shame, but also from the vivid memory, its warmth, and the myriad of possibilities it brought. Zita's loud squeal didn't help the situation any.

"You kissed! How dare you not tell me sooner?" She threw her arms up in exaggerated indignation, her cuffs clinging. "That should be priority information to share!"

"I'm sorry," Adèle protested. "Élise kind of crashed our party and arrested everyone!"

"Or you tried to hide your major unprofessional crush on the woman you were supposed to jail." Koyani's level tone made it impossible to guess if she was serious or teasing. Both, perhaps. Then again, maybe not.

"I want to hear everything," Zita declared. "Is it a one-time kiss, or are you a thing now? How much tongue? Did she remove her mask? Do you know—" She stopped short, and left her last question hanging. Adèle knew exactly what she'd meant to ask.

She struggled for an answer, though, stammering several beginnings, her words failing long before she could utter them. The more sexual-oriented question made her awfully uneasy, while the one pertaining to any future relationship sent her mind reeling with hopes and fears. How could she even start to untangle the whirlwind of feelings Claire brought forward? It was complicated, more so than Adèle had thought. Claire had spoken of layers, and Adèle now realized she'd seen only the one related to their positions as officer and thief. Now she needed to reconcile her two simultaneous crushes and to consider Claire's aromanticism, too. She did want a "thing," though, whatever that would mean for them.

"She had her mask," she said at last, clinging to that fact and avoiding the rest of the questions, unable to form the proper words to answer or to get the past the tightness in her throat.

The carriage lurched into a turn, sparing her the struggle. Adèle leaned to look through the bars. They'd left the main avenue to slip into a side street, down a gentle slope. Far ahead, above the rooftops, the massive Pont des Lumières loomed over the city.

"This is it." Adèle slumped into the cold seat. She did not add "we're all going to die," but the thought remained at the forefront of her mind, and when she tried to take a deep breath to steady herself, she only got a long, pitiful wheeze. The world around her seemed to grow dimmer and farther, and she focused on her companions to stay grounded.

Zita wrung her fingers, and the little ringing of her handcuffs' chain was the only sound breaking their subsequent silence. After several minutes of it, Koyani put a hand on hers to stop it. Though serious, she showed no sign of fear. Her composure impressed Adèle.

"Stay calm. A moment of clarity could save our lives. Zita, keep your senses open. Seek for a witch with sleep powers."

"Sleep…?"

Koyani nodded, and the heavy silence enveloped them once more. Adèle stared at her capitaine. What did she know that they didn't? Did she expect help? "Capitaine?"

"I trust my team above all else," Koyani answered. "I trust them with our investigations, and I trust them with my life."

The chain on the carriage's door rattled and the lock turned, interrupting Koyani. The carriage hadn't stopped yet, but its door swung outward and Élise stood in the opening. She held herself to the frame with one hand, pointing her gun at Koyani with the other. The capitaine had tensed, as if ready to bolt, and she unwound back into her seat under the threat.

"You should have kept your mouth shut," Élise told Koyani. "We could've made a deal. Montrant has several allies in the prosthetic industries and actively participates in the development of new models, you know. This could have been good for you."

Koyani scowled, and her prosthetic arm moved an inch closer to her body. "You thought I'd compromise for the sake of a better arm?"

Élise's eyebrows shot up at Koyani's obvious disgust. "I don't see how that's a stretch. You don't seem bothered by your current one being exocore-powered. Surely you've begun to understand what my gift meant when you walked between those tanks."

"I did." Koyani's voice hadn't lost a hint of its strength, but her gaze flickered to Zita, who had recoiled deeper into her seat. It felt like a silent apology. "I also know better than to try to remove my arm without medical assistance, and I worry doing so could not only harm me, but the witch imprisoned within. So I'm keeping it until I have a solution, thank you for your concern."

The sarcasm dripping from Koyani's voice pierced through Adèle's gloom. She snorted, not even bothering to hide how uplifting her capitaine's unrelenting anger was. Élise took it all in strides, her fake smile not moving an inch. "Very well," she said. "I came to offer you one last chance to share Claire's identity and location."

Of course. This morning Adèle would've had no idea, but now she did. The secret would stay locked inside, far from Élise's dangerous hands. A glance at Zita's determined frown told her Claire's friend also knew the truth and could be counted on not to reveal it. Koyani scoffed and shook her head. Resilient silence stretched between them, broken only by the crunch of wheels on uneven gravel roads. They'd reached areas so downtrodden they weren't fit for wheelchairs or vélocycles.

"Let me put it this way: accidents happen quickly, and you never know who might survive them. We're more likely to assist to whoever is of use to us."

Another silence. None of them were listening. Élise clacked her tongue.

"The worst thing about these accidents is how deep we have to investigate families, relatives, and other loved ones. To provide for them, of course. I understand Adèle's sister has already endured the difficult trials of grief. We wouldn't want her to struggle through it alone a second time."

Cold fear swept through Adèle and her ears rang at the implied threat. "Leave my sister out of this." Ironic, really. Emmanuelle had leaped into it without hesitation. But if Élise began investigating her, she might find everyone else now living under her large roof.

"Make me. Shouldn't this be an easy choice for you?" By the tone, Élise knew it wasn't. She pushed on anyway. "Your star sister, the brightest engineer Val-de-mer has had in years, or the thief who shattered your home safety? Think about how much you resented her, that first day."

Adèle clenched her teeth so hard her jaws hurt. She could not give in, even doubting Claire would want to protect herself if it meant the lives of everyone trapped in the warehouse. She'd entrusted Adèle with her location out of faith, and Adèle refused to betray her. She couldn't do that. But Em was a brilliant woman, and well aware of the risks she'd taken. She'd thwart attempts to ruin her. Adèle had to believe that. She stared right back at Élise, determined not to break. Zita didn't have her fortitude, however. Whether she'd reached the same conclusion as Adèle regarding what Claire would wish, or was affected by Élise's layering of threats, she shifted in her seat and started tapping her foot. Élise's attention turned to her.

"I'll find her eventually. I always do. The only question is who pays for it on my way there. Do you have family, informant? Most people have loved ones they want to protect."

Zita's head snapped up and Adèle had no trouble perceiving the horror spreading through her expression. In that regards, Zita was the exact opposite of Koyani: she could be read like an open book. "That's how you forced—that's horrible. You can't..."

"I can, I have, and I will again." Élise shrugged, as if none of her previous actions mattered. "Starting with Emmanuelle

Duclos, but leaving no one alone."

Zita flinched. "Claire is… she owns—"

"Paddlefish, enough." Koyani's commanding voice cut her off. More softly, she added, "It's okay. You can do this. Hold it in. Élise's word isn't worth shit. Just remember what I asked earlier and ignore her."

Zita bit her lower lip. Her gaze shifted from Koyani to Adèle, seeking permission. Asking silently if she could let the threat on Emmanuelle go unanswered.

"You don't have to talk," Adèle said. The words burned her tongue and heart, but she allowed them out nonetheless. She had to trust her sister to protect herself.

Élise stared at each of them in turn, her discontent obvious. Her gaze lingered longer on Koyani, frustration shining in her blue eyes, along with… envy? She must realize she could never exercise the same pull as their capitaine, even with an official sanction from the higher ups.

"Too bad," Élise declared. She gripped the door, ready to slam it shut.

Zita's head perked up. A slight movement—eyes widening, lips parting in surprise—and Koyani picked up on it. The moment Élise's position shifted the revolver away from her, she sprung into action, leaping from her seat.

The gunshot rang loudly in the carriage's cramped space, and their ride rocked hard before Adèle could get a sense of what was happening. There had been a metallic ring and a flash of red— the bullet hitting Koyani—then the capitaine crashed outside with

Élise, landing heavily in the gravel. Adèle leaped up, her heart pounding.

"The sleep witch!" Zita called as an explanation, scrambling up as Adèle jumped out.

A policeman almost fell on top of her, sliding off the top of the carriage. Knocked out? Adèle raised both cuffed hands over her right shoulder and motioned for Zita to stay inside as she tried to get her bearings. Quick orders from police officers preceded a salvo of shots—not as many as there should have been, considering their escort. A brief scan of the area revealed several police officers had slumped to the ground, snoozing. Two of those left promptly set each other back-to-back, moving towards cover. They managed three steps before they stumbled and fell, asleep like the others.

"And two more down!"

Marcel's high-pitched voice was the sweetest thing she had heard in... well, an hour at most. Claire's "kiss me" might forever hold that title, even though the continuous banter of Koyani's team was its own blessing.

"There's no point in a competition with you," Inha called back. "You don't even need to aim!"

Marcel tsked. "Don't be a sore loser, friend."

With a tired smile, Adèle refocused her attention on Élise and Koyani, still struggling on the ground. The capitaine was losing, stuck under the other woman, unable to wriggle free. A red stain spread across her shoulder above the prosthetic, growing as they fought. Élise punched her hard, twice, unleashing some pent-up frustration. Adèle dashed in before she could land a third, barrelling into Élise. Pain flared back to life in Adèle's stomach as they hit the dirt, and Élise dug an elbow right into her gunshot wound. Adèle's vision blanked at the sudden agony. She felt the scream rip out of her mouth but never heard it under the ringing of her ears. When her sight returned, she found herself once more staring at the barrel of a gun. Élise wasn't looking at her, however, but at Koyani, half-standing and obviously about to spring back into the fight.

"One move and your beloved recruit is dead," Élise threatened.

Well. Calisse. The last thing Adèle had wanted was to become the hostage. She gritted her teeth and turned her head, ignoring the increase of ringing pain that created. Gunshots no longer echoed around the nearby building, signalling the end of the battle. Yuri and Inha stepped around the carriage, and their respective pride transformed into uneasy shock when they witnessed the scene. Zita scrambled to Koyani's side, equally horrified.

Only Marcel didn't seem fazed. He exhaled a dramatic sigh and placed fingers on his cheek. "Élise, darling. That's not going to get you anywhere."

"To Hell, maybe," Inha said.

Élise snorted. Adèle's stomach squeezed and she prayed to Val-de-mer's nine saints and God above them. Air barely made it through the mucus in her throat, but she wanted to keep breathing, damnit.

"This is your last chance," Marcel warned.

"Until what?" She scoffed again. "None of you are in a position to threaten me unless you want Adèle to die. I don't know how you found us, but this is over. This case is closed, this unit will be dismantled, and no one will ever... hear of..." A slight frown marred her delicate features, and she crumpled without finishing her sentence, landing on Adèle's right.

"Until that," Marcel answered.

Zita whooped and rushed to Koyani, insisting on supporting her. The stain on her shoulders continued to expand but Koyani ignored it. "Good job, Marcel."

He saluted with a flourish while Adèle pushed herself back into a sitting position. When Inha's strong arms helped her up, Adèle leaned against the other woman without complaint. Her head spun from pain, exhaustion, and lack of oxygen, and she was glad for a colleague's support. "So... Marcel's a witch." It sounded like an obvious conclusion, but right now Adèle needed to voice things to make them tangible.

"Aah, yes, I do believe my little secret is out," he said. "One could say the capitaine and myself have been sleeping on this one for years."

Collective groans followed his declaration, but Adèle only grinned. She'd been convinced she'd never hear another of Marcel's bad puns again, and she couldn't resent this particular one. Marcel's power also reassured her about the group's stance regarding exocores and witches. "How did you know to rescue us?"

"Two things," Inha said.

"Nsia Kouna tipped me off, for a start." Yuri turned to their capitaine. "I returned to them and confirmed your suspicions about Élise's interrogation. She focused on the warehouse and Claire, disregarding orders to get Nsia Kouna to cooperate on Montrant Industries. Not that successfully doing the latter was easy. They rightfully didn't trust Élise and extended that attitude to me and most of the team. I couldn't draw anything out of them, except that yes, Montrant Industries was up to no good."

"We found a package at their private house, however," Marcel said. "A paper trail of Montrant's involvement in exocores. Many tiny elements spread over the years. And the last ones…"

"They had our friend's name on it," Inha completed. "Sometimes in covert words, sometimes her handwriting. Nothing direct, but she's so close to us—"

Where Marcel's voice had trailed off, Inha's cut off, the wound still fresh. She glared at the unconscious girl at her feet, anger and anguish mixing in her expression. Marcel ran uneasy fingers through his hair, so pale he looked nauseated. They had all worked with Élise for years and finding out she'd betrayed them had to be difficult. Yuri crossed his arms, and when he spoke, his tone was steadier than his two colleagues'.

"While one could say we've never understood Élise at all, we do know her. We collaborated for years. We barely debated whether they were authentic papers. We've watched her unravel cases, follow leads, tease out truths and answers from complex crimes. We've learned how she thinks, where she'd hide clues, how her mind functions. These papers… they rang true, somehow. I showed part of them to Nsia Kouna, and they opened up. They've been tracking the money to magistrates and political figures, all the way up to Gouverneure Lacroix. This is big, and the purpose her reinforcements would serve became obvious. We moved out."

Koyani smiled. "As efficient as ever. We have our work cut out for us. Where is Mx. Kouna?"

Yuri rolled his eyes. "Probably listening in from behind the carriage, thinking they're subtle."

"Well, now. I'm certain no one except you noticed!" came the answer, and Adèle had to repress a laugh. She hadn't, but with the messy state she was in, she shouldn't count. Nsia Kouna strode around the jail carriage, notebook and pen in hand. "I'm sure you will excuse my nosiness, considering how it has served you thus far."

"Forgiven," Koyani said. "We'll have some choice scoops for you, but I'd like to discuss when and how you publish them. I don't want Montrant catching on about how far we've dug sooner than necessary. It could stop us from reaching the top of this chain."

"I understand. Capitaine Koyani, I know what these exocores are. I value hundreds of lives over a good scoop, believe me."

"We're bound to get along, then!" Koyani replied with forced cheerfulness. "First, we need somewhere to settle down and work from. We'll build our case out of sight and present it to the mairesse once we're solid—you didn't have any dirt on her, did you?"

Kouna shook their head. "You can never be sure, but nothing leads me to believe the Spinster is involved."

"Good. I trust her. She forced the creation of my unit, and I think that means she wants people to clean up corrupted messes when they find them." Koyani rubbed her face, as if trying to push away the exhaustion slowly weighing down on her. How much did her shoulder hurt? "I suspect they'll break the portal magic leading to the labs, so we might never have that as proof, but I'm certain we can dig up more."

Silence stretched between the team as their resolve formed. Several of them glanced at Élise, sleeping in the middle of their circle, and after a moment, Inha searched her for the handcuff keys. They stood still as she freed Koyani, Zita, and Adèle. Despite the shade cast by the carriage and the surrounding buildings, the street was hot and stuffy, and Adèle could feel her skull buzzing. "Capitaine, the docteure who cared for my bullet wound could heal yours, too. My sister has many rooms in her manor, and she's already housing the witches I freed from the warehouse. Zita can lead the way if you don't remember the address."

"With great pleasure!" Zita said, before grabbing Koyani's forearm. "You have to get your shoulder seen to. You were shot! I'm sure that hurts a lot."

Koyani managed a smile. "It does, yes. I assume that, if you are not guiding us, Adèle, it is because you intend to join with the last person in the know?"

"I-I do." She shouldn't be surprised Koyani had caught on to her goals immediately. Now that the team had Élise under control and somewhere to go, Adèle found herself thinking of Claire and the *Croissant-toi* more and more. "I need to know she's okay, and I need to tell her I am."

Zita emitted a half-restrained squeal then clamped both hands over her mouth. Koyani rolled her eyes. "Calm down, Paddlefish. I'm sure you'll hear all about it in due time. Good luck, Adèle."

"Thank you." Adèle cast the group another long look, half-expecting one of them to protest, then turned heels and left. The first few steps demanded a lot of energy, but the farther Adèle walked from the team, the lengthier her strides became. A tiny part of her wanted to stay behind and work with the others as they unravelled *her* case, but her desire to see Claire took precedence over all. A strange pain gripped her chest, fear slowly bubbling up as she made her way through the city. What if she said the wrong thing and hurt Claire? She was a mess, her nerves frayed by the terrible week, and she doubted Claire would be in a better state, especially now. The memory of blood stains at the bottom of the elevator surged to the forefront of Adèle's mind, and she quickened her pace.

The *Croissant-toi* had been her safe place ever since she'd moved to Val-de-mer, and she couldn't wait to reach it, sit down with Claire, and recover from the last days.

-25-

PARTENAIRES

CLAUDE STARED AT THE BLOODSTAIN ON HIS BEDSHEETS AND the occasional drops across his floor. He'd tried to bandage the bullet wounds before his quick nap but his skills in the area left something to be desired. Even on someone else, he'd have botched the job, but on himself? Disastrous. Blood loss turned him almost as light-headed now as he'd been when crashing down earlier. With a weary sigh, Claude slid out of bed, struggling to muster the strength to fight the underlying nausea, remain standing, clean his bandages and redo them.

His feet dragged him to the bathroom. He had no idea what time it was—his sleep schedule had been thrown to the winds, and he hurt from wounds, exhaustion, and excessive magic. He'd used too much, leaving himself empty, a husk whose limbs felt distant and heavy, almost detached from his body. A dull buzz rang through the base of his skull, slowing all thoughts, and when he moved his head, it was as if the world waited a split moment to shift—as if his vision didn't quite keep up with the rest of him. He steadied himself with a hand on the wall, unconvinced he'd notice himself stumbling fast enough not to fall.

Claude's first-aid kit had remained opened on the floor of his bathroom. With a weary sigh, he started putting it back together. His stomach rumbled in a low protest. Food. Right. He should eat too. Later, after this—after tending to his bandages. One thing at a time, he chided himself, or he would never finish any of them. His hand hovered above the kit as he tried to remember what should go next, but his thoughts kept slipping away—sometimes to the labs, the tanks, Clémence or Adèle, and sometimes to sweet oblivion.

Loud knocks on a widow snapped him out of the reverie. A customer? They did that a lot, hammering despite the *Fermé* sign, but no. This came from another window, at the back, one you had to scale the tiny backyard fence to reach. Police wouldn't warn either, or at least they wouldn't wait after knocking. Except one. One police woman definitely would.

A surge of adrenaline and anxiety rushed through Claude. She'd done it. She had escaped Élise, and marched straight to the *Croissant-toi*. The ground spun under him and Claude set his hands flat on the floor, squeezing his eyes shut until the bout of dizziness passed. He'd thought he'd have more time, that he'd be rested and fed and a little better equipped to deal with this, but no such luck. Better that than Adèle remaining in handcuffs, however.

Claude struggled to his feet, paused to make sure his blood pressure wouldn't crash, then slunk out of the bathroom and towards the back door. His familiar home felt so strange, distorted by his nausea and fatigue. He stopped once more with his fingers

301

wrapped around the knob, the metal cold against his feverish skin. His chest hurt, but not in the same fashion his arm and leg did— these burned and throbbed, whereas his heart constricted from hope and fear. They had come such a long way.

"Please."

Adèle's voice was so soft the door almost muffled her word completely. Claude heard, however, and it sent a jolt of courage through him. In a slow, shaky movement, he turned the knob, pulled the door open, and stepped back.

She stayed in the doorway, staring at him, her expression schooled into a fragile calm. Claude had to wonder what she saw— what she thought of him. He stood there, in the middle of his dimly lit room, shoulders hunched from the exhaustion. The loose shirt on his back didn't conceal his unbound breasts and blood stained the sleeves. Sweat and grime had turned his hair into a heavy tangle, and he'd caught sight of streaks of purple in them— leftovers from the last days' magic. What a mess. His gender presentation had scattered to the high winds, and he couldn't even bring himself to care.

Adèle had seen better times, too. Her uniform sported several new tears and stains, and dark circles hung under her eyes. She studied him for a second or two, and these seemed to stretch into eternity. Then their gazes met, and her mask fell. She closed the gap between them and cupped his cheek in her hand, pulling him close.

The gentleness of her movement shattered his last barriers. He didn't have the strength to keep himself together anymore, to ignore the cumulative burdens of his magic drain, imprisonment, wounds, and the emotional vulnerability of letting Adèle in, of trusting someone else so completely with himself. He crumpled into her arms, and she caught him, holding him firm as he sobbed against her.

She said nothing, just tightened her grip every now and then, giving him the space he needed to piece some elementary thoughts together.

"Welcome to the *Croissant-toi*," he whispered. "I'm afraid it lacks coffee at the moment."

"I'll survive." She ran her fingers through his hair, tugging a little to unravel its tangles. Claude closed his eyes, revelling in the sensation, and in her warmth so close. Adèle squeezed him. "I'm glad you're here. And I imagine you'd like to talk… about us, and you, and the last few days, but I don't want to have this discussion while you're frazzled like this. Have you eaten? Slept? I can fix your bandages. How wounded are you?"

"Quite." Inside and outside, Claude added mentally. But Adèle wanted him to recover. He had time to find his words and stability—to just feel more like himself. "Bullets grazed me. A lot. I'm bad with… healing stuff. Docteure Adaho fixed you, not me."

"Then let me fix you," Adèle offered, before leaning back to meet his gaze. "Just… Should I call you Claude or…?"

"Please." He forced a smile out to reassure her. "I'm genderfluid. Claude is good at the moment."

"All right. That's all I need to know for now. Everything else can wait until you feel better. Sounds good?"

It sounded wonderful. Claude nodded, and her lips curved into a gentle expression that sent his heart hammering and his blood boiling. She'd always been beautiful, and now her kindness wrapped around him like a warm blanket.

"Good. You stay put, and I'll gather everything. I'll let you know if I need you to hold anything for me. We'll be a team—a real one, now."

A team. Claude's eyes watered at the thought, and he managed a weak nod. He settled down on the nearest couch while she went to the bathroom, to get his first-aid kit still sprawled there. Soon he found himself holding gauze, scissors, and other bandage implements while Adèle disinfected and cleaned his wounds, her deft hands working in soft and firm movements. How strange, to have someone care for him wordlessly, tending to every little woe. Adèle's presence allowed him to relax. She built a shield around him, the unspoken promise like a barrier against future fights. They were a team. They might need to talk, but she would never let him down.

Claude closed his eyes and leaned against Adèle's shoulder as she finished her work. She slid fingers into his hair again, tugging at the countless knots in it.

"All you need is a comb, and you're good as new," she said. He heard the smile in her words.

"You never have that problem, I bet."

"Neither do I have your glorious purple hair." She gently pushed him back. "Permission to steal croissants from your stocks?"

"They won't be fresh." He hadn't baked pastries in a while, and he didn't have the strength to now. The thought of providing anything but fresh croissants to Adèle bothered him. Some standards in their relationship should never change. "Besides, I'd rather not risk people seeing me through the display windows. Another day, perhaps. A better one."

"Understood, Master Baker. I'll prepare a little something else. You grab some rest."

Claude pouted. He didn't want to sleep, not with Adèle finally here, yet his energy levels still lay dead on the floor. And the solid sense of security she provided removed any urgency he had to drag his feet about and stay ready for a potential attack. He stretched out over the couch, pushing back his reluctance. "I suppose if I want to recover… but don't let me sleep too long."

She agreed, brought him a pillow and a blanket, and he nestled into them. A small voice whispered that Adèle would also need rest, that she seemed as pale and shaky as him, but he ignored it. He couldn't function at the moment. They could take turns, and he'd make sure Adèle woke up to fresh croissant once it was hers. He always had a frozen reserve, just in case. Satisfied with his decision, Claude slipped into blissful sleep.

As it turned out, he and Adèle had very different definitions of "too long". The sun had dipped low in the sky when he emerged from his rest. For one confused moment, Claude didn't recognize his surroundings. He jolted up, fingers digging into his sofa, eyes sweeping the area. His home. A cozy living room with two sofas, a bookshelf full of baking tomes and weird, sometimes creepy tales, and the large painting of a majestic cat in a forest of birch. The fear dropped as fast as it had surged forward, leaving him panting and slightly embarrassed.

Adèle came running, holding a long knife with both hands. She relaxed when she didn't spot any strangers. "Bad dreams?"

"Not really. I'm fine." In fact, now that the initial rush of fear had passed, he felt refreshed. The fog muddling his mind had vanished, and when he focused on himself, he detected a small swirling of magic. "I'm good, even. But still starved."

"Got you covered."

She grinned, and that alone could've staved off Claude's hunger for hours. His gaze lingered on the curve of her nose and the way the corner of her eyes wrinkled as she smiled until Adèle disappeared into his kitchens. She returned with a large plate of delicatessen, cheese, and fruits, along with a bowl of cut bread. Claude calculated how long ago he'd last baked a baguette and winced at how stale this one would be—until the characteristic rich scent of warm crust wafted over him. Adèle cleared her throat when his eyes widened.

"I… took a few liberties, and you had dough labelled," she said. "Hope you don't mind."

"No! Not at all." He had missed bread so much. Ridiculous, he knew, but it had always been a part of his life—from emptying the crust of fresh loaves as a child to preparing his own at dawn, it had accompanied every up and down, every hurt, and every success. Since Livia had been captured, however, the bakery had become an afterthought. He missed it and the peacefulness of his routine. Not as much as he missed his twin, though.

Claude's thoughts darkened as he shoved the first piece of baguette in his mouth. After all this time, he had finally learned where to find her. Le Pont des Lumières. Not a monument to human ingenuity, but one to their atrociousness—their willingness to do anything to profit off those they hated. And at the heart of it, to power its lights, Livia. He had less than a day now. The last weeks might have been difficult on her, but once they lit the Pont, she would never recover. Claude swallowed his bread hard, and its delicious interior tasted staler than it should have.

"There's still something else you don't know," he said. Better to get it out now—to put all cards on the table. "Throwing Montrant Industries to the ground isn't my main objective. It's nothing but a nice bonus, or a target for a later time."

"Then what…"

"Livia."

Adèle's skin paled and horror settled into her expression. He didn't need to explain the basics. She knew enough to understand Livia also had magic and figure out what Montrant would want with her.

"Her magic is deep and powerful. She vanished a week ago. Shortly after you met her when we started to dig the truth about exocores. I… only just found a trace of her." Claude snatched a slice of apple from the plate and picked at it, trying to focus his thoughts. He didn't want to dwell on what they'd done to her during that time. "She was with Celosia and the others, in the warehouse, before we arrived. Burning it down created a hole in their plans, however. They needed a new power source. For the Pont des Lumières."

"But she's not… is the process that fast? Can they make an exocore in a matter of days?"

"I don't know, and it doesn't matter. They would lose too much of her potential doing so. Instead, they found a way to use our bodies directly. Just… plug us in, and as long as we stay alive, we're batteries that recharge themselves. And someone with Livia's abilities? They'll burn her soul to light up the entire bridge, from one country to the other."

Anger kept Claude's voice from breaking. He hadn't even had time to tell Zita about this and hearing himself made it more real. This immense construction they had presented as a great prowess would be powered by their magic. For what? To further trade with Tereaus? Give them another handy source of witches? He used to believe the Pont was a huge waste of money, but now its looming shape filled him with dread.

A cool hand drew him out of his thoughts. Adèle squeezed his forearm and searched for his gaze. "The grand opening is tomorrow at dusk. We have time."

"We do."

Claude had no intention to waste it. Security would already be tight around the bridge, even more so after their escape. The gouverneure would expect trouble and want none. How many police officers would patrol the area? They'd encouraged the public to go and might plan for a riot in addition to infiltration.

Adèle squeezed his arm again and removed her hand. She

hesitated for a moment, then her fingers slid into his hair, drawing out one of the remaining purple strands. Everything else had returned to their usual brown. "How do you do this? Magic?"

"A hard trick to master, but yes. I loved the colour too much not to learn." He pulled the strand from her and reached into himself, for the thin pool of magic he'd regained while asleep. Fresh energy resting inside him, helping him stay focused. The purple spread from the strand to all of his hair as a quick demonstration, then he cleaned it all away. He didn't feel much like it right now.

"It's strange to see you use magic," Adèle said softly.

A wave of unease washed over Claude, and he needed a moment before he could put words on what bothered him. He shook his head. "You've seen me do so plenty of times. I am not a different person. Claire and Claude... they're the same. They're both me. Different aspects, if you will."

"I'm sorry, I didn't mean... I'm not used to thinking of you as one." She'd raised her hands as if holding two separate things and then squeezed them together with a sigh. "I'm glad you told me. Je crois en toi." With a tired smile, she met Claude's gaze. "So do I. I believe in you. I did even when it was just Claire in my head."

"I know. That's why I could finally reveal this to you." Claude ran fingers through his messy hair. "Before the warehouse, you always treated me... I didn't feel human to you. I couldn't risk telling you—not with Livia's life on the line. What if you hated witches? Or felt too betrayed to consider I needed help? But you freed the trapped witches in the warehouse, and that let me trust you. I just never had a chance to go through with all the details."

"Zita told me. She said you trusted me." Adèle whispered the words, with a wistful fondness to her tone. Claude turned squarely to face her, and couldn't help but snort.

"Of course she did."

The matchmaker had gotten the better of his friend. Even knowing he had no interest in romance proper, Zita had pushed for them to speak. She wasn't wrong. Adèle had carved a special place in Claude's heart. She made him want to take risks, to open up and allow her closer. To let her see his life, changing and fluid and complicated as it was. And this relationship with Adèle didn't resemble anything he'd experienced before—not his tight friendship with Zita, not his sibling back and forth with Livia, and not the short-lived attempts at romance he'd endured. "I love you" would never be right for them, but they had their own words—Je crois en toi—better and more tailored to him. They fit him, and he hoped they'd fit her too.

"Do you remember when you asked for a date? What I said about me and romance?" He waited for her to nod. Adèle stared at him in complete attention, listening like nothing in the world would be more important than what would follow. The sofa felt too small for both of them, yet he wanted her to stay every bit as close. "I'm still aromantic. I-I guess it's one of those layers of complicated, if you kissed me looking for romance. I—" His heart thundered across his chest, stealing his words. Adèle had always had a crush on him. What if they couldn't work anything out? He almost stopped and told her to forget it. He wasn't even certain what *he* wanted, so how was he supposed to figure out what to ask for? What he was ready to risk? But he wanted *something*, of that he was certain. "You do partners in the police, don't you?"

Adèle blinked, stunned, then a wide smile spread across her face. "We do. I'd offer you the spot, but… police partners usually don't kiss. Wouldn't we miss out?"

A little catch in her voice sent Claude's heart leaping, and his throat dried at the idea of *more* kisses. His body remembered how she'd pushed him against the test tank—of her surprising hunger. "Good thing I'm not police, huh? I like breaking rules."

This time, Adèle laughed. She slipped a hand around his waist, pulling him closer, and dropped a kiss on his lips. He closed his eyes and leaned into it until she retreated. "I'm becoming a pro at ignoring the law, too."

For a moment, the thrill washed his exhaustion away. He was home, on his couch, safe from Montrant Industries and law enforcement alike. Adèle dragged him close, and her warmth spread to his body. Under the pungent stink of sweat—an odour for which they were both responsible—she smelled of almonds and something darker, spicier. He allowed himself to daydream of cuddling for hours in the sun, perhaps under the Quartier des Bouleaux' massive birch Soul Tree, then forced his mind back to more difficult conversations.

"Aren't you… angry at me?"

Adèle stiffened by his side and took painfully long to prepare her answers. "When I think about it, I am," she said.

311

"You… you lied to me. I walked in your bakery distraught from finding a thief in my brand-new home, and you offered me a croissant and a coffee with that damn sweet smile, as if you had nothing to do with it! All those times I talked about Claire and how we progressed… And you even needled more information out of me at that non-date!"

Hot shame flushed Claude's cheeks, but he lifted his head and met Adèle's gaze without hesitation. He wouldn't deny any of these things, not when he stood by his reasons for them. "I had to save Livia."

"I know." Adèle's voice had become hard and pressing when she'd tried to explain, but now it regained its softness. "You don't need to justify yourself. I understand why. It stings all the same. Besides, I treated you like shit, too, and I don't even have an excuse beyond my personal hurt. I'm okay, Claude. It's already forgiven."

"Let me show you something. It's good for perspective." Even if she didn't seem like she needed it.

Claude grabbed the plate of cheese and fine meat then straightened. A bout of dizziness rooted him in place, and Adèle placed a gentle hand on his back. He offered the food to her, choosing a last slice of bread before he moved towards his office. She followed without a sound, a silent observer, still taking in information rather than commenting. He glanced at her— whenever Adèle listened to others or tried to unravel a puzzle, her face turned into this gorgeous expression of concentration. Lips pinched, slight frown, deep eyes tracking connections only she could see. They stared at him now, and a hot wave coursed through his body. He wanted to pause—to stop everything and kiss her again. Instead, he opened his trapdoor and climbed the ladder to the basement.

He relaxed at the sight of his mound of exocores, still safe in his home. When had he stopped seeing these lives as a stressful burden? Coming here while searching for Livia could almost paralyze him with fear. It had been so much to carry for his lonely shoulders. Not anymore, though. First he'd shared with Livia and Zita, and now Adèle was with him too. And behind them were Emmanuelle, Celosia, Docteure Adaho and the other witches— even Koyani. Claude had started this alone, sneaking into the night to safeguard exocores, but his secret had spread and support had come.

Adèle gasped when she reached the bottom and almost dropped the leftover food. Claude turned to her and sketched a smile. "My kidnapped friends," he said, echoing Koyani's initial reaction to learning these were people. Then he cast his voice out. "I'm alive, lovelies. Sorry I kept you waiting. I got caught, escaped, and had to rest. It's a long story, but first you should know Adèle is with me now. I mean, right now, with us, in this room."

Claude turned to Adèle. She startled, pointing to herself, then cleared her throat. "Hi. It sounds like I don't need an introduction…"

"I've been telling them everything. Their existence depends on it, so I figured it was only fair."

Adèle walked past the table, straight to his map of Val-de-mer and the exocores he'd tracked down. She touched the pin over her flat before moving on. Her eyes flitted from one pin to another with growing horror. "There're still so many left," she said. "So you gathered them, hid them in your basement, and talked to them? Told them our story?"

"I started that recently, sort of. Livia guessed they might be sentient, but I hadn't grasped what that could mean until we chatted with Basir and your sister told me more about her science. I have no way of proving they can hear and understand me, but it's not a risk I'm willing to take." Claude reached out to one of the many red pins—exocores still in the city, in one rich mansion or another—and thumbed it. "It hurts to think of how many are being drained out there. Stealing was like chipping away at a self-regenerating monster, though. Montrant Industries would have continued to produce exocores, and they would have shoved them into the Pont des Lumières no matter what. This is better. We're stopping it once and for all."

"You are." Adèle turned to him, her bony face hardening into a determined expression. "We are. I'm glad I won't be a hindrance any longer."

No, she definitely would not. Claude resisted the temptation to tell her she'd never been one, just to reassure her. He might not have lost Clémence in the first place if she hadn't drunk-tackled him on that first night, however, and Livia would be with him—with them—tonight. He saw no point in lying to Adèle and no reason to coddle her feelings.

"We're better together," he said, "and with the increased

security we'll find at the Pont, we'll have to be at our best."

"Do you have a plan?" Adèle asked.

"Get there, sneak in, save Livia, destroy Montrant Industries?" When was he supposed to have figured this out? Claude had never seen any schematics of the Pont and didn't know the first thing about security details on large events. Plans didn't agree with him. He rushed in and improvised. "Sorry. That's all I have. Better pray to the saints it'll be enough."

"It's fine. Zita, Nsia Kouna, Koyani and the rest of the unit can figure out the best approach."

"They're all… together right now?" Claude raised a hand to stall Adèle's answer, then gestured at the exocores. "You know what? We should grab a seat and start at the beginning. Last I told them, I was leaving for the labs. We have quite a bit of catching up to do."

Doubt flitted across Adèle's face, but she nodded. "All right. First, we explain. We might even figure it out as we talk."

Claude didn't think so, but he started without waiting. Adèle would find it easier after hearing him detail his expedition in the labs, the conversation he'd overheard, and Clémence's actions. As he recounted his time strapped into the test tank, Claude reminded himself he owed ol a service, and should speak to Zita. It didn't matter what atrocities Clémence had pulled: ols little brother didn't deserve to pay for them. Livia was not the only sibling to save in the coming day.

-26-

EN BONNE COMPAGNIE

THE LONG TALK WITH THE EXOCORES HAD LEFT ADÈLE IN A daze. Her life had taken a brutal turn for the weird and her mind still hadn't fully accommodated yet. Too many twists and brushes with death for them to sink in deeper than superficially. Lending her words to these events while retelling them had made everything more concrete but no less strange. She had sat with Claude next to a pile of exocores, explaining how Koyani's team had discovered Élise's treachery and rushed to the rescue, now aware that the anonymous papers that had saved her life had been another blessing from Claude. How close they had all come to failing! But it wasn't over, and, as they'd completed the narration, Adèle realized how much work still waited ahead of them.

"We should move to Em's manor," she'd concluded, and, although Claude had looked like he wanted to sleep for days before he returned to the fight, he'd agreed with a tired nod.

He hadn't retrieved Claire's typical outfit, preferring to disappear into his room to grab a clean shirt and brown wool pants. When he reemerged, he had his hair tied in his usual low ponytail, and Adèle couldn't fathom how she'd missed the body shape resemblance between her favourite baker and the thief she was searching for. Same soft arms, thick thighs, and roundness at the waist, but Claire's postures had always stayed more defiant, exuding confidence instead of a welcoming gentleness.

"I don't have the energy to deal with what the wrong presentation will do to my mind," he'd said. "This is a private group. I'll have to trust that all of them can keep a secret."

"One of them is a journalist," she'd pointed out.

Claude had laughed. "You'd be surprised how much they hide compared to what they publish."

And they'd headed out, Claude locking the bakery with a wistful sigh. He'd seemed better than when she had first arrived at the *Croissant-toi*—more himself, and more in control. Then again, that wasn't too difficult: he had crumpled in her arms almost immediately. Each smile and jest still felt forced, but she'd noticed that before their non-date. No amount of sleep would cure his bone-deep exhaustion until they'd rescued Livia. Only then would he start to heal.

Em's manor was a welcome sight to Adèle's tired heart. Most of the windows remained dark, and she wondered if Em had kept it like this on purpose. In theory, she lived alone. A dozen witches and Koyani's unit staying at her place wouldn't go unnoticed for long, but they only needed discretion to last for a day longer—hopefully, anyway. When Adèle started around the back, Claude caught her arm to stop her, mischief shining in his eyes. "Let's take my usual path."

Before she could protest, he swept her off her feet and leaped up. She yelped in surprise and clung to him, laughing as they landed on the balcony with ease. Claude set her back down and she pulled on her clothes, the uniform still dirty from rolling on the ground with Élise. At least Em had spare outfits since the warehouse, and a warm bath to offer.

"No wonder you like it so much," she said. "What now? We bust the door without warning?"

"Just because you call it breaking and entering doesn't mean I really need to break things," he quipped. "I tried to leave all non-exocore property intact. Besides, Em leaves this particular balcony unlocked. Someone should probably tell her."

He slid the door open and walked into the house as if it belonged to him. Adèle couldn't help but grin—how often had she railed against that very attitude? She quickly took the lead, heading towards the kitchens. The small plate of cheese and delicatessen hadn't fulfilled her hunger, and, at this time of the day, she suspected most of the guests would be finishing their dinner. She smiled as they passed several bedrooms with their doors open and obvious signs of habitation. The manor had felt so empty on her first visit, and Emmanuelle loved to play host. She must be enjoying this spontaneous occupation, despite all the risks it involved.

Zita's loud laughter echoed down the corridor, breaking the comfortable silence between Claude and Adèle. They caught hints of other voices, but the walls muffled the actual conversation. They both sped their pace without a word, their smiles growing with the noise coming from the dining room. Adèle reached the imposing double doors leading in, eager to join up with the group, but Claude's deep and steadying breath as she turned the handle froze her. When she met his gaze, he gestured for her to go on.

"I'm good."

She didn't need more. Adèle pushed the great door open and stepped into the dining room. The long table which had seemed so large on her first visit was now filled with plates, glasses, and even a handful of extra chairs. Between Koyani's unit and the witches, people were eating elbow-to-elbow, chatting eagerly. The extra chairs were all in the same rich wood and red cushion aesthetic—Em wouldn't break the pattern, after all. At one end of the table, Celosia and another older witch had been granted more space. The conversations died down as people noticed them, and Emmanuelle jumped to her feet.

"Adèle!" She was striding around the table within seconds, holding her skirts up for better movement until she could wrap her sister in a hug. Adèle returned the affectionate gesture with a grin. After a brief, tighter squeeze, Em released her and turned to the company. "And you're... oh!"

"We've met," Claude answered smoothly, extending his hand. "I own the *Croissant-toi*. Adèle drops by nearly every day." And then, after a slight pause, "Sorry for that night I burst into your room to ask about science."

Emmanuelle chuckled and wrapped an arm around his shoulder, guiding him towards the table. "No apologies needed. That was almost as thrilling as the first time my burner prototype

319

worked! Now, what can I do for you? I'm afraid we have no fresh croissants, but I made delicious tourtière if you're hungry."

"I'm hungry," Adèle piped in, triggering laughter from the table.

Before long, they were both seated with everyone else. Adèle squeezed between Em and Koyani, while Claude had wound up across from her, next to Zita. Adèle chomped down on the tourtière with enthusiasm, shoving potatoes and crust into her mouth shamelessly. It had been difficult to eat before leaving this morning, and except for small bits at Claude's she hadn't had a chance since. Besides, she always had room for tourtière and was more than happy to listen rather than talk.

Koyani was leading the conversation, and the plate in front of her had been replaced by a list of names. She had reviewed most of Val-de-mer's notable figures from politics and law enforcement with Nsia Kouna's help, filing them into three columns: safe, unknown, and unsafe. A few names in the "unsafe" column had been crossed out, while others considered safe had wide circles around them. One of the latter was the mairesse's, and Claude didn't fail to notice.

"Mairesse Denise Jalbert is an old family friend," he said. "Did you have plans to talk to her?"

"We did." Koyani tapped her name—with a dark blue finger, Adèle noticed, from a different prosthetic. She'd found a way to remove the exocore-powered one, then. "She is also the impulse behind my unit. I have a high opinion of her, and Mx. Kouna had nothing to indicate this should change. I think she would listen and help."

"Agreed. I can talk to her tonight." He set his fork down with a small laugh. "Who needs a full night's sleep anyway?"

A sharp cough down the table interrupted them, and Adèle shrank back into her seat when faced with Docteure Adaho's glare. "You do. I was given to understand you might have been shot. And how are your palms? Burns don't cease hurting overnight."

Claude immediately hid his hands under the table, and although he looked thoroughly chastised, it didn't stop him from countering with "Exocores don't save themselves either, sorry!"

"I could talk to her for you," Zita said. "I've met her once, and so if I name you…"

"No. You… you'll be needed elsewhere." His face dropped and he met Zita's gaze. "I promised Clémence help in exchange for the information we have now. You were right about ol—they were keeping ol in check with ols little brother. The moment Montrant Industries realizes ol's helped us, however… We shouldn't waste any time. Clémence thought you'd be able to find the boy?"

"I knew it! I knew they had something on ol, and when Élise mentioned family…" Her voice trailed off, horror stealing the rest of her words. Claude wondered how well she knew Clémence's brother, or if she'd played with him in the past. Zita's silence became contagious, and soon the entire table was watching her and Claude. Adèle shifted in her seat, unsure what to say. They couldn't risk a child's life, but how could they do anything if Zita couldn't find him? Koyani set a hand over Zita's forearm.

"Sounds like we have another rescue ahead of us, Paddlefish. Do you think this one will involve broken elevators?"

"Capitaine Koyani…"

Zuri Adaho started her protest, but Koyani interrupted with a raised palm. Even sitting, a tiny woman at a large table, she commanded attention. "I appreciate your concern, docteure, but my arm is fine. There is a child to protect. Marcel, Inha, you're coming with me. Adèle, Yuri, I would rather have you stay, in case Montrant Industries catches up to our whereabouts. With Élise here, I have doubts, but someone has to keep watch."

Adèle gritted her teeth, bitterness roiling at the bottom of her stomach. She knew she was being set aside, even though Koyani had reasons to back her order. And it made sense for her to stay: she still hadn't recovered from her gunshot, the day had been long and difficult, and this was her sister's manor. Yet she had wanted to go—to remain with the action and make herself useful— and the rebuttal stung. She turned back to her food as other witches volunteered and Koyani formed a small team from them. Adèle sulked, playing with her potato, knowing she was being childish but unable to stop herself. Em nudged her forearm and leaned forward.

"Don't let your boss see the pouty face," she said, "and come on, this means you'll be here with Claude most of the night. He's not going to chat with the old Spinster till dawn."

Adèle glanced at him, watching him silently pick at his tourtière while Koyani and Zita built rescue plans. He seemed just as disappointed at not taking part as she was, but when their gaze met he smiled. She blushed, smiled back… then heard Emmanuelle snicker right beside her. When it occurred to Adèle what two people sexually attracted to one another might consider doing with a night alone, Adèle grew red and shoved her sister.

"We both need rest, not sex!" she protested.

"Then cuddle up," Em said, showing her hands in mock innocence. "You do what you want, soeurette."

Claude was staring at them from right across the table — nowhere near far enough for him not to have heard the entire exchange. Eyebrows raised, his smile barely contained, he said, "I'm sure Docteure Adaho would agree with that assessment."

"I do," she said.

And if she had heard this conversation, it meant half the table had, too. Adèle groaned, then snatched her glass of wine off the table. "Hey, great bottle, huh? How about we *all* start discussing that instead? Em's taste in wine and décor and just about everything would make a way better topic."

It earned her a slew of laughter, but they did change subject after that. Adèle mouthed "I'm sorry" at Claude from across the table, but he shrugged it off with a smile. No blush, just a calm smirk acknowledging he had been thinking about it. She kept drinking, paying little heed to the conversations around her, which went from serious plans against Montrant to casual gossip about the next tournoi, including a long debate on the science behind exocores. As much as she wanted to be involved in the fight, it felt good to leave the talk to others for tonight, while she daydreamed of sleep and cuddles. She and Claude had earned a break.

By the end of the dinner, Claude's thin reserve of energy had been drained. He didn't remember when he'd last talked to so many different people at once, and the way the conversation had inevitably returned to Montrant Industries or his thieving nights didn't help. He'd known he would be the centre of attention and had tried to mentally prepare for it, yet, when Koyani and her small rescue team excused themselves to finalize their plans in another room, he sighed in relief. Six less people staring at him, and a little break from Zita's boisterous enthusiasm. He loved his friend, but right now he'd give a lot for some peace and quiet.

Docteure Adaho made him promise not to leave for the mairesse's office without a medical examination, then she declared she needed to corner Capitaine Koyani and exited, mumbling something about everyone in this household being way too eager to power through injuries. Emmanuelle forced Adèle to head to bed when it became evident she was hitting nails in her chair, and before Claude had quite realized it everyone had vanished except Nsia Kouna and him. The journalist had a long pad in front of them already covered in notes. They continued scribbling in silence until Claude rose to leave. Their head snapped up and they smiled, obviously preparing their request. Claude cut them off.

"No interview. Or anything of the sort."

Mx. Kouna's expression twitched but remained pleasant.

"I can understand, though I would have loved to hear how this started on your end. It seems highly unlikely that suspicious money trails and paperwork tipped you off." They flipped their pencil as they spoke, then stored it in a front pocket with a flourish and stood. "I have the utmost respect for your need for privacy and rest, however, and will hold my questions back. No… I wanted to thank you for blowing this story open, and answer any questions *you* might have."

Claude stared, taken aback by Kouna's lack of insistence. Respect for privacy had never seemed high on the list of most journalists' priorities, but perhaps the circumstances warranted it. Slowly, he nodded. "I could benefit from a quick rundown on the politics behind this, especially if I'm to talk with Denise. Care for some fresh air?"

The dinner room had grown stuffy, and he'd rather enjoy the rare summer nights remaining. Kouna agreed, and they even took a small detour by their room to leave the pad there. No notes, then. Claude relaxed—perhaps Kouna had indeed no professional interest in this. They threaded through the house in silence, as discreetly as they could, but as Claude slipped into the cool night he opened up.

"I do have personal reasons," he said. "Although I had started stealing the exocores long before they came into play. I could feel something off about them."

"Instincts rarely lie." Nsia's leisurely pace allowed Claude to keep up without struggling despite their long strides. Their entire body language exuded calm, as if nothing could unsettle them, and that eased him further. "You should know that I will not publish any information you wouldn't want me to. Sometimes my job is to get to the bottom of a story and expose the whole truth, but more often still it is to shed a harsh light on terrible stories while wrapping its victims in protective shadows. I would rather stay an obscure journalist with no prizes to their name than bring more pain and danger to your door with a public profile."

"You're a good egg." Part of Claude had wanted to quip about finding a rare journalist with a sense of ethics, but intense relief weakened his legs and stole his words, leaving only his mother's. "You're a good egg," she'd say whenever he'd gone along with Livia's complicated schemes to keep her safe, and she always followed it with "one day it'll get you into more trouble than you can handle". She'd been right.

"Thank you?" Kouna answered with a hint of confusion. One of Em's cats tried to dart between their legs then, and they scooped him up with ease, bringing the fluffy creature at eye level. "Hello, gorgeous. Have I drawn you yet? How many of you are there?"

"Six." Adèle had described each of them in great details over coffee, one morning. Claude reached out to scratch the kitty's head. He was all black, with a white stain on his chest and another above his nose. "This is Gravity, I think."

The cat struggled against Kouna, obviously already tired of the brief kitty love received. They put him down. "Good name. He sure wanted to return to the ground fast."

Gravity darted away, disappearing inside through the

little cat trap. Claude sighed. He would rather have petted Gravity for hours than return to the task at hand.

"All right." He clapped his hands, as if the movement could summon motivation. "Run me through the politics behind this. I know parts of who's who—my mother used to be involved—but I'm rusty. Then we can browse what you received for the most adequate proof to show the mairesse."

Nsia Kouna chuckled. "Should have brought my pad after all. These networks are better understood with charts and snide commentary. But here we go."

The journalist started at the top, with the information they had on Gouverneure Lacroix and which could confirm what Claude had overheard in the labs. They continued from there to the political figures more specific to Val-de-mer, and Kouna highlighted names, systems, and cliques. Memories of family dinner drifted back to the forefront of Claude's mind. How often had his parents discussed these same people? And in the last weeks before they had left for Tereaus, to join the thousands of witches who'd sought safety for themselves and their families, the topic had always revolved around who was safe, and who should never be trusted. Claude hadn't paid attention to the details—how could he have predicted he'd benefit from the information later? When his parents had left, he'd been glad to vanish from public life and to the tranquility of his bakery. He hoped this dip back into it would come to an end soon, and that the correct proportion of butter and salt in his dough could once more become his main source of concern.

-27-

VIEILLE FILLE,
NOUVELLE TOILE

MAIRESSE JALBERT WAS RARELY CALLED BY HER PROPER name outside of official spaces, and sometimes not even within them. Inhabitants of Val-de-mer's nine quartiers had long since adopted her nickname as an affectionate term: she was the Spinster, dubbed this way by political opponents eager to paint her as an old crooked lady without a husband or children and, as such, unworthy of trust. It hadn't worked—rather, Denise Jalbert had made it work... in her favour.

Campaigning on the imagery of a social security web and the capture of corrupted parasites, Denise Jalbert had demonstrated lone spiders could reach out and benefit many. It had taken countless knitting circles and a stubborn pride in herself, but her message had resonated loud and clear. Her web was benevolent; her lack of family proof that a woman's worth was not defined by children or partner. She had won her elections in a landslide and never lost since.

To Claude, however, she would always remain Denise, the family friend who stayed home playing games of bluff until unholy hours with his parents and the lady who hid maple candies in a small pouch and subtly dropped it when his father wasn't looking. He had been a teenager during the elections—old enough to understand why they'd tried to paint Denise Jalbert's single status as a mark against her humanity and to cheer on her victory. She had taught him aromanticism was no hindrance to a full and happy life, and that he should be proud of himself and even flaunt it if others attempted to diminish him for it. No matter what happened tonight, Claude would always be thankful for the path she had forged.

Still. As he stopped at the mairesse's two-storied house, he prayed Denise Jalbert would not balk at opposing Montrant Industries. They needed her support, and any rebuttal from her would stoke bitter disappointment.

The Spinster had never left the quartier of her youth, although she had moved from the impoverished northern section, where crooked buildings leaned against the fortifications, to the nicer area, with tall habitations and tiny lawns. It couldn't compare to the Quartier des Chênes, yet as the only residential part of Val-de-mer both near the sea and on water level, it was highly prized.

To his surprise, flickering lamps still illuminated the upper floor. Claude traced a route with his eyes: vault over the ironwrought fence, sprint across the narrow lawn, climb the vine-covered walls, break the lock on the rooftop glasshouse's door, and slip inside, towards the light. Then he went up and down the street

329

in case she had guards keeping watch. As soon as he believed himself in the clear, he drew upon his magic and dashed out.

Running without skirts, cape, or mask unsettled him for a moment. With the exception of his leap with Adèle, it had been months since he'd used his power without the costume—not since he'd shifted his nighttime partying to the less legal stealing outings. And it was… freeing. A strange elation filled Claude's chest as he worked his way up the vines. The various pieces of his life he'd forcibly kept apart as he'd investigated exocores had started mixing again. It hadn't been safe to do otherwise—it still wasn't entirely, in truth—but he was grateful for the growing number of people with whom he could be himself fully, croissants, magic, aromanticism and genderfluidity included.

All he was missing was Livia. Not much longer now.

Claude heaved himself on the roof and broke into the greenhouse with one magic-powered pull. At least the door stayed on its hinges this time—he'd had trouble judging the appropriate level of strength needed on his first attempts. The cloudy night sky offered little light to navigate through the array of plants, but Claude used what was afforded to him by the lit windows and pressed on. He had no desire to linger in the stuffy atmosphere, even if the soft scent of roses filled the air. His heart hammering loudly, Claude slipped out of the greenhouse and into the second floor's corridor. Music drifted into it from somewhere, sweet notes accompanying a tenor's voice as he sang of his language lost to foreign industries. No surprise there: Denise Jalbert had always toiled fervently to keep institutions in Bernéais first.

He stopped in front of the last door, already ajar, his courage failing for a moment. So much of their support would depend on whether or not the mairesse agreed to work with them. She could strike at complicit magistrates and protect Koyani and others from their direct superiors, and she could grant Nsia Kouna's article a legitimacy they would otherwise lack. They would forge on with or without her, but if she decided to oppose… everyone's livelihood and future was on the line here. He couldn't fail.

The nine saints willing, she wouldn't fail him, either. Claude pushed the door, and his heart flipped when it creaked — as if she wouldn't have spotted him after anyway.

Denise Jalbert lay in a long recliner in the middle of her living room, wrapped in a black bathrobe lined with white, web-like patterns, her back propped just high enough to allow easy reading. She held a thick tome with one hand, while the other swirled a glass of strong alcohol — whiskey, Claude remembered. Her hair had always been grey, but it had paled and thinned through the years, and new wrinkles marked her face. Part of the spider imagery had clung to her because of her tallness and spindly limbs, but Claude wondered if she hadn't grown even narrower and sharper, as if age had eroded her body. Her eyes hadn't lost any of their strength, however, and they snapped to him the moment he entered. She lowered her book and tilted her head, frowning. He forced himself to wait, even though every second heightened his desire to bolt. Then recognition washed over the mairesse's expression, and her concern turned into joy.

331

"You're Rico's kid! I'm sorry, I didn't recognize you. You've grown so much since we last had the chance."

He hadn't only grown: he had found his genders. When she had visited on a regular basis, he hadn't known how to explain the shift in them. He'd called them moods, and while at times he'd insisted on boyish clothes, he hadn't yet considered he could be a man one day, and a woman the next. He wondered how much his parents had told her afterwards—if they'd even talked about him beyond basic news. Knowledgeable or not, however, Denise Jalbert rolled with it with perfect ease.

"What earned me this midnight visit?" she asked, and as the question crossed her lips, she seemed to realize he shouldn't have reached her unannounced like this. "Young man, did you sneak into my home? Unless my memory is failing me, your sister is the reckless one, usually."

"I've been stealing exocores for weeks. What's one more breaking and entering, especially in an old family friend's house?"

Reckless indeed, he thought as the mairesse's eyes widened in understanding. He saw no point in beating around the bush, however. Either she was willing to listen, or she'd throw Montrant after him no matter how he broached the subject. She set down her glass of whiskey and studied him, perhaps silently considering the wider implications of his answer before replying. Good politicians knew to care for their every word.

"I had a strange report on my desk today. Two, in fact." Her voice remained calm and she sipped from her glass with deliberate slowness. "The first stated Capitaine Koyani had

332

changed her investigation target towards Montrant Industries. The second warned me she had been removed from her position in favour of Lieutenant Jefferson, and that charges would be brought against her newest recruit. When I tried to speak directly with Koyani, I was informed neither her, nor her two concerned officers could be found. Not since this afternoon. That wouldn't all be connected to your visit, would it?"

She swirled her whiskey with a slight smirk, and Claude couldn't help feel trapped. It was silly — she wasn't attacking him — but his defensive instincts reeled up the moment he recognized he was facing a skilled and witty interlocutor. As if she would pick on a single false step from him. Overwhelmed, uncertain where to start, he dragged his feet across the room and flopped down into the sofa opposite of her lounging chair. "It is."

"You look like you need a drink, son."

"No. I don't drink." He leaned forward, gathering his thoughts. Straightforwardness was probably his best bet here. "There wouldn't be enough alcohol in the world to make me forget about Montrant Industries' horrors anyway."

Denise's eyebrows shot up, but otherwise her features remained a mask of calm. She pushed herself up with shaky arms. "Well, then, let me at least refill my glass before you explain." She trudged towards the bar, knitted white slippers sliding across the floor, and she poured another drink. Claude watched in silence. A month ago, he would have squirmed from the awkwardness of staring at their aged mairesse while she prepared her midnight shot wrapped in a bathrobe, but between the exocores, his

333

relationship with Adèle, and the large dinner of fugitives earlier, he had lost his ability to wonder at the strangeness of life. When the mairesse was sitting back on the edge of her recliner, Claude started his explanations.

He was glad he'd already shared everything with the exocores in his basement. It helped him keep his voice steady and get straight to the point. The mairesse didn't need the whole story, as long as she understood the terrible hidden cost of Val-de-mer's precious new bridge and who had set the price. As Claude spoke, he withdrew the proof he had selected with Nsia Kouna, providing material support to his claims. Clémence had sent an impressive range of incriminating evidence, from ols notes on the exocore creation process to letter exchanges ol wasn't even involved in.

Claude presented them one by one with calm, but inwardly he was praying Koyani's strike team would make it to ols little brother in time. Denise Jalbert listened, mostly silent, only interrupting Claude for pointed and short questions. She didn't flinch when he explained he'd overheard Élise state the gouverneure supported this, or provided several messages implying it strongly. Her calculating eyes moved from the papers in her hands to Claude, then lost themselves over his shoulder as she considered the ramifications. At length, she downed the rest of her whiskey and focused on him.

"The Pont des Lumières opens tomorrow and Gouverneure Lacroix will be present. What is your plan?"

"Ruin the party." He smirked, but what amusement he derived from the idea of crashing the celebration vanished quickly.

"The exocores they had left are not sufficient to electrify the Pont, nor can their process fully drain powerful witches. So they... they're plugging people directly into the circuit. And one of these unfortunate witches is... it's Livia." It didn't matter how often he voiced this, it would always feel like a punch to his stomach. "The saints willing, the Pont's lights will never shine."

"Is that all?"

Claude scowled. "Is that not enough? I can't be everywhere, and I won't let them use Livia."

"But you are not alone." She bent with a groan and set her empty glass to the ground. "I'm sorry, I did not mean to sound dismissive. What are Koyani's plans? Kouna's?"

Claude rubbed his face and sighed. Yes. Of course. He was forgetting the others again—even his new partner. He had started this with Livia, and it was all too easy to focus only on her situation and omit the support he'd found along the way.

"Right," he said. "They'll be unravelling this mess, one person at a time. Any help you can bring to placate Montrant's agents and provide public legitimacy would be invaluable. If people don't believe this is real..."

"I believe you," she said, "and when you walk out of the Pont with your sister in your arms, so will they. Boy, am I about to call in some precious favours!" She clapped her hands, and her almost childish glee surprised Claude. She sounded thrilled at the idea of contacting others in the middle of the night to force them to help her as a deference to services once rendered. Denise Jalbert leaned forward, splaying her fingers mid air. "You see, the secret of a good Spinster is in her web. I have been mairesse for fourteen years now, and people in this city either love me or owe me. I have wrapped them into my web one by one, allowing many to believe they were profiting off my kindness, or that I had forgotten my due. Trusted allies will follow my lead without any prompting, and the others… I would enjoy nothing more than to let them know I have a long memory, and some important shit to get done."

She scooped the empty glass off the floor, grinning, then pushed herself to her feet again. Standing obviously demanded a lot from her old body, yet as Denise Jalbert straightened to her full height, she oozed perfect confidence—a powerful pull that established the mairesse as a force of nature, one you could trust in and follow without questions. With a quick speech and a smile, she had convinced him she could achieve anything, that even the large and still hidden network behind Montrant Industries didn't stand a chance against her. He grinned back at her and sprang to his feet.

"Thank you. Thank you so much."

"My dear, you and other witches in this city have suffered long enough. I was powerless to do much after the Meltdown, but my roots run deeper now. It pains me that your parents were right in leaving. Val-de-mer wasn't safe for them. It still isn't, but that is about to change." She stepped closer and extended a wrinkled hand. "I'm glad you trusted me with this information. Let Capitaine Koyani know I expect her to interrupt the ceremony tomorrow night, and that should she disrupt the peace she will have my full support doing so. No one's coming for her job without my say-so."

Claude grabbed the hand, and Denise Jalbert's firm grip didn't surprise him. "I will."

"And please take care. I can create logistical problems and disrupt tomorrow's security measures, but I cannot remove them entirely. I'll inform you all of what I successfully did for you." She released his hand and met his gaze. A fire burned in her eyes. "May the nine saints keep you safe."

"And may they guide your steps and words as you call in those favours."

Denise Jalbert laughed, a grating but honest sound that brought Claude back to his youth. It was good to know some childhood heroes never disappointed you—that people who had inspired you, forging a path of self-awareness and confidence, could continue to support and protect you even later in life, or even when seen from closer. He'd needed that almost as much as he had needed the mairesse's physical help, and the enormity of his relief left him light-headed. He stayed put, caught up in it yet unable to voice his thankfulness until Denise patted his arm.

"Now get going, young man, same way you entered! My night's work is cut out for me, and you have the looks of someone in great need of a bed, even more so than a drink."

Exhaustion laced his chuckle, and he nodded, his mind returning to Em's teasing about cuddling with Adèle. He wouldn't mind that *at all*, especially tonight, not knowing what would happen on the morrow. "You're right. Time to move." He shook himself out of his daze and started towards the living room's door, but stopped after a few feet. "Oh, Madame Jalbert? The name's

337

Claude now. I own a bakery in the Quartier des Bouleaux. If you wanted to drop by one day, after this is over... I'd love that."

"So would I, I think. And please call me Denise."

"Great." He wished to add something else, anything, but she gestured for him to go, almost shooing him out. With a grin, Claude turned heel and snuck back out of the mansion. Hope lengthened his strides as he crossed the greenhouse again. He was tired, true, but he had never been so certain of his future. Tomorrow they would take down Montrant Industries, and he would save Livia.

-28-

POUSSE ET POINTE

A STRANGE SILENCE REIGNED OVER EMMANUELLE'S household when Claude returned. More than twenty people occupied the manor, yet not one of them made a sound. Claude considered slipping into Adèle's room, to wrap his arms around her and rest with her nearby warmth, as they had mentioned of doing during dinner. Except there was something too... established couple about it, a vibe that felt wrong. Was it the timing? They hadn't discussed in depth what "partner" could mean for them, and while Claude fancied the idea of holding someone as he fell asleep in general, doing it *now, tonight* left him uneasy—a strong enough signal to stop him. He preferred to wait for Adèle to wake up and for them to talk things over.

As it turned out, his own bed was already occupied. Four of Emmanuelle's cats had split the space. Two fluffy orange ones were piled at the foot, a third stretched across the width, and Gravity had claimed the right pillow. Claude stifled a laugh. When had he last had so much company in bed? Smiling, he undressed and squeezed himself between two of the cats, displacing Gravity enough to fit in. Between the softness of the mattress under him, the weight of a quality blanket, and the warm feline bodies pressed against him, Claude fell asleep within minutes.

He woke up at dawn to the screams of an angry, terrified boy who absolutely did not want to eat breakfast. Claude rolled over, on his belly, and grabbed a nearby pillow to slam over his head, dislodging two cats and sending them scampering with his sudden movement. He wished he could laze in bed all day and forget the world until the inauguration of the Pont des Lumières, but everyone would want news of his meeting with the Spinster as soon as possible. Besides, he couldn't help worrying about Zita, and now that he'd woken up his mind wouldn't rest before he knew she was safe. Those screams no doubts came from Clémence's brother, but he hadn't heard Zita answer. Tiny paws climbed on his back and pressed into it, walking over Claude until they had reached his neck, and a cold nose pushed against his skin. He mumbled an "okay, I get it, I'm moving" into the mattress, and forced himself up.

Gravity leaped down his back and sat next to the door as Claude grabbed a change of clothes. The cat could have followed his friends out at any time, but instead hung near Claude's feet as he headed towards the kitchen. Maybe the poor fool expected free food—as if Claude didn't have years of training resisting the urge to overfeed strays roaming around his bakery.

Claude entered the dining room and found half the table dedicated to a morning brunch: eggs, grilled ham, sausages all glistening with grease, while a pile of crepes waited on the side, with some precious maple syrup Em must have kept since spring. A bowl of fruit salad and orange juice completed the offering, and his mouth watered at the luxury of it all. The sun was barely up, yet they'd already prepared a brunch, and Claude didn't remember when he'd enjoyed such a thorough breakfast. He filled a plate with a little of everything then moved to the other end of the table, where Koyani and Adèle picked at their food in silence. The screams of Clémence's brother still echoed through the house.

"Is no one else up?" he asked. "I would have expected everyone to hear that."

"Neighbours included, yes," Koyani said. "The team is trying to sleep. Marcel needed to replenish his strength, or this kid would be doing the same."

"Can't we bring him to Clémence?"

"If you want to drag a screaming child across the city to the evil scientist who created exocores and is without a doubt being watched by Montrant Industries, or working on the Pont des Lumières' premises this very moment, suit yourself," Koyani replied. "I'm staying here."

"Right. I clearly need more coffee."

Adèle gestured at the pot in the centre of the table. "It's nothing fancy, but I made it strong."

"Just like you enjoy it." He smiled at her as he reached for it, and Adèle grinned back. The combination of her genuine pleasure and dishevelled bed head made his head spin and his mouth dry, and he tore his gaze away to focus on pouring his cup. While Val-de-mer's dark green uniform granted her a sharp, assumed kind of sexiness, the loose shirt and latent sleepiness led to an understated, far more potent attractiveness—like she didn't realize how amazing she looked, and how little he needed the coffee to be awake now. Claude cleared his throat and hoped the fire in his cheeks didn't mean he'd grown bright red. "I take it the expedition went well?"

"I don't know about 'well', but everyone is safe and sound," Koyani said. "You can ask the Paddlefish for details. I'm sure she'd love to share the tale."

Of course Zita would enjoy that. Claude reminded himself he needed to prod his best friend about that nickname's origins, and if anyone except Koyani used it. He couldn't help but wonder at the fondness with which the capitaine pronounced the word. "I will."

"I can't believe you forced me to sleep through this," Adèle muttered. "Nothing happened here."

"Cats invaded my bed and you didn't stop them," Claude replied. "Besides, you had your head in a pillow before I even left."

"I try not to send officers who have been shot on the field," Koyani said. "You needed the rest. Now you'll be ready for tonight."

"We'll have the mairesse's support, in more ways than one, but her demand was clear." Claude let the sentence hang in the air and shoved delicious egg in his mouth. Needlessly dramatic, perhaps, but didn't he deserve to eat and enjoy himself? Koyani had frozen in place, fingers half-wrapped around a glass of juice. Claude swallowed. "We're duty-bound to crash the Pont des

Lumières' opening ceremony and, dare I say it, shed light on the horrors of Montrant Industries."

Adèle snorted at his pun—the saints bless her, if she hadn't, they might not have made good partners after all. Koyani released a sigh of relief and snatched her glass off the table, her smile widening. "Now that's the Denise Jalbert I know. For a moment, I worried she would demand compromises from me. She knows I wouldn't accept."

"It sounded like she did." These two obviously had a history, and it was none of his business. He focused on his meal, glad for solid food to put at the bottom of his stomach. Two of the witches he'd rescued entered while he was eating, followed by one of Koyani's men—Yuri, the pale one who'd stayed with Adèle. He greeted them with a nod while heading for the breakfast table. Claude turned back to Koyani. "She promised to disrupt security as much as possible and to get in touch with information about what she accomplished late in the day. Frankly, I don't care what happens at the ceremony. All I want is to go in there and save my sister."

"Then focus on that."

"There ought to be other exocores and witches with Livia, right?" Adèle asked. "You've been rescuing these people from the start. Finish what you started, and we'll deal with everything that added itself to the task. You don't have to do it all."

"In fact, you shouldn't," Koyani continued. "The longer you stay the central figure in this, the harder it will become to hide the rest of your life. Since we have a spider's blessing, I propose you try to go entirely unnoticed and let the attention shift on Mairesse Jalbert, myself, and Adèle. Mx. Kouna might even help us spin the tale away from you."

"Good. That... that would be really nice." Claude longed for the stillness of his bakery early in the morning, for a night cuddling against Adèle, or for a day of getting beaten at board games by Livia. He wanted his routine with loving and supportive friends and family, and for that, he needed anonymity.

Yuri slid at the table with his plate—a mountain of crepes and syrup, with no egg or meat whatsoever. "Already planning for tonight?" The fork and knife in hand, he attacked his food with great enthusiasm, stopping to speak in-between bites. "You could wait until after breakfast, you know. Clémence's Montrant Industries care package contained the full schematics of the Pont des Lumières and its surroundings."

"I'll set it up in the library," Adèle suggested. "Em has a large table for when her research spreads and becomes a little... out of control."

"Excellent." Koyani pushed herself up. "I'll clean myself up. Rendez-vous there in an hour."

The entire afternoon was devoted to plans. They examined schematics of the bridge and debated the best approach, they argued over who should come and who should stay safe, and they struggled to figure out when to seize control and what to say. Claude did his best to help, but the back and forth fried his brain. That was why he had never been a planner: the details slipped out of his mind as soon as they entered. After a while, he interrupted

344

to give Koyani instructions on how to reach the Spinster and left.

They could tell him the plan later. He, however, needed to relax.

Claude granted himself permission to use Emmanuelle's kitchen. Like the rest of the manor, it was elegant and airy, with enormous counters that he immediately envied. Large ovens occupied most of his bakery's small space, and while he had sufficient counter length, Em's surface stretched to almost double the size of his. Claude ran his fingers over it before seeking his most trusted allies: flour, water, salt, and yeast. He grinned when he found nuts and raisins, mentally making adjustments to his basic recipe. It'd been too long since he had baked anything—a few days, in truth, but they felt like a lifetime. Gnawing worry at the multiple ways tonight could fail disappeared as he measured ingredients, mixed them together, and created a sticky, humid dough. He didn't need plans. He needed bread, and a creative outlet for his nervous energy—nothing could beat dough under his fingers for that. Claude soon had the basics for baguettes ready for the five-hour wait of the first pointe. He wished he'd thought to mix poolish before leaving for Denise's house, the previous night—when had he last prepared anything without pre-fermentation? Too bad. Claude ransacked the kitchens until he found butter and started on the croissants' dough.

"Zita said I'd find you here."

Adèle's voice caught him off guard. He jerked in his surprise, and his elbow hit the sack of flour, tipping it over. A white cloud rose over the counter, covering him as he scrambled to right the sack. For a brief, chaotic moment he expected it to roll to the ground and create an even bigger mess, and Adèle's easy chuckles assuaged his frantic panic.

"I'm sorry," he said. "I was... very caught up. In my croissant-making."

"I could see that." Adèle laughed again, before stepping in and searching the many drawers for something to clean with. "They're still going over contingencies. I'm starting to believe Yuri is capable of conceiving every single scenario imaginable. It's fascinating."

"I think 'exhausting' is the word you're looking for," Claude replied. He gathered the flour off the counter with his hands, ignoring Adèle's offer of a cloth. "Don't mind me. I had too little sleep, and plans make my head spin. I'd rather be clear-headed than completely knackered."

"Fair enough." She leaned on the counter next to him, right over the flour. If the potential white smears bothered her, she didn't show. "Does that mean you'll improvise?"

"Clémence implied Livia would be in the upper parts of the Pont's structure. There's a doorway near the top. I'll enter from there and search unless Zita senses her elsewhere. What else can I plan? I don't know what state Livia will be in, or even exactly where to find her." He grabbed the bag of flour and closed it, before returning to his croissants' dough, turning it over and kneading as he talked. "One thing has held true throughout this entire ordeal, however: the saints have watched over my dangerously impulsive posterior and kept me in one piece. I can only trust they will do so again."

Adèle laughed, then reached for the amulet at her neck. "We can only hope they'll protect us all."

Silence slithered between them as Claude left the croissant dough alone and checked on the bread's mix, to see if it had raised any. At first, the silence bothered him. He and Adèle were always trading words, whether it was while he asked her for news every morning at the bakery, or during her brief but tense exchanges with Claire. But not all silences needed to be filled, and Claude enjoyed the discreet and solid company this afforded him. He'd wanted to relax, not to dwell on the myriad of ways tonight could end. Adèle continued cleaning up while he worked, taking care of the flour that had spilled on the ground broom in hand, much like Livia had swept the *Croissant-toi*'s floor on the day of her arrival. Only when they were done and Adèle was storing the broom did Claude speak again.

"Have you… talked to Élise?"

"No." Adèle clenched her teeth and slammed the cupboard's door close. "Koyani and Inha have been with her, but I see no point. In the end, I didn't know her that well."

It had been long enough for the betrayal to hurt, that much Claude could tell from the sharpness of Adèle's tone. He didn't push the issue, however. Élise could rot in a cell for decades for all he cared; she would deserve it. He had only worried Adèle would need closure of some sort. Perhaps not.

"I guess we're ready for tonight, then," he said.

"If such a thing is possible." The corners of her lips curved up in a shy smile. "What did you ask of me, once, at the warehouse? Promise me you won't die? I don't want to lose my new partner. It's... hard, letting you split up from the group so soon. I wish we could stay together."

Claude froze near the doorway. The depth of Adèle's caring left him breathless, both from the head-spinning warmth it filled him with, and from the incessant voice of doubts, at the bottom of his mind. She loved him—romantically loved him—that much was clear as day. Did she expect him to change? Eventually give it back? Would she grow bitter if his love remained different? But he had been honest from the start, and Adèle had acknowledged it. He had to believe she understood and accepted what it meant.

"I'm not dying anytime soon," he promised. "Imagine how many croissants are in our future? I want us to sit down and talk again, about us, but I want to do that with Livia safe, and with someone else taking care of Montrant. After that, we can enjoy some butter-filled goodness and define the shape of us."

"That sounds wonderful." Her voice had the same fragile huskiness Claude felt inside, and knowing they shared that uncertainty reassured him. Adèle crossed the kitchen in those long, determined strides that had always characterized her gait, and she set a hand on his shoulder. "Whatever the shape, I want you to be comfortable with it. It doesn't matter if it's unusual. We just need it to fit us, right?"

"Right." And that was why she was amazing. A soft smile brightened his face, and Claude opened the door. "I bet it'll be croissant-shaped," he added. "Because of the layers."

He had said it in jest and was rewarded with Adèle's heartfelt laughter, but his thoughts lingered on the imagery. When he had first spoken of layers to Adèle, he had meant complications—elements and secrets that hindered their potential relationship. Perhaps that had been wrong. Perhaps they had needed the layers, like how flaky dough required being folded over and over in order to rise. Would their bond be as strong without Claire's stealing and the shroud of mystery that had kept Adèle from perceiving all of him? He liked to think every one of their interactions, even the rocky ones, had contributed to the final result, and they had now reached the last step: baking.

He couldn't wait to see what would come out of the oven.

-29-

LUMIÈRE CRUELLE

EVEN WITH THE SPINSTER'S HELP, SNEAKING TO THE STAGE where political figures would inaugurate the Pont des Lumières proved a struggle. The first entrance had been unguarded, but other soldiers had moved around the premise, and Koyani, Yuri, and Adèle had needed every bit of coordination to take guards out before they were spotted. They had found themselves wishing Marcel had stayed with them, but he, Inha and several witches approached the area from the opposite side, closer to the bridge, opening a path for Claire and Zita.

By the time they made it to the front scene, Mairesse Jalbert was well into her speech. Her voice travelled over the gathered crowd, powerful even with the scratchy quality of old age threaded through it. "We can only hope that the Pont des Lumières will forever stand as a witness to what humanity is capable of. Many lives were sacrificed during the construction of this bridge—people who often go forgotten and unseen, but whose contributions we must remember. Today, we finally shed light on the Pont, and, as we celebrate, we must keep them in our minds."

Adèle grinned. Every single one of those words could be reinterpreted, and, when the day was over, people would look back to the Spinster's speech and notice the extra threads woven into her message. No wonder Koyani and Claude liked her so much. She had a way with the crowd, capturing their attention. Adèle had only ever read quotes from the mairesse before, and with a few spoken lines she understood why Val-de-mer had reelected Denise Jalbert for the past fourteen years.

"But enough about me," Jalbert declared. "Let's hear it from the true instigator of our brand-new bridge, the woman who pulled all the strings to make this happen in our beautiful city, the gouverneure of our state, Madame Annabelle Lacroix."

She stepped back with a wide gesture at the smaller woman by her side, who had chosen an elegant forest green dress for the occasion. Gouverneure Lacroix thanked the mairesse with a nod then strode forward under the thunderous applause. A delicate smile decorated her lips, and she moved with poise and purposefulness. It was a different kind of confidence than the Spinster's, but no less striking. In her fifties, the gouverneure had forged her way up through strength of character and, it seemed, a large network unafraid of shady dealings.

"Good evening, citizens." Her voice rose as she spoke, carrying across the crowd with ease, rich and warm. "It is with immense pleasure that I am at this grand opening tonight. The Pont des Lumières is more than a gigantic infrastructure. It is my life's work—a beautiful gift to this city I once inhabited, and which has suffered so much over the last decades. Many of you may know I was born in the Quartier des Épinettes, and my heart has grieved along with yours for the lives brutally wiped out in the Meltdown. Val-de-mer has endured difficult years, but today we move on!" A hard edge crept into her tone. "We move into a new era, one without dependence on witches' fickleness. Starting tonight, we are in control of our destiny. And this beautiful bridge? It will light our way!"

She raised a hand, fingers stretched towards the sky, then clamped it into a fist and lowered her arm. At her signal, the Pont the Lumières blazed to life. Soft white lights ran along its main towers and the bridge behind, illuminating the structure, but the most impressive change came from the glasswork. Spotlights must have been installed on the other side, because the darkened piece of art turned into an intricate pattern of colourful tiles. A great tree stretched its branches, roots digging into red soil, the purple sky alive above it. And smack in the middle of the illustration, as if clinging to one of the branches, was Claire.

Adèle's heart plunged as the brightness highlighted Claire's shape, with Zita on her back. The crowd gasped and pointed, Gouverneure Lacroix cursed, and the soldiers raised their guns. Adèle sprinted forward, yelling "Marcel!" and gesturing at the line of guards between herself and the stage, now taking aim at Claire. They crumpled to the ground, put to sleep by her colleague's well-placed spell, and chaos followed their fall. The crowd backed away as one, people pushing at each other to get farther from the stage. On the other side, bright flames erupted from Celosia as Docteure Adaho's small team of witches kept the soldiers busy. Several still shot at Claire, but she smashed the glasswork in. As the shattering of glass rang above the many screams, she disappeared within the Pont des Lumières, and Adèle returned her attention to their task. They needed to take control.

Koyani and Yuri had surged past her, leaping over the sleeping guards and climbing onto the stage. The capitaine clamped her hand over the gouverneure's shoulders, the other holding handcuffs. Two bodyguards tried to rush in to help Lacroix, but Yuri put two sleeping darts into them with exemplar calm. Adèle joined them and surveyed the crowd. Inha and Marcel had been hard at work neutralizing what security the mairesse hadn't managed to remove, and both the constant blasts of gunshots and Celosia's fire stopped quickly.

"What is this?" the gouverneure demanded. "An arrest?"

"Hopefully," Koyani said.

The gouverneure scoffed, but before either could continue their low conversation, a strange hush fell over the plaza. Most of the crowd had dispersed with the first gunshots, shoving their way to the closest streets, but those remaining stilled their flight and turned to listen. Many now edged back, their curiosity overcoming their need for safety. Adèle easily found Nsia Kouna within the spectators: they had ditched their quick disguise and stayed near the front lines. They were sketching furiously, eager not to miss a moment. Adèle slid closer to Capitaine Koyani, and she noticed Yuri naturally did the same on the other side and grabbed the gouverneure, allowing his capitaine full freedom of movement. Koyani set her hands on her hips and cleared her throat, to cast her voice across the plaza.

"My unit has been investigating the creation of exocores. We believe you, Gouverneure Lacroix, have been involved into this thoroughly inhuman process, and we have questions you must answer."

"Do you, now? You must be Capitaine Koyani." Just like Koyani, she made certain her firm and cutting affirmation would be heard by all. Adèle gritted her teeth and forced herself not to look in her direction—to continue staring at the crowd ahead. The bridge still cast bright light upon it. She hoped Claire would find Livia before this monstrosity could drain too much of her sister away. "I was told to expect a rogue police squad—people who haven't hesitated to kill Lieutenant Élise Jefferson after she took over their investigation. To think you would ally with *witches*, too! You, Capitaine Koyani, have no authority to place me under arrest. You have been discharged."

"She has *my* authority," Denise Jalbert declared, stepping forward. When the gouverneure glared at her, she countered with a smile. "You are on my city's grounds and have perpetrated crimes against my citizens. I trust Capitaine Koyani's team above all else, and I—"

Thundering hooves interrupted the mairesse, growing closer by the moment. The gathered residents understood what they meant immediately and surged towards the exits, eager to flee, but the Bernéais National Guard blocked their paths. They stood proudly atop their horses, rifles at the ready, their lines cutting off every road leading out the plaza. Adèle's grip tightened on her pistol. Denise Jalbert had no authority over these soldiers — only the gouverneure did.

If the Spinster realized that, she didn't show it. She turned to Koyani with a smile. "I did warn you they would bring the cavalry."

Koyani grinned back. "Right as—"

A gunshot cracked across the plaza, coming from the Pont's heights, and Yuri gasped. He stumbled back, his grip on the gouverneure slipping as blood flowed out of his side. In the second it took for Adèle's brain to scream *sniper*, Koyani dove to catch her man before he hit the ground, and Gouverneure Lacroix dashed away. The attack command followed—"À l'assaut!"—and the national guard rushed forward.

Immense walls of fire burst before them, intercepting their charge and causing the horses to rear. Inha's calm orders rang even above the screams of citizens and high-pitched neighing, and Adèle struggled with her desire to help fight the police back. They'd predicted all but the sniper, and everyone on the team had their role. She needed to trust that Inha and Marcel could direct the witches with sufficient efficiency to regain control of the plaza. Her job was to grab the stage, unravel the conspiracy, and arrest Gouverneure Lacroix. Yet here she was, standing still on the wooden boards with Denise Jalbert, an obvious target.

"Madame la mairesse, get to cover!"

Adèle spared a moment to check on Koyani, and, once certain her capitaine was carrying Yuri away, she sprinted in the opposite direction, running after the gouverneure. The woman had made a beeline around the scene, avoiding the crowd in favour of the back ways through which Adèle'd sneaked in moments ago. Adèle followed, trying to predict the route, and her stomach twisted. The only person anywhere near their entrance and the gouverneure's path was Emmanuelle, waiting for her turn in their planned speech. Her sister would never allow the gouverneure to escape without a fight, no matter the risks.

"I'm not letting you through." Em's voice echoed down the small alley, firm and confident.

"You're not? Now that remains to be seen."

Something in the gouverneure's tone chilled Adèle to the bone, and her strides lengthened. She could sense the woman's threat—her absolute certitude that she was escaping safe and sound—and that didn't bode well for Em. If only Adèle could arrive in time...

A second gunshot rang, and Adèle turned the corner as her sister buckled. She fell to her knees with a moan, and standing behind her, gun smoking, was Élise. Free and smiling. Their gaze met, and Élise shifted her aim immediately. Adèle flung herself back into the building's cover just in time to avoid the bullet.

"Adèle Duclos, my dear new colleague. I do believe your sister is bleeding to death. Are you really going to stay hidden?"

Despite her quick dash and the frenzied beating of her heart, Adèle felt cold. Ice in her veins and muscles, ice in her mind, slowing her thoughts, allowing only for one: Em was dying. And it froze her in place, her back against the wall, her numb hands around her own firearm. She couldn't move, couldn't imagine a

356

solution.

"Took you long enough," Gouverneure Lacroix said to Élise. "I was starting to worry."

"Then you'll want to review your national guard's efficiency. They hadn't gotten the message about leaving me in charge and disputed my authority."

"Heads will roll. Now do your job and silence this. People have already heard too much."

They needed to hear it all, Adèle added mentally to herself, and Em should have explained the science to them. She couldn't, not if she died. Adèle gritted her teeth, and her hesitation thawed away. She might not have Claire's superspeed or the years of experience Koyani boasted, but she knew a few tricks, and she understood human nature. She risked a glance to evaluate the two women's positions. Élise had moved closer to cover, while the gouverneure was striding over Em, out in the open.

And then she noticed that Em was staring right back at her, eyes open and quite aware. Pain contorted her expression, but as soon as her gaze met Adèle, she nodded. Relief flooded through Adèle, and she flicked a thumbs-up at her sister. Emmanuelle's hand snapped out, grabbing the gouverneure's ankle and yanking her off her feet. Lacroix cried out, and Élise reflexively reached out to catch her. As soon as she left her cover, Adèle leaned forward and shot twice. The first bullet hit the wall, but the second touched Élise's arm and caused her to drop her gun. Without wasting a moment, Adèle stepped entirely out and pulled her trigger again, aiming for Élise's leg. Her old partner fell to the ground with a yelp

357

of pain, but she immediately stretched towards her firearm. Adèle sprinted, arriving just in time to kick it far, far away from Élise.

"This is over," she said, pointing her gun at Élise. "Don't make me shoot you."

The gouverneure had wriggled back into a sitting position, leaning on the wall, but she didn't seem of a mind to run again. Perhaps she wasn't keen on her knee becoming like Élise's.

"Adèle…" Emmanuelle's voice was weak, and the red stain at the back of her sky-blue dress worried Adèle, but her sister smiled. "We make a great team. Do you know… how far Zuri is?"

"Not far," she said, even though she had last been on the other side of the area. She hoped Docteure Adaho had noticed Yuri fall and had run in their direction. The cries from the plaza seemed to have calmed. "Hang in there. Someone will be there soon."

It ended up taking several painfully long minutes. Adèle wished she could help her sister and apply pressure on the bullet wound in her back, but between the fire burning in Élise's eyes and the gouverneure's tense stance she didn't dare. The moment she relaxed her vigilance, they would jump her and escape—or the gouverneure would, at least. Emmanuelle seemed to understand. She stayed unmoving, her teeth gritted, and at one point muttered something about "not being in shape for her speech." As time passed, Em was obviously struggling to cling to consciousness, and Adèle could feel her heart shrivelling as her sister slipped away. They had come all this way to save Claire's sister, and now Adèle risked losing hers? It wasn't fair, and she couldn't accept it. When Mairesse Jalbert finally rounded the corner, she snapped, unable to contain the panic rising in her.

"Get Zuri *now*! Docteure Adaho. Please."

Denise Jalbert's gaze went from Adèle to Élise, then the gouverneure and Emmanuelle. She nodded, her wrinkles deepening as she frowned. "Of course. No one is dying today—not Monsieur Osinov, and certainly not Madame Duclos."

She turned on her heel and left as quickly as she'd arrived. As they fell back into waiting, Adèle could only hope her words would come true.

Claire clung to the solid metal bars keeping the Pont's impressive glasswork together. When she'd told Adèle she would improvise, she hadn't expected to be climbing the front façade of the Pont des Lumières with Zita holding on for dear life on Claire's back, her arms wrapped around her neck. But that happened, when your best friend recognized your twin's signature magic within the Pont after weeks of searching for her.

They had been in the middle of yet another planning session, this time right under the Pont's shadow, led by Inha and Marcel, who were intent on discussing tactics to keep control of the plaza and how to spread around it, ready to act once things became heated. Claire couldn't have cared less. She had been staring at the looming structure, trying to decide how to enter, when Zita had pulled her sleeve. "Claire! I can feel her. It's very faint but I can feel Livia!"

Just a few words, and any pretense of caution Claire had had vanished. "Where? In the Pont?" A nod from Zita. "Do you need to get closer?" Another nod. "Hop on my back, then."

She had flooded her muscles with magic, and before any of Koyani's team or the accompanying witches could protest, Claire had dashed for the Pont and started climbing. Darkness had shrouded the entire structure for now, waiting to be lit, and it was the fastest way to reach the estimated location. It might not have been her best decision. Magic compensated for the slim holds and the extra weight of Zita on her back, but already her strength had diminished. She'd only climbed about halfway up the towers.

"Are we close?" she asked, hoping Zita's Seeking powers would have homed in on Livia.

"No, I—it's so hard! I'm sorry, I catch hints of her but there's so many others!"

"Don't worry. Just—"

Intense light erupted from behind the glass and transformed Claire's words into a surprised cry. She squeezed her eyes shut at the bright assault, freezing where she hung, well in sight of those below. Zita screamed even louder, her fingers digging holes in Claire's shoulders, her voice turning hoarse from the high-pitched plea.

"No please stop—it's too much! I can't…"

Zita trailed off and her grip loosened. Claire could swear she felt every finger slip one by one, and the pressure from her friend's legs vanished. Claire released one of her thin holds, twisting over, her heart stuck in her throat as her best friend peeled away, falling. She caught Zita just before she was out of reach, her fingers stabbing into her friend's darker hand, clinging so tight the skin whitened around their edges. Magic surged through Claire's muscles, compensating for the shock and extra weight, and she wished she had a power to steady her frenzied heart.

Far below them, policemen lined up, raising weapons in their direction. Claire yelped as the first gunshot rang. A thousand colourful swears crossed her mind, but even alone with the unconscious Zita she couldn't bring herself to utter them. Her shoulders hunched in a desperate attempt to make herself smaller, Claire braced one boot against the metal railing and kicked hard at the beautiful stained glass. It shattered under her enhanced strength, leaving an opening barely large enough for her and Zita despite their size. Claire pulled her friend up and into a close embrace, her nerves flaring with every new bang from a gun. They would die. She would get hit by a bullet and her fingers would relinquish the too-thin hold and they would fall to their deaths.

Familiar shouts echoed from below. She couldn't parse the words at this height, but Adèle's voice went straight to her heart, cradling it reassuringly. She wasn't alone, not truly. Holding Zita tight, Claire shut her eyes and swung her body through the hole, barely squeezing through. Two sharp blades of pain flared in her forearm and side—the broken glass taking its toll for their passage—then she was on the other side.

Falling.

Her stomach heaved as they plunged downward and she regretted the forceful swing through. Claire twisted her body midair, wrapping her legs and arms around Zita to cushion her as best as she could. Her friend moaned, slowly coming back to her senses. Just in time for the pain, Claire thought. She had a brief glimpse of the scope of the room—wide walls glowing red despite the bright light inside—then they hit the ground. Claire's breath snapped out of her lungs and sparks flew before her eyes.

For a long moment, everything went black and silent. Claire lost track of time, of everything except the burning in her back and the sharp flare in her chest every time she tried to breathe.

Sounds returned first. Zita's weeping, to be exact. Claire's eyes opened but couldn't focus past the blur of her bright surroundings.

"No, please. There's so many... Everywhere—I can't..."

Zita's voice cracked with every word, interrupted by the occasional sob. Claire shifted her head towards her, and the bulky brown mass of her friend slowly became an actual person in her swimming vision. She was clenching her head, eyes squeezed shut.

"Zita," Claire croaked. "Zita, what happened?"

Zita turned her ears as if to better listen. "I can... I feel them all." She gestured at the wide room around them, and it hit Claire.

The red glow. She hadn't paid it any mind when falling, but now her gaze came into focus, and every gleaming exocore jumped before her eyes. So many. Entire walls embedded with them, one row after another, stretching to the very top then across the ceiling, where they hung like red eyes in the shadows. Had they stolen witches from all across the country? In Tereaus too? There had to be hundreds... and all of them had been brutally awakened when they'd turned on the bridge, leaping into Zita's consciousness and overwhelming her.

Claire struggled to her knees, wincing at the pain, and crawled to her friend. She squeezed Zita's shoulder, hoping the firm hand would anchor her.

"I'm here. I'm right here. Zita, listen to me. You can control it. Shut it down."

Zita answered with a keen moan and leaned into her. Claire wrapped her arms tight around her. This had happened once before, when they were still teenagers. Witches from every quartier had gathered for a quick competition, as they used to before the Meltdown. Zita's unhoned skills hadn't handled the massive amount of magic well. She'd panicked, unable to deal with the sudden surge of pain, and —

Just like then, Zita's head snapped up, as if something had caught her attention. She scrambled up, pushing Claire away, and sprinted straight for the closest door. Her strides were uneven, as if she was drunk, and more than once Claire thought she would fall back to her knees.

"Zita, wait!"

Claire struggled to her feet, the hot pain from her glass cuts almost keeping her down. She gritted her teeth, fighting against the spinning world and the blackening of her vision. Her best friend was stumbling away, panicked and agonized, and Claire had no idea how many soldiers patrolled inside the Pont. They would all be on high alert now, perhaps ready to shoot Zita on sight. Claire couldn't risk leaving her alone, no matter how much blood was gushing from her wounds. She dashed after Zita through a side door, down a narrow corridor of pristine grey walls, and into a second, much smaller room.

Two very distressing sights awaited her.

First were the three witches held into a vertical apparatus by a translucent film: two masculine figures on the left and right, and stuck between them, Livia. The film also glowed red, giving all three humans a striking and nauseating resemblance to functioning exocores in their sockets. Livia's cheeks had turned unnaturally thin, as if the device sucked away her physical form as well as her magic power. Claire stared at her sister's sickly brown skin, the brutally shorn hair, and her bone-thin wrists, unable to move beyond the horror the sight inspired her. All along, she had known what she'd find. She had known what was happening, what they were doing to her, but no amount of preparation could have saved her from the shock. Darkness encroached at the edge of her vision, threatening to overtake her, and she started shaking so hard her legs almost gave in. Claire tore her gaze away from the sight to focus on Zita—the second disturbing element.

Her friend stood next to Clémence, tears streaming down her cheeks, clinging to ol and struggling to breathe. Clémence had an arm wrapped around her shoulders, and Claire couldn't tell if it was meant to hold Zita or comfort her. Both, perhaps.

"Let her go," she growled.

Clémence straightened and snorted. "I'm not restraining her. I'm appeasing her."

Zita wiped her tears away with a wide gesture and turned

to Claire. She managed a slight smile—not the most reassuring expression. "I-I'm sorry. It was just too much. All those exocores… all those witches suddenly flaring to life. Then I felt Clémence, and that perfect sphere of emptiness, and I ran. I couldn't think of anything else."

Claire gritted her teeth. It made a lot of sense, and she was glad Zita had found some peace, but she couldn't bring herself to be *relieved* Clémence was in the Pont des Lumières, not to mention right next to Livia. "It's fine, Zita. We should have expected this and avoided bringing you here. This entire building is like a catacomb of exocores. And we know who's to blame for that."

If she could have drilled holes in Clémence with a glare, she would have. Zita must have caught her meaning because she stepped aside, away from her old friend. Clémence lifted ols chin, and if ol had any guilt over ols actions, none of it showed.

"Is he safe?" ol asked.

"Of course. We wouldn't have let them hold a kid hostage just because I hate your face," Claire said. "Now can you free Livia, or must we have this conversation while this accursed bridge drains away her entire being?"

Clémence clacked ols tongue. "It's not that simple."

Claire was upon ol in a flash. A burst of speed carried her into the range of Clémence's nullifying power, and even without enhanced strength, she grabbed the much-taller Clémence and pushed ol until ol slammed into the closest wall. Zita let out a terrified exclamation and implored her to stop, but Claire didn't listen. "I don't care if it's complicated. We rescued your brother, and you're going to save my sister. Do whatever it takes. It's already stretched on too long, and soldiers will be on their way. Do it *now*."

"It could be dangerous. Their own raw magic forms a film that draws the rest out, as if trying to reach a new physical shell. Exocores function in the same manner, except that the more the magic fills the gem, the less pressure it applies to suck out what is left. I refined the technique to obtain the most out of any witch, but even then... This works better. The pressure never diminishes because the power is consumed as—"

"I couldn't care less about what horrors you conceived to drain her. You knew I would return, so you better have designed a way to get her out."

"I did... In theory. The film is their magic. I should be able to nullify it."

"Time to make theory into a reality, my friend."

"Please," Zita added, her voice almost a squeak.

Ever since Claire had reminded her of Clémence's contribution to this horror, Zita had looked nauseated. Clémence turned to her, and ols expression softened. With a slight nod, ol headed for the wall and placed a hand on Livia's forearm. The film seemed to curl away from ol, like paper near a flame. Claire scuttled closer to her sister, ready to catch her. Her heart hammered as Clémence worked ols way up. What if she hadn't arrived fast enough? What if after all of this, Livia was lost? Could any of the people in the exocores truly be saved, or had they risked it all for nothing?

Warm fingers snatched up Claire's hand and squeezed it, stopping her panicked thoughts from wandering any farther. Claire glanced at Zita, standing by her side with a tired but confident smile. Warmth spread through her. Her best friend's optimistic view of life never failed to calm her. It would be okay. They would put an end to the exocore creation and fix the damage done. Adèle was down there with Koyani and the mairesse, exposing the gouverneure for her heinous crimes. They would prevent police forces from stomping up the Pont des Lumières and arresting Claire. And while they were cleaning up the exocore mess across the city, Claire could bring Livia home and welcome her back with the best croissants she had ever baked.

Sweat rolled down Clémence's forehead as ol worked, and the film stopped peeling away. Before Claire could complain, ol raised a hand. "I need a moment to recover before the hard part. I have to release them all together. This... Because the power is turned on, freeing your sister is applying more pressure on her two companions. Either I do all three, or they will die within minutes. I don't want to mess it up because I was careless."

Claire gritted her teeth. She wanted to scream. "Wonderful. Just... hurry as much as you can."

Pressing Clémence might have been unnecessary, but she'd needed to release some frustration. With every moment Livia spent in this half-cocoon of magic, her life force slipped into the bridge, perhaps lost forever. Somehow, she doubted Livia's deep pool of magic would remain unaffected by this technique. A look at her emaciated body destroyed any hope of that. Claire prayed

367

that time and care would allow her sister to recover from this ordeal, and as she watched Clémence free the two other witches, she extended that thought to all of those stuck in exocores, whether as a thin film of magic or as a gem.

Long minutes passed, and Claire wished she could see outside, or hear enough noises to know what was happening. A dull throb in the back of her head covered the din of whatever chaos Adèle and the others had created, muffling out even gunshots. She suspected the ambient magic, the constant pain from her wounds, and the blood loss were causing it. Perhaps once they'd shut down the Pont and received treatment, it would vanish. The lights started flickering as Clémence neared the end of ols work, and when ol finally removed the last of Livia's glowing cocoon, they fizzled out entirely. A long moan escaped Livia and she tilted forward, no longer imprisoned by the film. Claire slipped out of Zita's grasp and caught her twin as she fell.

Livia felt ridiculously light even without augmented strength, as fragile as thin ice. Claire wanted to squeeze her tight but feared breaking her sister's bones. She settled for a quick kiss on her temple and securing her hold. At least she had her. She could hardly believe it—her sister was in her arms, alive despite everything. Darkness had fallen around them, and Claire suspected the entire Pont des Lumières no longer shone bright and strong. They had cast it back into obscurity, right where it belonged.

-30-

OMBRES PROTECTRICES

WHEN ADÈLE RETURNED TO THE PLAZA, SHE CAUGHT A glimpse of the chaos that had unfolded without her. The Pont des Lumières was still shining bright light down on them, most of it white, and some coloured by the panels from the glasswork partly shattered by Claire's entrance. Trash cans were smoking near the plaza's exits, where Celosia's magic had set them on fire, and several soldiers of the national guards were lying on the floor, hopefully asleep. Riderless horses milled around the crowd, remaining at the edges of the confused mass of humans. Adèle had no idea what had happened to the sniper, but the mairesse stood defiantly in the middle of the front platform, so they must have had been taken care of. Marcel had knocked Élise out once more, and they had walked the gouverneure onto the stage.

Unwilling to leave Em's side as the docteure wove her healing net again, Adèle had stayed back with Zuri. Her sister had kept trying to shoo her off, promising Adèle she was feeling increasingly better and that if Yuri was fine she would be too, and it hadn't been until Koyani gripped Adèle's shoulders and asked for company on the stage that Adèle had agreed to leave. She'd hated every moment of it, but duty called, and deep down she knew she could count on Docteure Adaho.

She and Koyani flanked the mairesse on each side, with the capitaine holding the gouverneure steady once more. Adèle hoped that although their outfits were now bloodied, they still cut impressive figures. She found Kouna drawing again, at the exact same spot, as if they hadn't doubted for a second that they'd return. Reassured by their confidence, Adèle smiled.

The Spinster turned to the crowd with the poise of someone whose speech had not been interrupted by snipers and cavalry. "Thank you for staying or returning to us. To those worried, the officer shot while by my side earlier is in good hands and will survive. If you need to seek safety, please don't hesitate to leave the premise. What we have to say tonight will be printed in time for tomorrow's breakfast. If, however, you want to hear here and now why your lives were put in danger, remain here, with us." She waited, and a few made their way towards the exits. Once most of the crowd had stopped moving, she started weaving her tale.

"Citizens of Val-de-mer, I have told you earlier... Today, we shed light on the Pont's true nature! Many perished for this bridge, often unnoticed and forgotten—those who built the structure, and those who power it even now. And that is the heart of it. The exocores are witches, imprisoned within a gem, slowly being drained of their life force. The Pont des Lumières is an abomination—a testament to our cruelty—and it should never have been allowed to brighten our cityscape!"

The Pont's lights flickered as she finished her sentence, as if their power source had become unstable. Adèle's heart lifted at their first good sign from inside. It had to be Claire and Zita. Who else? Claire had found her sister, and she would shut the entire bridge down. Excitement and hope rippled through Adèle in a head-spinning wave, and she struggled to focus on her situation instead of imagining Claire's relief.

"This is nonsense," Lacroix said. "We have forsaken witch magic. It's unreliable and destructive, and the technology to force it into gems does not exist. You would do well to watch your words, Spinster. That web of yours won't hold against bigger prey."

The mairesse laughed, a brief and dismissive sound. "People here have had fourteen years to learn I do not spin my webs from lies, Madame la gouverneure, and nothing is more robust than the truth. Why else would you resort to snipers and soldiers? But we can explain in more detail, provided Madame Duclos feels up to it despite her very recent gunshot wound. Emmanuelle, would you care to demystify the science in general terms?"

Adèle spun on her heels as her sister strode upon the stage, wrapped in a golden light. The loose healing web circled Em's entire frame, more tightly knit around her belly and back. Docteure Adaho held her arm, supporting her, and they walked with a deliberate calm that gave both an air of regality. Em had pinned up her curls again, and her hair looked sterling, as if she had never been attacked. She exuded competence and confidence, and as she

371

took the centre stage, Adèle couldn't tear her eyes away.

"Good evening, everyone," Em begun with her science-lecture voice. "I'm afraid I have had little time to prepare charts and graphs to facilitate comprehension tonight. I have, however, had ample opportunity to examine those used to devise the exocores, and the conversion of magic into a solid support for energy is a specialty of mine. We will keep this simple, as I'm sure none of you attended this event or stayed through the violence for a science lesson." A smattering of chuckles spread across the crowd and Em smiled at them.

"Magic is a form of energy. It exists in the air around us, like a great many other things we've yet to properly fathom. Witches pull upon this ambient energy and create an internal pool of it. Exocores steal this pool. One must understand, however, that although we use the image of a reservoir to describe a witch's magic, it is not… gathered in such a manner. Their magic is threaded through their very being. You cannot tear the magic away without taking the witch, too. It *must* be freely given, or the person is trapped in the gem alongside their power."

She paused, letting the full implication of her words sink in, the deafening silence sign enough that most were putting one and one together. Behind her, the bridge's lights kept flickering more and more. Emmanuelle shifted towards it. "Right now, as we speak, people's life force is being drained everywhere across the city."

"But someone saw it coming." Adèle stepped forward, half-surprised at her own intervention. She hated public speaking, and now all eyes had turned to her. She could feel them drilling through her, judging her, and her heart sped under the pressure. "When I arrived here, I was tasked with finding and arresting a purple-haired thief—one whom Mx. Nsia Kouna dubbed 'the Exocore Thief' in an incisive article. You saw her climbing the Pont des Lumières earlier. From the start, she and others knew something was wrong with the exocores. She saved hundreds of them already and she is saving even more right now." The lights went down for longer than usual, and Adèle was certain Claire had almost finished. The crowd had hushed in a reverential silence. Adèle smiled; they were listening, believing. "Lieutenant Jefferson isn't dead: she was involved in the large-scale kidnapping and transformation of hundreds of witches, and shot Emmanuelle less than an hour ago in one last desperate attempt to stop us."

"And yet we're here," Koyani continued, picking up right where Adèle had left it. "Gouverneure Lacroix said the Pont des Lumières was her life's work. She put everything she had into it, coercing one of Madame Duclos' colleagues into developing a brand-new form of energy and throwing her political weight behind Montrant Industries. It's over now. Adèle, would you like the honour?"

Adèle's heart jumped as Koyani extended manacles to her. The gouverneure was staring ahead, pale and stiff, her chin lifted with as much dignity as she could muster. She was no longer arguing. Either she recognized the pointlessness when faced with an increasingly hostile crowd, now filled with angry mutterings, or she had another plan, secret cards to play later. The idea sent chills down Adèle's spine, but she pushed it away. Tonight, they were exposing Montrant Industries. They could think of the consequences later.

Accepting the handcuffs, Adèle walked solemnly to the gouverneure and grabbed her wrists before clipping the cuffs around them. The soft click echoed across the near-silent plaza, as if the hundred citizens gathered were holding their breath, waiting for the sound's finality and the undeniable confirmation of the events unfolding before them. And as Adèle pressed the handcuffs close, her hands steady despite the wild hammering in her chest, the Pont des Lumières' lights went out, leaving only the occasional gas lamp to stave off the darkness.

"She did it," Adèle whispered.

She allowed relief to flood through her as her eyes readjusted to the moonlight. The crowd clustered under the gas lamps around the area, seeking its light. One such lamp hung right above the front stage, and it now shed its light directly on Denise Jalbert, who had somehow known exactly where to stand. The mairesse began explaining the city's plan to retrieve every exocore installed into people's homes, offering financial compensation straight from Montrant Industries' coffers so Val-de-mer would recover. Adèle tuned out the details, her mind returning to her new partner, the brilliant baker who had started it all, still inside the Pont des Lumières. This wasn't over—of course not—but for now Adèle was ready to celebrate. Claire had found Livia, and they had arrested the gouverneure. It had almost cost Yuri and Emmanuelle their lives, but they had done it, and they deserved a break. She only hoped it would include fresh croissants and coffee.

No one came after Claire in the Pont des Lumières itself. She had expected troops to invade the corridors, booted feet echoing down the darkened paths and instead she received complete silence. Every step resonated loud and clear, and at first she had cringed at the sound announcing her presence. She had become so used to stealth and shadows. As Claire and the others progressed towards the exit, guided by Clémence's mental map of the building, Claire grew accustomed to her own loud striding. She held Livia tighter, straightened her back, and lifted her chin. The Pont des Lumières belonged to them now. They had taken over — why else would no one come after them, ready to shoot them down? Koyani's small team must have successfully kept the plaza under control.

Claire sped up her pace, eager to join the rest of the group and see what was left to be done. The Pont still contained hundreds of exocores, and someone needed to care for the two witches that had been installed with Livia. Zita had found a blanket for them and tried to make both as comfortable as possible while Clémence was recovering from the staggering drain of magic freeing the three witches had represented. They could ask Denise Jalbert to send allies — any ally but Claire. She had her sister, and the exhaustion of the past weeks was starting to settle in. She had done her part, and until she felt like more than an automated husk again, someone else would need to step up.

Claire strode out of the Pont des Lumières main entrance flanked by Zita and Clémence—a tiny barrel-shaped woman on one side, and a tall, dapper scientist on the other. A thin crowd was still milling around the plaza, forming groups of discussion, and the earlier chaos had left burning trash cans and downed guards. People hushed as they spotted the trio, nudging each other and pointing. Claire almost backpedalled into the Pont, her breath catching at suddenly being the centre of attention. Zita's small hand against her back steadied her, and she forced herself to inhale deeply. It would be okay. They had torn down the Pont des Lumières and the awful lies behind Montrant Industries. This crowd was *nothing* she couldn't handle. Claire sought the stage, across the plaza, and took her first confident stride in that direction, followed by Zita and Clémence.

To her surprise, people parted before them. Many whispered about the exocore thief, others shouted thanks at her. Clémence hunched ols shoulders, as if trying to occupy as little space as possible. Zita, however, grinned at the sudden influx of love. She waved at the crowd on each side, glowing at their enthusiasm. Halfway through the trek across the plaza, she leaned towards Claire and whispered "I can't believe they're so happy to see a bunch of witches." And she was right, that was incongruous. Would their reaction be so positive if they knew Claire held the very witch who had iced the Lark Soul Tree? Doubtful, but she had no intention of shattering their illusions. Claire couldn't remember the last public show of support for magic users, and she hoped this one would last. She summoned the confident façade she'd always donned with her mask and started nodding back at those who called out to her.

By the time she reached the elevated platform, Denise Jalbert stood on it, ready to welcome them. Zita climbed on it excitedly before helping Clémence up. Claire looked back at the smattering of people still gathered, staring at her intently, then tested her power. Clémence's negating field must be contained, because she could access her remaining magic with ease. Claire's smile grew—if they wanted a show, she could give them one.

"Good evening, Madame la Mairesse," she declared. She made sure she had a solid hold of Livia before pushing strength into her legs and springing up, leaping higher than the mairesse's thin frame, vaulting over her and landing neatly on the stage. Denise turned, startled but grinning. The crowd gasped and clapped, as if they had just witnessed great circus acrobatics, and the sound rushed to Claire's head. Still clutching Livia, she bowed and retreated, away from the scene and away from them. As *fun* as their awe was, she had no patience for public appearances.

Most of their team had formed a small secure perimeter behind the stage, stealing the tent structure that had been set up for the gouverneure and repurposing makeshift tables into… hospital beds? Her heart stopped as she stared at Yuri and Emmanuelle, both pale and bloodied. Zuri bent over the former, lowering a golden web over his wounds, her expression set in intense concentration. Emmanuelle seemed in a better state, already wrapped in soft light, but Adèle stayed by her side nonetheless, her sister's hand tight in hers. Claire hesitated at the edge, unsure where to put Livia down, or how urgently her twin needed help compared to Yuri and Emmanuelle. As she stood there, frozen and indecisive, Nsia Kouna spotted her and headed her way.

"Claire," they greeted. "Welcome to our temporary headquarters."

"Where is everyone?" She couldn't find Koyani or her team besides Adèle and Yuri, and many of the witches who had been in the warehouse had gone, too. Gouverneure Lacroix was nowhere around either.

"Getting our two criminals behind proper prison bars and making sure Emmanuelle's manor is safe to return to. Lieutenant Jefferson showed up while the gouverneure tried to escape and almost killed Em, so we think troops might have raided her house."

"Oh."

Words escaped her. Livia was starting to feel heavy in her arms, and she knew it was as much emotional exhaustion as carrying her sister around for so long. Nsia seemed to understand, because they set a hand on her elbow and slowly guided her closer to the beds. "Let me prepare a clean area for you to lay your twin down. It won't be much, but I'll ask Docteure Adaho to check on her after she is finished with Mister Osinov. You must not worry for Emmanuelle—she is only resting and was up on the stage earlier."

Relief flooded through Claire and she allowed Nsia to lead her around, listening to their instructions until Livia rested on a mix of coats and clothes, one of them bundled under her head as a pillow. At first, Claire wanted to sit by Livia's side and stay, irrationally certain that if she left her twin would disappear again. Nsia gently convinced her to take a break, insisting Adèle might be in need of some friendly company. When Claire glanced at the police officer's crestfallen expression, she couldn't help but agree. Adèle had rarely looked so stricken. Claire found a chair, dragged it close, and collapsed into the seat next to Adèle.

"Nsia told me she'd be okay," Claire said.

Adèle startled, as if she hadn't heard Claire settle nearby, too caught up in her fearful thoughts. She swallowed hard and flicked a smile. "I know. My guts won't accept it, but I know. I just... I knew this would be dangerous, but I was ready for *me* to... Not for her." She let go of Emmanuelle, clasping her hands together and setting them on her lap. They were shaking. "I don't understand how she lived. Élise shot her right before my eyes, almost at point blank. She... All the blood. It was—"

Claire wrapped an arm around Adèle's back, pulling her closer until they could lean against each other. "It's okay. It's over now. We did it, Adèle. No one's dying, from gunshots or being turned into exocores, or *anything*. Livia is safe, and so is your sister, and soon the four of us can sit around a table and play cards and chat, or eat fresh bread and make whatever plans we want."

"That sounds nice," Adèle said, and she leaned further into Claire, closing her eyes. "I'm glad you're here."

Warmth spread through Claire at the words and she whispered "me too" as she squeezed Adèle closer. She felt small, almost buried under the taller woman's frame, but Adèle's weight against her was full of reassuring promises. It was enough to be reunited with her, to be able to comfort Adèle and project into a common future—to know they had one, away from Montrant Industries' plots and the conflict that had plagued their early relationship. Claire closed her eyes, enjoying the press of Adèle's body as she imagined their next morning chat in the *Croissant-toi*, Adèle sitting at the counter while Claire prepared her strongest coffee and picked her best croissant out of the lot. She liked to think these brief exchanges would now end with Claire leaning over the counter to steal a kiss before sending her police officer to work.

-31-

DU PAIN ET DU REPOS

LIVIA SNATCHED A FIFTH CROISSANT OFF THE PLATE AND tore a large chunk from it before shoving it in her mouth. She had opened her eyes about an hour ago and, after being reassured by Claude that she was safe, she had caught a whiff of the fresh pastries. Her first words had been "are those croissants?" and she had said nothing but the occasional thank you since. She didn't need to. Tears had filled her eyes after a bite, and Claude knew that while she was probably famished, Livia was also using this prolonged break to sort through her feelings. He gave her the space she needed, sitting nearby with Gravity on his lap. Two more cats had elected to occupy Livia's bed and piled one upon the other within the single ray of sunlight falling on it. Sometimes Livia stopped eating to stare at them and the faintest hint of a smile curved her lips. She finished her croissant, then reached for Sol, running a hand through her thick orange fur. After long minutes scratching her around the ears, Livia voiced her first question. She hesitated, as if she couldn't decide what mattered the most. She met Claude's eyes, and determination shone behind her exhaustion.

"How much did you stop?"

Claude heard the determination nestled within her question: Livia meant to fight until Montrant Industries was destroyed if necessary. He smiled at his sister, glad she wouldn't have to.

"Everything," he said. "We found who and where, and Denise is helping us put an end to it all and retrieve all the exocores sold. Adèle and her capitaine are building a case on everyone related to Montrant Industries. It's over, Livia. I'm… I'm so sorry I brought you into this, and you suffered so much."

"There was a warehouse with women…"

"We saved them, too. There were a lot of exocores in it, and Zita could sense them. That's how I found your trail." Threads of guilt weighed him down again, but he pushed them away. He had rescued as many as he could—more than anyone else. He should mourn the others without blaming himself. Claude reached out, placing his hand over Livia's. "I know you want to participate, but you need to recover. It's under control now. You and I can rest."

He couldn't wait to return to his bakery, although he suspected he would take a few days off before reopening. Claude tried not to think of what his finances might look like after the time spent closed. It shouldn't matter, considering what he'd used that time for, yet it bothered him that he had let down faithful customers without an explanation. Would they ask questions? Might any of them recognize him from Kouna's first newspaper article? He had no desire for fame; he wanted his slow life back.

Livia clearly had different goals, however.

"What about the witches stuck in exocores? Can we do anything for them?" She slipped her hand out of his and turned her head away, to stare at the bright window. "They can't stay in there, Claude. It's too awful."

For a moment, he felt guilty. It hadn't crossed his mind that he should be there for the trapped exocores. Hadn't he done enough already? But in truth, he didn't grasp the science behind this and would have no idea where to start. "I know. Emmanuelle understands something of how they created these gems. If anyone can figure out how to undo them, it'll be her. She'll get a grant for it, too."

"Then I want to help," she said, and Claude realized instantly nothing could stop her.

"As long as you rest first."

"Sure."

And they both knew, from that simple answer, that she wouldn't—not unless forced to. Claude made a mental note to warn Emmanuelle about it so that Livia wouldn't burn herself out, then he grinned. "It's good to have you back, stubbornness and all."

Livia laughed, and the sudden loudness scared Sol away. She watched the cat scamper out of the door before turning to Claude. "It's... It's good to be here and feel human again. You don't need to be in a gem to feel like an animal—or even less than that. And those in exocores... they didn't have an awesome twin to come and save them. No one was there to convince them it's not true, that they're worth so much more than their magic."

"I've been talking to those I had, at least. Just in case they were sentient. I kept them up to date about my efforts." It had been weird, but Claude hoped they had heard him and understood they weren't abandoned. Still, for every exocore in his basement, a dozen others existed out there, perhaps more. And there were all of those he had lost in the warehouse. "Some... some people were still destroyed. I'll see with Denise if we can hold a ceremony for them."

They would have justice, but it felt important to also honour their memory. No one would ever know who had perished that night.

"You look exhausted," Livia commented. "You keep telling me to rest, but you're really no better. Will you be taking time off?"

"I'm going back to my bakery, yes."

Livia laughed and pushed at him. "That's not a break, Claude. That's a different task. Let's make a deal: I'll rest for three days if you do the same. Complete rest. No work!"

"Baking is not work," he muttered, but he saw her point. No baking for customers. That could be a good time to try out recipes and explore his ability to create something new, without the pressure of having to sell it. He could ask Adèle to test them... Claude smiled at the idea of preparing an oven-full of pastries and having her and Livia test each, one by one. He wondered if Adèle would take a few days off to rest as well. They could spend it together and figure out the details of their relationship. "Do you remember Adèle? The police woman who came by on the day you arrived?"

"I do." Livia's eye brightened, and her tone turned to teasing. "Hard to forget the way you looked at her, especially when I know how much tall and strong brunettes are your type."

Claude choked, but he had to admit most of the girls who struck his fancy fit that description. Livia hadn't seen most of them, however, so how did she guess? Had he always been obvious? He felt himself flush and released part of his shame in a chuckle. "We're… something now. I'm not in love with her, that much hasn't changed, but she's… unique, to me. You'll be seeing more of her, for sure."

"Powerful love comes in many forms, and not all of them need to be romantic. I daresay most aren't." She tilted her head back, leaning against the bed, and smiled softly. "I've been trudging happily alone, but… can I ask you something? It's been… bothering me for a while, but it never felt right to ask in a letter, and I don't really talk about these things with my friends in Tereaus. Sometimes I think I want to be with someone, like a couple, but it never lasts. It's… a flicker—a few days of intense pining for romance, and then it's gone. Does that ever happen to you?"

Claude considered the question for a moment. Did it? He had certainly experienced a rush of *want* for Adèle, but it had nothing romantic in nature. In fact, the idea that she'd demand anything resembling an "I love you" from him had left him cold and hesitant to approach her. But they had their own words—their

385

Je crois en toi—and it suited them better than romance ever could. What Livia described felt different. "I don't think so. I never pined for anyone that way. All I wanted was for Adèle to trust and understand me as fully as I did her."

Livia let out a pensive "hm" and nodded. She could not entirely hide her disappointment from him, and he wished he'd had a better answer for her. They used to spend hours late at night, staring at the stars or a ceiling, talking through their problems. When his parents and Livia had left, Claude had finished his journey alone, with Zita as an outlet as he experimented with presentation. Livia, it seemed, had never found someone else to speak with.

"It makes me feel like I don't know what I want," she said, her gaze intently refusing to leave the spot where Sol had. "Like I'm needlessly complicated."

"You're fine, Livia. Believe me, all humans are needlessly complicated." Claude tapped her knee so she would turn to him and smiled until she returned it. "You'll figure it out, and now I'm here to help. There's more to aromanticism than the complete absence of romantic attraction, and yours is no less important. Give yourself time. You used to tell me getting to know myself was a process that'd never end, remember?"

This time, Livia laughed. "You're right. I ought to take my own advice, eh? Besides, I'd already decided not to pursue anyone for a while. It's just too complicated, and it feels so much like leading them on. It's not, but… Whatever. Now there are exocores to save, and I'll focus my limited energy on them. That, and on recovery. I… don't think my magic is gone, but it's a tremendous effort to reach for it. Like all that power has been locked away. Perhaps it'll come back, with time."

"I'm sure it will. Don't overdo it, and it'll return." Claude set Gravity down on the bed, then pushed himself to his feet and picked up the now-empty plate of croissants. "I'll let Zuri know you're awake and already have a healthy appetite. She'll be thrilled, I think, especially considering half the household requires her attention."

"She should stay with them," Livia said. "I'm fine, really, and I have all the cats I need to keep me company." She gestured at the purring friends in the bed around her.

"I'm sure Docteure Adaho can decide for herself, Livia. She'll want to give you at least a last check-up." Claude suspected she *would* return to the others. Yuri and Emmanuelle had been in a particularly terrible state when he'd emerged from the Pont des Lumières, Livia in his arms. Interrupting the ceremony had been costly for everyone. But they were all alive, and Montrant Industries would never take another life. Despite the bone-deep exhaustion and the work left to be done, Claude smiled. Tonight, he would invite Adèle over to dine, with great wine and fresh garlic bread, and they could talk in peace and figure themselves out and, maybe, *maybe*, seal it all with a kiss.

Adèle's vélocycle trip through Val-de-mer on the

following morning felt surreal. The Pont des Lumières still towered above the rooftops, but a powerful sun bathed the city in light, brightening its front façade. Even with the broken glasswork attesting to yesterday's events, Adèle had the distinct impression she'd dreamed it. Certainly, her mind refused to accept that Emmanuelle had been shot. It had already shut out the details of her encounter with Élise—she remembered the gunshot, the echoes of her sister's moan, the way Gouverneure Lacroix had casually stepped over her... but the rest had become vague. Just a solid ball of horror settling at the bottom of her stomach and pushing her to pedal faster.

She hadn't slept at all last night, constantly getting up to check on Em, then returning to bed only to turn over and over. The nervous energy had continued through dawn, until Zuri and Koyani had grown sick of it. The capitaine had ordered Adèle to go by Yuri's place to pick up essentials for him. The sniper's bullet had ruined his uniform and the new binder he had so excitedly talked about on her first day of work, and in his brief moment of consciousness, he'd given Zuri a list of his medical needs and very clear, insistent instructions on how to take care of George, his pet iguana.

For a flat in the poorer parts of the Quartier des Saules, Yuri's home had been surprisingly clean and well maintained. She had been in and out as fast as she could, yet it had been hard to miss the massive wall of romance and erotica novels in his room. She preferred stories with less sex herself—it always felt awkward to read—but if any of these crossed into the mystery genre, she might give them a try. She wondered if Yuri would lend her any, then set aside the thoughts to look for his binder and pills, and to care for George. The creature stared at her, unmoving, while she refreshed the water in his bowl and prepared a plate of fresh lettuce ripped into shreds along with bits of carrots and a few figs. Once the food offering was completed, she checked the temperature of his environment, made sure the curtains were wide open to let sunlight in, and promised him Yuri would return soon. George, it seemed, liked being talked to: he flicked his tongue and tilted his head to the side.

Once she was done, Adèle decided this would be the perfect time to replenish her stock of vivifiants. The last few days had left her airways painfully tight and, while biking from the Quartier des Mélèzes to Yuri's home took her down the cliff's slope, she knew the way back to Em's manor would finish her off. She'd need help to unclog everything between her throat and lungs.

She used the stop at a pharmacy and the long wait it always brought to further calm down. Emmanuelle had been safe from death within an hour of being shot, yet the terror it had provoked lingered on. Adèle hoped her sister would wake in a better state of mind than her own, that her brain wouldn't replay the events over and over. She rested against the pharmacy's counter and closed her eyes, trying to empty her thoughts of the previous night—all but the end of it, leaning against Claire, taking comfort in her warmth and her assurance that the future would be better.

She'd been right, too. Em's house had a few broken doors—nothing major, however, and no national guard had been waiting for them there. They'd been able to reclaim possession of the place without resistance and install Em, Livia, and Yuri in isolated rooms. The two witches left to watch over Clémence's little brother had hidden safely, and the kid had jumped into ols arms as soon as he caught sight of ol. Clémence had been allowed to return to ols home with him, but Denise Jalbert had assigned trusted policemen to ol—as much to keep Clémence from running as to protect ol from potential retribution from Montrant. Zita avoided ol, instead spending much of her time with Koyani and the mairesse, eager to use her Seeking to find exocores across the city.

Claire had remained with Adèle for most of the night, trusting Nsia Kouna with Livia's safety. Adèle had no idea how she had managed to stay away from her lost twin, but she had been grateful for the company. They had cuddled in a large sofa, Zephyr climbing onto their lap, and Adèle's panic had eventually receded. She clung to that memory now, pushing herself back to that calm place, and the tightening of her throat lessened in part. The vivifiants would have to do the rest.

Adèle returned to Em's manor shortly before noon and forced herself to bring Yuri his things before she hurried to her sister's room. Em sat up in her bed, awake and smiling, a healthy pink colouring her cheeks. She had a heavy tome on her lap and her nightrobe seemed to glow from the inside—probably Zuri's healing net underneath it. Zephyr and Aurora formed a cat pile within reach of her right hand, in perfect position for occasional petting. Relief washed through Adèle and she grinned.

"Don't tell me that's a science book," she said.

Em laughed but didn't bother to deny it. "It's Clémence's, and it has ols notes on exocores."

Adèle traversed the room and sat across from the cats, unwilling to disturb them. "Don't you want to rest first?"

"I do. In fact, I need to get out of the city." She brushed the top of the book with her fingers before playing with the corner of the page, refusing to meet Adèle's gaze as she did. "Do you think Uncle Fred would lend us his cottage by the Lac? Would you come, or does Koyani need you?"

"I'll ask her. She'd be down half her team." Between Élise's betrayal and Yuri's wound, now might not be the best time for a vacation. Adèle would love to spend her days by the Lac Saint-Damase, however, reading in the shades of trees with the water lapping nearby, or fishing in the perfect stillness of dawn. And yet... that would mean leaving Claude before they'd had a chance to talk properly. "Maybe we should plan it for next week, or the one after? It would give us all time to prepare, and Yuri might be in better shape."

"Sounds great." Em finally lifted her gaze from her tone. Amusement shone in her eyes and a wry smile curved her lips. "You should tell our good baker and his twin that they are welcome to this retreat."

Adèle's face grew hot and red, and she wondered if Em had read her mind. She tried to answer, but her words came out as a jumbled, excited squeak which made Em laugh again. Adèle waited for her sister's mirth to die down before finally whispering "Thank you."

"This is entirely self-serving. Imagine how much better this vacation will be with fresh croissants and warm bread every morning."

Adèle pushed at her sister's shoulder with a chuckle. "You're inviting him to rest, not to work for you." She knew he would do both, however. Baking had been his way of relaxing yesterday, and she wouldn't be surprised to learn it was helping him recover from the ordeal. "I'll go to invite him, then. Try not to overdo the science."

She stood while Em stuck out her tongue at her, and left in search of Claude, her heart aflutter with visions of a long vacation with him, away from conspiracies and politics. Would Claude teach her some of the basics of breadmaking? Come fish on the Lac in her uncle's old boat? Perhaps they'd just sit on the porch and talk, or find a private corner to cuddle, kiss, or more. Her dreamy thoughts distracted her so much she almost bumped directly into Claude as he exited Livia's room.

"Adèle!" he exclaimed, and grinned. "I was about to go look for you."

"I—me too."

"I have an invitation for you," he continued, and his excited enthusiasm gave way to the shy smile she had always loved. "For dinner. Tonight. I-I think we should talk? About the whole…" He gestured at both of them vaguely. "That thing."

Adèle's soft flutters at imagining their potential vacation earlier turned into an almost painful twist. Part of her wanted to run away from this discussion, to avoid putting words on what they might feel, and on what it meant for them. Was she ready for that? What if either of them panicked or otherwise ruined it? Couldn't they continue leaning onto one another for support without explaining more? She told herself they had gone through worse and, more importantly, that Claude needed this. What good would their relationship be if she already refused him the right to clarity and boundaries? Adèle pushed back at her doubts and nodded.

"It would be a pleasure," she said. "I also have an invitation, but it might be best to wait until we've talked."

He perked up, his eyes shining. "Now I'm intrigued. You couldn't help but keep me on the edge of my seat until tonight, could you?"

"It'll make two of us," she countered, and her anxiety seeped into her voice more thoroughly than she had wanted.

Claude's expression softened. "It'll be good, some time alone from the flurry of events. Just the two of us at my place, with a nice meal and all the evening ahead of us."

"But no candles or flowers, huh?"

He laughed and his mirth was a calming balm on Adèle's stress. Perhaps he was used to these discussions, much like she had gotten skilled at explaining to potential lovers she might never feel sexually attracted to them. "I like candles. No idea why everyone believes they're *so* romantic, but they're good ambiance and they smell great when you snuff them out. You're hereby in charge of bringing them. Grab wine for yourself, too, if you want any. I don't drink."

"Understood."

"And Adèle?" He hesitated, his body tensing as his doubts spread clearly on his expression. "Please take some time to think about what you want, or any questions you could have. It might make it easier and I... I really want this to work."

He reached for his elbow, as if to hold himself smaller, and she intercepted his hand. They stood in the corridor, silent for a moment, near enough to feel each other's warmth—almost as close as in the laboratory, when Claire had teased her with charges of seduction. Her blood had pounded so hard then, the rush of adrenaline from their rescue and the horror of the tanks compounding her desire, fraying her control. Adèle was calmer now, and she pulled Claude closer slowly, dropping a soft kiss on his lips. It didn't last, but Claude's smile had returned as she drew back.

"Me too. We'll figure it out." As she said it, she found her confidence more solid than ever before. She stepped back, releasing Claude. "See you tonight, then! I have to talk with Koyani."

At Claude's request, she promised to greet Koyani and thank her for the help at the Pont, then she reluctantly left his side. Part of her wished to linger around for the entire day and contribute to their dinner, but she suspected Claude needed the space to better define *his* wants and questions. After a meeting with her capitaine, she decided to return home too, and spend the day on her own and follow his sound advice. How strange, to enter her flat, where it had all started. She sat on her bed, where she'd first heard Claire sneaking into her office, and smiled at the memory. Her home no longer felt unsafe, and she had since connected with the city's gas lines. Her future in Val-de-mer had never looked as promising as it did now.

-32-

LA FORME DU NOUS

THEY MANAGED TO EAT THE ENTIRE MAIN COURSE without a word on their relationship. Claude had slowly baked a salmon wrapped in the leftover flaky pastry from this morning's croissant, stuffing it with fresh cheese and herbs. Adèle had devoured it with great delight, promising it was better than almost anything she could prepare, and they'd spent most of dinner chatting about their favourite food and her questionable cooking skills. It had been fun and left them both in good spirits by the time he brought his mini chocolate muffins out of the oven, but the unresolved questions about their relationship hung over them through it all.

Over the course of the afternoon, Claude had tried to untangle what he wanted from this relationship with Adèle. He hadn't expected anything like this to happen to him—not after years of living comfortably on his own, building his business from scratch and enjoying the occasional outing at night, with Zita or alone. The closest thing he'd entertained in the recent years was with Fiona, a quick-witted dancer in the Quartier des Sorbiers, and it had been very strictly sexual in nature. They would spend nights together, enjoying the flirting and the physical intimacy, and eventually it had fizzled out, both of them slowly moving on.

It had been good while it lasted, but his feelings for Adèle were completely different, and could never take the same shape as his brief time with Fiona. He recognized the way she looked at him, eyes shining, her blush easy and her laugh light, and he remembered how she had asked him out. Adèle was *not* aromantic, and he hadn't yet learned how to deal with that. He needed to know what she expected of him, and this. He needed boundaries that would prevent him from feeling trapped, as he had with Zita, or from convincing himself he was stringing her along and lying. He wasn't. Neither had he been to Zita, while he was trying to understand who he was and what relationships meant to him, but those thoughts were not easy to dispel.

With a sigh, Claude set the plate of muffins in the centre of the table. "This is bait," he declared, "and we don't get to enjoy it until we've had our talk. Let's... get it done before they grow cold?"

Surprise flashed across Adèle's expression, but she put down her glass of wine and nodded, looking serious. "You're right. I... thought about this a lot today. You don't want romance, do you?"

"What even *is* romance?" Claude countered, before slinking back into his chair. He hadn't meant to drop the question like that—it was too big, too impossible to answer—but it had plagued him for so much of his life. "We won't get anywhere if we

397

go too large. I don't fall in love, and when I tried to follow relationships the way others did... It was stifling and wrong. I know that much. But I have one certainty nestled in my soul, as strong and true as any others, and it's that you mean the world to me. Being with you feels *right*, and I want that to stay. Whatever that means..."

He was being confusing. He could tell by the hesitation in Adèle's eyes and how she'd folded her hands over the table. She didn't *get* it, but how could he explain the way his heart expanded when she walked nearby, or how she just fit, like she had always belonged to his life. But there was kindness in her pose too, and no hurt at all.

"I want the whatever that means." She leaned forward, and Claude was once more caught by the striking beauty of her brown eyes, of her long nose and smattering of freckles running over it, her narrow visage and her determined smile. "I love you. There's no going around that. I... crush on people a lot, ages before I experience any sexual attraction. That latter... doesn't happen often, actually, but since I enjoy the occasional sexual encounter I don't usually wait for it." She coughed, intensely red by the candlelight. "So that can be part of our equation every now and then if you want it."

"Oh yes." The words escaped on their own—that was the easy bit for him, the one that had always been obvious.

Adèle laughed at the speed with which he answered, then sipped at her wine. "So we're a non-romantic pair with occasional sex. Is pair okay? I don't think polyamory is for me."

"A pair is good." Setting the boundaries of one relationship was proving complicated enough for him, and who would they add to this anyway? Maybe one day someone else would come up, just as Adèle had dropped on him unexpectedly, but they could talk about it again if it happened. Claude had his doubts. "I don't want to *only* be a pair. You know how couples sometimes can't seem to exist without one another? That freaks me out. I want to go out and do stuff on my own, and I want to know you have your own friends and activities. I need my own discrete life or I'll drown in the one we'd share."

"No moving in together, then."

Claude's heart squeezed in horror at the idea, and he grabbed the table. "No."

"Great!" Adèle said. "My flat is *finally* growing on me, despite your best efforts. I didn't relish the thought of moving again so soon."

"I am *not* a living-together person. I love my bakery, and my weird hours, and having a space that belongs to no one else but me—well, me and the fifty exocores in my basement. Sleepovers are fine, though."

"What about something longer, but still temporary?"

Adèle had hesitated before asking her question, and Claude felt stones drop at the bottom of his stomach. He leaned back, trying to force himself to stay calm and relaxed. This had been going very well. "What do you mean?"

"Like a vacation." A genuine smile spread across her lips and melted away chunks his reluctance. Still, he waited for more details, afraid to agree to something he'd regret. "That's why I was looking for you earlier. I have an uncle who owns a cottage by Lac Saint-Damase, and Em and I will be retreating there for a few weeks. Livia and you would be welcome along. So it's not even the two of us alone, really, and I think we could all use the time away from Val-de-mer."

"That sounds wonderful," he said, and it truly did. He had promised Livia he would rest—and made her promise the same— and a cottage wasn't *his* space. It didn't feel like an intrusion. "Livia loves large bodies of water. She says it makes her magic easier, and it might help her recover. I'll ask her if she wants to come."

"Deal, then."

Adèle leaned forward, reaching across the table to grab a muffin. Immediately, Claude snatched the plate away, his heart hammering. He didn't understand his sudden surge of panic at the idea that they'd covered everything they needed, but his magic had flowed out on its own, and now he stood by the table, holding the muffins high, a little breathless, and confused at himself. Were they *really* done? Shouldn't there be so much more to discuss? What if they forgot an important element and it shattered them down the line? Shouldn't they take more time, and go over everything again, and—

"Claude," Adèle said softly. "Are you all right?"

"I'm… I feel like we're missing something." He shifted away and forced himself to look at Adèle. "That can't be it, can it?"

"It can." Adèle pushed herself up and slowly made her way around the table, to him. She removed the plate from his hands and set it down. "We'll never unearth every potential detail of our future, Claude. We don't need to. We'll figure it out as we go and it'll be okay. I know this like I know my last name. And do you know why?"

It took him a moment. Adèle's proximity calmed him and allowed him to return to the foundation of their relationship. "Je crois en toi."

"Je crois en *nous*," Adèle corrected. "*We* can do this."

She was right. They didn't need more precise rules any more than they needed romantic love. They had faith—the kind that destroyed industries and changed the cityscape forever. All they needed was to keep communicating, and they would get through fine. Slowly, Claude reached for the chocolate muffins and handed her one.

"We can do anything," he said, "but right now, I think we should start with muffins and a long, well-deserved vacation."

THANK YOU FOR READING!

If you enjoyed *Baker Thief*, there are a few simple ways through which you can support me!

The first is to leave a review on retail sites such as Amazon or Kobo! These provide invaluable help in allowing others discover my books.

You can also join my newsletter to receive monthly updates, sneak peeks, and book recommendations from me by heading to http://eepurl.com/cSekDf

Finally, you can support me directly on Patreon, at patreon.com/claudiearseneault, and gain access to exclusive bonus short stories and other amazing extras for as little as $1 per month!

But, always and most importantly, keep reading and keep loving. Your support matters, no matter its form.

WANT MORE?

At The Kraken Collective, we know how frustrating it can be to reach the end of a book and want more. Within the following pages, you'll find books with a similar feel to help you scratch that reading itch and why we're recommending them.

We hope our suggestions will help you find your next favourite read!

Cheerleaders from Planet X,

by Lyssa Chiavari

THE INVASION HAS JUST BEGUN

CHEERLEADERS FROM PLANET X

LYSSA CHIAVARI

If you're looking for more delightful stories with classic SFF creatures and a happy f/f ending, check out *Cheerleaders from Planet X*. Laura Clark thought she was just your average college freshman—until the day she saw a cheerleader on a skateboard get into a superhuman brawl with a lightning-wielding stranger in a trenchcoat. And the only person who saw it is the beautiful, standoffish Shailene, one of the possibly superpowered cheerleaders of her Laura's rival school. Fun and fast-paced, *Cheerleaders from Planet X* is a perfect blend of old tropes and fresh twists wrapped around a romance that might just be … out of this world.

Learn more at krakencollectivebooks.com

Stake Stauce, Arc 1:

The Secret Ingredient is Love. No, Really,

by RoAnna Sylver

If you're interested in more urban fantasy lead by an aromantic spectrum character, check out *Stake Sauce, Arc 1: The Secret Ingredient is Love. No, Really.* Once a firefighter, now a mall cop, Jude is obsessed with the incident that cost him his leg and his friend, five years ago. He is convinced a terrifying vampire was involved, and that they haunt Portland's streets. Every night he searches for proof and is about ready to give up... until he runs into one—a fuzzy, pink-haired vampire named Pixie. Cuddly, not-at-all scary, Pixie needs his help against his much deadlier kin. *Stake Sauce* is a perfect blend of dark and amusing, while giving a wide space to trauma healing and found families.

Learn more at krakencollectivebooks.com

REMERCIEMENTS

Baker Thief is in many ways a book of self-discovery and self-affirmation. At the risk of sounding like I have an overblown ego, I want to thank myself for writing, for daring to put so much of myself into it.

Books don't happen without a team, however. Thank you to Marianne, first reader and eternal cheerleader, to Laya Rose for the wonderful cover, to Ren, Janani, Gaven, and Lynn for the help with both story and representation. In fact, double thanks to Lynn, who also patiently fixed all my grammar mistakes and blessed me with long chats about how we could play with French and English.

Many thanks to my wonderful family for the continued support, to my friends who make me laugh and love every week, to everyone on twitter who ever got excited about this project, especially the aromantic community, to my patrons who love every single tidbit of *Baker Thief* posted and encourage my work in such a wonderful and direct way. I would never have the courage to pour so much of myself into *Baker Thief* without all of you.

A particular thanks to my punmaster partner, Eric, who got me into actual baking and is always there by my side, even when all I do is stare at the screen and mutter angrily about plot holes. Our life together is full of croissants, delicious cheesy bread, and love.

Merci à tous et au prochain roman!

Milton Keynes UK
Ingram Content Group UK Ltd.
UKHW012300080124
435686UK00007B/418